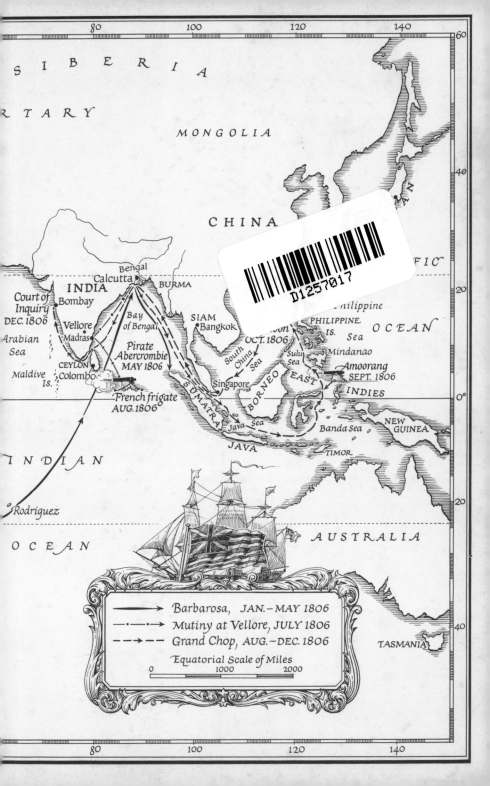

SIBERIA

TARTARY

MONGOLIA

CHINA

PACIFIC

INDIA
Bombay

Court of
Inquiry
DEC. 1806

Vellore
Madras

Arabian
Sea

CEYLON
Colombo

Maldive
IS.

Bengal
Calcutta

BURMA

Bay
of Bengal

SIAM
Bangkok

Pirate
Abercrombie
MAY 1806

French frigate
AUG. 1806

OCT. 1806

South
China
Sea

Singapore

BORNEO

SUMATRA

Java Sea

JAVA

Philippine

PHILIPPINE
IS.

Sulu
Sea

EAST

Mindanao

Amoorang
SEPT. 1806

INDIES

OCEAN

Sea

INDIAN

Rodriguez

OCEAN

Banda Sea

TIMOR

NEW
GUINEA

AUSTRALIA

TASMANIA

D1257017

Barbarosa, JAN.—MAY 1806
Mutiny at Vellore, JULY 1806
Grand Chop, AUG.—DEC. 1806

Equatorial Scale of Miles

0   1000   2000

The East Indiaman

To James B. Robinson,
my friend + client,
with the continued
admiration of
Ellis K. Meacham
5 Nov. 1968

The East Indiaman

BY ELLIS K. MEACHAM

with decorations and map by
Samuel H. Bryant

LITTLE, BROWN AND COMPANY · BOSTON · TORONTO

LIBRARY OF CONGRESS CATALOG CARD NO. 68-25906

FIRST EDITION

*Published simultaneously in Canada
by Little, Brown & Company (Canada) Limited*

PRINTED IN THE UNITED STATES OF AMERICA

To Dean Jean

PART ONE

Barbarosa

CHAPTER 1

ONLY a single captain on the active list of the Naval Service of the Honourable East India Company was in England this raw January morning. This was by no means remarkable, since the normal theater of operations of the service was half a world away and its officers had little occasion to come to Britain except as invalids or upon retirement—if they were fortunate enough to survive so long.

The popular name of the service was the Bombay Marine, often called with grudging admiration by officers of the Royal Navy "The Bombay Buccaneers." The Marine was the only private navy in the world and was employed by the Honourable Company to protect its far-flung operations, which extended from the Red Sea and Persian Gulf, across the Indian Ocean and the crowded East Indian archipelago, to China. It was a service small in numbers, but already possessed of a hundred and ninety-three years of honorable tradition in this year of 1806. While it sailed frigates of as many as fifty-six guns, it was more often concerned with ketches, snows, brigs, sloops, schooners and grabs of shoal draft, carrying six to fourteen guns, which met and defeated French, Dutch, Portuguese, Spanish, Chinese, Arab, Malay and Moro ships and forces under adverse conditions.

The officers of the Marine served not only at sea but as diplomats in remote areas among savage peoples; as commanders of units in combined operations ashore with army siege trains; as expeditionary forces with elements of the Marine Battalion; and as surveyors charting the eastern seas. Few sprigs of the nobility or sons of landed gentry chose the arduous service of the Bombay Marine as a career in preference to His Majesty's Navy or Army.

Some officer candidates entered as volunteers or midshipmen; others rose from the ranks if they possessed sufficient education and ability. Cannon and musket balls, tropical fevers, accident and shipwreck, provided a constant attrition in the lower commissioned ranks and left promotion to captain in the Service largely a matter of fortune and influence in the Court of Directors of the Company.

This one captain in the Bombay Marine was in London for the first time in nine years by pure chance. He bore the somewhat pretentious name of Percival Merewether, but had risen to his exalted rank from humble origins in life by way of the lower deck. He was a man of a little more than middle height, broad in the shoulders, not yet stooped by life below decks, and carried himself with the alert air of agile grace often seen in the practiced seaman. His face, with lively blue eyes under dark brown hair, was unremarkable except for a broken nose, badly set, a long disfiguring scar along his right jawline, a missing right earlobe and blue-tinged powder burns on his cheek, the combination of which gave him an expression of ruthless determination. He had held the rank of captain less than twenty-four hours, though sixteen of his twenty-eight years had been spent at sea in the service of the Company.

Yesterday, Merewether had been a first lieutenant in the Service, junior to at least a score of other officers of vast experience, courage and ability, equally deserving of promotion to the one vacancy in the list of captains. It had been his fortune to distinguish himself under the eyes of an Indiaman's captain, who was also Ship's Husband of three other Indiamen, owner of a large number of shares in the Company and a member of the Court of Directors. Merewether had waited on the New Year's session of the Court of Directors outside the massive chamber in East India House in Leadenhall Street yesterday, subject to interview if the Court so desired, in full-dress uniform as required by regulations, brave in his blue coat with buff lapels, black velvet cuffs and collar, cocked hat under arm, dress sword at his side. The motion to promote, so important to him, made by an influential director, passed unanimously without debate as a matter of routine. The commission was signed in open meeting, and he was one of six-teen captains in the Bombay Marine.

Merewether, still in full dress with sword, came to the door of the Crown and Sceptre just after daylight this gray London morn-ing, tested it, found it unlocked and went in. He felt furtive, unaccountably embarrassed to be returning to the inn at this hour, though no one here knew him; as he went along the hall to the stairs, he found himself almost tiptoeing. He heard voices in the dining room to the right, passed the open door quickly, and ascended the stairs. Outside the door to his room, he found a jug of water, still hot. He picked it up and went in.

He looked about the pleasant room with its unrumpled bed and curtains at the windows, and reflected that he had spent ten shillings for about ten minutes' use of the room since yesterday morning. Until then he had occupied quarters in *Lord Exmouth*, anchored down at Blackwall. He had moved here only yesterday for his appearance before the Court of Directors. Setting the jug on the washstand, he threw his hat on the chest, unbuckled his sword, hung it on a peg and quickly stripped off his clothing. Opening his sea chest, he removed his shaving kit, laid out razor, brush, soap and washcloth. He poured the basin half full, wet the washcloth, applied soap and began to wash himself from head to toe.

The back of his head still throbbed, the legacy of the brandy consumed last night. He wondered briefly if Beth Watkins, or whatever name she called herself now, had awakened yet. It had been an evening of gaiety in celebration of his promotion yester-day to captain in the naval service of the Honourable East India Company, the Bombay Marine. After the tailor had added the gold lace to his blue coat denoting his new rank, he had gone to a public room off Drury Lane, extravagantly ordered Spanish brandy that was undoubtedly contraband, and had sat sipping appreciatively. Others were in the room, including a group of three, two women and a swarthy little man at a table close by. One woman and the man had their heads together, conversing in low tones while the other woman gazed across the room.

Merewether started slightly. He was sure he knew this woman with the bold brown eyes, tilted nose, wide mouth. He thought a moment and a name popped into his mind. Certainly, he thought, they had been children together sixteen years ago; she was the daughter of the upstairs maid at Bell Flower House. He caught her eye, saw her draw herself up with a spurious air of hauteur, and said, "I beg your pardon, Miss, but aren't you Beth Watkins of Bell Flower House?"

She held her pose of hauteur a moment, looked at him and said, "Why yes, that was my name, and now I know you, Percival Merewether! It's been a long time since Bell Flower House."

From that point, matters had developed rapidly. He found her receptive to his offer of brandy, available for an extravagant dinner, delighted to attend the theater, thirsty again after the final curtain, but not fuddled or nostalgic enough to forego the fee for her ultimate favors. Half an hour ago, he had left her still asleep in a sleazy room two squares away, looking blowsy enough in daylight. Beth, his childhood playmate, he thought cynically, was a common whore. He hoped she had not presented him with anything more to remember her by. The evening, he computed, had cost nearly seven pounds, but after four months at sea, it was worth it.

Standing naked before the mirror, Merewether mixed lather in his mug as he examined the image in the glass. Deeply tanned by sixteen years at sea, his face under straight brown hair had high cheekbones, flat cheeks, firm jaw, bright blue eyes under level brows. The flaws were obvious: a nose with a hump on its bridge, crooked to the right; a white scar, half an inch wide, running from almost the right corner of his mouth back just above the jawline; and a missing right earlobe. On either side of the scar, blue specks stood out on the roughened skin. The broken nose was a souvenir of a wild night ten years ago off the Cape of Good Hope when a block swinging loose on a line caught him on his way to the foretop. The scar and embedded powder grains were only a few months old, evidence of the passage of a pistol ball fired by a thug in the guise of a lascar stevedore at point-blank range.

Merewether applied the brush to his face, evenly distributed the lather, and stood waiting a moment for it to soften the bristles, while he absently stropped his razor. That lascar thug had died a fraction of a second after he fired the pistol, cut almost in half by the charge from a blunderbuss; but, Merewether mused, he owed his promotion largely to him and his band, one of many roaming the Ganges Delta in these times.

It had been an unusual circumstance. The Indiaman, *Lord Exmouth*, had anchored off Matla Station at the entrance to the Hooghly River and made a distress signal. HEIC twenty-two gun sloop of war, *Sir John Shore*, was close by and responded. Merewether was first lieutenant of the sloop and took the boat to the Indiaman. He found her captain had suffered a stroke and was partially paralyzed. Her chief mate had died off Ceylon, the second officer was ill and the third officer lacked confidence in his ability to take the big Indiaman eighty-three miles up the treacherous Hooghly River, with its bars and tidal bores, to Calcutta. Even with the advice of the Indian pilot and the southwest monsoon, working a big Indiaman up the river was always difficult. The Captain, his speech somewhat affected by the stroke, requested the services of a qualified officer. Merewether was designated that officer.

The *Lord Exmouth* had come to anchor two miles above Budge-Budge at dusk, expecting lighters and stevedores alongside at daylight. The third officer had the watch, passengers were still asleep, and when the lighter came alongside and hooked on, all seemed routine. Suddenly nearly fifty lascars had scrambled up the side and seized the watch; some went racing to the companionways leading to the passenger quarters aft, others sealed off the ladders to the forecastle and officers' quarters. By merest chance, Merewether had been up early in the roundhouse on the poop, preparing his request for pratique for the Captain of the Port, when he heard the disturbance. In the roundhouse was a rack containing four blunderbusses, prudently kept there close to the helm for just such an event as this; they had probably been loaded and primed at the commencement of the voyage in The Downs. As he snatched up one in either hand, Merewether wondered if they would fire after six months at sea.

He had slipped out the door, down the side of the roundhouse to the companionway leading to the officers' quarters. As he became visible, a thug with a white sweat rag tied about his head had leaped from the companionway, pistol in one hand, knife in the other. The pistol belched fire and smoke, Merewether felt a blow to his face, was momentarily blinded; without conscious effort, he fired the blunderbuss in his right hand like a pistol. The smoke blew away and he saw the twitching thug on the deck, belly ripped open.

At the companion, Merewether had shouted down, "All hands, all hands, arm yourselves, on deck to repel boarders!" He heard doors slam, a voice shouting that the armory was unlocked. Merewether looked forward. The mate and three of the watch lay at the gangway, a thug just removing from the neck of one a loop of cord on a stick. Done for, thought Merewether savagely, strangled. He pitched the empty blunderbuss aside. There were a dozen thugs guarding the companionways to the forecastle, holding the crew below while their fellows ransacked the passenger quarters. He ran back to the roundhouse, snatched up the two remaining blunderbusses, ran forward just as the Purser emerged cautiously from the officers' quarters, a pistol in hand.

"Here!" snarled Merewether shoving one of the blunderbusses into the Purser's hands. "We've got to get the crew on deck, shoot those bastards forward!" He ran up the port side of the weather deck, past the main mast, dodged around the small boat stowage cradles, emerged thirty feet from the group of cutthroats on guard at the forecastle. He swung up the short ugly weapon in his right hand and pulled the trigger. There was a deafening roar, and the recoil wrenched the gun out of his hand to clatter to the deck. Close beside, he heard the Purser's shot, and through the smoke could see at least six of the thugs down.

Merewether called, "Follow me!" to the Purser, ran a few steps and then, aiming carefully this time, blasted into the group still in the companionway. One man tried to run; the pistol barked behind him and the man stumbled and fell. One of the wounded thugs struck feebly at him with a knife and he kicked the man savagely in the face. A moment later, Catlett, captain of the main top, axe in hand, had led a party up on deck, armed with clubs, knives and axes.

Lord Exmouth had lost its third mate and three seamen, all strangled. They had counted thirteen thugs dead, thirty-one captured; several had leaped over the side, their fate unknown. The captured outlaws had been handed over to the Captain of the Port for trial and execution.

The surgeon had patched up the long red furrow and powder burns along Merewether's jaw with court plaster and trimmed the shreds of the earlobe off neatly, while the fat old Captain listened to his report, propped up in bed. No passenger had been injured; most of the articles the outlaws had seized had been recovered.

Commodore Land, Master Attendant at Calcutta, had granted the Captain's request that Merewether be loaned to *Lord Exmouth* to work her back to London.

Most people thought Indiamen were owned by the Company, but they were not. Such ships were built, manned and hired to the Company by owners who held a monopoly with hereditary rights to furnish the bottoms for the trade. It was this that had caused Merewether to transfer to the Bombay Marine nine years ago when his apprenticeship in an Indiaman was up. With no family or connections, he would never hope for promotion in an Indiaman where commands were purchased for as much as ten thousand pounds and the investment earned back in a single voyage. The monopoly had been broken temporarily in '98 but the Shipping Interest had almost regained control.

The old Captain, disabled though he was, was most influential in the Court of Directors and had made a handsome report of Merewether's actions at Calcutta and his ability to command a ship to the Operations Branch here in London, thus leading to his promotion. He was reasonably assured that back in India he would receive a command in the Naval Service, though some noses at Bombay might be out of joint. He had now to await passage back with the next convoy. Merewether carefully brought the edge of the razor across the corner of his upper lip, surveyed the results in the mirror and washed off the remnants of lather. The scar might be a continuing nuisance in shaving, but it was responsible for the gold lace now adorning his coat and he could live with it. He put on his undress uniform and went down to breakfast.

In the big dining room of the Crown and Sceptre, he found

two couples just rising from the table. The maid indicated a place laid at the other end and brought him a steaming cup of freshly brewed tea. He helped himself to bacon, eggs, biscuits, noting with appreciation the gleaming silver and white napery. He remembered once as a very small child slipping down from the dingy room over the kitchen at Bell Flower House, while his harried mother held open the door a crack so that he might see the great table, blazing with candlelight, laid with gleaming silver and china, Sir Jeffrey presiding at the head, bright colors, flashing jewels, the buzz of conversation. It was another world to a backstairs child, he thought, one he had never expected to reach, even a week ago.

As he ate, Merewether thought how far he had come during the past sixteen years. Who would have thought a snot-nosed Cockney lad, illegitimate son of a kitchen maid in Bell Flower House, the London residence of Sir Jeffrey Meigs, would ever sit at table in the Crown and Sceptre, for that matter? He caught the eye of the maid and she refilled his cup.

His mother had died, worn out with consumption, at twenty-nine, only a year older than he was now. She had never told him who his father was, though he thought she had tried at the last, as she drifted into a final coma. Her father, an old man, had come up from Surrey where he was a groom on Lord Spencer's estate, loaded the coffin in a cart, and had grudgingly taken Merewether back with his dead mother. The old man was ashamed of this bastard grandson, he realized now; in two days he had brusquely taken him back to London, signed articles of indenture for Merewether with the Ship's Husband of *Dunvegan Castle* of the Honourable Company, and departed forever from his life.

Merewether knew officers in the Company service who were fond of recalling that they had commenced before the mast. Well, he could hardly say that; he had commenced as a scullery boy, washing dishes, scouring pots, pans, dumping the garbage overboard, in the passenger galley of an East Indiaman. It was unpleasant work under harsh taskmasters, but Merewether had persevered, endured the blows and hazing, and in three years' time, had grown and filled out to the point where the Boatswain asked for his transfer to the deck force.

This had been a stroke of luck. Merewether was a natural seaman, quick, agile, strong, with the instinct to use his strength effectively. In a year's time, he was a foretopman, in two years captain of the foretop, at nineteen, one of the boatswain's mates. He had been even luckier in another respect, Merewether thought, as he put jam on the last of his biscuit. Dawson had been one of the purser's mates, a frail, nearsighted man who had been a schoolmaster in Liverpool. He had romantic illusions about the sea, threw up his appointment in the school and sought employment in a Company vessel after the Royal Navy refused him a warrant as midshipman. A qualified mathematician with no experience as a seaman, he made a passable purser's mate, able to keep accounts, prepare bills of lading, deal politely with unreasonable passengers.

As a child, Merewether's mother had managed two years of school for him; he could read and write, but not cipher. Dawson, out of kindness and to pass the time during long voyages, had formed a class for the apprentices and had undertaken to give them instruction. He had corrected Merewether's speech, grounded him in mathematics, and carried him far enough into the theory of navigation so that he was able, at twenty, to pass an examining board and obtain an appointment as second lieutenant in the Bombay Marine during the shortage of officers in '98.

Merewether, mind still faraway in reminiscence, pushed his chair back and started to rise, when he saw the maid approach, followed by a man in the blue livery of the Company's shore establishment.

"Captain Percival Merewether?" inquired the man. "Commodore sent me for you, sir. He wants to see you at once. I've a coach outside."

"Very well, I'll step up and get my hat," said Merewether looking at the tall clock in the hall. It showed nine o'clock. He wondered for a moment if his adventures of the night before had somehow come to the Company's attention, if the Commodore might be calling him to account. Nonsense, he decided.

The coach rattled rapidly over cobblestone for a mile, drew up at a small building on Downing Street where the Operations Branch of the Board of Control had its London offices. The doorman passed Merewether in to a crowded room where a super-cilious clerk had him write his name on a slip of paper. In a mo-ment the clerk was back beckoning and led him through the large room filled with high desks at which other clerks stood. Mere-wether entered the tiny chamber where yesterday he had received his commission and taken the oath as captain in the Bombay Marine.

The Commodore, Edward Welchance, was a tall, taciturn man who had distinguished himself three years ago in command of the Bengal Squadron. "Ah, Merewether," he said briskly. "We must go to Leadenhall Street." The Commodore clapped on his hat; together they went out and reentered the coach. In a few mo-ments' time, they drew up before East India House, with its six Ionic columns, ornate facade, the whole surmounted by an un-gainly statue of King George. Here there was delay, even for the Commodore; finally they were escorted down a long corridor past the sacred rooms of the Proprietor's General Court and the Court of Directors, where Merewether had waited yesterday, and en-tered a lavishly furnished chamber. Here a tall, elegantly dressed man sat behind a desk dictating in clipped, precise accents to a secretary. He finished, then waved the secretary out.

"Good morning, sir," said Welchance. "I have Captain Mere-wether with me."

"Oh, yes, Merewether, good morning," said Sir William Foster. "You may be seated, this may take a little time."

Merewether knew Sir William was Secretary of the Committee of Secrecy, most powerful in the operations of the Company, and responsible for the safety of its shipping. He sat down self-con-sciously in the presence of this man and looked briefly about him. On two walls were charts: Europe, the Mediterranean, Africa, North and South Atlantic; and India, the Indian Ocean, English, French, Dutch and Portuguese East Indies, China. His mind considered briefly the magnitude of the Company's far-flung operations, the reality of the distances it took a ship months to traverse.

"This man's safe?" demanded Sir William. The Commodore nodded. "Most confidential, hell to pay if this leaks out in Eng-land," he continued in his high precise voice, fixing Merewether's gaze.

"I understand, sir," said Merewether.

"So," said Sir William. "Cornwallis is dead, died last autumn, two months after he reached India as Governor-General again after Wellesley resigned. Everything in confusion, fight in the Court of Directors, fight in the Cabinet over the appointment. News came three days ago, and with it something vital to the Company." He paused, pulled a little pile of papers toward him.

"Suppose you never heard of the Right Honourable John William Cecil Lynde?" he demanded.

Merewether answered, "No, sir."

"Son of the Earl of Lincoln, Proprietor in the Company; married to the daughter of the Duke of Ascot, Proprietor in the Company, both rich as sin," continued Sir William approvingly. "Last spring, before Wellesley resigned, certain people in Cabinet and Company decided Government needed a man in their interest out there, fellow who's Governor of Madras didn't get along with Wellesley, and they decided to remove him. So, Government got King George to make an *in camera* appointment of Lynde as Governor of Madras, issue commission to him. He would just walk in and relieve the Governor. Lynde was delighted, was in the Cabinet back in '98, been an ambassador, but this was a better post." Sir William paused, picked up a silver carafe, poured a glass of water and sipped.

"Not a word leaked out in England, Lynde took passage in *Lord Mornington* of the Company, arrived Bay of Bengal last July. Caught in a storm, convoy dispersed, *Mornington* blown east, lost spars, cargo shifted, put her on her beam ends. No one knows how to stow cargo any more," grumbled Sir William.

"Anyway, she was helpless when the weather moderated; crew got to work shifting cargo, and a dhow came in sight, pulled alongside, and a hundred odd men, Atjenese Malays mostly, came over the side." Sir William consulted a paper, "Trapped three quarters of her crew below, killed six, wounded eighteen and took her. Understand you've had some experience of that sort, Captain."

Merewether responded, "Yes, sir. I had a little better luck."

"Remarkable thing," continued Sir William, "The dhow's captain was an Englishman. Rest of her crew were Atjenese pirates from Sumatra, not too far from where *Mornington* was blown. Have had trouble with those pirates for a long time, lost country ships and native vessels, but this is the first Company ship they've taken."

Sir William went on. "Of course, they gutted the ship, over twenty thousand in specie, that much again in jewelry from the passengers, cabin stores, spirits. And then, some blabbermouth let it be known the Governor Designate of Madras was on board. Lynde had talked during the voyage. This Englishman grabbed Lynde, wife and daughter, made them pack their belongings and took them aboard the dhow. He left this with the captain of *Mornington*."

From the pile of documents, Sir William extracted a single sheet and handed it to Merewether. It was written in a large scrawled hand, unmistakably English. Merewether read it quickly:

To the Governor-General:
You want your governor back, do as I say.
First I want 100,000 pounds in gold, quarter in escudos, quarter in Louis d'or, quarter in guilders, quarter in mixed English coin.
Second bring gold to Port Cornwallis harbor, Andaman Island in unarmed dhow week of May 1, 1806.
Third No tricks or you never see your governor again.

BARBAROSA

"Barbarosa," said Merewether wonderingly. In the course of his tutoring by Dawson in the old *Dunvegan Castle*, the class had read the history of Europe. "He was an early German emperor, sir."

"Yes, more recently two Algerian pirates called themselves by that name," said Sir William. "This Englishman wore a full beard, quite red, this report says. Unfortunately for Barbarosa, there was a man on board *Mornington* thought he recognized him." Sir William turned, picked up another document.

"Ever encounter an assistant purser in the Company's service named John Abercrombie, Merewether?"

Merewether started almost imperceptibly, and Sir William continued, "I see you did."

"He was a purser's mate in *Dunvegan Castle* in '96, sir," answered Merewether. He did not amplify that Abercrombie had made a vicious attack on his friend Dawson and might have killed him, except for Merewether's vigorous intervention. Abercrombie had left the ship after that voyage and Merewether had not thought of him for ten years.

"Thoroughly bad egg," grumbled Sir William. "Had a warrant as midshipman in the Royal Navy. Cashiered in '95. Crippled another midshipman, sold rum to the crew. Came from a good county family in Devonshire, they got him an appointment as assistant purser with the Company. Made one voyage, jumped ship at Calcutta. Short in his accounts, family made good. Got hold of a dhow, did some illegal trading and smuggling. Dropped out of sight with peace in 1802. People out there think he went to the Dutch Indies."

Sir William paused, poured another glass of water, and drank, as his eyes ran down the report. "Several country ships, independent traders, disappeared. Could have been lost in storms, taken by Malay or Moro pirates, but people out there think it was Abercrombie, all in eastern sector of the Bay of Bengal and the Straits."

Sir William paused, then said incisively, "We've got a caretaker government out there now, don't know which way the cat will jump. No one would take responsibility to act on this, six months for the word to reach us. Certain elements in Company and Government got Lynde into this, feel they should rescue him. Crown agrees to put up a quarter, Company a quarter of the ransom. Lynde and his wife's families will put up the rest. Time is short. This is where you come in, Captain. You seem to be the only captain in the Bombay Marine in England at the moment."

"I don't quite understand, sir," said Merewether carefully. "Am I to deliver the ransom, sir?" There seemed to be an element left out of the account.

"Oh, quite, Captain," said Sir William. "Forgot to mention we have a fast ship available, ex-slaver, just out of graving dock, new copper, standing and running rigging. Should reach India in half the time an Indiaman takes, and you have to be there before May first."

Sir William picked up a packet of papers, looked briefly

through them. "Named *Rapid*, built in '95; most profitable, but the Abolition Act nearly passed last year, would have but Pitt was sick, and is sure to pass next year. Her owners were afraid, and the Company bought her advantageously. Should, with a little more armament, serve as a very effective sloop. Also, with the slave deck, should be able to carry a half battalion of troops." He paused again, and looked at the papers.

"Mounts ten guns, nine pounders, been logged at fifteen knots. Excellent ship," he said.

"What about a crew, sir?" asked Merewether anxiously. With the shortage of seamen and the constant depredations of the press gang, he might never fill his complement. He doubted enough Bombay Marine men could be enlisted in England to man her.

"She's manned," chuckled Sir William. "Gave her hands a choice, enlist with the Company in the Bombay Marine two years, or lose their exemptions from the press gang. Silly fellows were delighted to sign up, expect to break their shins on piles of rubies and pearls out there. Captain and two mates left her, retired. Third mate, an American, incidentally, in charge, commissioned second lieutenant in the Marine."

Merewether felt a surge of relief. His first command would have an experienced crew. "I'll need two more watch-keeping officers, sir," he said.

"There are two Bombay Marine officers, both first lieutenants, in London now, awaiting transportation to India," broke in the Commodore. "Both are qualified watch officers, though they have lately been stationed ashore. I have in mind ordering them to *Rapid*, letting them work their way back to their duty stations.

"Your orders are being written, Captain," continued Sir William. "As soon as I sign them, you take command. You may indent on the dockyard at Blackwall for supplies. When will you be ready for sea?"

Merewether started to expostulate that he could not say before he saw the state of readiness of the ship, then decided that that would be a confession of weakness, indecision, in a newly promoted captain entrusted with so important a mission. "Three days, sir," he said firmly.

It was Sir William's turn to expostulate. "But Captain, we

cannot get together the ransom in less than a week, scouring the city now for guilders and escudos."

"I shall be ready, wind and tide permitting, sir," replied Merewether.

Outside the chamber in the corridor, Merewether and the Commodore perched on a hard bench. The Commodore fished out a long West Indian cigar, went in search of a light, came back puffing blue smoke, and reseated himself.

"Ever been to the Andaman Islands, Merewether?" he asked around the cigar.

"No, sir."

"I was there in '96, evacuated Port Cornwallis when it was abandoned. The natives are pygmies, Jarawas, shiny black, kill on sight. Have to watch out for them if you go ashore. Some say they're cannibals too." He continued, "Don't go too far into the bay, Abercrombie will be watching, no doubt. I'd anchor off Perserverance Point, about twelve fathoms, where you can see the entrance between Ross Island and Dundas Point. No charts here, you'll have to get them at Calcutta from the Master Attendant when you pick up the dhow."

Merewether thought a moment. "Perhaps this is covered in the orders, sir, but what about Abercrombie, shall I try to capture or kill him?"

"It will be covered in the orders," replied the Commodore, delicately flicking the gray ash from his cigar. "But your primary mission is to rescue Lynde and family. Crown is most interested. Never hear the last of it if he comes to grief. We can catch and hang Abercrombie anytime."

A clerk stepped into the corridor, beckoned. Merewether and the Commodore arose and re-entered the chamber. Sir William put the pen back in the shot bowl, sanded his signature, blew the surplus sand into a cup. The clerk, candle in hand, melted wax, and Sir William applied the seal. He handed over the packet to the Commodore, who read the orders. The Commodore handed them to Merewether.

"Very well put, Sir William," the Commodore said. "Attached also are orders to the Master Attendant at Calcutta to furnish you a suitable dhow. Say as little as possible of your mission out there.

Company and Crown would just as soon this venture not be known."

"Aye aye, sir," said Merewether. "Have I permission to proceed to my ship?"

"Yes," said Sir William. "Orders to sail will accompany the gold. By the way, there is an adequate strong room below the master's cabin in *Rapid* to stow it in."

Outside in Leadenhall Street, the Commodore signaled for the carriage. "We'll pick up your chest and then your officers. They should be at my office by now."

At the Crown and Sceptre, Merewether had the porter bring down his chest and stow it in the boot. He paid his reckoning, and the coach rattled back to Downing Street.

"I'll give you the carriage to Blackwall for your officers and baggage," said the Commodore as they entered.

In the tiny chamber were two men, both in the uniform of first lieutenants in the Bombay Marine, crowding its space. They greeted the Commodore respectfully. The elder was a burly, red-faced man, with a protruding belly, the other small and dark, with a cast in one eye.

"Mr. MacLellan, Mr. MacRae, Captain Merewether," said the Commodore. "Mr. MacLellan is senior and will serve as your first lieutenant."

Merewether thought, heaven help him if MacLellan had to go aloft. Two more Scots, it was a wonder any Highlanders were left, so many had taken service with the Company. He greeted them civilly, extending his hand.

"You gentlemen are ready to go aboard?" asked Merewether.

"Yes, sir," replied MacLellan. "Our chests are outside on a barrow."

CHAPTER 2

The ride down the Thames to the East India Company Dock-yard at Blackwall was silent. Possibly these officers resented being required to work their way back to India. At the yard, the dockmaster provided a boat, the coachman loaded the chests, and Merewether took his seat beside the coxswain.

"Shove off," he told him.

As the boat pulled beyond the slip, he could see his new command anchored half a cable's length off. Freshly painted, black trimmed with buff, she had towering raked masts, a graceful shear, exquisite lines. Undoubtedly she possessed the speed Sir William had mentioned. Anchored below her, close by, was another ship with a boat alongside, a Royal Navy sloop. He heard the squeal of a boatswain's pipe and looked around to see side boys manning the gangway, while a tall figure in a uniform trimmed with gold lace, from which the pale January sun glinted, climbed the ladder.

The coxswain followed his glance. "*Atropos*, twenty-two," he volunteered. "She's sailing to the Mediterranean to fish up treasure from a wreck." There were few secrets kept from these watermen.

Merewether wondered briefly about the value of such ceremony, whether it aided discipline. After all, it was the ability and force of personality of an officer, not ceremony, that instilled the respect and loyalty necessary to maintain true discipline. The boat grated alongside *Rapid*, and Merewether mounted the ladder.

As his head came level with the deck, Merewether heard a command, "Attention on deck!" A boatswain's pipe squealed and he stepped off the ladder between four side boys. A tall, slender man with long blond hair stood at the end of the files at salute, a man beside him blowing trills on the pipe.

"Welcome aboard, Captain," said the tall man, as Merewether returned the salute. "Decided to greet you man-o'-war fashion." Merewether extended his hand. The tall man murmured, "Larkin, sir. Formerly third mate, now second lieutenant. Tompkins here allowed he could still pipe the side like he used to do in *Leviathan*."

"Very good, Mr. Larkin," said Merewether. "Please call all hands. May I introduce Mr. MacLellan and Mr. MacRae, my first and second lieutenants."

In a moment, the hands poured aft, curious to see this new captain they would have to serve under for the next two years.

From the break of the poop, Merewether read the portion of his orders giving him command of *Rapid*, adding briefly: "Men, we sail within the week for India. Do your duty and I'm easy to live with. Dismiss the crew, Mr. MacLellan." He saw the sea chests swaying up from the boat to thump on deck.

A short, fat man bustled up. "Davis, sir, Purser. May I show you to your cabin?"

The man led him aft, down a companion to a passageway, with doors on either side. At the end of the passage, he threw open a heavy door and stood aside for Merewether to precede him in. The cabin was spacious beyond any quarters Merewether had ever occupied at sea. It extended from side to side across the stern of the ship, with windows looking aft, portholes along the sides, a skylight in the center, vents in the overhead, now closed, that Merewether recognized as openings for windsails to cool the cabin in the tropics. A handsome brass bed was bolted to the deck, a desk set under the skylight, a leather-covered transom with drawers underneath across the stern. Lockers were set against the forward bulkhead, and beside the door was a rack containing four blunderbusses, four cutlasses, four pistols and four trunch-eons with leather-wrapped grips.

Davis, noting his glance, said, "I guess you never served in a slaver, sir. Every now and then, some of those big bucks get loose, handy to have them things here." Merewether heard footsteps, and two hands came in with his chest.

"Ask Mr. MacLellan, Mr. MacRae, Mr. Larkin, the Boatswain, Carpenter, Gunner, Cooper, and Sailmaker to meet here at their convenience," said Merewether. "And yourself." Davis departed.

The meeting was brief. Each department was directed to pre-pare lists of requirements and turn them over to the Purser for requisition from the dockyard. By midafternoon, Merewether had signed the stack of requisitions, working parties had been told off and dispatched ashore. Merewether decided it was time to look at this ship of his.

On deck, he went aft to the helm, tested the play in the tiller ropes controlled by the big, brass-trimmed wheel. Removing the canvas hood from the compass binnacle, he checked the ship's heading against the sun, looked briefly at the table of corrections for deviation on the board. He would have to swing ship once he had all his arms and ammunition aboard, to see if these corrections were still valid before he set out halfway around the world.

Just aft of the helm was a pivot gun, a long brass nine pounder, now snugly covered with its canvas jacket. Merewether had seen pivot guns before, but had never used them. The gun, in an ordinary carriage, was mounted on a platform which was pivoted in the center and had small iron wheels at ninety degree intervals around the circle to support it. The gun tackles were secured to the platform and timbers formed a track in which the carriage wheels ran. A brake operating against the deck allowed the gun to be locked at any point in its train, which could cover an arc of almost two hundred and twenty degrees, astern and to either side. Merchantmen had been mounting such guns since '98, but, quite naturally, the Royal Navy had rejected them: pivots being able to fire to either side tended to reduce the number of broadside guns, and since the rate of Navy ships and the pay of their captains depended on the number of guns carried, no board of Royal Navy captains would approve such an innovation. Forward, he could see another pivot on the forecastle, and four guns a side on deck. With the pivots, he carried quite a respectable broadside of six guns, as much as some Royal Navy brigs or sloops. He looked astern. *Atropos* had gone with the tide on her mission to recover gold, while he made preparation to deliver gold. Merewether wondered briefly if her captain ever had feelings of inadequacy or doubt such as he was now experiencing in his first command.

Merewether prowled forward examining every detail. The top hamper was up but yards were not yet crossed. He inspected the capstan, tested with his foot the strain on the anchor cable. If he used the forward pivot gun as a bow chaser, he would have to yaw slightly so the shot would clear the bowsprit, he decided. There was a complex arrangement of tackle on the forecastle, apparently for the sheets to control the headsails and flying jib this ship undoubtedly carried. He made a mental note to speak privately with the Boatswain as to the use of this tackle before getting under way.

Merewether heard the watch hail. He turned and saw a water

hoy coming along the port side, the Cooper and his party on her deck. He had decided to fill all water casks, though it might be more than his crew required, so as not to change the trim of the ship too much. This ship was designed to carry a light, highly perishable and valuable human cargo, with water and rations accordingly. He desired to make the ship as independent as possible and had indented for her capacity of supplies. With all regard for the Bombay Marine, its supply department in India often was lacking in necessary stores. He heard the watch hail again, and saw a lighter pulling along the starboard side. Ordnance stores, forty muskets, a hundred pistols and cutlasses, powder, a thousand flints, spare locks for the ship's guns, round shot, a full allowance of cannister and grape, serge cartridges, quick and slow match and a double allowance of pyrotechnics—all hard to obtain in India. It would be dark by the time these were stowed.

"Out all fires!" roared the boatswain's mate of the watch. "The smoking lamp is out throughout the ship." The messenger dived below to the forecastle to extinguish the lamp that burned there twenty-four hours a day, furnishing a source of lights for the crew's pipes. Two cook's mates carried the galley fire in its iron basket to the gangway and dumped the coals into the water. Merewether hoped the cook had foreseen this and had dinner for the crew already prepared. He came aft, went below.

At the end of the third day, *Rapid* was provisioned, filled to capacity with water, ordnance stores, cordage, spare canvas. Merewether had also bought his cabin stores: wines, spirits, raisins, preserves, dried fruit, the small things that made a long voyage bearable. The Commodore had come aboard that afternoon, Merewether was certain, to see if he could in fact be ready for sea in the three days he had told Sir William and had found that yards were now crossed, sails bent on and furled, the ship indeed ready for sea. After loading the ordnance stores, Merewether had established true bearings on the shore, had the launch swing the ship around at slack tide while MacLellan and MacRae took the compass bearings, and corrected the deviation table.

"At least two days more," replied Welchance gloomily to Merewether's question. "Still trying to find enough guilders." Merewether decided to risk the starboard watch on a run ashore at liberty tonight, the port watch tomorrow. He thought briefly of Drury Lane, then decided to invite MacLellan, MacRae and Larkin to a tavern outside the dockyard. It might be well also to ask the Commodore.

"I plan a small dinner tonight for my officers ashore," Merewether said carefully. "Might I hope for the honor of your presence and that of any members of your staff?"

"I should be delighted, Captain," replied Welchance. It was quickly settled as to time and place. The Commodore mentioned that only three of his staff were presently in London. Actually, the Naval Service had only the barest representation in London: the Commodore and a few other specialists to give counsel to the Committee of Secrecy, and through it, to the Court of Directors, when some major decision of policy was to be transmitted to Bombay. The post was largely a sinecure, awarded for services rendered and through influence in the Company. Commodore Welchance was an able man, however, and Merewether respected his abilities.

Merewether sent for the Purser, dispatching him ashore to the Bull Tavern to make the arrangements. It was his intention to get better acquainted with these officers over a bottle and bird, even at the cost of hiring an officer from the dockyard to keep the watch. He decided that he had no complaints as to their industry and ability thus far. In fact they seemed to be making every effort to please him.

In late afternoon, Merewether called for his steward, the youngest of the cook's mates, a weedy Cockney youth with the accent of Bow Bells that Merewether had spent sixteen years trying to eradicate. He requested hot fresh water for shaving. The lad departed with a rush, came back in a moment with a jug. Merewether, shirt off, said, "Pour the basin half full."

The lad poured, slopped, almost upset the basin, set the jug down and fled. Merewether wondered a moment at this agitation. He stepped before the mirror, picked up mug and brush, absently working up the lather. He looked into the mirror just as a cloud shut off the sun from the skylight. In the half light he saw the face in the mirror, almost as though he were a stranger observing it. The crooked nose, the white scar, the rough blue powder burns, the missing earlobe, all combined to give the face an expression of cruel determination, quite different from the doubt and inadequacies Merewether had felt the past few days. He realized suddenly that the agitation of the lad, the brisk manner in which his officers and men had carried out the orders he had given in his quiet, civil way, were based upon their fear of him. They evidently thought his manner was a pose to conceal a disposition as hard and cruel as his scarred face appeared. He snorted a mirthless laugh as the realization sunk in; perhaps he was a paper tiger, as they said in China, but, he resolved, he would conceal the fact as long as possible.

The gig put his party ashore at a landing upstream from the dockyard. They walked through the dusk a few hundred yards to the Bull Tavern. The host met them at the door and ushered them into a private dining room where a bright sea-coal fire blazed on the hearth. He had set out a table in one corner on which were ranged bottles of port, rum, brandy, gin.

"Serve you, sir?" inquired the host.

"No," said Merewether. "We expect others." His back to the fire, he waited for the arrival of the Commodore. He heard the sound of hooves outside. In a moment the host ushered in the Commodore, all smiles, with three other officers. The Commodore introduced them around, Lieutenant Mason, Operations; Lieutenant Abbott, the Dockyard; Dr. Spencer, Surgeon General of the Company in England. Merewether signaled the host to serve his guests.

Dr. Spencer was a rotund man, almost completely bald. Drink in hand, he approached Merewether by the fire. "Ah, Captain, this is a most felicitous occasion. By the bye, I'm sending you another officer, coming up from Kent, Dr. Buttram, Assistant Surgeon. Sir William thought it might be well to have a surgeon aboard for your mission." The Company from its beginnings had always been liberal in providing medical attention for its servants.

"Very good," replied Merewether. No telling what condition he might find the Lyndes in after all these months in the clutches of a pirate in the tropics.

The real purpose of this gathering as far as he was concerned was to get to know his officers. He could not offend the Commodore or his staff, but Merewether began a careful circuit of the room, a few words here, respectful attention to an anecdote there, making himself as agreeable as he could. He discovered that MacLellan had quietly prevailed upon the host to find a bottle of what he called Scots whusky, which he was sipping with the air of a connoisseur. In a few minutes toasts were being drunk and by the time the host called the party to dinner, all were in high good humor.

The affair broke up after midnight, everyone a little tipsy. Merewether saw the Commodore and his staff into his carriage and made his way to the landing through the chill darkness. He was satisfied that liquor was no great problem for his officers, and had realized his purpose in learning something of the background and abilities of each in a casual manner.

In his cabin, Merewether found himself quite unable to sleep. He finally arose, struck a light, lit his lamp and took his orders from the strongbox. As Welchance had mentioned, they were well put, specific as to objective, but allowing for the exercise of discretion as the situation might develop. The primary objective was to ransom and rescue Lynde and family. He noted the standard closing directive that he should render all aid and assistance within his power, commensurate with his mission, to any public vessels of the Crown. Little chance of that, he mused, ten guns and a ship lightly constructed for speed would stand small chance against even a corvette or brig.

Merewether laid aside the orders and began to sort out the facts he had gathered during the evening as to the backgrounds and abilities of his officers. MacLellan was ten years older than he, the son of a Scots gunsmith. Apprenticed as a lad in a Company ship, he had risen to gunner before the ship was lost on the Coromandel Coast. His passion was guns, ordnance, explosives. He had confided that he had invented some improvements in carriages, tackle and sights. After joining the Naval Service, he had risen from warrant to commissioned rank and been assigned to the Company arsenal at Calcutta. There he oversaw the repair and refitting of ordnance, the testing and issue of powder and shot, the arming of ships. He expressed himself as most anxious to test the abilities of the long nine pounder pivot guns with his improved sight. Merewether hoped he was competent to stand an efficient deck watch under way,

MacRae was a somewhat different kettle of fish; small and dark, a Scots as was MacLellan, he had first gone to sea in a North Sea trawler, had risen to command and then, on the death of his wife, had gone out to India to seek his fortune. He found this not so easy as expected for a man without capital or connections, and had taken service as a mate in a "country ship," Indian built, lascar manned, European owned and commanded, which carried on the local coastwise and island trade. He had been to the pearl fisheries off Ceylon, had, he said, learned to dive for the pearl oysters where the depth of water was not too great. He could, he had boasted, stay underwater for nearly two minutes. He had come into the Bombay Marine, as Merewether had, during the shortage of officers in '98, though their paths had never previously crossed. He had come back to England on leave to settle his father's estate.

Larkin was American, born in Canada, a year younger than Merewether. His family had moved south after the American War, settled in the wilderness of Kentucky, taken up land and tried to scrape a living from it. His mother and father had died when he was sixteen, his sisters were married and he decided to go back east to try the sea after listening to the tales of a keelboat-man on the Ohio. At Baltimore, he had signed on the first ship he saw, a British merchant brig, was paid off at Liverpool and then found a berth on the newly constructed slaver *Rapid* in '95. Native intelligence and industry had resulted in his rise to mate. He also appeared to have a love of firearms, describing the shooting matches on the frontier, the range and accuracy of the Kentucky rifle, promising to demonstrate his marksmanship to Merewether at a suitable time.

Larkin had made one remark that puzzled Merewether.

"Have you found my pigeon cote yet, Captain?" he had asked.

"No," said Merewether. "What and where is it?"

"I keep my birds in a little compartment just forward of my room, Captain. It was built as an extra bosun's locker but never used. Six generations I've raised. Every so often I swap cocks to bring in new blood, and I've some dandies now." Merewether resolved to see for himself in the morning. Six bells in the mid-watch struck, he yawned, put the orders back in the strongbox, blew out the lamp and retired. Sleep came easily enough this time.

At eight bells of the morning watch, Merewether heard the watch hail. He looked out and saw the liberty boat coming alongside. Clapping on his hat, he went unobtrusively on deck. The starboard watch came over the side. They all seemed happy; a few were bleary-eyed and dirty. No wholesale desertions, he thought, turning to go back below. Just then, Larkin emerged from the companionway.

"Good morning, Captain," he said. "Just about to feed my birds. Usually exercise them just before dark so they come back quick. Would you like to see them, sir?"

"Yes."

Larkin turned and went below, Merewether following. At the foot of the companion on the left was a door he had not noticed, secured by a large padlock.

"Some of the crew like squab," Larkin grinned apologetically, turning the key. He stood aside and Merewether entered. He noticed a slightly acrid smell, not unpleasant. Larkin must keep the compartment clean, he thought. Ranged against the forward bulkhead was a cote composed of wooden-barred cages. In each were pigeons, usually two, a cock and a hen, strutting about on their short legs, preening, fluffing their feathers. Along the after bulkhead were secured casks containing grain, crushed shell, gravel. Larkin opened a door, took a cock gently, held him, stroking his grayish feathers.

"Watch," he said and opened the deadlight. He launched the bird and Merewether craned his neck to see him fly out across the Pool, circle several times, then come back to the porthole and enter. Larkin put him back in the cage. "Knew he wouldn't stay long," he chuckled. "This pair's beginning to court again."

"Amazing," said Merewether. "Will they always come home?"

"So long as the ship don't move too far. This is the only home they've ever known. I might lose them if the ship went fifty miles or so while they were off, haven't tried that. Some of the other mates on ships trading into the Congo have 'em, too; we have races for a pot. I'm over three hundred pounds ahead last three years," continued Larkin with satisfaction. "Secret of it, sir, is selection. I only keep eight or ten pairs, sell, trade or eat the squabs that don't come up to snuff. That way, I've got the fastest and best of each crop to breed. Have to trade or buy occasionally, else they'll get too inbred."

"Amazing," said Merewether again. These were a far cry from the pigeons he saw fouling London rooftops. He went on aft to his cabin.

Working over the inventory of supplies an hour later, Merewether heard a knock. "Come," he called and the Purser entered. "Yes?"

Davis seemed ill at ease, shuffling his feet, clearing his throat.

"Sir," he said. "It's Jones."

"Who?"

"Jones, sir, your steward. He's gone." Merewether had not learned his name, but Jones must be the weedy Cockney cook's mate.

"Enlisted in the Royal Navy, sir," the Purser continued in a rush. "Men say Jones and some of 'em were at a tavern. Press gang came in. Of course all of 'em had certificates, but Jones wouldn't show his, so they took him. Some of the men said Jones told them he was afraid, beggin' your pardon, of you, sir, and intended to enlist in the Navy. Anyway, he's gone."

Merewether recalled the episode of the afternoon before, his conclusion that his scars gave him a sinister aspect, quite at variance with his true nature. Poor lad, he thought, in his fear he had exchanged the frying pan for the fire.

"I wish Jones every success in his new career," said Merewether. "Report the facts to Mr. MacRae and have him enter them in the log."

"Aye aye, sir."

At four bells of the forenoon watch on the sixth day, the gangway hailed a lighter heading for the ship under sweeps. Merewether looked out the port, saw it carried at least eight soldiers and a sergeant armed with muskets. He recognized the Commodore in the little group in the stern, then saw Sir William Foster beside him, as well as Lieutenant Abbott from the dockyard, and Dr. Spencer. In the center of the lighter were four iron-bound chests, not very large, each with a line with a bouy on the end tied to a handle. Sir William was taking no chance of losing this treasure if the lighter swamped or a line parted while the chests were being hoisted aboard.

Merewether was at the gangway to greet Sir William and the Commodore as Tompkins piped the side. "Day early, Captain," said Sir William. "Found a Dutch émigré willing to exchange guilders for guineas. Commodore says high tide in three hours. Are you ready for sea?"

Merewether looked up at the vane. The wind was almost due north. "Wind will have to draw a point or so west, sir," he replied carefully, "for the ship to weather the point. If it pulls east, we're stuck." The Boatswain and Larkin were supervising rigging the slings about the chests. The hands tailed on to the line: the first of the chests swayed up and thumped on deck.

It was all two hands could do to lift each chest. Grunting and straining, they took them down the companionway, along the passage to Merewether's cabin. There, Merewether opened the hatch set flush in the deck, made of two layers of oak with iron plates between them, to expose the ship's strong room. Slavers had to carry large sums of money, and *Rapid*'s builders had constructed this room so as to be inaccessible from any other point in the ship. The chests were lowered into the strong room and wedged fast; the hatch was closed. Merewether turned the keys in the two heavy locks, straightened up. Sir William handed him four keys and a receipt. Merewether signed and handed it back.

"No doubt what was in those chests, sir," he said cheerfully.

Sir William handed him another sealed document. "Orders to get under way immediately," he said, "wind and tide permitting, of course. Oh, and there are twenty pouches of mail and dispatches came aboard too."

"Aye aye, sir," Merewether replied. "By the way, Doctor, your Assistant Surgeon has not reported."

"Due any minute," said Dr. Spencer anxiously. "Hope the

young fool hasn't got drunk along the way." The party was piped over the side and now pulled back toward the dockyard.

"Mr. MacRae, you may send the hands to dinner. Then pass the word to make all preparations for getting under way." Merewether turned to go below, looked aloft at the vane again, saw little change, walked aft to survey the position of shipping in the Pool. With the tide still making, the ship had swung around until she headed almost due east. It would be simple to take her out now, if the wind were only favorable; but at slack tide that northerly breeze would bring her head north again and the ebb would swing it almost west. A big Indiaman was anchored outboard only half a cable's length away, another on the other side, the same distance toward the dockyard. Unless the wind veered almost west, it would be a trick to get *Rapid* under way east toward the channel in these tight quarters with the Indiaman so close aboard to windward.

Merewether turned, started forward again. He became aware of a sort of chant behind him, "Mark! Mark! Mark! . . ." He turned and saw MacLellan crouched behind the after pivot gun, Larkin standing alongside with his eye to a brass tube that appeared to be over the touch hole. The Gunner and two of his mates stood by, tools in hand, intently watching the antics of these two officers.

"Ah," said MacLellan straightening up. "That fixes it." He appeared to tighten a bolt, and turned about, catching sight of Merewether.

"Just completed bore-sighting, Captain," he said. "Had to make sure my sight is lined up with the axis of the bore at point-blank range."

"Meaning what?" inquired Merewether, honestly puzzled. He had often enough fired cannon. It was just a matter of catching the target in the notches on the breech and muzzle, estimating the range, adjusting the quoin for elevation and pulling the lanyard.

"Let me show you, sir," said MacLellan self-consciously. Merewether stepped forward. Mounted on the breech of the long nine pounder, offset to the left to avoid the lock, was a highly polished brass contraption, a sort of horizontal bar containing numerous marks cut into its surface, with its edge cut into teeth like a saw.

Sliding on this bar was a brass piece on which was mounted a tang pivoted against a brass quadrant, which also bore lines cut into its surface radiating out to its arc. A threaded bolt with a knob on the end protruded from the sliding member on the crossbar. A collar bearing an upright blade also offset to the left had been fixed about the muzzle of the gun.

"Here," said MacLellan. "Look through the notch of this rear sight at the front sight on the target, sir." Merewether bent over, looked. The notch and blade lined up squarely on a bollard on the dock some three hundred yards away.

"Now, sir," continued MacLellan, twisting the knob and moving the sliding member. "Now look." Merewether looked, the sights unaccountably lined up ten feet to the right of the bollard. MacLellan raised the tang a fraction and the sights now lined up not only ten feet to the right, but at the water level of the pier. Merewether felt confused, looked his question at Mac-Lellan.

"Now, sir," continued MacLellan. "Look down this tube." Merewether came to the side, applied his eye to the end of the tube over the touch hole. Seemingly at a great distance he could see light, a circle, quartered by crossed wires and beyond the crossed wires he could see the bollard on the pier.

"Sir," said MacLellan. "You're as well acquainted with the theory of ballistics as I am." His Scottish burr had become quite pronounced. "You just have not seen my solution of the problem." He took on the manner of a schoolmaster about to expound the Pythagorean Theory to a rather dull class.

"When a gun is fired, Captain, the ball actually begins to drop as soon as it leaves the muzzle, though this is not apparent for a few hundred feet. From what we call point-blank range, it begins to slow up by reason of air resistance and gravity. Thus, in order to hit at longer ranges, the gun must be elevated so the ball travels above the line of sight and descends at the proper point to strike the target. My sight here provides an exact measure of elevation, allows corrections to either side for windage, or the tendency of guns to throw right or left, and permits the gunner to keep his sights on the target at all times, regardless of the range of the target and elevation of the gun. What we have just done is set the sight at zero elevation and deflection to coincide with the axis of the bore." MacLellan paused.

"How can I see out the bore by looking down the touch hole?" inquired Merewether curiously.

"Ah, Captain, another of my inventions." MacLellan removed the brass tube and handed it to Merewether. "You see, I have a magnifying lens in this tube. In the bore under the touch hole is a prismatic mirror so arranged that it transmits the image of the cross wires in the muzzle at right angles to the lens in the tube, thus allowing me to aim the axis of the bore at a target and adjust my sight to the same mark. I can then set my sight for the proper range."

"Very ingenious," said Merewether. "Very." MacLellan removed a brass ring from the muzzle containing the cross wires, then pulled a cord and withdrew another brass ring in which was mounted a triangular piece of glass. Just then, Merewether heard the boatswain's mate of the watch roar, "All hands! All hands! Make all preparations for getting under way!"

The vane had changed its direction a little, maybe as much as two points west. With another hour to the ebb, perhaps there was hope of getting under way. Merewether went below. In a few minutes' time, there came a succession of messengers reporting the various departments ready for getting under way. Damnation! Merewether suddenly remembered the Assistant Surgeon was not yet aboard. Well, if he was not aboard in the next few minutes before slack tide, Merewether would sail without him.

On deck, the vane showed a further shift west in the wind. The ship was headed now directly into the wind, almost north north-west. Close-hauled, she could now sail down the estuary without great difficulty. He went forward to the forecastle, noted that the anchor cable tended dead ahead. "Haul in to short stay," he told MacLellan. "Set the jib, but do not sheet it home until I give you the word."

"Aye aye, sir." The windlass clanked around, hands pushing easily enough on the bars as the messenger brought the dripping cable in. Merewether hurried aft. Never before had he had the sole and ultimate responsibility of getting a ship under way from tight quarters. Except for the two Indiamen anchored so close aboard on either side, there would be no problem, but by the time the anchor broke ground, *Rapid's* bowsprit would be little more than a hundred feet from the side of the inboard Indiaman.

On the quarterdeck he told Larkin, "Hoist the spanker."

"Aye aye, sir." The huge fore and aft sail rose slowly, halyards were belayed.

From the forecastle came the hail, "Anchor's at short stay."

"Hands to the spanker sheet," ordered Merewether. "Haul the boom out to starboard." The hands tailed on and hauled the boom over. Now the canvas filled, and it was all the hands could do to hold the sheet even with a turn about the bitts. "Waisters!" shouted Merewether. "Tail on here, haul out!"

He looked at the head of the ship. The stern, forced to port by the backed spanker, was swinging slowly around the anchor as a pivot. "Heave round, Mr. MacLellan, till she's straight up and down!" he shouted. He heard the windlass clank and in a moment the hail came back, "Straight up and down!"

Merewether watched the ship swing, the stern still moving slowly to port, forced by the immense leverage of the backed spanker, the wind now just abaft the beam. "Heave round!" he shouted to the forecastle.

"Anchor's breaking ground," roared MacLellan. "Anchor's aweigh!"

"Sheet home your jib," shouted Merewether. "Port your helm!" The jib flapped violently, then filled on the port tack with a thunderous report. The ship spun on her heel, no longer pointing into the side of the Indiaman as the jib brought her bow around. He could see lascars lining the bulwarks in the Indiaman's waist staring curiously, and hear the blue-jacketed officer of the watch raving warnings and maledictions from her poop through a speaking trumpet. The spanker flapped. Larkin and the after guard took in the sheet until it was close-hauled on the port tack. The stern was still swinging to port.

"Shift your helm, meet her, steady as you go!" said Merewether in a volley of orders. This vessel was instantly responsive to her helm, he found. The stern of the Indiaman slid by, fifty feet away, the watch officer now leaning silently over the side to see *Rapid* pass, speaking trumpet still in hand. Just then, Larkin pointed, "Boat coming alongside."

Merewether stepped to the rail and saw a four-oared wherry

frantically pulling toward the port gangway, a young man in the uniform of a surgeon crouched in its bow, bellowing for a line. A hand snubbed a line on the bitts, dropped it to the officer, who took a turn about a cleat in the bow of the wherry.

"Put over a ladder," called Merewether. "Haul in those chests." The officer, red-faced and perspiring in spite of the January chill, came over the side. The two chests were swayed up and the officer leaned over and dropped a gold guinea in the hand of the stroke oar as the bow oar cast off the line. He made his way aft, mopping his face with his handkerchief.

"Set the tops'ls," roared Merewether. "Come to port two points," he commanded the helm. Now clear of the Indiaman he wanted to stay as far to the left of the channel as possible to give himself room to weather the next bend. With the topsails braced up, close-hauled, the ship moved rapidly with the ebb down the estuary.

"Take the watch, Mr. Larkin," he said and turned to greet the newcomer. "That was a near thing, Doctor."

"Yes, sir," replied the young man. "Buttram, sir, Assistant Surgeon. The stage lost a wheel this morning."

"Very well," said Merewether. "Mr. MacLellan will assign you quarters."

CHAPTER 3

The run from Land's End to the Cape Verde Islands was uneventful, a few squalls, but generally favorable winds, thirteen days, averaging almost ten knots. Merewether took a new departure, and set a course for the Cape of Good Hope, seeing no need for stopping at St. Helena with his water and supply situation so favorable. Near the Equator, for the first time the wind failed him, left him becalmed in stifling heat on a mirrorlike sea for two days.

"Mr. MacLellan," he called, the first morning of the calm. "I take it you would like to exercise your gun crews?"

"Yes, sir," replied MacLellan. "Could we put out targets, sir?"

Merewether sent for the Cooper, had the gig lowered, and directed MacRae to drop a cask a third of a mile to starboard.

A competition seemed suddenly to have developed between the port and starboard batteries. He heard chaffing remarks passed and concluded that wagers had been made. He hoped both batteries would acquit themselves with some distinction. MacLellan had assumed command of the starboard battery, Larkin of the port. The guns had their jackets pulled off, tompions removed; locks were attached and tested. Merewether saw the cask dropped and the gig pull hastily to one side.

"You may fire when ready," he told MacLellan.

"Load your guns and run them out," commanded MacLellan. The powder monkeys came running up with the cartridges, shot and wads were rammed home, quills inserted, the locks primed from the powder horns carried by the gun captains. Merewether noticed the pivot's crews had not loaded.

"Sir, with your permission, Mr. Larkin and I have a little private wager going. Both have been fitted with my sight. Larkin will lay the forward gun and I the after, five shots each."

"Very well." Merewether was interested to see how well these officers and guns performed. MacLellan went forward, stationing himself behind and to one side of number one gun.

"Stand by," he commanded. "Take your aim, you may fire when ready."

Merewether took the glass from the rack, found the bobbing cask in the narrow field, and steadied himself against the mizzen shrouds. He had told Dr. Buttram to bring a sheet of paper to tabulate the shots. Forward, the gun captain was painstakingly adjusting the quoin, looking up at the target to estimate range. He peered through the sights, motioned the man with the handspike to train the gun about a fraction, then stood aside and pulled the lanyard. The lock snapped, a tiny puff of smoke shot up from the torch hole and the gun roared out.

In the field of the telescope, Merewether saw a spout of water rise, fifty feet right and a hundred feet short of the target. He called to Buttram, "Number one, one hundred short, fifty right."

"Aye aye, sir," replied Buttram, making entries in a column.

"Number three gun, stand by," commanded MacLellan.

Five shots each for the starboard battery and the cask still floated. Many shots came close, but hitting a three-foot target at seven hundred yards with a nine pounder would be mostly a matter of luck. There was just a breath of breeze, but enough to enable Merewether to work the ship about and bring the port battery to bear. Larkin took over. The shots continued. Misses, near misses. The last gun was laid absolutely true, but the shot was short and ricocheted right over the cask. There would have to be a tedious computation of Buttram's tabulations to determine which battery had won this competition.

MacLellan and Larkin approached. "Captain, would you spin a coin to see who goes first?" MacLellan won, turned to the crew of the after pivot. "Load and run out," he commanded.

The gun on its platform was trained out to port, loaded and primed. MacLellan crouched behind it, adjusted the sight tang against its quadrant, tested the motion of the air, twisted the deflection knob a half turn, took careful aim, gingerly moving the quoin a fraction, signaling the hands at either side of the pivot platform.

"Mark and lock," he called, stepping hastily aside and jerking the lanyard. The long nine's spiteful, ear-splitting report cracked out. Merewether caught the splash, a hundred feet over, slightly right, almost in line. The crew sponged out, reloaded, and hauled the gun back to battery. MacLellan adjusted the elevation, turned the deflection knob a fraction, took his aim, fired again.

"Short a hundred, dead in line," reported Merewether.

The gun was readied again, another sight adjustment made and the gun fired. In the field of his glass, Merewether saw the cask suddenly disintegrate, staves flying into the air. "Hit, third shot," he said to Buttram. The starboard gun crews raised a cheer, while the port crews looked glum.

"Over, short and halve the difference!" crowed MacLellan. "Works every time!" He was beaming with satisfaction while the sweat ran down his big red face and his shirt stuck to his back. This equatorial sun was fierce. The gig was pulling over to set out another cask.

"Ready, Mr. Larkin?" inquired Merewether as he took his place forward to observe the fall of shot.

"Yes, sir," replied Larkin. The gun was loaded and run out. Larkin set the sight, took careful aim, locked the pivot and fired.

"Over fifty, right ten," reported Merewether. Larkin made a quick correction, sighted as soon as the gun was loaded and back to battery, fired again. "Over fifty, dead in line."

Larkin made an infinitesmal sight adjustment, fired again. The cask exploded. "Hit, third shot," Merewether said to Buttram. "Gentlemen, we need waste no more casks or powder. I declare the honors even." He turned. "Mr. Davis," he called to the Purser. "It appears the mainbrace is in need of a splice." Cheers erupted from the grinning hands as he went aft. "Hoist the recall," he told the signal quartermaster. He had no morale problem as yet, he reflected. The crew had shaken down.

Merewether invited MacLellan, Larkin and Buttram to dine with him that evening in the dead calm. "There's a bottle of your peat-smoke whisky," he told MacLellan. "And port, claret, brandy or gin." For the first time this voyage he had broken out some of the cabin stores he had so extravagantly laid in. The vents in the overhead were open, windsails rigged, but they hung limp in the stifling heat. A dram of claret would be sufficient for him, he decided. Larkin exclaimed, as MacLellan beamed, that he desired to test the "Scots whusky," to see for himself how it compared with the corn whiskey of Kentucky. Merewether noted that Dr. Buttram contented himself with a single glass of claret.

After dinner, Larkin excused himself to go on deck for the first watch. Merewether during this cordial period had learned that Buttram was the younger son of a landed gentleman in Kent and had read at Cambridge; this was his first experience in practice after completing his medical education and serving an apprenticeship under a London surgeon. He confided that the second chest he had brought aboard contained a complete surgical outfit, every specific drug he could obtain, together with the latest pharmacopoeia and texts on medicine and surgery. The Company always provided its ships with an ample supply of medicines, so *Rapid* should be doubly well-equipped. Buttram was twenty-four, with fair complexion and close-cropped blond hair, a pleasant manner and real enthusiasm for his new career with the Company.

"Would you excuse me, Captain," asked MacLellan. "I forgot

my pipe." He was back in a moment, puffing contentedly, a bright object in his hand.

"You know, Captain, the Company sent me to England at the invitation of the Admiralty to demonstrate my sight to a board of Royal Navy captains. Damned fools wouldn't buy it, said all they need to do is lay alongside the enemy and keep the guns in action." MacLellan snorted at the recollection. "Four months I wasted at Portsmouth and Plymouth, showed them time after time how the sight improved the accuracy of their guns, but no luck. Did learn a few things myself, the armorer at Portsmouth had some very good notions. I met some others too, a German clock maker. He made this." MacLellan laid on the table a brass device that appeared to be the works from a clock to which was fitted a small flintlock. Merewether and Buttram both looked closely at it.

"What is its use?" asked Merewether.

"It is a time mechanism for exploding demolition charges," explained MacLellan. "I furnish the salvage ships for the Company with powder, quick and slow match, other supplies needed to blow a wreck open, recover specie and cargo. It's dangerous work when you use either a flying fuse underwater or a hose pipe; we lost eleven divers last three years. Quick match is too unpredictable and slow match burns unevenly. I've been working a little on improving the quality myself," continued MacLellan self-consciously. He extracted a key from his pocket, inserted it in the mechanism and turned it, making a clicking sound. He laid it on the table, pointed a finger at a small dial on the side divided into six segments with a slot cut into its rim.

"You may set the time of explosion up to six hours. Clock mechanism turns this wheel till the slot comes opposite a spring, just like a striking clock. Spring is released and trips the sear on the lock." MacLellan put his pipe carefully away, extracted from his pocket a vial, opened it and poured a pinch of powder into the priming pan of the lock. He turned the dial until the slot was almost upright. "Two, maybe three minutes," he said. Merewether instinctively leaned back away from the device, and waited. Surely, the dial was turning almost imperceptibly.

Suddenly the mechanism gave a sharp snap, the hammer fell

with a shower of sparks as flint met frizzen, and the powder flashed with a minute puff of smoke. MacLellan beamed.

"Most remarkable," said Merewether.

"And you can set that thing for as much as six hours?" wondered Buttram.

"Yes," said MacLellan. "Normally a diver wouldn't need so much time to place the charge, unless the water is vurra deep." At moments such as this, his Scottish burr became quite pronounced. "This device, of course, is sealed up in a watertight keg, coated with pitch, to hold the powder charge. I've already improved on it," he continued with pride. "Old Benziger had it in his head he had to light a quick match to carry fire to the powder charge. He missed lighting the quick match three out of ten tries." MacLellan pointed at a tube extending from the priming pan. "Fill that tube with powder, stick it in the main charge and no misfires; my improvement."

"You are a man of many parts, Mr. MacLellan," said Merewether. "But, after you fire this device, it's gone. It must be quite expensive."

"Twenty-five guineas," said MacLellan sorrowfully. "Not pounds, guineas, he wanted. Of course," he brightened, "there was a bit of bargaining. Fifteen pounds, at last, not a shilling less. I drew a bill of exchange on the Company. No doubt," he looked gloomy, "some treasury clerk will protest it and I'll have to make good, pay it myself. Ah, well, I have a Chinee artisan works for me. With this as a model, he'll turn out a hundred. I bought that many springs, four shillings each, only part the Chinee couldn't make.

The gathering broke up, MacLellan to snatch a nap before the midwatch, Buttram to read Frazer's *Notes on Naval Surgery*, Merewether to go on deck in the sweltering night, seeking some relief from the heat.

Conditions were unchanged the next day, except that a long greasy swell had developed that kept the ship in motion, slack canvas and rigging flapping and creaking. Idleness, heat and monotony were beginning to take their toll after the excitement of the target competition yesterday. Tempers were short, the men uncomfortable in this oppressive atmosphere. Merewether considered briefly setting out targets again, renewing the gunnery practice, but that was expensive sport. Just after the issue of spirits, words passed between Jackson, maintopman, and Eldridge, ordinary seaman. In an instant they were locked together in a flurry of blows, straining each to throw the other. The leading boatswain's mate separated them under the indignant eye of Mr. MacRae and brought them to the mast before Merewether. He heard the complaint, looked at the two sheepish men. Both were young, splendidly muscled, without much weight advantage, and they belonged to different watches.

"Very well," said Merewether after the boatswain's mate had concluded his testimony, looking from MacLellan as officer of the starboard watch to MacRae of the port, "I think this matter should be settled between these men. Johnson," he called to the Sailmaker. "Will you rig a ring on the forward hatch, cover it with canvas, and these men shall have it out, man to man, catch as catch can. Mr. Larkin shall be the referee, two falls out of three, half hour time limit."

"Aye aye, sir," said the Sailmaker. In an hour the ring was ready, the two champions, barefoot, stripped to the waist, in opposite corners with their seconds. Every man on the ship was present, even the quartermaster and helmsman at the idle wheel peering forward to see the match.

It was a good show. Both men were strong and agile, possessing some skill in the sport. Jackson finally pinned Eldridge in the last two minutes, to the cheers of all hands. It was even enough that there was immediate talk of a rematch. In the late afternoon, a squall built up in the west and struck the ship with blinding rain, thunder, lightning, and enough wind to keep all hands busy. By the next day they were out of the doldrums, on a long reach to the south against the southeast trades, thence to beat up for the Cape of Good Hope.

Regulations required Company ships to fly the red ensign north of St. Helena in the Atlantic. As *Rapid* crossed sixteen degrees south latitude, to his own surprise, Merewether found himself calling all hands aft, making a solemn ceremony of hoisting the colors of the Bombay Marine, telling the crew in ringing tones that this was the flag under which they would henceforth serve and fight. The hands, and even his officers, seemed impressed. He felt curiously exhilarated to see the thirteen red and white stripes, quartered by a red cross, St. George's Cross in the left canton, snapping in the breeze again. He was back in home waters, no longer an alien.

CHAPTER 4

It was a warm, pleasant day, summer in these latitudes, with the wind almost south. *Rapid*, on the starboard tack, was steering northeast on a course Merewether had calculated would just weather Cape Agulhas, the southernmost tip of Africa. He had had to reach down almost to the Roaring Forties to get enough southing against the southeast trades to weather the cape and enter the Indian Ocean. Over the horizon, on the port beam, was Cape Town, safely in British hands since last month.

Merewether and MacRae were on the quarterdeck, sextants in hand, quartermasters standing by to record the noon observation. Merewether raised the sextant to his eye, adjusted the vernier, brought the sun down to the horizon through the smoked glass, continued to adjust while the quartermasters, watches in hand, waited.

The sun dipped. "Mark," said Merewether. "Mark," said Mac-Rae in almost the same breath. The quartermasters recorded the time. Merewether and MacRae compared the readings on the scales of their sextants.

"Close enough," said MacRae. "I'll compute the latitude."

"Very well," replied Merewether, handing the sextant to the quartermaster to be stowed in its box. MacRae had a passion for navigation and mathematics. Merewether at the outset of the voyage had insisted on MacLellan and Larkin alternating with MacRae in doing the day's work in navigation. Each had proved to be fairly competent, but in view of MacRae's interest, he decided to entrust the task to him. After being so long out of sight of land, he had, the last few days, taken the observations with MacRae. Their accuracy shortly would be tested.

"Land ho!" came the hail from the maintop lookout.

"Where away?" cried MacLellan.

"One point on port bow, sir." Well, thought Merewether, Mac-Rae may have scored a bullseye, if this was Cape Agulhas. They could, of course, be a hundred miles out of reckoning on longitude, but the star fix last night did not indicate it, and the latitude was correct.

Within half an hour, the Cape was visible from the deck. Mac-Rae requested permission to take a new departure and changed course to east northeast by east until they weathered Cape Elizabeth. On the new course, Cape Agulhas was soon on the port quarter, as close-hauled under all plain sail *Rapid* headed into the Indian Ocean.

"Sail ho!" came the hail from the masthead.

"Where away?"

"Dead ahead, sir."

Merewether was not concerned. It was probably a Royal Navy vessel, if alone. Indiamen would be in convoy.

"Sail ho! I see two more sails astern the first," came the hail. Well, possibly it could be a convoy. Merewether took the glass, went forward and up the foremast shrouds. At the crosstrees, he steadied the glass, focused it. The leading ship was large. She could be one of the Company's, but the cut of the topsails did not look right. He shifted the glass astern. Unless his eyes were playing tricks, there were three ships astern, close-hauled, all sail set. There was no doubt as to their identity: the rig was distinctive, Royal Navy seventy-fours. He shifted back to the ship ahead, almost hull up now, and realized she was a Frenchman, a ship of the line.

Merewether slid down and hurried aft. He was rapidly closing and almost on collision course with her. Admiral Linois had a sizable French squadron based on Mauritius; there had been just enough time for the news of Trafalgar last October to reach him, and orders to return to France for some strategic maneuver in mind by Bonaparte. The seventy-fours were three miles astern of the Frenchman and appeared to be losing ground. Their bottoms must be foul for a three decker to sail away from them like this. If the Frenchman held her course, she would just weather Cape

Agulhas and could then wear around with the wind on her quarter and escape into the Atlantic. Merewether made his decision.

"Send the hands to quarters. Clear the ship for action!" Pipes shrilled, the boatswain's mates passed the word, the hands came pouring up, jackets came off the guns, the galley fire was dumped over the side, sand was spread on deck, fire buckets filled. Dr. Buttram went below, shouting for the two cook's mates and the Purser, who constituted his staff, to move his medical chest to the slave deck midships where he had established his surgery.

Merewether had no illusions. This ship resembled in rig the new thirty-six-gun frigates just now being commissioned in the Royal Navy, but it was much more lightly constructed. Even a frigate could not stand a moment against the broadsides of a hundred-gun ship. He must try to herd this battleship in toward Cape Agulhas, force her to go about, give the seventy-fours time to come up and engage her. His nine pounder popguns could do little harm; her twenty-four pounders could blow him out of the water in a single blast.

"Mr. Larkin, you have excellent eyesight. Tell me what guns the Frenchman mounts as bow chasers."

Larkin took the glass. In a moment he reported, "Looks like two twenty-four pounders, sir, not long guns. By the bye, her name is *Canonnière*."

"Very good," replied Merewether, making up his mind. The direction in his orders was to render all aid and assistance to the Navy within his power, commensurate with his mission. Being sunk by a single broadside would be no assistance to those seventy-fours. *Canonnière* was less than two miles ahead, closing rapidly.

"Hands to the braces!" roared Merewether. "Wear ship, starboard helm." *Rapid* spun about as the hands hauled on the braces. "Midships, meet her, steady as you go!" He completed the hundred-and-eighty-degree turn, steadied on the port tack, close-hauled on the same course as *Canonnière*, two points on her port bow, a mile ahead. In this position the Frenchman could bring only one bow chaser to bear without yawing. Close-hauled as she was on the port tack, she would have to turn at least forty degrees to leeward to make her port broadside bear, even at the limits of the guns' train, and the Frenchman could not lose that much ground to leeward and expect to weather Cape Agulhas.

Merewether measured the distance to *Canonnière* with his eye, gave quick orders to the helm, yawed to port until the wind spilled, sails flapped a moment, brought her back to course, repeated, using the old tricks of station keeping to reduce the distance to the Frenchman. He saw a puff of smoke from her port bow chaser, saw no sign of the fall of the shot. At little less than a mile, hitting with a twenty-four pounder would be luck. He could count on his long nine pounders having a quarter again more range, he thought, but without the deadly weight of metal.

"Mr. MacLellan," he called. "Try a ranging shot, if you please."

"Aye aye, sir." MacLellan bustled back to the long nine, tested the force of the wind almost at right angles to the line of fire, twisted the sight knob for right deflection, raised the tang almost to its limit, crouched behind the gun signaling to the gunners for train, adjusting the quoin for near maximum elevation.

"Mark and lock!" He stood aside, jerked the lanyard. The spiteful, ear-splitting report rang out; with smoke blown instantly to leeward, Merewether caught a minute splash in the field of his glass.

"Short one thousand, right two hundred," reported Merewether. He saw smoke puff again from the bow of the Frenchman and a towering splash arose a hundred yards off the port quarter. This was too close for comfort. He heard MacLellan give the mark again, watched the fall of shot, dead in line, but at least five hundred feet short. As the gun heated up, it would throw the shot a little better. The gun appeared to be at maximum elevation. He yawed to port, again reduced the range to *Canonnière*.

MacLellan said something to Fleming, the Gunner, who departed at a run. He fired again. Short. Something howled close along the starboard side, a splash arose just off the starboard bow. The twenty-four pounder had the range!

The gunner emerged on deck, his arms full of half cartridges. Apparently MacLellan intended to overload the gun with half again its usual charge. Dangerous, it could result in a burst gun; but he had to take the chance. Unless he could shoot away a spar in the next shot or so, he would have to pull out, or risk being crippled or sunk himself.

Just then, there came a shattering crash forward. A twenty-four pounder ball had struck the starboard bulwark, ranging forward, sending a shower of splinters about number one gun, tearing a gash ten feet long. Merewether saw men down, blood spurting. He turned just as the pivot gun fired and leaped off its track with the excessive recoil. He caught *Canonnière* in his glass, saw no sign of the fall of shot. Then the fore-topgallant sail changed shape, the topgallant mast bent, hesitated a moment, and folded down over the fore-topsail. The two jibs disappeared; evidently the forestays had parted. Now *Canonnière*, relieved of the balancing pressure of the headsails, came around into the wind.

"Well done, MacLellan!" shouted Merewether, just as the starboard side of *Canonnière* erupted in a cloud of smoke. She had fired her entire broadside, forty-five guns, at this insolent terrier that had brought her to bay; but they were hastily laid and fired, and most of the splashes were well astern. One ball howled through the spanker, barely missing the mizzenmast, and plunged into the sea ahead.

Merewether saw the three seventy-fours plowing ahead, rapidly closing the gap. One was flying the broad pendant of a commodore and had signal flags hoisted.

"Engage the enemy, sir," said MacRae, signal book in hand. Merewether could see the frantic seaman on *Canonnière* cutting away the wreckage, while another party set a sail under the bowsprit. It filled and *Canonnière* began to pay off. Just as she did, two of the seventy-fours fired their broadsides, almost together, from either side, a third of a mile distant; *Canonnière* replied in kind. The third seventy-four came up directly astern of the Frenchman, yawed and fired a raking broadside. The three ships closed in, guns thundering, as the greasy clouds of smoke blew along the surface of the water to leeward. Merewether looked forward. The men from number one gun had been moved, but dark stains still glistened on the sanded deck. A new crew, the Cooper, his mates, waisters, stood by in their stead at the gun. Cape Agulhas was dead ahead, too close for comfort. Merewether gave the orders, brought *Rapid* around, ran toward the battle, just as the tricolor fluttered down.

As he came down to the scene of the battle, Merewether saw launches, crammed with men, sun glinting on arms, pulling for *Canonnière*: the prize crew. All four ships were now hove to, but drifting uncomfortably close to a lee shore. There was other damage apparent now to the Frenchman, mizzen-topsail yard shot in two, braces and shrouds dangling. Her wheel had also been shot away. The seventy-fours had poured it in, making sure she did not escape. She was in no danger of sinking, and with a little work could be brought in to Cape Town as a proud and valuable prize; money in the pockets of all hands, from ten shillings to thousands of pounds for that flag officer. Merewether felt a flush of resentment that the Bombay Marine and *Rapid* would not share.

"Make the recognition signal and our number, Mr. MacRae," said Merewether. The flag ship hoisted the response. Then another string of flags went up. MacRae spelled out, "Well done."

"Acknowledge," said Merewether turning away. "Pass the word to secure from quarters, set the underway watch, resume course."

"Aye aye, sir," said MacRae. "It *was* well done, sir." Merewether plunged below and sought out the surgery on the slave deck midships.

In the surgery, in the light of the battle lanterns, he found Dr. Buttram, sleeves rolled high, shirt splatterd with blood. On the improvised table, he had stretched Sullivan, captain of number one gun, face down, buttocks exposed. Through the right cheek was a two-foot jagged oak splinter, which had entered from the side and protruded several inches from the rear of the buttock. Sullivan lay quietly, apparently unconscious. Buttram looked around. He saw Merewether.

"Ah, Captain, the only serious wound we had." He motioned to four men who sat or lay on the deck, bandaged about arms and shoulders. "No more than flea bites for them, but this fellow's hurt. I've just administered a dose of laudanum, waiting for it to take effect before I try to remove this." He stepped to Sullivan's head, lifted an eyelid. "I think we are ready," he told the Purser.

From his open surgical chest he took a small saw and began to cut off the longer protruding end of the splinter. "Can't ever get one out the way it went in; barbed, just like fish hooks," continued Buttram. "Try to pull it out the other way. Fortunate it came clear through." The end of the splinter was severed and pitched aside. Buttram took a pair of forceps, gripped the end, pulled. The splinter did not budge, Sullivan groaned and twitched as the cook's mates held him down.

"On the off chance," said Buttram, shifting the forceps to the other end and pulling. The splinter slid smoothly out, followed by a considerable hemorrhage. "Well," said Buttram, "old Dr. Gray said it might happen once in a lifetime of practice and this is my time." He watched the hemorrhage for a moment, applied compresses and dressed the wound. "Blood is the best cleanser," he said. "This man will be off duty awhile, but barring infection, should be good as new in a fortnight."

"Very good," said Merewether. "Make your report, with a copy to Mr. MacRae for the log." This young doctor appeared to know his business. He had been lucky to escape so lightly under the fire of a ship of the line.

Back on deck, he saw the warships far astern, the group still etched against the sunset. Larkin was exercising his pigeons, a half dozen flying out and returning to the ship.

CHAPTER 5

Merewether intended to give Mauritius a wide berth. French held, she was the base of a powerful French squadron under Admiral Linois, and also supported a number of fast, well-armed privateers, any one of them probably more than a match for *Rapid*. In March, the northeast monsoon still blew, but fitfully; by April, it would have shifted to the southwest for six months. Now the prevailing wind was near dead foul, but interspersed with squalls, local breezes, changeable weather. Even so, *Rapid* continued to make good progress; not the speed with which he had come south, but sufficient, if all held well, to ensure his arrival in ample time to mount the rescue mission.

Unable to sleep longer, Merewether came on deck just after dawn. He saw MacRae and the quartermaster in the cubbyhole computing the star fix. He knew Mauritius was a hundred miles to port, it should now be broad on the beam. He had ordered double lookouts at the mastheads. Just now, one of them sang out, "Deck there, sail ho!"

"Where away?" cried Larkin.

"About four points on the starboard bow, sir."

"Can you make out her course?"

"Looks like she's crossing our bow, heading west."

Merewether conjured up a mental picture of the situation and came to a conclusion. He opened his mouth to give the order to Larkin, when the masthead hailed again.

"Deck, there, she's hauled her wind, headed toward us, running free."

The local breeze had been just west of north; close-hauled, *Rapid* had been able almost to make good her course northeast-wardly. That other ship, eight, ten miles ahead, quite evidently had the benefit of the fading northeast monsoon, and with the weather gauge was running down to investigate him. Her bold reaction indicated a ship of force, possibly a frigate.

"Hands to the braces," roared Merewether. To the helm, he said, "Port your helm." He squared off before the local wind running south southeast. For a moment he had considered some fancy maneuver, then concluded that the surest way of escape was also the simplest; to run away, even though it might delay his voyage. He set studding sails, flying jib, skysails. By eight bells of the morning watch, the enemy was out of sight. He altered course, close-hauled, reached far eastwardly before he again resumed his course for Ceylon.

They made their landfall on Ceylon and altered course up the Bay of Bengal, steering for the mouth of the Hooghly River with the new southwest monsoon. In late afternoon they were at anchor off the Company dockyard at Calcutta. MacLellan had the glass, searching the dockyard where the arsenal was located.

"Aha!" he snorted indignantly. "Not yet six o'clock and those lazy good-for-naughts already coming out the gate. Wait till I get ashore, I'll change all that!" The bell struck four times, signaling the end of the first dogwatch. MacLellan was a hard taskmaster. He saw a boat pull away from the landing. "Captain's coming aboard," he called to MacRae.

Merewether spoke briefly to MacLellan, "I would like to see you at your convenience." He went below. In a moment, the knock came. "Sit down, Mr. MacLellan. In view of your previous shore duty here, I want to talk to you privately about the local situation. Are you acquainted with Sir George Barlow?"

"Yes," said MacLellan. "Met him a time or two at receptions. He's senior member of the Council, appointed provisional Governor-General, 1802, under Wellesley. He was passed over last year when Cornwallis was appointed, but should be Acting Governor now."

"He is," said Merewether.

"A cold, hard man, they tell me," continued MacLellan. "Almost as cold and hard as Wellesley, though they seemed to get along remarkably well. He's no blue blood, though. Son of a silk mercer in London. I don't believe he has a real friend in the world, but he has good backing among the Court of Directors in the Company."

"Very well. Now, Mr. MacLellan, the Commodore has invited me and the officers of the ship to a reception tonight. Sir George will be there late. The Commodore wants me to meet him. Can you, MacRae and Larkin decide who keeps the watch? I'll want to take Buttram too."

"I'll find out, sir," said MacLellan. In a few moments he was back. "MacRae says the last thing he wants is to attend a reception. He'll keep the watch. The others are delighted to go ashore, sir."

"Very good. Commences at ten, though the Acting Governor won't be there until later. He has a dinner first. Have the gig ready at three bells in the first watch."

"Aye aye, sir." McLellan departed. Merewether sat back and considered the interview he had had this afternoon with the Commodore.

Commodore Land, the Master Attendant for the Bombay

Marine at Calcutta, was a tall, excessively thin man of middle years, noted in the service as an avid gambler. Merewether had rowed ashore in the gig, followed by the launch loaded with the mailbags and dispatch pouches. After making arrangements for their delivery, Merewether went to headquarters in the dockyard and sent his name in to the Commodore. He had met him on only one other occasion, when he received orders to take *Lord Exmouth* back to England.

"Well, Merewether," greeted the Commodore. "I see you have advanced in the service. My congratulations."

"Yes, sir," replied Merewether. "Thank you. Promoted in London, sir." He was uncertain of this officer and did not know what side he might be on in the dispute as to the succession of the Governor-General, or the politics that had resulted in the capture of Lynde. But he had to take him into his confidence, since counterparts of his orders were undoubtedly in the dispatch pouches now being unpacked and routed outside, and he was senior officer of the Bombay Marine at Calcutta. He drew out the orders, handed them to Land. "My orders, sir."

Land took them, unfolded and read them, whistled. "Of course, I knew about this last summer, wasn't asked for any decision or action. Point of fact, told it was none of my business by Sir George. Matter for London." He looked keenly at Merewether. "Do you know how hot this was?" he demanded.

"No, sir," replied Merewether.

"So hot," continued Land, "that if Lynde had actually reached Madras, attempted to carry out his commission, he would have been arrested, perhaps even shot. Wellesley was gone by then. Some mighty rough people in charge, Sir George just holding on for Cornwallis. When *Lord Mornington* finally limped in with the ransom message, strong school of thought was to let Lynde go. Still some sentiment here, Sir George fighting for the appointment and Lynde's people pushing for Lord Minto now."

"I require only a dhow and crew to make delivery," said Merewether. "There shouldn't be much difficulty about that. As Master Attendant, you must have control of dozens."

"Master Attendant takes orders from the Governor here.

There's a reception tonight, all the European community invited I want you and your officers to be my guests," said the Commodore slowly. "Governor will be there late. Possibly I may get a chance to introduce you. I'll get his counterpart of your orders over to him by messenger now." Land shouted for his clerk, issued brisk orders, and turned back to Merewether. "Affair commences at ten o'clock. I expect to foregather earlier for a few rubbers of whist with friends. Do you play, Captain?"

"No," said Merewether. "I never had the opportunity to learn."

"Great game," said the Commodore. "I shall expect to see you later."

Merewether bathed, shaved, dined, and put on the full-dress uniform with care. He admired the new gold epaulets; buckled on the sword he wore so seldom; and extracted from its box the cocked hat he had bought in London, but never worn before. At last he went on deck. These affairs in Calcutta always started late, after heat subsided. In fact many Englishmen did not dine until ten o'clock, but often entertained into the early hours of morning. The gig was waiting. Buttram, Larkin and MacLellan embarked. Merewether followed. He certainly did not want to be the first arrival, but it was his duty to be prompt. They landed, went up the walkway, and proceeded to Government House.

The building was ablaze with lights. Servants held flaring flambeaus outside the entrance as carriages pulled up, deposited their passengers, drew away. He would not be the first guest, Merewether decided, then straightened himself, put hat under arm, adjusted the hang of his sword, looked his officers over critically, and approached the entrance. A majordomo bustled up and listened attentively to the recitation of names. He stepped forward and in faultless English rattled them off. Merewether entered, blinking in the light, and was greeted by a man of pontifical bearing in civilian full dress.

"MacIntosh, secretary to Sir George Barlow, Captain. The Governor has not yet arrived. May I present Mr. Locksley of my staff," he said as another well-dressed young man stepped forward and bowed. "Mr. Locksley will present you to some of the guests present."

Merewether heard the majordomo announce Commodore Land. MacIntosh excused himself and went to greet him. In a moment he was back with the Commodore.

"Ah, Captain, Mr. MacLellan," greeted Land. "I do not believe I have had the pleasure."

"Lieutenant Larkin, Assistant Surgeon Buttram, sir," interposed Merewether.

"I'll take responsibility for these gentlemen, MacIntosh," said the Commodore. All bowed and Land led his party across the room.

"Have to meet the dowager queens first," he whispered. Merewether met a succession of people, bright dresses, glittering gems, shy and bold eyes. They drank punch, discussed the heat, the news from England, the heat again. They had made almost the circuit of the room when they came to a party of five seated women about which a cluster of Army, Royal Navy and Company officers had gathered. The group parted grudgingly to admit the Commodore and his party.

"Madame, the Vicomtesse l'Hereaux, may I present Captain Merewether, Lieutenant MacLellan, Lieutenant Larkin and Dr. Buttram." The Vicomtesse was gracious, evidently a French émigré. In only slight accents, she introduced the Commodore and his party to the young ladies seated with her. Merewether bowed, murmuring at each presentation. He caught only one name, which went with the young woman at the end of the row.

"Miss Flora Dean." She was no great beauty, but her brown eyes were bright and intelligent, her color good. The other officers attendant on the party crowded back and conversation resumed.

Merewether had become inured to his disfigured face over the past few months, but suddenly became self-conscious. He tried to present only the unscarred side to Miss Dean while he made small talk.

"Oh, Captain," she said suddenly, fanning herself. "Would you be kind enough to escort me to the window, I find the heat most oppressive." Merewether could agree wholeheartedly. The many candles and increasing press of guests had made the room stifling.

"Delighted," said Merewether, offering his arm. There was a bit of breeze through the window and they stood silent before it, enjoying the cooling effect. Miss Dean was on his left hand.

"Have you been long in India, Captain?" Her voice was low and pleasant.

"Sixteen years, most of the time, Miss. Just arrived from London this afternoon."

"London! My home is London, but I've been out here only three months, visiting my elder brother and his wife. He's a writer for the Company." Merewether became cautious. He had seen hundreds of her kind, girls without suitable prospects in England, sent out to India in hope of finding a husband, or to escape the attentions of an ineligible suitor at home. There was little place for wives of officers in the Bombay Marine, hard, bitter and demanding as service in it usually was.

He soon discovered her father was a small merchant in the City. She had three brothers, three sisters, all older than she, and a new step-mother she detested. She expressed herself as quite refreshed and Merewether turned to escort her back to her party, exposing the scarred side of his face. He heard a slight gasp, looked sharply at Miss Dean, who looked straight ahead, and delivered her to her party, just as the Commodore came up.

"Captain, the Acting Governor-General has arrived."

"Yes, sir," said Merewether. "Miss Dean, you'll excuse me. Duty calls. May I hope to see you again?"

"Possibly. Au revoir, Captain." Merewether thought bitterly for a moment of apparent effect his scarred face had on her, then dismissed the thought. He turned and followed Commodore Land across the room.

Sir George Barlow was an icily composed man of medium height, with piercing blue eyes. He spoke in a clipped, brisk manner, barely acknowledging the introduction. Without preamble, he said, "You're ordered to rescue Lynde. I want to see you at nine o'clock in the morning."

"Yes, Your Excellency," replied Merewether. He and the Commodore were abruptly dismissed. He wandered back toward the group of young women and Miss Dean, but found all space now preempted by Army officers. He decided to take a turn outside.

It was cooler outside. He walked along the street, past several carriages waiting for the affair to end, made a turn intending to circle the square. He took a wrong turn, came out farther away from Government House than he intended, and walked leisurely back. It was after midnight and as he came up to the entrance, a barouche drew up, a footman sprang down, lowered the step, draped a cloth over the wheel and stood at attention. Merewether stood aside. In a moment, MacIntosh and Locksley, the secretaries, emerged. They beckoned to the servants carrying flambeaus, formed them in a double file lighting the path to the barouche, for all the world like side boys at the gangway. A moment later, Sir George and his wife, a faded beauty with a bitter mouth, walked between the flambeau bearers and were assisted into the barouche. Now the footman remounted and they pulled away. MacIntosh and Locksley hastened to board a four-passenger tonga and trotted off in the wake of the Governor.

Back inside, free to leave now that the Governor had departed, Merewether looked for his party. Larkin, he saw in a distant corner, tête-à-tête with a young lady, Buttram was at a window chatting with two assistant surgeons of the Royal Navy. Mac-Lellan, he found, after a short search, in a cloakroom with three other Highlanders, seated about a table with a bottle of Scots whisky. He gathered them together, took leave of Commodore Land, and returned to the ship.

Merewether and the Commodore were at Government House well in advance of the appointed hour next morning. They waited in an anteroom while Locksley came and went, bearing baskets of documents, answering an imperious bell. Thirty minutes after the hour, MacIntosh appeared. He beckoned.

"Don't lose your temper, no matter what, Captain," growled Land, sotto voce. "And remember, address him as Your Excellency!" They entered the chamber.

Sir George was seated at a large table, baskets full of documents on the corners, its center bare except for a small stack of papers. Merewether to the left of the Commodore marched with him to a point six feet from the table, stopped at attention, hat under arm, hand resting lightly on the pommel of his sword.

"Good morning, Your Excellency," said Land carefully.

"Morning," rasped Sir George. "I don't know what the Company's coming to, appointing persons of no family, bastards in fact, to high rank in the Marine. Incredible!" Merewether felt a wave of heat flood upward. He knew his face must have flushed, but he strove to remain impassive and not flare out at this harsh, insulting man. He saw Sir George's eyes peer up under his brows, observing, thought Merewether furiously, how he was taking it. He fought for control, mastered himself.

"Can't imagine what that gathering of fools, that call themselves Committee of Secrecy, think they're doing," continued Sir George. "If they had been doing their duty, protecting shipping, this situation would never have arisen. Goes to show how rotten politics corrupts everything it touches." He paused and tinkled the bell on the stand beside his chair. Locksley appeared as though by magic. "My morning bitters," barked Sir George. In a moment, Locksley was back, carrying a small glass of dark liquid on a silver tray. Sir George sipped, grimaced, sipped again, set the glass on the tray. He glared at the Commodore.

"The Committee's orders are asinine. Deliver one hundred thousand pounds to a damned pirate, say 'Thank you kindly,' tamely sail away! Well, I rule this part of the world, including the Naval Service, and I say it won't be done!" he almost shouted. Sir George settled back in his chair, picked up the glass of bitters, sipped, grimaced, then tossed the remainder down at a gulp.

"Now, Merewether," said Sir George in his usual clipped, incisive manner. "I've read your record, read the report of your voyage out here. You may possess sufficient courage and determination to carry this off. If not, I've got a dozen officers who'll jump at the chance. Getting involved in a naval engagement that's none of your business speaks well of your courage but not your judgment."

"But, sir . . ." began Merewether.

"I am addressed as Your Excellency, and don't you forget it," grated Sir George. "And wait until you're invited to speak." Merewether felt the heat of suppressed fury mount until his temples throbbed, saw Sir George through a red haze, held himself rigid lest he lash out at this arrogant man.

Sir George glared at him for a moment. "I've endorsed your orders," he continued, "changed them; at your peril, mind you, you're to capture or kill Abercrombie and his crew. I want them dead or alive! You may have to deliver the ransom, but you must recover it. Except part of it is private funds, I'd seize it now, sequester it, so there's no chance of giving it to a damned pirate. Of course," Sir George looked pious, spoke in a milder tone, "out of common humanity, try to rescue Lynde and family unharmed. But," he said again incisively, "that is no longer your primary mission. Do you understand?"

"Yes, sir—I mean Your Excellency," murmured Merewether. Sir George registered the slip of the tongue.

"Master Attendant says five days to bring a dhow around from Chalna; that leaves nearly two weeks to make plans and sail to the rendezvous. Now, any questions?"

"Sir, I mean Your Excellency . . ." began Merewether.

"Young man, one more failure to address me properly and I place you under arrest for willful disrespect!"

"Yes, Your Excellency," stammered Merewether, his question forgotten.

"Have we Your Excellency's permission to retire?" asked Land.

"Yes; report when you are ready for sea." The Commodore about-faced, strode out, Merewether marching stiffly at his heels. In the anteroom, MacIntosh handed over a new packet of orders bearing the seal of the Governor-General and took a receipt. They went out, past the sentry and doorman to the street.

"What . . ." began Merewether.

"Silence!" growled the Commodore from the corner of his mouth. He strode down to the next square, turned the corner, said, "He watches out the window and calls you back for cross-examination, if he sees you talking after such an interview. A hard, hard man, merciless!" The Commodore launched into a string of invective acquired during a lifetime at sea, paused, and pointed down the street to a small public house. "I need a drink. Portugee runs it. I go there after every time I see Sir George."

In the public house at this hour, there were few patrons. Drink in the morning in such a climate usually made short work of a man. Merewether agreed with the Commodore, however, that it would be a therapeutic measure; he was still trembling and felt the heat of his anger yet burning in his face.

The host, a swarthy old white-headed man, served them London gin with half a lemon; each took a quick swallow, then tossed off the glass. The Commodore signaled for another; Merewether followed suit. He sat back with the second glass before him. He felt the gin take effect; his trembling ceased, he could see clearly again, his mind resumed its function.

The Commodore said suddenly, "I hope you weren't disturbed by that 'bastard' bit. Sir George will never get it through his head I'm not Commodore William Land, excellent officer, dead now, who was a by-blow of Sir William Allison by way of his chamber maid. I've even considered calling him out for satisfaction, but you noticed, he's not direct in his insults and besides, I have conscientious scruples against dueling." He sat a moment contemplating the gin. "He often goes on worse than that, must have admired the way you crippled that Frenchman; fond of quoting some Member of Parliament who said, 'The miliary forces of the Company are composed of the scum of Europe.' Spared us that bit anyway."

Merewether hoped his face did not betray him, so certain had he been that the allusion was to him, that somehow Sir George had access to the history of his low origin. He felt better already. The heat in his cheeks subsided. He began to give sober attention to the changed nature of his mission.

Staring at the glass of gin, Merewether began to sort out the situation. Aside from the gratuitous insults, the action of the Governor-General was not without logic. From his viewpoint, it was important that a dangerous pirate, particularly an enterprising Englishman, be eliminated. Payment of a fantastic ransom for a man, even though an aristocrat and important politically, created a dangerous precedent, and would encourage repetition by other desperate men. The Committee of Secrecy, the elements in the Court of Proprietors and Government who felt the obligation to rescue Lynde, would have no control over Barlow. Any retaliation would be long after the fact and useless. It would be nearly a year before a report could reach London, action be taken and a decision return to India. In the meantime, the responsibility rested squarely on Merewether.

"Of course," Merewether broke the black silence, "I intended to take every measure to capture Abercrombie, and recover the ransom, after making sure of Lynde."

"Of course," replied the Commodore. "But now you have no latitude, no discretion. Only sure thing is sail into Abercrombie, guns blazing, to hell with Lynde and his family. Only thing, the man's no fool, he won't come meekly into a trap; probably he'll have Lynde hidden on another island somewhere; never find him. Most difficult situation; Barlow's orders probably cover you so far as punishment is concerned, but unless you rescue Lynde, I'd say you're finished with the Company." He drank off the second glass of gin, called for another.

For a moment Merewether considered the offer Sir George had made to resign his command and let another officer try to carry out this impossible mission. He shook himself, put the thought of quitting out of his mind. Whatever might result, he knew he could not live with himself unless he made the attempt.

"I have nearly two weeks, sir. Possibly something will occur to one of us to solve this problem. By the way, sir, I should be most obliged if you would leave MacLellan and MacRae with me until the mission is completed. They are under temporary orders to serve in *Rapid* at the present."

"Oh, quite," said Land. "I'll endorse their orders to that effect immediately.

"And," continued Merewether, "quarter day is past. Can my officers and men draw pay here?"

"I think so,' replied Land slowly. "Will have to be in rupees, no gold available. Send your Purser to the Paymaster and I'll authorize it."

"Thank you. No objection to giving the crew shore liberty?"

"No," said Land. "But your men haven't been out here before. Best warn them of disease, and the danger of too much drink; there are lots of desperate poor people, dark streets, few watchmen, and most of them conniving with the thugs. It's a dangerous place at night. Best limit liberty to daylight."

"Thank you, Commodore, I'll bear it in mind."

The Commodore finished his gin, bit into the lemon, rose and paid the score. Merewether followed him out into the glaring sunlight and back to headquarters. The gin coursed through his veins. He felt almost cheerful again.

Back aboard ship, Merewether summoned Davis, the Purser,

and sent him to wait upon the Paymaster. He then called for Mac-Rae and Dr. Buttram.

"I've arranged with the Commodore for all of us to draw a quarter's pay," he told them. "Also, I had in mind giving the crew, by watches, daylight liberty in Calcutta, to see the sights, do a little trading. Do them good, I think." MacRae's sallow face clouded. Merewether continued, "I want you, Mr. MacRae, to call them together, give them the most explicit advice, how to stay out of trouble. Doctor, I want you to advise them of the danger of disease from these women, how to take precautions, and you must inspect them when they return and see they bring no vermin aboard, disinfect them if necessary. Is that clear?"

"I'm afraid, sir," said MacRae carefully, face still clouded, "we're asking for trouble. Sir George runs quite a tight establishment."

"Exactly why I want you to advise them in detail. You're an old hand out here, and know the problems. We can't wet-nurse them, these men have been slavers, served in Africa and the West Indies. Just point out the local situation."

"Aye aye, sir," said MacRae reluctantly.

Merewether felt the gin still at its work. With it came bravado. Sir George would not deprive his crew of a chance to see the sights. "I do not wish to be disturbed," he told MacRae in dismissal. The windsails were rigged, with windows and ports open, the monsoon was diverted into a cooling zephyr. He removed his sword belt, coat, stock, shoes and stretched out on the bed. The gin took full effect. In a moment he was fast asleep.

CHAPTER 6

Four days later, the dhow was alongside. A tiny forecastle accommodated her crew of thirty lascars and there was a small cabin aft under the poop for her captain, a wizened, elderly master's mate. Two masted, the mainmast much taller than the mizzen, she carried lateen sails, now furled on their yards. These Indian dhows were not as large as the Arab version, differed in minor details, but were essentially the same vessel. There was no galley; such cooking as was done was on charcoal braziers on deck. Merewether had seen hundreds like her in the past sixteen years, but had never had occasion to examine one closely. He went aboard.

"Jenkins, sir," the old man introduced himself. "And you'll be Captain Merewether. I'll need water and provisions."

"Make a list and I'll indent on the dockyard," Merewether told him. "I'd like to see your ship." Jenkins led him forward, pointing out the features of her rig, explaining her handling qualities. Merewether noticed sweeps stowed on deck and saw her sides were pierced for them.

"Can you move her under sweeps?" inquired Merewether.

"Oh, yes, Captain. Four on a side, two men each, move right along. Up some of those channels in the Delta, it's the only way we can move. She's not very deep, draws five feet."

"How fast can she sail?"

"Almost six knots before the wind wing and wing. Of course, she won't lie very close to the wind, goes sideways about as much as ahead," explained the old man. Merewether made a mental computation. He would never reach the rendezvous in time relying on sailing qualities such as these, close-hauled against the monsoon. He made a decision.

"How does she handle under tow?" he inquired.

"Dunno, never had her under tow, sir." Merewether stepped aft, swung over the side, hanging on the mizzen stays until he could see the rudder under the long, overhanging poop. He swung back on deck and tested the long wooden tiller. He felt the rudder bite in the current, the stern push out against the mooring lines.

"Ever lose a rudder, Jenkins?" he asked.

"Yes, sir, twice. She'll just lay four points off the wind no matter what you do. Sweeps are too short to use to steer, poop's too high. Only way to get her off the wind is to rig a Danube rudder."

Merewether came up short. "What's a Danube rudder?" he demanded.

"Well, sir, the way I make one is to take a large cask, attach lines to each end, and stream it over the stern, lines around each side of the poop. Have to fill the cask, either water or sand, so it barely floats. That way the drag holds the stern so it don't swing; you can steer by taking in on one line or the other. I brought this ship from Chittagong to the mouth of the Hooghly once using one. Saw 'em used on river barges years ago." The old man spat over the leeward rail in self-satisfaction. He had educated this fancy captain a bit.

Merewether again swung over the side to look at the rudder. It appeared to be about six inches thick forward, tapering only slightly aft. It was braced on either side by substantial wrought-iron straps. The wrought-iron pintles were fitted into gudgeons on the stern post, secured by smaller bolts through the ends below the gudgeon sockets. An idea was beginning hazily to take shape in Merewether's mind. He wanted more time to examine it thoroughly.

"Come aboard *Rapid*, Jenkins. Give your requirements to Mr. Davis, my Purser, and he'll make out the requisitions for you." This was a small reward for enlightening him as to an obscure bit of seamanship and giving him the germ of an idea.

"By the way, is this trick of yours generally known?"

"Dunno, sir. Never saw anyone else use it, or hear about it around here."

Merewether returned aboard and sat at his desk. If Abercrombie had a dhow similar to the one alongside, its characteristics would not be much different. If he lost his rudder, he would be helpless. Even if he knew enough to rig a Danube rudder, his progress would be reduced to a snail's pace by the drag. If he could contrive to make him lose the rudder at the proper time, his problem might be solved. He called for his gig.

After the Commodore had endorsed the orders for MacLellan and MacRae to remain with the ship, MacLellan had urgently requested leave to attend to his duties in the arsenal. He had, he said, to see what ruin had occurred during his absence. Merewether had consented while he awaited the arrival of the dhow. He landed, walked through the dockyard to the arsenal. There he found MacLellan, coat off, on his knees peering at the underside of a field carriage for a six pounder.

"Axle's cracked, sure as thunder," he said to a rating standing by. "We'll have to dismount the gun and replace the axle."

"Aye aye, sir," responded the rating. MacLellan arose. He dusted off his trousers, turned and saw Merewether.

"Good morning," said Merewether. "I wanted to see how the other half lives."

"Delighted, Captain. May I show you around?"

Merewether looked at lathes turned by manpower, augers, saws, forges, grindstones, all the machinery necessary to repair ordnance. Most of the workmen were Europeans, but he saw several Chinese about.

"By the way, has your Chinese artisan copied the device you brought from London yet?" Merewether asked.

"Oh, yes, quite accurately. Works fine. It took him three days for the first, the rest he'll make up in a day's time each. Only making five now to have on hand.

"You still have the original in working condition?"

"Yes."

"All right, Mr. MacLellan, I've a problem to pose for your ingenious mind." Merewether explained in detail the physical situation and the result he hoped to obtain.

"Bottom of rudder's about five feet below surface," mused Mac-Lellan. "Six inches thick, top's out of water. Bolts securing pintles, lower end, about half inch. You know, sir, water's quite incompressible, most of the force would go up. Half pound of powder about right; blow off pintles, and not damage gudgeons or hull."

"Exactly," said Merewether. "You understand what I have in mind. You'd best look at the rudder of that dhow out there for yourself. The device must fit exactly and be quickly and easily attached by a man underwater, and withstand water pressure for six hours."

"I understand, sir," said MacLellan, his big red face taking on the rapt, remote expression Merewether had so often seen when he discussed his inventions. "I'll get right to work. I must do a little computation. By the way, who's to place the device?"

"MacRae. He claims to be able to dive for two minutes. Arrange your fastenings for thirty seconds at most. He may be out of practice."

This was a desperate device, Merewether mused. Barbarosa, Abercrombie that is, would undoubtedly disable the Company dhow to delay any pursuit. By the time repairs were made and he could beat back to *Rapid* lying fifty miles west of Port Cornwallis over the horizon, Abercrombie would be hard to find unless he were able to immobilize him. Uncertain of the day Abercrombie might choose to reach the rendezvous, Merewether could not leave any arbitrary instructions to come in lest he spring the trap too soon. He walked down to headquarters and called on the Commodore, proposing to get under way tomorrow morning, if the dhow was provisioned. He said nothing of his plan. It was far too desperate a thing to talk about.

As he left headquarters, the Commodore's clerk called and came out, a letter in hand.

"Messenger delivered this a few minutes ago. Just about to send it out to your ship, sir." What now, thought Merewether, another impossible order from Barlow? He broke the seal and opened it.

"I'll be damned!" he ejaculated.

"Sir?" inquired the clerk.

"Nothing, thank you." Merewether read it again, laughed shortly, and placed it in his pocket. Perhaps Miss Dean was not so offended by his disfigured face as he had concluded. An invitation to dinner tonight, probably some of the local parlor games afterward. Well, he would accept. It might be the last such affair he would attend as an officer of the Bombay Marine. He borrowed a pen from the clerk, wrote a brief acceptance, found an Indian messenger boy and dispatched it.

Back aboard ship, Merewether sent for the Boatswain and Sailmaker.

"I want a large drogue, a sea anchor, made large enough and weighted sufficiently to hold this ship against the monsoon," he told them. "Can you agree on the size and rigging?" A brief technical discussion followed and the two warrant officers departed.

Merewether dressed with care that evening, then called away the gig to take him to a landing two miles upstream that would put him close to the Dean residence. This dinner was set for nine o'clock. Presumably the Deans were not as fashionably late in dining as some of the others in Calcutta. At the landing, he stepped ashore, gave the coxswain explicit instructions, and made his way up a flagged walkway to the street. He found the bungalow of Jason Dean and knocked on the slatted door. He could hear voices and laughter inside. An Indian manservant opened the door, salaamed as he entered, took his hat, and escorted him down a hall to an open door. The servant stood aside for Merewether to enter. The room was brightly lighted. He saw two captains of Bengal cavalry and a Royal Navy commander, all of whom he had briefly met at the reception last week. There were three of the girls from the reception, as well as Miss Dean and an older couple that Merewether concluded were Jason Dean and his wife.

"Come in, Captain," called Miss Dean. "May I present Captain Merewether, my brother, Jason Dean and Mrs. Dean." Merewether bowed and murmured amenities. Jason Dean appeared to be about forty, well fed, complacent in appearance. Possibly he had been fortunate, able to trade a little and accumulate some funds to take him back to England for retirement. His wife was a little younger, plump, able to chatter at a great rate.

"Oh, Captain," she exclaimed. "I hear you're going to catch that pirate, Barbarosa." Merewether started. The eyes of the entire party were on him.

"Well," he replied, feeling a complete fool, "can't believe all you hear." Mrs. Dean looked at him reproachfully.

"And I was expecting you to entertain my party with an account of your plans."

Merewether laughed, still feeling foolish in the gaze of these other officers. "What plans? I only carry out orders." At this, the commander and captains laughed too, and the conversation veered into safer channels. Toasts were soon being drunk, the party livened and soon dinner was served. Then the ladies withdrew, reappeared, and the gaiety continued.

By midnight, the possibilities of charades, whist and several simpler games had been exhausted. The group began to pair off,

Captain Daniels with Mary Phillips, Captain Williams with Lucy Morgan, Commander DeLuce with Abigail Warner, Merewether with Flora Dean. It had taken Merewether most of the evening to sort out the various names of the guests. Jason Dean and his wife seemed discreetly to have melted away, leaving the party to the younger group. Merewether and Miss Dean were seated on a rattan settee at one end of the room close to the window. He listened to her chatter about social life in Calcutta compared to her life in London: the easier social lines out here, the fact that the Vicomtesse l'Hereaux was planning to establish a young ladies' finishing school and had asked Miss Dean to be an instructor in it. She thought she might accept, since she was proficient in French herself. Out of nowhere, she said brightly, "I learned how you acquired your distinguishing scars. I think you must be frightfully brave to fight such a murderous party of thugs."

Merewether flushed and stammered. No one had mentioned his scarred face since it had healed. He had hardened himself to the fact it existed and possibly offended or frightened some people. She gently touched the scar and ran her fingers over the blue powder burns. She did not appear offended. He felt a sudden surge of heat, told himself cynically that he was being unduly susceptible. He could not at this point become involved with any young lady, no matter how attractive, faced as he was with an impossible mission that probably would wreck his career. He gently changed the subject and soon found the party breaking up.

Captains Daniels and Williams departed to walk to their quarters. Commander DeLuce had a tonga waiting. Merewether, too, prepared to take his leave. He found himself at the door with Miss Dean, the others gone.

"Au revoir, Captain," she murmured. "I wish you the greatest fortune in your mission!" Without willing it, Merewether found his arms about her, his lips upon hers. For a moment she pressed her firm body against him, then gently touched his chin and pushed him away. "A token to take with you," she whispered, "and you'll return?"

"Yes," said Merewether brusquely, coming to earth. "Should return within a fortnight." He turned away, made his way down to the landing, alternately despising himself, then feeling a sense of elation at the involvement. The gig was waiting.

CHAPTER 7

Shortly after daylight, Merewether sent for MacLellan and the Boatswain. The ship was anchored bow and stern to hold her against the tidal bores that occurred almost daily at the beginning of the southwest monsoon. Anchors in this river quickly became silted over and most difficult to dislodge. They sometimes had to be left to be recovered by the Captain of the Port with his barge mounting a heavy pair of shears. Merewether had no intention of leaving an anchor.

"Mr. MacLellan, I want to hoist in the stern anchor and heave in the bow anchor to short stay. I intend to leave with the ebb to take advantage of the freshet."

"Aye aye, sir." MacLellan and the Boatswain departed.

The stern anchor broke ground with more ease than Merewether had anticipated and was hoisted on board. The hands manned the windlass again, hauled *Rapid* upstream toward the bow anchor, brought the cable to short stay, and attached stoppers to it. The tide was making, pushing the river current back so that the ship swung around until it headed downstream. Merewether had the launch in the water along the port side, the dhow still moored to the starboard side. He called MacRae, had the signal hoisted requesting permission to get under way, and received an affirmative from the dockyard. As he waited for the ebb, he made polite conversation with the bearded Indian pilot.

The run down the Hooghly with the current was always chancy. The dhow cast off and followed, sweeps ready to aid in negotiating the bends in the channel. The launch was manned, towing alongside, ready to pull *Rapid's* bow around the more treacherous stretches. In late afternoon of the second day, after anchoring during darkness and surviving a tidal bore of at least seven feet, *Rapid* was off the Sandheads pilot station. She hove to, dropped the Indian pilot and signaled the dhow to take position astern. With the launch still in the water, it took only a short time to carry the towing cable over to her. Late in April, the monsoon was still variable; it now came almost out of the west. *Rapid* got under way, took up the slack, fought her helm for a few moments until the dhow also got way on, then began the tow south southeast across the Bay of Bengal. Once the strain was taken, Merewether set more sail. He found the ship handled reasonably well, but signaled the dhow to set sail to take some of the strain off the cable. The log showed eight knots. At this rate, three days would bring him to the point where he had determined to leave *Rapid*.

MacRae obtained a five-star fix at dawn the third day and computed a course that would lead to a point fifty miles due east of Port Cornwallis. By dead reckoning, *Rapid* reached this point by midafternoon. The dhow was signaled to cast off the tow line and heave to. On the forecastle, the Boatswain and Sailmaker had the drogue rigged, the anchor cable bent on to the four lines fastened through the spreaders at the mouth. At the much narrower forward end of the drogue, sixteen twenty-four pounder balls had been stitched into the heavy canvas to ensure its sinking to a proper depth. The whole thing looked like nothing so much as a gigantic stocking, its foot cut off at the narrow ankle. Once launched, the force of the monsoon would blow the ship eastward and the drogue would sink deeply, provide massive resistance in the water and minimize her drift.

"Launch the sea anchor," ordered Merewether. It was hoisted over the bow, cable payed out and stoppers attached. The cable became rigid. The Boatswain tested the strain with his foot and reported to MacLellan.

"Sea anchor's taken a strain, sir," called MacLellan.

"Very good," said Merewether. The evening and morning observations would indicate the amount of drift, he hoped. He wanted the ship to remain as close as possible to this spot. If too much drift was noted, she would have to beat back to her station. He signaled the dhow to come alongside. It was time for a council of war, though he had at least two days before the dhow must depart for the rendezvous. He called the meeting for eight bells of the morning watch. A heavy thunderstorm broke after midnight, with drenching rain and some wind; it was still overcast at dawn.

The officers seated themselves along the transom in the big cabin, Mr. Jenkins somewhat ill at ease among so much rank, and assuming a vast dignity in compensation for it. Merewether asked MacRae, "Any star sights this morning?"

"No, sir," he replied. "But I don't believe we're going to leeward more than a quarter mile in the hour."

"Very well. Now, gentlemen, we must make our final plans. You all know in general the nature of our mission. The Acting Governor has changed our orders, however, and our primary concern is to capture Barbarosa and save the ransom. My original orders still have force with me, however, and I intend to rescue Lynde and family as well." Merewether paused, looked from face to face.

"Only common humanity, sir," said Larkin, almost in the words of Sir George.

Merewether continued, "We load the ransom in the dhow. I will accompany it. I want you, Doctor, with medical supplies along." Buttram nodded. "I want you, MacRae, ready to dive and attach a mine to Abercrombie's rudder." MacRae's mouth popped open; he appeared bewildered, then nodded. "And, Doctor, I want an ointment prepared, goose grease probably, mixed with soot, to spread over MacRae's body, to color him so he's not so likely to be seen in the water. Can you accomplish that?"

"Yes, sir, I have the goose grease and there should be plenty of soot in the galley smoke pipe."

"Very good. And now, Mr. MacLellan, have you prepared your diabolical device?"

"Yes, sir." MacLellan arose. He stepped outside, returning in a moment.

The device appeared to be a box made of sheet copper, rectangular in shape, six inches wide, three inches thick, possibly a foot long. A soldered seam ran along one edge; one end was soldered shut, the other open. Two brackets extended up from either side. MacLellan held in his other hand the clockwork mechanism connected to the flintlock. He laid it carefully on the desk. His big red face bore the rapt, distant expression it assumed when he was called upon to demonstrate his inventive abilities. He held out the copper box for all to see.

"This end," he said, putting a finger on the closed end, "contains nine and one-half ounces FFFG powder, quite fine, for better ignition and faster burning. My computations, Captain, convinced me I needed an ounce and a half more than I first thought. Powder's firmly compressed behind this plug," he continued, pointing in the open end. "A hole in the plug fits the ignition tube from the lock quite exactly. I have a rod in the hole now to prevent the powder leaking out." He paused, picked up the clockwork device, and moved it toward the open end of the box.

"At the last possible moment, fill the ignition tube with powder, prime the lock, wind the spring, set this wheel at the sixth mark, and insert the mechanism in the box, pushing the tube into the hole, being most careful not to spill any powder," he went on in his pedantic burr.

"I recommend you be most careful also not to jar this mechanism. Then," he laid down the mechanism, picked up a piece of copper, whose edges were bent down in the shape of a lid, "fit this over the open end, solder it about the edges, being careful to let no heat touch the other end. Then coat the whole box with pitch to take off the shine and eliminate any small leaks."

"Solder on the end!" exploded Merewether. "I never soldered anything in my life. Have you, MacRae, Buttram?"

"No, sir," they replied in chorus.

MacLellan chuckled. "Thought probably you hadn't," he said. "So I brought my best Chinee along, same one made the mechanism. He'll load and solder it for you." He chuckled again at the sighs of relief from Merewether, MacRae and Buttram.

MacLellan indicated the two sets of bracket arms extending up from the box. Fixed in the end of each was a needle-sharp steel spike. "Put the box under the heel of the rudder, force these spikes, which you'll notice are barbed, into either side. That should hold it very securely against the drag of the water." MacRae tested the sharpness of the spikes. He nodded.

"Very good, MacLellan," said Merewether. "Now, Mr. Larkin, you and MacLellan will keep the ship. Possibly you'll think me mad, but how are your pigeons faring?"

"Why, Captain, very well. Six of my pairs have young now. With no one out here to sell to or trade with, I expect we'll have to eat the ones I can't keep."

"If we took some of your cocks on the dhow, could they find their way back here?" demanded Merewether.

"Honestly I don't know, Captain. I would think if they were kept on deck as you sailed to the islands, they'd keep their bearings and find the ship, if she don't move too far. No landmarks, but I don't think they use landmarks anyhow. Most of them found their way back from a hundred miles off the Congo."

"Nothing to lose," said Merewether. "If they do, we save time, with a better chance to catch Abercrombie. If they don't, we'll have to sail back to the ship anyway. I'd be most obliged for the loan of six of your best cocks, Mr. Larkin. Now, any questions, gentlemen?" A short technical discussion followed between Mac-Rae and MacLellan.

"By the bye, Captain," said Dr. Buttram, "we have only two cases of the clap. There shouldn't be any more now, since the last run ashore. Little too soon to tell about the syphilis yet."

"Very good. You're giving treatment?"

"Yes, sir. They're not incapacitated for duty."

The group broke up. Merewether sat reflecting on the chances for success of this impossible scheme. It might be better yet to try to find Abercrombie, and overpower him, no matter what the consequences to Lynde and his family. He decided again he could not stomach such callous disregard of human life, even at the risk of his career. He shrugged, spread out the charts Commodore Land had found for him, and began to check the sketchy soundings through Cleugh Passage, just north of Great Andaman Island. He had been assured *Rapid* could negotiate the channel with ease, and it was much the shortest route to Port Cornwallis.

CHAPTER 8

At dawn two days later, a working party hauled the chests of specie out of the strong room, carried them aboard the dhow, and lashed them securely under the break of the poop. MacRae, Buttram and the Chinese artisan were aboard; provisions, medical supplies, tools, a few arms were stowed. Merewether checked his list with MacLellan and made sure the six small cages, each containing a pigeon cock, were secured on the deck of the dhow and the supply of grain was aboard. He concluded he was as prepared as he ever would be for this venture.

"Remember," he told MacLellan and Larkin. "If a pigeon returns, this is your signal to sail at once for Port Cornwallis. I'll try to meet you outside."

Merewether boarded the dhow. Now the lascars cast off, sail was set and she commenced her sluggish journey east, heading for Cleugh Passage to pass between Great Andaman and Landfall Islands. By four bells of the forenoon watch, they had the hills of the island in sight. By midafternoon they were east of Great Andaman, beating down to the entrance of Atalanta Bay. The island was high, wooded, with some mangrove along the water's edge. Merewether had decided to anchor just inside Atalanta Bay. There was plenty of water there for dhows, and it was well sheltered from the southwest monsoon. As the wind was foul, Jenkins called his hands to the sweeps. They crept slowly in.

Glass to eye, Merewether surveyed the island. Port Cornwallis had been a supply base, abandoned in 1796. He could see no sign now that man had ever been here before, but of course, the settlement was out of sight, several miles up the bay. He swung the glass upward, passed along the saddle-shaped crests of the hills. There was one bare spot on top of a hill, a large dead tree standing in it, which looked as though it had been cleared by man or fire. He listened to the chant of the lascar leadsman, automatically transposing it to fathoms; slowly the dhow glided in.

"Way enough," he said to Jenkins. The dhow rounded to and let go her anchor. It was still an hour to sunset. He started to put the glass in the rack, but looked shoreward up the hill. Something was on a high limb of the dead tree in the clearing. He raised the glass and focused. It was a large flag, black against the sunset, flying apparently from a line passed over the limb, secured on the ground. It had not been there a quarter hour ago, he was sure. Undoubtedly it was the signal from a scout posted by Barbarosa!

Instinctively Merewether turned and looked out to sea. He laughed at himself. There was, of course, nothing in sight; yet somewhere within sight of that tree, Barbarosa must be lurking. He focused the glass again on the flag. It was impossible to tell its color against the sunset, but he confirmed that there was no device on it. For a moment he was childishly disappointed that there was no skull and crossbones displayed. He handed the glass to MacRae, pointing.

"Our arrival has been announced. Mr. Jenkins, I'll thank you to set an adequate anchor watch for the night, armed with muskets." There was the distinct possibility in these remote parts that Abercrombie was not the only pirate about, and there were Jarawas too. Merewether dined frugally with MacRae, Buttram and Jenkins on rations heated on a charcoal brazier, then ordered all lights out and settled himself for a sleepless vigil. He was asleep in three minutes. The night passed without incident.

At dawn, the first day of May, Merewether breakfasted on ship's biscuit and hot tea, then began the uneasy wait for something to develop. At full daylight, he put the glass on the dead tree. The flag was gone; evidently there had been some sort of acknowledgment of the signal.

"Mr. Jenkins, I'd like you to hoist a white flag," he said. It might mean nothing to Atjenese pirates, but Abercrombie had served as a Royal Navy warrant officer and must know its significance.

An hour after daylight, one of the lascars hailed the poop and pointed. Out through the harbor entrance, not more than a mile away, a dhow had come into view around the point, moving slowly against the monsoon under sweeps. Merewether felt his pulse quicken. The critical moment was at hand. He measured the progress of the dhow and decided it would take half an hour for it to come to anchor in the bay. He called MacRae, Buttram, and the Chinese artisan into the tiny cabin. MacRae stripped, and Buttram began to rub his ointment over the small, compact body. The artisan had his irons in the brazier outside. Merewether filled the brass tube on the ignition device with powder, primed the pan, wound the spring, set the wheel for six hours, cocked the lock, and gingerly inserted the ignition tube through the plug into the powder charge. He called the bandy-legged, perpetually smiling little artisan into the cabin.

The lid slipped on, and the Chinese, soldering iron in one hand, bar of solder in the other, a pot of flux on the deck, began his skilled task. The solder ran smoothly around the edge of the lid, urged by the hot iron in a firm bead, and joined at the point of beginning. With a brush, the Chinese dipped pitch from a bucket, coated the copper box smoothly. He stepped back. In the moment of silence, the box emitted an ominous ticking sound.

Merewether turned around, startled by the apparition of a Mac-Rae black from head to toe. He stepped out on deck and, deciding that the dhow was still nearly half a mile away, said to Jenkins, "Call a half dozen men aft here for a screen, please." The lascars came aft, lining the rail. MacRae crept out of the cabin, slid over the port quarter into the water. The explosive device was lowered to him on a cord. He pulled himself astern where a line had been rigged that he could stand on, hidden by the overhang of the poop and the rudder post, his nose barely above water.

Merewether watched the slow progress of the dhow bearing Barbarosa through the entrance of the bay; with the glass he could see she was crammed with men. He tried to make out Abercrombie and finally saw him move into view on the poop close to the man at the tiller. He still wore a full red beard. There could be no doubt now about his identity.

Merewether noticed something else: this dhow had been decked over amidships, differently from the one he was on. Trained out to port he could now see two bronze guns mounted on rude carriages. At two hundred yards, the detail was apparent through the glass; the serpent-shaped handles on the decorated barrels he had seen only once before. He realized that these were Spanish or Portuguese demiculverins, possibly two hundred years old, such as Magellan or Vasco da Gama might have mounted on their galleons. He had seen one once preserved at Portuguese Goa years ago. They looked to be about ten pounders. Those on the dhow gleamed and were apparently in good condition, capable of hurling a formidable charge, probably scrap metal or musket balls. He saw standing beside the breach of each gun a man with a lighted slow match in hand. Barbarosa was taking no chances!

At a hundred yards, the sweeps ceased moving. A hail came across the water.

"Dhow ahoy! What dhow's that?"

"Company dhow, to meet Barbarosa," roared back Merewether.

"Have you the gold?"

"Yes. Come alongside." Abercrombie looked suspiciously about and called an inaudible order to his crew. Merewether saw that many of them were armed with muskets and pistols, each with a kriss in his belt. They manned the rail threateningly, as the sweeps moved again and the dhow crept forward pulling to starboard. A heaving line soared from the forecastle; a cable snaked across and was made fast. The port sweeps were taken in, the starboard sweeps backed, and the pirate dhow creaked alongside. Instantly a party of Atjenese leaped across to forecastle and poop. They took position to command the entire deck with their muskets, while the two demiculverins pointed, slightly diverging, into the waist.

Abercrombie swung himself over the bulwarks to confront Merewether. "Well, I'm damned!" he roared. "If it isn't little Percy Merewether from *Dunvegan Castle*. And a captain! I'd heard the Bombay Marine had gone to the dogs and now I know it."

"Good morning, Mr. Abercrombie," said Merewether civilly. "I am here to arrange the exchange."

"You have the gold?" demanded Abercrombie again. Merewether pointed to the four chests lashed to the deck under the break of the poop.

"Open them," barked Abercrombie. Merewether produced the keys and laid back the lids. The coins were wrapped in heavy paper, apparently in rolls of fifty each. Abercrombie extracted a roll, broke it, poured out a cascade of gold escudos into his palm. One escaped, rang on the deck, and rolled overboard through the scuppers.

Abercrombie roared with laughter. "Plenty more," he shouted. "Let it go!" He quickly checked each of the other chests, the guilders, guineas, louis d'or. He held out his hand for the keys.

"Where are Lynde and his family?" inquired Merewether. "As you may guess, I have rather strict instructions to make sure of their safety before delivering the gold."

"As if you have any choice," sneered Abercrombie. "But I'm a man of my word." He turned, shouting to an Atjenese on the poop of the other dhow. The Atjenese went below and emerged in a moment, preceding a woman of early middle years, a girl who appeared about eighteen, and a man. Merewether noted that the woman and girl each had hold of one of the man's hands, leading him while he walked as though in a daze. At a word from the pirate they stopped on the deck.

"Do you mind if I talk a moment with Lynde?" Merewether asked.

Abercrombie brayed with laughter again. At close range he was not greatly changed from the man Merewether had known ten years ago, though he must be at least forty now. The red hair and beard were streaked with gray. He had acquired a hard, round, protruding belly, bulging his madras cloth shirt and white trousers, about which he wore a broad leather belt in which were thrust two handsome double-barreled pistols. His arms, hanging from very broad shoulders, were corded with muscle, and he undoubtedly yet would be a nasty opponent in a hand-to-hand match. On *Dunvegan Castle*, he had boasted that he fought for prizes at the English fairs.

"Talk to him if you wish, so long as it's not more than two minutes. Little you'll get out of him. He's had a fit of some sort. Won't talk."

A fit, wondered Merewether; it might explain the two women leading him. "Dr. Buttram," he called. "Come with me." They swung across to the pirate dhow as Abercrombie idly jingled the handful of gold coins.

The older woman came forward to meet them. "Thank God!" she said. "You've come."

At close range, Merewether saw that her face was lined, haggard, dark circles under her eyes. She once had been a beautiful woman, he decided. Her clothing was worn, but carefully preserved.

"Captain Percival Merewether of the Bombay Marine, Madame, your servant. And this is Dr. Buttram."

"Oh," she said, "I hope you can do something for my husband. Gradually, the last six months, he's become like this. He will not speak. I do not think he even knows Jennifer or me."

Merewether turned and addressed Lynde, a medium-sized man with long, iron gray hair falling almost to his shoulders and an unkempt beard. He wore trousers and shirt, a plaited straw hat.

"Sir," said Merewether. "Mr. Lynde!" The vacant stare continued; Lynde gave no sign of hearing or comprehending. "We are here to help you." He turned to Buttram who was examining Lynde with every sign of professional interest.

"Sir, I believe he is in a catatonic trance," whispered Buttram. "A brain disorder brought on sometimes by shock or ill treatment. Nothing I can do for him here."

"Very well," decided Merewether. "You ladies are well, I trust, and ready to go to Calcutta?"

"Oh, yes," they cried. Merewether swung back aboard the dhow, confronted Abercrombie, and handed him the keys. He hoped MacRae had already attached the mine. He had to restrain himself from peering over the side.

"I am satisfied," said Merewether. "The man is in some kind of a trance, but perhaps the doctor can help him later. You may move the specie and I'll bring the party aboard."

"Oh, no!" growled Abercrombie. "I'll keep hold of my little prizes till I'm well away from here, just in case you've got ideas of calling down a sloop or frigate on me!"

Merewether kept his face impassive, Abercrombie was not stupid; he had anticipated this reaction. "Then how will I get them? It is inhuman to torture these people further," he said rhetorically. "I call upon you in the name of common humanity to release this sick man and these women." He had no hope of changing Abercrombie's mind, but had felt the accusing gaze of Dr. Buttram upon him.

"I'll take them to a safe place and leave them. My word is my bond. Now, where's your chart?"

Merewether unrolled the chart and spread it out. Abercrombie thrust a dirty fingernail at a tiny dot east of the Andamans.

"There, they call that Barren Island. 'Tis an old volcano, over a thousand feet high, you can see it a long way off. There's a beach and cove on the southeast side and a spring close by. I'll leave them there. It's about seventeen leagues due east of North Point on Barratong Island, which is about sixteen leagues south of here." He stabbed again at the chart.

Merewether's mind was in turmoil. His carefully contrived plan had fallen apart in his face. Barren Island was more than sixty miles off. Yet the mine was on Abercrombie's rudder by now and would explode in a little more than five hours. Even at five knots maximum speed, Abercrombie would be less than halfway there, still in control of the hostages, able to slaughter them out of hand or use them as shields until he could make repairs and escape. The alternative, of course, was to disregard the fate of Lynde and family and carry out the brutal orders of Sir George Barlow. He wished desperately there were some way to surprise this arrogant pirate, kill him now, but a glance at the fierce faces of the Atjenese crew was enough. Abercrombie alive or dead, they would destroy him and this tiny crew. There must be eighty of the Atjenese. Abercrombie was still talking. Merewether hauled himself back and gave attention.

"I beg your pardon, I did not catch what you said."

"Sail not more than two miles offshore south to Barratong. The monsoon is diverted by the hills and most of the time you can catch a northwesterly breeze close in. Off North Point, head due east. You can't miss it. Of course," Abercrombie smiled, "I've never seen a captain yet would take advice."

"Can't you leave them a little closer, Abercrombie? Would not a few miles down the coast serve your purpose just as well?" inquired Merewether hopefully. "That man needs treatment and it will be a long beat back against the monsoon from that island all the way to Calcutta."

"No, these are my terms." Abercrombie turned and called to his crew in their language. Two came forward. They attempted to lift one of the chests, grunted, called others. Finally four of the small men lifted each chest, took them to the rail, and passed them over to the pirate dhow. Merewether watched glumly. The loss of the ransom meant the end of his career, unless it could somehow be retrieved, together with Barbarosa.

Abercrombie turned and again shouted to his crew. Instantly, blades flashed, as nearly every man drew his kriss and began to slash at the rigging. The yards fell. In two minutes not a whole line was left in the dhow. This ruin would take hours for a British crew to repair, Lord only knew how long for these lascars. Abercrombie turned back to Merewether. "Of course," he said, "what

I should do is kill you and this crew out of hand and leave no witnesses, but I always was softhearted."

"You were recognized by a man on board *Lord Mornington*. I knew you were Barbarosa before I left England," Merewether told him carefully. "I advise you to govern yourself accordingly. This war will not last forever. I urge you to deliver these people now."

Abercrombie sobered. "Recognized, hey? Well, that makes little enough difference. I hold Bonaparte's Letter of Marque issued by Admiral Linois. 'Tis full protection against any charge of piracy. I can go anywhere in the world King George don't control, and I never wanted to go back to England in any case. With that," he gestured to the chests, "I can set up as a king myself. 'King John the First.' " He roared with laughter. "No, I'll not change my mind. You can pick up your people on Barren Island, once you get your rigging put back together."   Letter of Marque, thought Merewether, accepted from Bonaparte, made Abercrombie not a pirate in the eyes of the law, but a traitor to England. Pirate or traitor, it made no difference, he had incurred the death penalty in either event. As traitor, however, Abercrombie had safety anywhere in the non-English world, while as pirate, the forces of all nations would be against him. No doubt, the man was cunning and intelligent. He watched Abercrombie climb across to his dhow, shout orders, cast off and begin to work out of the bay under sweeps. The two women were standing on the poop weeping bitterly, Lynde standing staring vacantly across the widening gap. Merewether looked at his watch. It was forty minutes since he set the timing device. There were five hours and twenty minutes to go.

"Mr. Jenkins, get your men to work, please. Doctor, see if Mac-Rae is ready to come out of the water." He looked down the bay toward Abercrombie. It was probably safe now. In a moment a dripping black MacRae came over the side and dived below. Merewether followed with Buttram who had towels and a liquid soap he said would remove the black grease.

"Attached very solid, sir," reported MacRae. "Right under the rudder post. Ought to lift it straight up." Under vigorous application of the soap solution and rubbing of towels, his skin was coming clean.

Merewether stepped back on deck. Abercrombie was at the

entrance, sails now set, apparently ready to head south. In a few
minutes, he cleared the point and went out of sight. Merewether went to the locker where the pigeons had been hidden. He
took out a cage, turned and opened the lid. The bird hopped onto
the rim, looked about, then lifted leisurely into the air, circling
about the masts, higher and higher, heading off on a tangent
westwardly. Merewether watched him rise to clear the hills.
Suddenly another speck appeared above the cock, diving downward. A hawk! It struck the pigeon, seized it, glided down out of
sight behind the trees.

"Damnation!" exploded Merewether. "Jenkins, MacRae, Buttram, come here!" They rushed on deck. "Hawk got the first bird
I released. Best release the others together. Better chance of
getting through."

They took the other five cages out and lifted the lids. The birds
rose higher and higher, then peeled off in a long ragged formation, heading westward. Merewether seized the glass, caught them
in it, saw the leader flare sidewise as a hawk dived. Apparently it
escaped. Soon the pigeons went out of sight over the hills, with
another ten or twelve miles of danger to traverse across the island.
All he could do was hope; if they found *Rapid*, it would not be
much over an hour until it was under way. In the meantime, he,
MacRae, Buttram, Jenkins and the Chinese artisan turned to with
the lascars, splicing braces and reeving new halyards, trying
desperately to re-rig the dhow and make it seaworthy again. It was
not yet six bells in the morning watch, but it felt as though it
should be noon.

By noon, the crew had accomplished a considerable amount in
setting up the standing rigging. Another four hours and the dhow
might be maneuverable. Merewether looked at his watch, noticing the raw ends of his fingers, unaccustomed to handling and
splicing hemp the past seven years. He made a mental computation. *Rapid*, if a bird had returned, should have been under way
four hours ago with a fair wind; in one, possibly as much as two
hours, she should arrive. He could only wait and drive the crew in
the meantime, counting off the minutes now left before Abercrombie might see his rudder blown suddenly into the air. He
might be as much as thirty miles away by then.

Merewether was in a fever of impatience. He had to get this

dhow moving, heading back for *Rapid*. He called Jenkins, had the anchor hoisted, the sweeps manned to move her toward the entrance of the bay, while he and his party continued setting up the running rigging. Outside the entrance to the bay, he found Abercrombie had been truthful. The backlash of the monsoon was out of the northwest, dead foul for the dhow to get back through Cleugh Passage. He steered northward toward the passage, the sweeps moving in slow rhythm. How long these lascars could pull them, he did not know, but he intended to keep on until they dropped from fatigue.

MacRae was at the foremasthead, just completing the reeving of the halyards through their blocks. Merewether was on deck tending the lines. He heard MacRae shout, looked up. There rounding the point was *Rapid!*

"Thank God!" cried Merewether. Jenkins was already steering to close the ship as it came running down to meet them. Half a cable's length away, it spun on its heel, hove to and the dhow hastened to pull alongside. Merewether, MacRae, Buttram and the Chinese clambered up the pilot ladder to the deck where Larkin met them. Buttram's medical chest followed. Merewether leaned over. "Take her back inside the bay," he commanded Jenkins. "If we are not back in five days, make your way to Calcutta."

Now *Rapid*'s hands boomed off the dhow, the ship paid off, and close-hauled, headed south in the backlash of the monsoon.

Merewether had considered briefly setting a course for Barren Island, mistrusting the gratuitous advice given by Abercrombie. He remembered, though, that Abercrombie had never displayed any aptitude for navigation, had in fact once remarked that this lack of ability had kept him from being promoted to lieutenant in the Royal Navy. He decided that Abercrombie would run down to the landmark, North Point, then take departure due east to raise the island, both out of mistrust of his ability to set a direct course to so small a mark and to enable him to run before the wind on both legs. Under all plain sail, *Rapid* was logging ten knots; in two, at most three hours, he should have the pirate dhow in sight, if it had followed this course.

Engrossed in his thoughts and calculations, Merewether had

paid little attention to anything other than the course and speed of the ship. Now, he found Larkin at his elbow.

"A near thing, Captain," he was saying. "Look at this fellow." On deck was a pigeon cage; in it one of the cocks. Merewether bent and looked through the bars. The cock was huddled in a corner, breathing in rapid palpitations, blood on the floor of the cage. One eye seemed to be torn out and many feathers were missing.

"He's the only one came back," continued Larkin. "Don't believe he'll last out the day. Struck by a hawk."

"Yes," said Merewether. "I saw the first one caught, then released the rest in a group and saw them attacked over the island. It is most fortunate one got through. And now, I'll have cutlasses served out and the boarding parties told off. Have the pistols loaded and ready for issue."

"Aye aye, sir." Larkin departed seeking the Gunner. He seemed close to tears.

"Mr. MacLellan," he said, "Our plans are changed. Abercrombie intended to land the Lynde party on Barren Island. If your device functioned, the dhow won't be a third of the way there. It will be dangerous to fire our guns with the Lyndes on board, not to mention the gold."

"Yes, sir. MacRae told me he placed the device exactly as planned. If the soldering was well done by the Chinee, no reason why it didn't work," he replied confidently.

Merewether began to pace the quarterdeck, gloomily turning over in his mind the situation in which he found himself; Abercrombie in possession of the ransom and the hostages, infuriated by the explosion and the loss of his rudder, willing to go to any lengths to escape. The plan which had seemed so astute at Calcutta now appeared to be a childish conception. He was back where he had been at the termination of the interview with Sir George. He cursed himself for a fool. Any simpleton would have realized that no pirate with his life and a hundred thousand pounds at stake would lightly part with the guarantees of his safety. Force and arms were the only solution, and he was faced with a large, well-armed crew of born fighters. He continued to pace in his black mood, subconsciously noting that the Gunner and his mates had arms laid out on the forward hatch and were busily charging and priming pistols and muskets.

A little more than two hours after getting *Rapid* under way in pursuit, the masthead hailed. It had the dhow in sight two points on the port bow.

"What's her course?" demanded Merewether.

"Looks hove to, sir. Head's almost in the wind." Well, no doubt now the rudder had been blown off, Merewether thought.

"Mr. MacLellan, I'll have the pivots manned and loaded with canister, if you please."

"Aye aye, sir." MacLellan passed the word for the gun crews and gave the orders. The jackets came off, powder and canister came on deck, the captains shortly reported, "Manned and ready, sir."

Rapid was closing the dhow, now hull up, so as to engage her port side. Merewether intended to go alongside, if there were any opportunity, to fire one or both pivots at close range, grapple and board. He put the glass on her, saw her decks were crowded with men, that the two demiculverins were trained out to port and manned. He made a sudden decision.

"Come to port two points," he told the helmsman. The ship swung, the watch manned the braces, and he headed to cross her bows and engage the starboard side. Instantly there was a flurry of activity in the waist. The Atjenese tailed onto the guns, and in a moment had shifted them across the deck to meet the new threat. "Come to starboard two points." He resumed the original course, saw the guns shifted without delay to the port side. He might be annoying Abercrombie, tiring to some extent his men, but there was no advantage to be gained with such an active and well-trained crew.

The ship was closing rapidly on the dhow. Larkin had his boarders formed up, armed. Seamen were stationed along the port side with grapnels laid out, lines bent onto the lengths of chain attached to them to prevent cutting them loose. He would have to sustain at least two shots from the demiculverins, probably at close quarters. He doubted they had round shot to fit; probably they were loaded, instead, with metal scraps and musket balls, capable of deadly execution at close range.

"Mr. Larkin," called Merewether. "Have your men lie down on

deck." No use of exposing them unnecessarily. No glory here, just a nasty task to perform, like stamping on the head of a venomous snake, taking sensible precautions meanwhile to avoid harm.

In the glass, from a mile away, Merewether saw Abercrombie come out of the cabin under the poop. He was pushing the two women ahead of him, up the ladder. Merewether could now see that the tiller indeed was missing. There was a stack of lumber on the deck and what appeared to be a stage rigged under the poop. Evidently Abercrombie had been at work constructing a new rudder. He saw the party stop. Now Abercrombie beckoned and two Atjenese mounted the ladder. The group remained there as *Rapid* ran down little more than half a mile off its port bow. Abercrombie stepped back, waved, pointed. The Atjenese had gripped the women by the hair, pulled their heads back, and were holding a kriss at the throat of each!

Merewether took stock of himself. He concluded instantly that he was absolutely incapable of coming alongside the dhow at the cost of having the throats of two women cut in cold blood. His career was finished; he would head *Rapid* back to Calcutta. He himself did not intend to land there, however. He would be buried at sea. Only a terse formal entry in the log would document his failure and suicide. He turned to give the word to sheer off, to go about.

Before he could open his mouth, someone brushed by him. "Don't go about, Captain," shouted Larkin. "We'll diddle this fellow yet!" Merewether took his eyes off the dhow, turned and looked stupidly at Larkin, conscious even in his moment of crisis that a subordinate officer had presumed to give a direct and arbitrary order to the captain of the ship.

Larkin had in his hand a long, slender gun, brass mounted, stock of curly maple, gleaming with polish. Behind him was MacLellan, holding the mate of Larkin's gun. Merewether realized suddenly that he was seeing the American Kentucky rifle, famous even in England for its range and accuracy. *Rapid* was within a cable's length now of the dhow.

Larkin and MacLellan, kneeling side by side, braced against the bulwark and took aim. The rifles cracked out, almost as one. Small puffs of smoke instantly whipped forward, and as Merewether whirled to look, he saw the two Atjenese were struck.

As one slumped flat on his face, the second, flinging the kriss in the air by some muscular reaction, staggered backward two steps and fell off the poop into the waist. Abercrombie had been standing at the foot of the ladder in the waist. When the two men fell, he started back up, drawing a pistol from his belt, apparently intent on murdering the women himself.

Merewether snatched up the speaking trumpet from its rack beside the wheel. "Behind the lumber!" he bellowed to the two women. He was conscious of Larkin ramming home a new load, priming, firing at Abercrombie. He hit, but evidently not fatally. Abercrombie whirled to see *Rapid* a hundred yards away. He shouted to his gunners. The two demiculverins fired almost together, two great flashes, reports, clouds of smoke. Merewether heard the charges howl across the deck. A length of rusty chain wrapped itself about the mizzenmast, broke, as half of it howled the length of the ship forward. Musket balls and scrap iron had cut rigging, peppered the decks. Men were screaming. Some had been hit.

"Number one pivot, fire into the waist," commanded Merewether. The long nine roared out, discharging its canister at point-blank range, cutting a swath through the waist, killing the men toiling to reload one of the demiculverins. The women were now lying behind the pile of lumber on the poop, reasonably sheltered. "Clear the forecastle!" called Merewether to number two pivot. "Port your helm! Grapnels there!" The jib boom almost touched the starboard shrouds of the dhow as *Rapid* turned, the grapnels sailed out, bit into bulwarks and rigging, lines were hauled in, belayed. The pivot fired a little high; its charge did little execution on the forecastle. As the side of *Rapid* ground into the side of the dhow, the two ships locked together, the forecastle of the dhow against *Rapid*'s waist.

Merewether shouted to Larkin and MacLellan, "Stay here, keep that poop clear!" He raced forward to the waist, and snatched up a cutlass. "Boarders away!" he called, swinging over the bulwarks and dropping six feet onto the forecastle of the dhow. The boarding party poured across. Muskets were banging, pistols popping in the hands of the Atjenese. One of the group on the forecastle leaped toward him, wielding the deadly kriss with its scalloped edge. Merewether made an elementary outward parry with his cutlass, and felt the blade of the kriss slide down outside and bite into the brass hilt. He disengaged instantly and thrust the cutlass through the man just below the breast bone, taking him by surprise. He forced his way into the group, swinging, thrusting, mad with blood lust. He was conscious of two figures by his side, hacking away as madly as he did. The three made a bull-like charge aft, cutlasses flailing. The remaining pirates jumped into the waist.

Merewether paused a moment to catch his breath. He looked about. On one side of him was Jackson, maintopman, on the other, Eldridge, ordinary seaman, the wrestling antagonists of two months ago, both splashed with blood, breathing stertorously. Merewether called his party together, urged them forward, plunged again into the tangled mass in the waist. The attack from the forecastle upon their flank disconcerted the Atjenese; some turned to meet it, giving the boarding party in the waist room to press home their attack with renewed vigor.

Aft, still close by the ladder to the poop, Merewether saw Abercrombie. He was holding back from the melee, his right shirt sleeve soaked with blood, firing a pistol with his left hand. Larkin had hit him, but had not disabled him. Merewether saw an opening behind the mass in the waist and ran along the starboard side aft toward Abercrombie, intent on cutting him down. Abercrombie saw him, whirled and snapped a pistol at him. Whether unloaded or a misfire, Merewether never knew; but it did not fire. Abercrombie threw the pistol, striking Merewether squarely in the face, stunning him for a moment, bringing him to a dead stop. He shook his head, felt the blood running, its salt taste in his mouth, as he panted for breath. Abercrombie leaped up the ladder, ran to the starboard side and dove into the water.

All about him, Merewether heard cries, apparently for quarter. Atjenese were throwing down their weapons, holding arms outspread, palms out in token of surrender. Merewether shook his head again, gathered his wits, ran up the ladder, peered over the side. Abercrombie was swimming a steady breaststroke; obviously his arm was not broken. A powerful swimmer, he could quite possibly reach the shore two miles away.

Merewether saw a heaving line, coiled, hanging on a peg on the bulwark. He snatched it up, threw a slip knot in its bitter end, spread the noose, leaned over the starboard quarter. He had subconsciously noted a moderate swell, which was quite apparent now that the ship was not under way. Abercrombie came into view, swimming under the stern to cross the bow of *Rapid* and head toward shore. Merewether dropped the noose over the red head as it bobbed up and the stern of the dhow subsided in the trough. He twitched the noose tight, as he saw Abercrombie turn his furious face toward him, then took a turn about the quarter bitts. The poop heaved up on the following swell; the line jerked tight; Abercrombie came half out of the water, inexorably hoisted by the pitch of the dhow, with an audible snap. There was a brief commotion in the water from his involuntary spasm. Merewether looked around, suddenly tired and weak, fighting to hold down the nausea that assailed him. He had just hanged a man with his own hands. Pressing close to him were Jackson and Eldridge, bloody cutlasses in hand; they apparently had stayed with him on his dash from waist to poop.

"Haul him out," directed Merewether. In a moment Abercrombie's body, streaming water, was stretched on deck.

Merewether took his fascinated gaze from the body and looked for the women. He found both stretched on deck behind the pile of lumber, eyes closed, biting clenched knuckles. He approached them, "Mrs. Lynde, Miss Lynde, you're safe."

Eyes popped open, the two sat up and, aided by Merewether and Jackson, regained their feet. Larkin and MacLellan were in the waist, pushing Atjenese into lines under the threat of a dozen muskets. MacRae and the Boatswain were supervising the gathering up of weapons. Wounded men were being assisted or carried by their mates across to *Rapid*. The sun had descended below the hills of Great Andaman. Merewether shook himself, gingerly touched his throbbing, swollen nose. He drove himself to cope with the situation, to get lanterns rigged and guards posted and dinner ordered for the crew.

CHAPTER 9

"Captain," said Buttram, "I can reset this nose. I'll use a bit of whalebone for a splint and make it straight as the day you were born, once it knits." Buttram's sleeves were rolled to the shoulder. There were blood stains on his shirt. However, Merewether noted with relief that he had washed his hands.

"No," replied Merewether firmly. "I've worn it for ten years. Plaster it up, let it grow back the way it's been." Buttram threw up his hands in mock despair, then applied the plaster. Merewether thought for a moment of dazzling Flora Dean with a new nose, almost reconsidered, decided not.

The surgery on the slave deck midships had been a busy place. Buttram's report showed three killed, thirty-four with wounds of varying degrees of severity, of which he expressed the opinion that four would be mortal. One man had been struck by a length of chain fired from one of the demiculverins and cut right in two. Stab or bullet wounds into the body cavity were almost uniformly fatal. Other wounds, even barring gangrene or blood poisoning, would cause disability, making the ship shorthanded. No amputations were necessary yet.

"Once you've caught up here, as a matter of common humanity, see what you can do for those pirates. Not much mercy though in saving them for the hangman." Merewether winced as he said the word. He wondered if he could ever forget hanging a man with his own hands, even though it was largely an accident. He went on deck.

The dhow was still alongside, properly secured now, fenders between the ships. With *Rapid*, she was drifting southeastwardly, safe for hundreds of miles before there was another island group. Merewether needed time and daylight to make necessary repairs, to shift the gold back to his strong room, to get a rudder on the dhow, to bury the dead. He saw Davis, the Purser, and called him over.

"How is our supply of spirits?" he asked.

"Ample, sir. We have ten ankers untouched, something over a hundred gallons all told, sir."

"Good. Have the Cooper prepare a large barrel; be sure it's tight. Bring it on deck as soon as possible. And I'll want four ankers of spirits broken out on deck with the barrel."

Davis showed his puzzlement.

"Aye aye, sir, right away."

"And, Davis, while you are in the spirit locker, you have my permission to serve out a double ration to all hands including the wounded, if Dr. Buttram will consent."

"Aye aye, sir." In a moment the pipe twittered. The word, "Up spirits," was passed. Huzzahs rang around the ship in the gathering darkness.

On the forecastle, Merewether found the Sailmaker and his mates by lantern light, just finishing sewing the third body into its canvas shroud, final stitch taken through the nose, and round shot at its feet. He would have to find the Book of Common Prayer, read the Service for the Burial of the Dead at Sea in the morning. He flinched from the task. He had often enough seen and heard it done, but this would be the first time he had officiated. The body of Abercrombie, clothing still damp, was stretched out close by, a sheet of canvas spread over it.

In a few minutes the Cooper and his mates appeared with the barrel. Merewether saw Buttram emerge from below. He called to him.

"Doctor, I propose to take Abercrombie back to Calcutta. Will spirits preserve the body sufficiently?"

Buttram stopped dead, mouth open. "Take him back . . ." he stammered. "Oh, I see. I believe they will, not indefinitely in this climate, but certainly should delay decomposition. The Royal Navy brought Nelson back from Trafalgar last year by that method. I'm told the body was quite recognizable two months later, sir. Have to add some spirits from time to time. Body absorbs a good deal."

"Thank you." The Purser's party came up, ankers thumped on deck. Under Buttram's directions, the big body, not yet stiff, was folded and fitted into the barrel. The spirits were poured in until it was covered. The Cooper fitted the lid, tightened the hoops, and announced all secure. Merewether had it lowered to an empty storeroom midships. He became conscious of the throbbing pain in his nose, now swollen twice its size. He felt weak in the knees and decided he needed a ration of spirits and some dinner himself. He could see Buttram aboard the dhow with his assistants in the light of the battle lanterns, under the watchful eye of the prize crew with their muskets, ministering to the Atjenese. There had been no shortage of handcuffs and leg irons in this former slave ship to secure them. He went to his cabin, called his servant, ordered gin and lemon, washed, changed his clothing. Suddenly he realized he had guests of high quality aboard.

MacLellan had preempted the supercargo's cabin, which was not as elaborate as this one, but large, airy and comfortable. When the Lyndes came on board, he had asked him to surrender it for the women. Possibly by now they had completed their toilet and would be receptive to dinner at his table. The servant came in with the gin and lemon. Merewether sent him to bring part of his precious stock of wines, then went down the passage and knocked lightly at the supercargo's cabin.

"Who is it?" called Mrs. Lynde.

"Captain Merewether, Madam. May I invite you and Miss Lynde to be my guests for dinner?"

The door opened a crack. "Why yes, that would be delightful." Merewether ascertained that she preferred port and returned to his cabin, giving instructions to the servant for dinner.

He thought again about Lynde, still in his trance, who had been found sitting in the tiny cabin of the dhow oblivious to the turmoil about him. Buttram had moved him to his sick bay where there would be someone to look after him. A terrible fate for a nobly born and ambitious man! Merewether decided not to wait for his guests and poured a glass of gin. Drank. This was medicinal, he told himself.

Mrs. Lynde and her daughter Jennifer put in an appearance a few minutes later, followed by Larkin and MacLellan. Merewether made the introductions. He was informed gently that they preferred to be addressed as Lady Catherine and Lady Jennifer. He then opened the last bottle of Scots whisky, poured port for Lady Catherine, a glass of white French wine for Lady Jennifer. He noted that the women, whose baggage had been on the dhow, had changed their clothing. Their faces gave evidence of attention, and in lamplight they were much more attractive than their appearance at Port Cornwallis this morning. Was it only this morning?

"Mr. Larkin and Mr. MacLellan are responsible for your safe rescue," Merewether told the women, who made appropriate exclamations, to the embarrassment of the two officers.

"Bring your rifle, Mr. Larkin," Merewether said, "I would like to examine it." In a moment Larkin was back with one of the rifles. He handed it to Merewether as the women leaned forward to see.

The rifle was long, the full-length stock quite small and light by comparison with a musket. It was extremely muzzle-heavy, balancing well forward of the trigger guard. The barrel was pinned to the stock, no bands. The front sight was a silver blade, the rear sight a series of leaves, which folded up and down.

"Lowest is fifty yards, next one hundred, highest, two hundred yards," Larkin told him. "It will carry well beyond that range, but that's about maximum for accurate shooting, sir." He chuckled. "If my paw had been here today, he'd have whupped me for shooting from a rest. He always said, 'a man can't shoot standing on his hind legs don't deserve a rifle.'"

"How do you happen to have two?" inquired Merewether.

"Well, the last year my father lived, we found a whole stream full of beaver ponds, trapped them out that winter, caught a high market and had more money than we ever saw before." His pale blue eyes under the straight yellow hair had taken on a distant expression of reminiscence. "Old Pennsylvania gunsmith lived over the mountain, still made a few rifles. Bought barrels and locks from Philadelphia, but rifled the barrels himself. Paw had him build these two rifles for him and me. Paw died before he ever got to fire his. When I came east, I brought both with me. I had no brothers, only sisters, and I wasn't going to let one of their husbands get a rifle like this." He tossed off the remainder of his whisky.

"Mr. MacLellan did quite well, too," said Merewether.

"Yes," replied Larkin with an elaborate wink. "If Mac had a little practice, he might develop into a fair shot."

"Fair shot!" exploded MacLellan. "My group, five shots, was less than one-eighth inch larger than Larkin's! Fair shot. Foosh!"

"We had a little competition on targets while we were riding to the sea anchor," explained Larkin. Merewether put the deeply curved brass butt plate to his shoulder, sighted down the long barrel, felt the steadiness of his hold. With a rifle like this, many men might become marksmen. He handed the rifle back to Larkin just as Dr. Buttram knocked and entered.

Buttram had bathed, shaved, and donned clean clothing. His fresh young face lighted up at the sight of the women.

"You met Dr. Buttram this morning," Merewether reminded the women. Buttram chose a glass of white wine. Dinner was soon served. Larkin shortly excused himself, to relieve MacRae for the watch. MacRae, small and quiet, was presented to the ladies, and had little to say. Not so, Buttram; he and Lady Jennifer appeared to have found friends in common, were chattering away at a great rate about hunt meetings, Christmas parties, the success or failure of various marriages. Merewether and MacLellan kept a desultory conversation going with Lady Catherine, and tried to engage MacRae, without much success. Merewether felt he should be on deck, to see that all was well. It was a relief when Lady Catherine made her withdrawal.

The next morning, repairs were soon completed to the rigging of *Rapid*. The Boatswain and MacLellan worked out a way to make new pintles for a rudder; the gudgeons were still intact on the dhow. The Carpenter and his mates soon commenced hammering together an adequate rudder, and the Boatswain would oversee its lowering into place.

Merewether went aboard the dhow soon after breakfast. The prize crew, with years of experience aboard a slaver, had the prisoners secure. The wounded were sheltered in the forecastle; the others in handcuffs and leg irons sat on deck, a long chain passing from one to the other through rings in the handcuffs, secured to ring bolts in the deck at either end. There were sixty-one prisoners, including the wounded. The dead had been unceremoniously dumped over the side last night. Merewether started as he heard a call in English from one of the prisoners.

"Sir, I am no pirate! I was forced man, cook and steward for Abercrombie!" Merewether saw a small man; obviously, now that he looked at him, a Hindu. He was naked like the rest, barely five feet tall, chained to the deck.

"How did you come to be here?"

"I was in Abercrombie's crew in India, back when he was trader. I was cook and steward for him. When he went east, we thought it was only a trading voyage. All the others are dead now, some killed trying to escape from the island, some of fever, some killed by these pirates." The little man whimpered, his huge eyes brimming with tears.

"Island?" wondered Merewether. "What island?"

"Pulu Rondo, sahib. A small island about twelve miles north of Sumatra. Abercrombie's been there nearly five years. Old Dutchman had it, spice groves, a good stone house. Abercrombie found him, old man, got thick with him. The Dutchman spoke Atjenese, was friendly with them, bought slaves from them. When he died, Abercrombie took over. He helped the Atjenese on their slave raids, got enough slaves to work the plantation for him, but mostly they just went out as pirates, up the Straits. Captured thirteen vessels last three years."

A crafty look crossed the small man's face. "His treasure is still there. I know where."

"Quite interesting," said Merewether quietly, turning to go back aboard *Rapid*. It was time for burial services. "Thomas," he called to the boatswain's mate of the guard, "Bring this man aboard *Rapid*."

It was an elementary precaution. These villainous pirates having seen the Hindu talking might very well strangle him out of hand. Merewether climbed over the gangway.

MacLellan had the crew formed up at quarters by divisions. Merewether made his way forward to the gangway where five canvas-shrouded forms, each with the ensign of the Bombay Marine spread over him, were ranged on planks. Two of the mortally wounded had died during the night.

"Attention on deck!" roared MacLellan. "Off hats."

Merewether took his place at the rostrum, opened the Book of Common Prayer, and began to read the service. He was conscious that his voice was high and nasal, his nostrils were swollen almost shut. He concluded, "Unto Almighty God we commend the bodies of our brothers departed, and we commend their bodies to the deep; in sure and certain hope of the Resurrection unto Eternal Life . . ."

A man at the end of each plank raised the end, at the same time deftly catching the edge of the flag. The bodies slid off, making sullen splashes over the side.

"Dismiss from burial services, Mr. MacLellan." Merewether went back to his cabin.

The little Hindu had posed an interesting problem. Merewether at this point had fully executed his orders and was free to return to Calcutta, under no obligation to risk ship or men any further. Yet, if the Hindu was not lying, there was a pirate nest on that island that still might support a band of fierce Atjenese pirates. Also there was possibly some of the funds and property of the Company, or of its passengers from *Lord Mornington*, that might be recovered. The Dutch had tried for a hundred years to suppress Atjenese piracy; nor would they be finally successful for over seventy years more. Merewether pulled down the chart, stepped off the distance with his brass-mounted dividers. Less than five hundred miles: close-hauled, against the monsoon, a run of three days with luck. Less than one fifth of his crew were dead or temporarily disabled; he still had to supply an adequate prize crew for the dhow, but he was sure he had enough able-bodied men to make the effort. He made up his mind, subject to one veto.

Lady Catherine and Lady Jennifer had been in respectful attendance at the burial services. He found them still on deck, chatting with Dr. Buttram. Merewether courteously joined the party. Dr. Buttram departed for the dhow to see the wounded pirates.

"Lady Catherine," commenced Merewether somewhat nervously, conscious of the nasal tone of his voice, "I know you're anxious to rejoin your friends, but . . ." He made a bold presentation of the project.

Lady Catherine evidenced little enthusiasm but Miss Jennifer was a young lady of spirit. "Of course you must go, what's a week after all this. And a chance to get back what they stole too!" Lady Catherine somewhat reluctantly agreed. Merewether's heart rose.

"Thank you," he said, and took his leave. Naturally, Lady Catherine had little desire to go back where she had spent the last ten months. Under discreet questioning at dinner last night, Merewether had determined that neither of the ladies had any real idea of the location of their place of imprisonment.

By noon the rudder was complete, had been lowered, pintles worked into gudgeons, the tiller shipped. Supplies and water had been loaded aboard the dhow, sufficient for its long, slow voyage back. The prize crew had been told off, Larkin appointed Prize Master with the Boatswain and Carpenter as his mates. Merewether bade them Godspeed and cast off. They would have to work out of the lee of the island and its backlash breeze with sweeps, but he could depend upon Larkin getting some use out of the prisoners for this. Sail was set on *Rapid*, she paid off, and began to run south in the lee of the island. In less than two hours, the dhow was out of sight.

That night, running free, the crew seemed to be in excellent spirits. They had met their first real test and acquitted themselves with distinction. After dark in the warm night, most of the crew were on deck. A Welsh cooper's mate led them in song, interminable ballads, apparently well known, in which all joined in the chorus. Merewether leaned against the weather shrouds, with Lady Catherine and Miss Jennifer in canvas chairs close by, listening to them sing halfway through the first watch. He had thought it was only fair, with Larkin gone, that he should take a watch under way. Just as the last song came to an end, Buttram came on deck.

"Sir," he said, sotto voce. "Smith and Blandford are gone. Internal hemorrhage. No way to stop it." Smith had been a topman, Blandford one of the boatswain's mates.

"I'm sorry. Thank you, Doctor." Merewether moved aside and let Buttram join the ladies. The peace of mind he had enjoyed during the singing dissolved, to be replaced by gloom; two more burials in the morning. He hoped these would be the last this voyage.

At eight bells of the morning watch, the crew was again at quarters for burial services. The ship hove to, Merewether read the service; there were two more sullen splashes alongside, MacLellan looked expectantly at Merewether for the order to dismiss.

"Jackson, Eldridge, come forward," commanded Merewether.

There was a bustle in the ranks, a snicker or so from some of their mates who anticipated some disciplinary action. "By authority of the Regulations for the Government of the Honourable Company's Naval Service," recited Merewether to the two anxious men, "I hereby rate Jackson, boatswain's mate, and Eldridge, maintop-man. Make the proper entry in the log, Mr. MacLellan, and correct your pay records accordingly, Mr. Davis. You may dismiss ship's company."

"Aye aye, sir." It was a small enough reward, thought Merewether, for two men who had so valiantly fought by his side the day before yesterday. He went below to write his report of the operation thus far.

At his desk in the cabin Merewether wrote out the formal commencement, the reference to his orders, then stopped to organize the matter in his mind. The report must be concise, factual, free of boasting, self-praise; it must give credit where it was due. He thought of MacLellan, designer of the device which immobilized Abercrombie and one of the marksmen who saved the women; MacRae, who dived to attach the device; Larkin, who conceived and carried through the rifle practice at a time when Merewether had decided to abandon the whole project. Aside from his leadership of the boarding party, Merewether concluded, he had done very little on this operation. Not much of a captain, where his subordinates had accomplished so much and were so directly responsible for the success.

He wrote a draft, decided its praise of his officers was too fulsome, tore it up; wrote another, decided it was sketchy; commenced a third, then laid it aside for further consideration. He sent for the Hindu prisoner.

Merewether spoke enough of the language, acquired by simple exposure to it over a period of years, to express himself and understand at least some of the natives. Dialects were a different matter. He wanted an adequate description of the island, its defenses, garrison, depths of water, and any other intelligence. The Hindu obviously had a very fair command of English and Merewether would conduct his interview in that language. The boatswain's mate of the watch brought the Hindu in.

"Your name?" barked Merewether.

"Sangh, sahib."

"Your village?"

"Chittagong, sahib."

"Who did you serve before Abercrombie, why did you leave him, and how did you become steward for him?"

"Velloso, sahib, who keeps the public house in Calcutta. I left because Abercrombie offered me more wages to serve as steward on his ship. He came into the public house many times, I knew him there."

Well, considered Merewether, it was not unreasonable. Velloso was the Portuguese proprietor of the tavern where he and the Commodore had calmed their nerves after the interview with Sir George. "Tell me about the island, is there a harbor, how much water?"

"There is only a small cove on the southeast side, about a mile from the house. The dhow can anchor there but I do not know the depth, I am not a sailor. The house is surrounded by a palisade made of logs set in the ground. There is a tower and guard post at the gate, and towers at each end. Usually, only the gate is manned by one guard. The back entrance is kept barred. Abercrombie left ten men on guard, to watch the house, slaves and his harem. He has a stone-lined chamber under the house for his treasure."

"Harem!" exclaimed Merewether.

"He has five women, two Atjenese, three Indians."

"Now, beside the guard posts, what fortifications does he have? Any guns?"

"Yes, sahib, a battery concealed beside the path to the house overlooking the cove where he anchors. It is manned only when a ship stops for spices or trade. He never allowed a crew ashore, only the captain and supercargo."

"How many guns?" demanded Merewether. "And how heavy?"

"Two, sahib. They are mates of the ones you saw on his dhow."

"Where did he get them?"

"The old Dutchman had them, said the natives on the island had them in their house when he came." They must have come from a wreck of centuries ago, Merewether concluded, some

Spanish galleon seeking the Straits, driven ashore in this wild place, her crew drowned or killed by the bloodthirsty Atjenese.

"By the way, Sangh," asked Merewether curiously, "what happened when the mine on the rudder exploded?"

The little Hindu rolled his dark, liquid eyes upward and spread his expressive hands. "Oh, sahib," he said, " it was as though a giant had struck the bottom of the ship with his fist! The rudder flew up against the poop, then sailed a great distance through the air and fell into the sea. The man at the tiller was thrown over the side, but was fished out."

"What did Abercrombie do?"

"It was as though he was struck dumb, at first. Then he did much shouting, cursing you, threatening to hang the women! Then he went to work to make a new rudder since the old one was quite shattered." Merewether chuckled at the little Hindu's description of Abercrombie's consternation and rage.

"Very well, Sangh. If any of this information proves false, you hang with the rest," said Merewether. "If you are accurate and we recover the treasure, I shall try to save you. Understand?"

"Yes, sahib," the little man said humbly.

That afternoon, Merewether again took the watch. He leaned against the weather shrouds, looked upward at the mainmast with its towering pyramid of sails to the royals, considering what a fragile thing a ship was. These towering masts would not stand a moment under the pressure of the wind except for the stays and shrouds that supported them, balanced exactly, one against the other. Make the stays too tight and something would part, carry away; too loose and again an essential part might fail, permit the whole to fall in ruin.

Suddenly, it occurred to Merewether that he, as captain of this ship, occupied a position analogous to that royal mast, balanced so precariously, high above the lower masts, supported by its stays and shrouds, but essential to move this ship. MacLellan, MacRae, Larkin, Buttram and the entire crew might be considered his stays and shrouds, without which support he would have inevitably fallen to ruin under the pressures of this operation. His perspective was restored. Captain, officers and crew were all mutually dependent; they could not long survive without the balancing support of one another. At the end of the watch he went below and wrote his report without difficulty.

CHAPTER 10

A little before noon the third day, they raised the island, running down the eastern shore. Merewether took the speaking trumpet and climbed to the foremast crosstrees. From here in this clear water he could see reefs, shallows, obstructions. In a half hour they were off the cove. MacRae worked the ship to windward, Merewether watching for discoloration, shadows in the water. The leadsman chanted, "No bottom with this line," monotonously. Finally he got a sounding only a quarter mile off the cove, ten fathoms. Ahead, Merewether could see the outline of a narrow channel, reefs and rocks on either side. It was much too dangerous to enter.

"Heave to, let go the anchor," he shouted. The ship came to anchor in eight fathoms.

Merewether observed the shore from the masthead. He could see no signs of life. He tried to find the battery and thought to send for Sangh, but finally concluded it was covered with vines and hidden two hundred yards up the hill. He fancied he could see the muzzle of a demiculverin through the growth. The launches were being hoisted out; the landing party of fifty men had been told off and armed. Merewether intended to lead it himself. He swung the glass slowly along the side of the hill. Catching a glimpse of movement, he swung back, but could now see nothing. He slid down to the deck, armed himself with Abercrombie's double-barreled pistols, a cutlass, and ordered the embarkation. Sangh was in the boat in Eldridge's charge.

To MacRae in command of the second boat, Merewether said, "Land on the south side of the cove and approach the battery so as to flank it." He took his boat straight across the cove, expecting any moment to receive a hail of chains and musket balls. He saw

MacRae had landed and sent out scouts; he was taking his party along the side of the hill toward the battery.

Merewether sent his scouts, three men led by Jackson, to approach the battery from the north. He had the men shelter themselves in the event the guns fired. In a few minutes Jackson appeared above the tangled mass of vines, hallooed, and shouted, "Battery's not manned, sir!"

Immediately, Merewether called his party to attention. He sent his scouts ahead on each side of what was actually a narrow roadway. He directed MacRae to follow his party at an interval with a rear guard posted and hurried up the road toward the crest of the hill. Just as his party approached the crest, he heard distant shots.

Looking down the valley, Merewether could see the house and stockade in a grassy clearing on a knoll half a mile away. He stopped and put the glass on it. The gate was open, he saw, and men were running about inside. He heard more shots, urged his party along at a trot, told MacRae to take a dozen men, circle the stockade, enter from the back. The main party approached the open gate. An ominous silence had fallen inside. Merewether wondered if an ambush was laid, sheltered himself behind the gatepost, peered in. He saw several bodies strewn across the enclosure, apparently Atjenese, although two obviously were not. He signaled his party, entered, sent one group to the left, the other to the right to seize the towers at either corner, and led his main party toward the squat stone bungalow.

The scream, quickly repeated, made Merewether jump. He went across the verandah, found the heavy door open, and entered cautiously. The light inside was dim and came from high windows which were mere slits, designed as loopholes. The first room appeared to be empty except for heavy teak chairs and a table. Merewether pressed on, cocked pistols in hand, toward the rear from where the screams had come. He burst into a large room, and found a milling mass of men in breechclouts, armed with krisses. Several women were pressed in a corner against the wall, some with children in their arms. Two women lay dead, throats cut, on the floor; two dead Atjenese lay close by and three more were in another corner defending themselves with pikes.

"Here, now!" roared Merewether. "What's all this!" His men pressed in behind him, muskets at the ready.

The small dark men in breechclouts, seeing the threat of the muskets, reluctantly dropped their weapons. The three Atjenese held their pikes at the ready, watching the small men, stealing glances at Merewether and his crew.

"Sangh," called Merewether. Eldridge led him forward. He had looped a line about his waist, taking no chance of having the little Hindu bolt to liberty during the march. "Who are these?" he demanded.

"Slaves, sahib, taken by Abercrombie from Borneo." He jabbered rapidly with one of the men. "He says they have revolted and have killed all the Atjenese except these three men and would like to complete the job. The women," he pointed to the two dead women on the floor, "were also Atjenese, most cruel to the slaves. They have no desire to harm the other women."

The slave jabbered again. Sangh interpreted to Merewether. "He says, let them go. They have hidden dugouts with outriggers and sails. They can sail back to their homes in Borneo." The slave spokesman looked hopefully at Merewether.

"Very well," decided Merewether. "I give my consent. Now march this group out. Hold them under guard outside." Sangh again translated. The party of slaves marched out in orderly fashion, Merewether's party opening to let them through. "Now tell these three to lay down their arms. I will not harm them."

The three reluctantly laid down their pikes and two krisses and came forward, hands outstretched. They marched out under a separate guard. The three women still cowered in the corner. Merewether could now see there were four children, three in arms, one little boy of about three holding on to his mother's skirt. The child was obviously Abercrombie's; he showed little of his mother's Indian blood and was fair and red-haired, the spawn of the pirate. Under questioning, Merewether quickly found they wanted to go back to India. He wondered briefly about the probable future of the red-haired child, but put the matter out of his mind.

"Get your belongings together," he told them. "I can deliver you to Calcutta." They might be of service to Lady Catherine and Lady Jennifer on the way.

"Now, Sangh, where is this treasure?"

Sangh led the way into still another room, evidently the very lair of the pirate. Muskets stood in racks, pistols were laid on a table in a row beside two blunderbusses. On shelves against the wall was a great supply of spirits: brandy, rum, wines of every variety, apparently the whole cellar of *Lord Mornington*. Sangh stopped. With his manacled hands he pulled aside a Persian rug and pointed. There was a trap door set in the floor secured by a heavy lock. Merewether sent Eldridge for one of the pikes. The lock snapped under prying, and he pulled up the door. Underneath was a cellar, walled with rough stone, deep enough for a man to stand in. In the cellar were many more arms and several sea chests. It was the work of a moment for Eldridge to fasten lines to the chests and for willing hands to haul them out.

Merewether pried open the lid of one. It was half full of specie, gold guineas, wrapped in paper—the loot from *Lord Mornington*, no doubt. The others contained various coins intermingled, silver, gold, copper, rupees, guilders, louis d'or, escudos, square Chinese pieces, booty from the thirteen ships taken the last three years. There was no jewelry.

"Abercrombie gave the jewelry to the Atjenese as their share," explained Sangh. "They had no desire for the coins."

Outside Jackson had found a cart and two donkeys. He brought the cart around to the door, loaded the treasure and arms on it, and started under escort back to the ship. Merewether called Sangh and had him tell the slaves to gather all the supplies they wanted from the house for their voyage. It was a shame to destroy this sturdy house, but it was in the power of the Atjenese and might serve again as a pirate nest.

Merewether reluctantly gave the order to apply the torch. He watched the fire take hold until it was roaring through the thatch with a great column of smoke rising into the sky. He called the balance of his party, together, took the women, children, the three sullen Atjenese and went back over the hill to the landing. MacRae had dismounted the two guns in the battery and had them in slings being carried by his party to the launch.

By dusk, *Rapid*, close-hauled as she would lie, under all plain sail, was sailing northwestwardly, the column of smoke still visible from the island. The three Atjenese had been left to shift for themselves. Merewether considered he had no valid case against them for piracy. The former slaves had left in three dugouts, woven sails hoisted, paddles flashing, on their long voyage toward Borneo through the Straits of Malacca.

It was a slow but pleasant voyage back, fair weather, the middle of May. Lady Catherine and Lady Jennifer spent much of their time on deck in their canvas chairs, attended by Dr. Buttram. Merewether's nose lost its swelling. He could again speak in his normal tone. Only four men remained in sick bay, which was now established under an awning on deck forward. The rest were mending and ambulatory.

"Captain," said Buttram one evening, a hundred miles off the Hooghly. "This fellow Lynde, I've been experimenting a little, giving stimulants, trying to improve his general condition. Don't know any specific remedy for it, but I notice some improvements, an occasional lucid flash. The books say recovery may come spontaneously. I think possibly kindness and good treatment may help. I've had Sangh cut his hair, shave him, clean him up. If you could see your way clear, could you have him to dine with Lady Catherine and Lady Jennifer, sir? I'll be responsible for him. After all, he'll be my father-in-law soon."

"What!" ejaculated Merewether. "I had no idea. My congratulations, Doctor." He shook Buttram's hand as the young man beamed and blushed.

"Of course, Jennifer's family is of higher rank than mine, though no older. Lady Catherine was a little upset at first, but reconciled now. It isn't as though the title descends in their branch," he continued.

"Do you intend to remain in the Service, or return to England?" inquired Merewether.

"Oh, she wants to stay out here awhile. Fortunately, I'm in receipt of an income. I have enough to live on quite comfortably, sir. Then too, she's an only child, and will have quite a fortune someday."

"Certainly," said Merewether, harking back to the original question. "Bring Lynde to dinner tonight."

"Thank you, sir." Buttram went forward to his sick bay.

The transformation in Lynde was startling. Hair trimmed,

unkempt beard shaved clean, he was revealed as a man of strong features and quite distinguished appearance. Buttram propelled him gently along by a touch on the elbow, seated him, tried to include him in the conversation, gave him a glass of brandy. Lynde did appear more alert—or at least conscious of his surroundings, but was still speechless.

There was a break in the conversation.

"Could I have another glass of brandy?" said Lynde in a perfectly normal tone of voice. Dr. Buttram glanced warningly at the startled Lady Catherine, and Merewether rose and poured the brandy.

"Thank you," said Lynde sipping.

Dinner was served and consumed with no further remarks from Lynde. As Lady Catherine and Lady Jennifer made their withdrawal, Lynde made one further utterance.

"Thank you for a pleasant evening, Captain." He went back with Buttram toward the sick bay. Well, thought Merewether, Buttram's analysis of the disorder must have been accurate; the man was recovering.

By eight bells of the morning watch, *Rapid* was in sight of the pilot station. Merewether hailed the pilot boat and inquired as to the dhows; they had not arrived. He anchored off Matla Station to wait for them. In view of the lubberly qualities of the dhows in beating against the monsoon, they were by no means overdue.

Two days later, the lookout reported the dhows in sight. Merewether had the gig lowered and rowed to meet them. He boarded the pirate, and found all in order, with Larkin cursing the slow progress. It would be easier now steering north up the river. He returned to *Rapid*, hoisted anchor and began the tedious trip up the Hooghly, adjusting his speed to that of the dhows.

CHAPTER 11

Rapid let go her anchor off the Company dockyard at Calcutta soon after noon the second day. She made her number, received an acknowledgment, and signaled Larkin to bring the pirate dhow alongside. The sullen prisoners looked about in some understandable apprehension at this termination of the voyage. Merewether hailed Jenkins in the Company dhow, called him along the other side.

"Jenkins," he said. "Have you a vacancy for a cook and steward?"

"Yes, sir. Short two hands as it is."

"Over you go," Merewether told Sangh. "You have just enlisted in the Bengal Branch of the Bombay Marine."

The little Hindu's dark eyes moistened. He salaamed, scrambled over the side, dropped to the deck of the dhow as it pulled away to report to the Master Attendant. Merewether had no misgivings. If ever there was an unlikely pirate, it was Sangh.

The gig was in the water. Merewether now embarked and headed for the landing. Halfway there he saw the Commodore hurrying down the walk, followed, it appeared, by every officer, rating and workman in the yard. By the time the gig hooked onto the landing, there were civilians and members of the European community of Calcutta flooding through the gates to the waterfront. Merewether stepped ashore and saluted Commodore Land.

"Report my return, sir," he said. "I'll need a lighter and an armed guard to land the prisoners."

"Very well," replied Land. "I'll have to notify the Captain of the Port." Messengers were dispatched. "I've already notified Sir George Barlow of your return, Captain. By the way, did you find Lynde and family?"

"Yes, sir, they're on board. Lady Catherine says Lady Houghton, wife of the comptroller of the Calcutta headquarters, is an old friend and possibly may invite them to stay until they can get passage back to England."

Just then there was a flurry in the crowd, hoofbeats sounded, and a barouche came impatiently through, followed by a tonga. Sir George was as impassive as ever, deigning scarcely a glance at *Rapid* with her prize. MacIntosh and Locksley leaped from the tonga and hastened to assume station on the Acting Governor-General. The Commodore and Merewether came to attention.

"Good afternoon, Your Excellency," the Commodore greeted.

"Afternoon," snapped Barlow. "You have Abercrombie, the prisoners and the ransom, Captain?"

"Yes, Your Excellency," replied Merewether.

"I'll have them paraded for my inspection at once."

"Yes, Your Excellency," said Land. "Lighter is embarking the guard from the Captain of the Port now." Upstream, Merewether could see the barge, its sweeps manned by lascars, with two squads of soldiers carrying muskets with bayonets fixed. Mac-Lellan had hoisted the barrel out of the storeroom and had it on deck in slings, ready for loading in the lighter. According to the noon report, fifty-two Atjenese pirates survived. The lighter came down with the current, backed her port sweeps, and tied alongside the dhow.

"What about Lynde and family?" Sir George inquired abruptly.

"Safe, Your Excellency. Mr. Lynde is recovering from an illness, but Lady Catherine and Lady Jennifer are quite well," said Merewether. Sir George stared at the scene. The crowd had now occupied every point of vantage: wives, children, Company officials and servants. Merewether decided this would be an unprofitable afternoon for the Company in Calcutta.

The lighter pulled alongside the landing; willing hands from the dockyard made it fast. The guard disembarked to the commands of a huge sergeant major, and formed ranks along the quay. Merewether saw that Larkin had the Boatswain, Cooper and a working party in the lighter. There was a boom on the dock sufficiently strong, it appeared, to hoist the barrel to the shore. A corporal took one end of the chain and urged the leading Atjenese out of the lighter to the landing. The rest followed sullenly, glancing about these strange surroundings. The corporal pushed them into line, a burly soldier holding each end of the long chain.

Behind the ranks of soldiers and pirates, Merewether saw the boom lift the barrel and swing it ashore. The Cooper and two hands rolled it up the landing, upended it at the righthand flank of the line of pirates. The Cooper stood behind it, tools in hand.

The footman lowered the step on the barouche, and spread the cloth over the wheel. Sir George dismounted and proceeded in icy dignity toward the left flank of the line of prisoners. The guard presented arms as he passed, then grounded the muskets with a single crash. Barlow proceeded along the line of pirates, the Commodore and Merewether keeping station on him a step behind and to the left, the secretaries following. Three quarters of the way down the line, Merewether caught the Cooper's eye and nodded. The hoop and top came off the barrel like lightning, releasing a gust of the heady scent of strong spirits, mingled with an unmistakable odor of corruption; the Governor reached the end of the line. Merewether, craning his neck anxiously, could see the big red head, hair floating, just under the surface of the spirits. Thank God, the face was still recognizable!

"John Abercrombie, Your Excellency," Merewether said firmly.

Merewether stood naked before the mirror in his cabin, cooling zephyrs diverted down the vents by the windsails on deck playing pleasurably over his still damp body. He scraped the edge of the razor carefully along the blue scars on his cheek. The recent scars on his nose and forehead were healed and almost unnoticeable. Earlier, Buttram had tested the nose gently with his fingers and decided it had knitted sufficiently to require no more plaster. It was a relief to Merewether for the women to be ashore, to be able to bathe and shave in naked comfort, unworried that they might catch a glimpse of him through vent or skylight.

The Lynde family had moved ashore yesterday afternoon, guests of Mr. Alexander and Lady Mary Houghton. The three Indian women—Abercrombie's concubines—and their children had been put into the hands of the Master Attendant to be transported by dhow to their villages a hundred miles east. Merewether wondered briefly again as to the future of the little red-haired boy, what his grandparents in England might think if he were suddenly delivered to them. Again he concluded that it was not his affair.

Half the crew was on liberty, prowling the grog shops and alleys of Calcutta; they were due back aboard at sunset. Commodore Land had sent two relief officers over from the dockyard to keep the in-port watch and permit MacRae and Larkin a holiday. Mac-Lellan was back at the arsenal with his Chinese artisan. Dr. Buttram was, Merewether presumed, dressing himself for the evening.

They had both been invited by the Houghtons to a dinner in honor of the Lyndes. The Acting Governor had, of course, regretted, but others of the Company hierarchy would be present. Lady Mary had, at the special instance of Lady Catherine, invited Miss Flora Dean to be a guest. Dr. Buttram had confided this afternoon that his wedding would take place within the week in anticipation of the departure of Lady Jennifer's parents for England in the big Indiaman now anchored upstream. He had been frantically searching for suitable quarters for his bride.

Merewether pulled on his best uniform. It was still too early to go ashore, so he sat at his desk and read again the receipt of the Governor-General's treasurer for the one hundred thousand pounds, less one gold escudo piece lost over the side, to be shipped back to England on the Indiaman. He read the second receipt of the Comptroller of the Company for the twenty thousand pounds taken from *Lord Mornington*. The third receipt covered mixed coins, arms and spirits of the appraised value of twenty-three thousand pounds—the spoils Abercrombie had taken from many small traders in country ships. It was a tremendous sum to have passed through his hands, Merewether reflected bitterly, and leave him as poor as before.

He reviewed in his mind the contents of his report submitted to the Commodore yesterday. Once written and irretrievably delivered, he could think of many ways to improve the story, place himself in a better light. In any event, the Commodore, and even Sir George, seemed to be pleased with him. He chuckled at the recollection of Sir George's loss of his dignity, of his openmouthed sputtering astonishment, when Abercrombie was produced.

"Damme, Merewether," he had cried. "You're as hard and literal a man as I am!"

Merewether put the receipts in his strongbox and buckled on his sword. Hat in hand, he went on deck. In the cooling evening, waiting for his gig, he felt a flush of anticipation at the prospect of seeing Flora Dean. He told himself again he would not become involved and felt the exhilaration mount in spite of himself. He swung light-heartedly after Buttram and down the ladder to the squeal of the pipe.

PART TWO

Mutiny at Vellore

CHAPTER 12

MEREWETHER came awake with a start, the echo of the watch officer's hail from just above his head still ringing in his ears. It was light enough so that he could read the telltale compass set in the overhead and see that *Rapid* was still sailing northeast along the Orissa Coast of the Bay of Bengal. He listened intently and heard the attenuated reply from the masthead, "Two points, starboard quarter, sir. Looks like a schooner." Well, he thought, that was encouraging. The two French privateers that had swept shipping from this coast the past month were reported to be large schooners, American-built for the slave trade, fast, handy, and armed with eighteen pounders. The recollection of the four twenty-four pounder carronades added to *Rapid's* battery last month was comforting.

Out of the handsome brass bed, Merewether slipped into his shoes, put on a shirt, slid into his undress uniform in anticipation of possible action, and waited to see how long it would take for Dobbs, the passed midshipman and acting second lieutenant, to realize he should notify the captain of this sighting. Dobbs had come aboard three weeks ago from Bombay Castle, ordered by the Superintendent of the Bombay Marine to replace MacLellan, now again permanently assigned to the arsenal at Calcutta. No doubt young Dobbs was a competent seaman, excellent at ship handling; but he tended to treat lightly his obligation to keep the captain informed of all developments, no matter how trivial they appeared, and this sighting could be anything but trivial.

A knock on the door. "Come," invited Merewether. The door opened, and a small dark figure, not quite five feet tall, glided in with a tray in hand, containing cup, pot of tea, lemon and sugar, slices of toasted bread, and a crock of jam. He slid them deftly onto the table, laid a napkin and silver like lightning, salaamed and withdrew, almost colliding at the door with a very tall, thin young man in the uniform of a midshipman.

"Sir, masthead reports a sail, looks like a schooner, on the starboard quarter, heading toward us."

"Very well, Mr. Burcham. Ask Mr. Dobbs to pass the word to the cook to serve the crew breakfast as soon as possible."

The tall, gangling boy went out, bending carefully to avoid striking the overhead. Seventeen years old, Merewether remembered, six feet four inches tall, probably weighed no more than ten stone; but he appeared bright, intelligent, learned rapidly, and might have possibilities as an officer. He moved to the table, poured a steaming cup of tea, added a bit of sugar and lemon, picked up a toasted slice to munch, added jam, finished off the toast, and drank the tea.

Merewether clapped on the round lieutenant's hat he still wore at sea and started on deck. The small dark figure slid by him in the passageway. Sangh, the Hindu ex-cook and steward for the pirate Abercrombie, had lasted exactly four days as a deckhand for Jenkins on the dhow. Merewether chuckled as he recalled the dhow pulling alondside *Rapid* and the visit from Jenkins.

"Sir, I can't use this man," he had said. "He tries, but he's too small and light. Look," he called to Sangh. The little Hindu came forward timidly. "Hold out your hands," instructed Jenkins. Merewether was shocked to see they were raw and swollen, the fingers like sausages, stiff and unbending. "He can't handle lines, pull a sweep, carry cargo," continued Jenkins. He'll never make a seaman nohow. I don't need a steward, maybe you could use him, sir," he said hopefully.

Merewether recalled the desertion of his steward in London and the heavy-handed service he had received from the fat cook's mate since. He made a decision. "Transfer him back aboard," he told Jenkins. "Notify the Purser to take him up temporarily as a volunteer on our books. May be quite a while," he said to Sangh, "before you draw any pay. Have to get permission from Bombay Castle to enlist you in a European-manned ship." Sangh had salaamed profoundly, fetched his pitiful bundle of belongings and come aboard *Rapid*. Merewether reflected he had had no complaints on his service since.

He emerged from the companionway and turned automatically to look aft to see if the schooner was in sight from the deck yet. However, the raw timber framework, the canvas stretched tightly over it, blocked his view. He returned the salute from the short, thickset, carrot-topped Dobbs, stepped over to a rickety ladder lashed to the framework, climbed to a narrow scaffold hung four feet below the top of the structure, and looked aft. With the naked eye, he could see a speck of white astern. It must be seven or eight miles, he thought, possibly two hours for the schooner to come up. He looked forward, wincing at the sight. Built amidships was a huge roundhouse, filling the waist, destroying the symmetry of the ship. He looked up and winced again: the towering masts had become stumpy things, wearing their sails like a dowdy old woman in a Mother Hubbard dress.

Well, Merewether thought, it would be worth the time, labor and affront to his seaman's sensibilities if this disguise would lure one of the privateers into range. It was a legitimate enough ruse, after all. He had sent down the royal masts and erected these structures of wood and canvas on deck to simulate a roundhouse and the high poop often seen on the "country ships" built out here. Another structure, invisible to him now, extended from the bow to hide the graceful stem of *Rapid* and give it a bluff-bowed appearance. Yards had been sent down from the mizzen and a staysail rigged in place of the spanker to give, over all, the appearance of a clumsy, stumpy barque.

He looked along the starboard side. Behind the false canvas bulwarks, he could see the squat black mass of the two twenty-four pounder carronades crouched on their slides at either end of the battery of nine pounders. *Rapid* had grown teeth—fangs in fact—since his return from the Andaman Islands. He looked astern again, but saw no appreciable change in the appearance of the schooner. There was nothing to do now but wait.

Merewether's thoughts went back to the two months just past since he had brought Abercrombie's body back for Sir George, in literal compliance with his orders. The marriage of Dr. Buttram and Lady Jennifer in St. John's Church had been a brilliant affair. The entire European community had been present, and at a handsome reception at Lady Houghton's afterward. Repairs, refitting, victualing, supplying had been accomplished; he was ready for sea but without orders, lying at anchor off the dockyard. The crew, with regular liberty, was beginning to learn the ways of Calcutta. He hoped the fresh water in the Hooghly was preventing the growth of barnacles on *Rapid's* hull. Boredom touched him, but as he told himself, war at sea usually consisted of long periods of boredom, exploding suddenly into more action than he desired.

The American brig had come to anchor a cable's length astern and dropped a boat. It had started for the dockyard, then changed course, and come alongside *Rapid*. "Is that a ship of the Bombay Marine?"

"Yes. HEICS *Rapid*."

"Request permission to come aboard." The bearded captain, decked out in a blue frock coat and beaver hat in spite of the heat, came aft to Merewether's cabin with sweat pouring down his cheeks. American ships were becoming a problem; they traded illegally as they pleased within Company areas, with the French, Dutch, and Spaniards, daring the Company or Royal Navy to interfere and create an incident. Merewether wondered what had brought this captain aboard, dressed so formally.

"Andrews, master of the brig *Liberty* out of Philadelphia," he introduced himself. "I was going to find the authorities ashore, then recognized your flag."

"Yes, Captain. What is the problem?" inquired Merewether.

"Goddamned Frenchies!" exploded Captain Andrews. "Three days ago this big schooner, built at Salem for a slaver—oh, I know those pious New Englanders say they don't trade in slaves, but they sell ships to those who do—ran me down off Godavari Point, fired a shot cross my bow. Naturally, I hove to, only carry one nine pounder pivot gun." He paused, and mopped his face with a huge blue-dotted handkerchief.

"Why don't you take off your coat?" Merewether invited.

"Move your chair under that vent, catch a little breeze." The Captain gratefully struggled out of the coat, which Sangh took from him and hung carefully on a peg.

"Anyway, this schooner hoisted the tricolor and sent a boarding party. They tried to accuse me of carrying contraband. Damn lucky my papers are in order. I was in ballast, heading for Java." He paused, cut his eyes at Merewether for reaction, saw none, and continued, "He is a privateer, already captured three prizes in two days, he said. Paraded my crew, found a Frenchman I picked up in Martinique, claimed he was a deserter, and took him. Whole thing just made me mad as hell. Thought I'd report it and let you Bombay Marine boys teach him a lesson!" The breeze diverted down the vent by the windsail had evaporated some of the sweat, but had not cooled the temper of Captain Andrews.

"Where was this, Captain?" Merewether asked.

"About a hundred miles north of Madras off Godavari Point, right in the shipping lane to the Hooghly. He had ten eighteen pounders. Looked like over two hundred men."

"Very well, Captain. Shall we go ashore and inform the Commodore?"

Ashore, Commodore Land was quickly told the story and made an immediate decision. "Must inform Sir George," he said, picking up his hat. He called his clerk and when they emerged into the blinding sunlight, a four-passenger tonga was pulling up.

The interview with the Acting Governor-General was brief, not unpleasant. Possibly the presence of the American captain had a restraining influence. In conclusion, Commodore Land said carefully, "Your Excellency, this privateer carries ten eighteen pounders. The arsenal has just received some twenty-four pounder carronades, came off *Royal Princess* when she was wrecked. I'd like your permission to mount four of them in *Rapid*."

Sir George flicked his hard blue gaze from Land to Merewether and back. "Very well," he said, "so long as you are under way tomorrow."

"Thank you, Your Excellency. Have we your permission to withdraw?" The party marched out.

"Don't think we need visit Velloso's grog shop today," said the Commodore cheerfully. They clattered back to the dockyard, took leave of Captain Andrews and went to the arsenal.

MacLellan, as usual, was in the midst of activity. He was supervising a party carefully lowering a twenty-four pounder carronade, lifted from its carriage with a rope cat's cradle. The task accomplished, he came over, sweat pouring from his big red face and shirt stuck to his back.

"Good morning, Captain, Commodore," he said. "What brings you to my chamber of horrors?" He was quickly informed. " 'Tis a chore," he whistled. "Have to reinforce the deck, mount the slides, get ammunition aboard. Usually figure about four days." His face took on the faraway expression it assumed when his technical abilities were challenged. "I'll see what I can do, sir," he concluded, turning to shout for his leading artificer.

Back aboard ship, Merewether called his officers together to tell them of the developments. He sent the Carpenter, Gunner, and Boatswain to the arsenal to obtain specifications for deck reinforcements, to make arrangements for ammunition and for assistance in moving the squat monsters into a lighter with shear legs to lift them aboard.

Twenty-four hours of turmoil had ensued. Battle lanterns burned on deck all night. Pounding, sawing, all hands tailing on as tackles hoisted in the parts necessary to mount the guns. Merewether had the Cooper empty some of the extra water casks he had carried full to preserve the trim of the ship, and compensate for nearly twelve tons of guns and shot added to *Rapid*. By noon the next day, however, some order had been made out of the melee. The slides were in place, guns mounted, powder and shot stowed, the smoking lamp relighted. The ebb was an hour away.

"Make all preparations for getting under way," roared the boatswain's mate of the watch. Merewether caught MacLellan's eye. "You have time for a drink and lunch with me before we weigh anchor," he said quietly. "It was a magnificent performance." MacLellan looked actually haggard. There were circles under his eyes; his plump red cheeks were sunken. Merewether led him below.

"Sangh! Scots whisky, gin and lemon, lunch for five." The little Hindu vanished.

"Well, Mac," Merewether smiled. He could afford to unbend since MacLellan was no longer under his command. "If that Frenchman has ten eighteen pounders, we now can throw exactly six pounds more weight of metal than he, thanks to your efforts."

"Aye, Captain. And I wish I could go along, though Larkin is vurra knowledgeable with guns." He mopped his brow. The door opened and Sangh slid in with his tray.

"Your health!" Merewether said, lifting his drink.

"All success and damnation to the French!" responded Mac-Lellan. They downed the toast, poured again. MacRae, Larkin, Dobbs came in. Dinner was served.

Finishing, Merewether inquired. "Has anyone heard from Dr. Buttram?" Apparently no one had, though a message had been sent yesterday informing him of *Rapid*'s departure. He had been on leave granted to enable him to settle his bride in a new bungalow in the European settlement just north of the Governor's Palace. Well, Merewether thought, I'll sail without him if he doesn't arrive in time. He and his officers went on deck; Mac-Lellan departed.

"Haul in on the anchor cable to short stay," Merewether told MacRae.

"Aye aye, sir." MacRae went forward to join the Boatswain and his party already on the forecastle and start the windlass clanking around. The ship was now headed downstream with the last of the tide pushing against the river current. The wind might hold her there at slack tide, but he wanted to weigh anchor and be under way before the ebb commenced. The launch was towing alongside, her crew stretched on thwarts asleep, oblivious, in their exhaustion, of the sun and swarming flies.

"Heave in," shouted Merewether. To Larkin, he said, "Set the jib and spanker, have topsails ready."

"Aye aye, sir."

"Anchor's straight up and down, anchor's breaking ground! Anchor's aweigh!" came a volley of reports from MacRae.

"Sheet home, Mr. Larkin. Starboard your helm," he told the quartermaster, watching the sails fill. "Midships, meet her, steady as you go." On the starboard tack, he might weather the bend below Budge-Budge. "You have the watch, Mr. Larkin."

Merewether turned to look at the dockyard. He saw frantic oars pulling a boat for the side, a tall figure in the uniform of a midshipman standing in the bow and Dr. Buttram crouched behind him. Both men bellowed for a line. The watch hauled them alongside. As they came up the ladder, Buttram turned and dropped a handful of silver rupees into the boat and came aft with the towering midshipman.

"This is beginning to be a habit, Doctor," said Merewether reprovingly. "Stage lose a wheel again?"

Buttram flushed. He looked at the tall youth beside him. "No, sir," he said, "not exactly. I got to the dockyard, but Commodore said wait to pick up Mr. Burcham. Neither of us realized you'd move so soon. Sorry, sir."

"Burcham, sir, midshipman, Bombay Marine, sir. Reporting for duty, sir." The boy towered six inches over Merewether.

"Glad to have you aboard, Mr. Burcham. Give your orders to Mr. MacRae and see Mr. Davis, the Purser. He'll assign you quarters." He turned away as he heard Larkin's orders to the watch and helm, changing course to weather the point. Satisfied with the maneuver, he turned again, to discover Burcham still staring at him, mouth agape with fascination. Merewether realized that his scarred cheek had attracted the attention. Burcham flushed and went forward.

The run down the Hooghly was uneventful. They had arrived at the Sandheads the next afternoon and had seen an armed transport, HEICS *Antelope*, hove to awaiting the pilot. As soon as *Rapid* came in sight, flags blossomed on *Antelope*'s mizzen signal halyards. Burcham took down the signal and consulted the book, while *Rapid*'s flags hung at the dip. Finally, MacRae could stand the delay no longer.

"Two block," he told the signal quartermaster, wrote rapidly on the signal slate, and sent the messenger below.

Merewether read the terse message. "Have men on board for you."

"I'll come on deck," he told the messenger. This was puzzling; he had no knowledge of any draft of men allotted to *Rapid*. Emerging from the companionway, he could see *Antelope* half a mile away.

"Signals!" called Merewether. "Will send boat." The bunting

soared up, was acknowledged and executed. "Call away the launch, Mr. MacRae. You better take her. See what this is all about, and be sure to get all endorsements on the orders."

The ship came up into the wind a cable's length astern of *Antelope*. The launch was hoisted out and manned.

Merewether, pacing the quarterdeck, saw the launch tie up at *Antelope*'s gangway and MacRae climb the ladder. Still curious, he focused the glass to see MacRae come forward from the Captain's cabin, putting papers in his pocket. Something else caught his eye: a double line of men, ranged rigidly across the waist, muskets grounded. Through the glass he caught the glint of gold epaulets and could see green facings on the jackets. He realized it was a detachment from the Bombay Marine Battalion, the famous Sepoy Marines of the Company service. A moment later, he saw them right face, march to the gangway and embark in the launch. He counted thirty-two.

MacRae came over the side, followed by a Sepoy wearing the insignia of a Jemadar—a senior noncommissioned officer—followed by two naiques. The Jemadar was middle-aged with gray showing in his beard; but he carried his erect square figure with superb military bearing. He saluted the ensign from the gangway, and then Merewether. Then he gave a terse command as his men, kits on their backs, muskets slung muzzle down over their shoulders, climbed the ladder. They formed instantly into two ranks, were dressed by the two naiques, and stood rigidly at attention.

"Sah, detachment from the First Bombay Marine Battalion to serve in this ship. My orders, sah, I am Sheikh Gunny, Jemadar in command."

"Glad to have you aboard," said Merewether, accepting the orders. "Mr. Davis, you will show the Jemadar and his detachment to quarters?" He turned to MacRae, "Come below."

In his cabin, Merewether looked at the orders. They seemed in proper form. "Any explanation, Mr. MacRae?"

"No, sir. The captain of *Antelope* was directed to transport the marines to us at Calcutta. He was very happy to sight us here. Didn't want to have to go up the Hooghly. I never served with marines, sir, don't know much about them."

"I have, several times," replied Merewether. "Battalion was

established in '77; when I became a second lieutenant in '98, my first ship was *Viper*, sloop. She carried a detachment under this same Gunny and beat off a Joasmi pirate attack in the Persian Gulf. He was decorated. Top-notch officer. Very happy to have him aboard." He lifted the packet of orders and removed a printed sheet, handing it to MacRae. It was headed "Articles for the Government of Marine Sepoys on board the Hon. Company's Cruisers." "Read this," he told MacRae, "and have all other officers and noncommissioned officers read it. Any dealings you have with the detachment is through the Jemadar. They have well-established duties and privileges and their officers will see they attend to them."

MacRae took the printed sheet and scanned it curiously.

Bombay Castle, April 28th, 1806

The Honourable the Governor in Council has been pleased to order the following regulation to be framed for the government and conduct of the Marine Sepoys, serving on board the Hon. Company's cruisers, with the view of defining their duties, so as to prevent the recurrence of complaints between the two branches of the Marine service:

1st. The Sepoys are to assist in working the ship below, in hauling up and paying down cables, in hoisting in and out of boats, water and provisions, and in manning the tackel-falls on all occasions.

2nd. They are to draw and hand along water for the purpose of washing the ship, and are personally to clean out their own berths.

3rd. They are not to wash their clothes but upon days specifically approved by the regulation of the ship.

4th. They are not to be compelled to go aloft, to scrub the decks, or perform any menial office.

5th. In case of misconduct a noncommissioned officer to be confined, and (if the havildar) a naique, or (if the naique) a private is to be selected to perform his duty till he can be tried, or upon due sense of this misconduct, it shall be deemed proper to release him.

6th. In no case is a noncommissioned officer to be struck, or to have corporal punishment.

7th. Privates are, for crimes of a serious nature, to be confined, till they can be brought to trial, but for offenses of less importance, when absent from the Presidency and the support of discipline requires immediate punishment, they are to be punished with a "rattan," according to the degree of the offense, by the drummer or fifer, in presence of the detachment to whom the cause of the punishment is to be clearly explained, or for misconduct not demanding corporate punishment, they may have alloted to them the task of picking oakum or knotting yarns while their comrades are relieved from duty.

"Well, I'm damned!" said MacRae. "Particular buggers, aren't they?"

"Yes," replied Merewether. "But worth their weight in gold if we have to board or land a shore party. By the way, Burcham seemed most upset. I inquired and learned of his trouble with the signal. I'd be most obliged if you would take a little time to impart some of your knowledge of signals and navigation to him."

"Aye aye, sir. I do get a little impatient when it appears we're not a smart ship." He went forward.

Rapid was still hove to, the watch idly gazing at *Antelope* as she paid off and got under way again east. Merewether came on deck. "Get under way," he told Larkin. "Course as near south as she'll lie."

"Aye aye, sir. Hands to the braces, starboard helm." *Rapid* paid off, and close-hauled on the starboard tack, headed a point west of south. In an hour, they were out of sight of land.

Just at the end of the afternoon watch, the hail had come from the masthead, "Sail ho!"

"Where away?" bellowed Dobbs.

"Two points starboard bow. Looks like a schooner."

"All hands make sail!" roared Dobbs as the boatswain's mate of the watch repeated the word. *Rapid* set studding sails, flying jib, sky sails, and lay far over to port as her wake foamed from under her counter.

"Deck there! Schooner's hauled her wind, running due south.' Merewether hurried forward and climbed to the foremast cross-trees. In addition to the two huge fore and aft sails, he could now see through the glass that the schooner had an immense flying jib and staysails set, and was heading away almost on the same course as *Rapid*. These fore-and-aft-rigged ships often could lie a point or so closer to the wind than a ship-rigged vessel such as *Rapid*. He heard a call from just below him. Looking down, he saw Larkin with a glass to his eye. "Captain, unless I've gone blind, that's the *Claudia Peabody*, built at Salem, and sold to Rucker Brothers for the slave trade. She's the only ship that ever beat *Rapid* in a race!"

Merewether focused again. He imagined the sails were diminished in size, rested his eyes, and looked again. There was no question: the schooner was sailing away from *Rapid* and a point nearer the wind, to boot. He descended to the deck. In an hour, the masthead lookout reported he had lost sight of her in the gathering dusk. Merewether kept *Rapid* plunging on her way on the off chance the schooner might have a rigging failure or accident of some kind during the night. At dawn, however, the horizon was empty.

"Well, Captain," said MacRae, "That's one we'll never see again. She knows our rig and the cut of our sails now. We'll never get close to her."

"Call all hands," said Merewether abruptly. "Heave to. Take in all sail."

The hands poured up; sails came in. Merewether called the Carpenter, Sailmaker and Boatswain aft.

"How is your lumber supply?" he asked the Carpenter.

"Plenty, sir. Picked up some last week."

"Canvas?"

"Enough, sir," replied the Sailmaker, "and all the old canvas we replaced at Blackwall besides."

"All right," Merewether told them. "Now, I want a framework erected around the stern. Make it look like a high poop. Cover it with old canvas, paint it enough to match the ship. Then I want a roundhouse in the waist, same way, and maybe you can figure out a way to disguise the bow—make it look plumb. You get me?"

"Aye aye, sir," responded the Carpenter and Sailmaker in unison.

"And, Sails, I'll want a sail rigged above the spanker gaff. You and the Boatswain decide what you need. Now," he told the Boatswain, "let's have a little drill. See how fast you can strike the royal masts and yards below."

The warrant officers were dismissed and went forward calling for their mates. The topmen assembled, each party at the base of a mast, as MacRae, watch in hand, surveyed the scene. "On your mark, get set, go." Topmen leaped for the ratlines and raced aloft. Royal sails and yards came off and were struck below by eager hands. The bands securing the royal masts were loosened. The wedges were knocked out. Stays and shrouds disconnected, slings attached, and the deck crews lowered away. As the masts touched the deck, willing hands secured them

"Twenty-eight minutes, forty-two seconds!" cried MacRae. "Mainmast wins, mizzen second, foremast third!" Eldridge, maintopman, was grinning widely as his mates pounded him on the back and set themselves for the harder task of sending masts and yards back up. "Make sure those masts are made fast," continued MacRae. "Secure from drill."

The hands looked about, open-mouthed in astonishment. Usually the losers counted on being able to redeem themselves on the second part of the exercise. "We'll complete the drill another day. Now, all hands turn to," said MacRae in partial explanation.

Soon working parties were moving lumber aft, while the Carpenter and his mates fastened studs to the bulwarks and connected them with stringers. The sailmaker's mates took measurements and began to cut and sew threadbare sails into strips to fasten over the framework. The boatswain's mates came aft with pots of paint and brushes to rig stages over the side and help stretch the canvas over the framework against the pressure of the breeze. They held it while the carpenter's mates nailed battens down to secure it. Seamen went over the side on the stages. As their mates tended the lifelines fastened to their belts, they began to paint the canvas under the artistic eye and supervision of Dr. Buttram. (Buttram himself was swung over the side in a boatswain's chair, suspended from the end of the mainyard.) The framework of the roundhouse was erected and covered. A party nailed planks together, and fastened them under the stemhead to give the appearance of a bluff-bowed vessel.

By the end of the afternoon watch, the disguise was completed. The paint was still wet; but in the gig from a cable's length off, Merewether, Larkin and Buttram could scarcely believe that this clumsy, stumpy, barque-rigged vessel was *Rapid* and not one of the country ships. Back aboard now, sail was set. The ship continued southwardly, running on a long reach well below the latitude of Madras before going about to beat northeastwardly again toward Godavari Point on the Orissa Coast.

CHAPTER 13

The operations of the past thirteen days had run through Merewether's mind as he balanced on the precarious scaffold, his forearms braced on the top stringer of the spurious poop. So far not a sail had been sighted, though *Rapid* had dawdled along in the regular shipping lanes up the Coromandel Coast past Madras, then slanted northeastward along the Orissa Coast. It was as though the French privateers had vanished from the sea. Possibly they were satisfied with the prizes already taken, or had felt some alarm at the appearance of *Rapid* and her bold approach, or had simply run out of men to furnish prize crews. Merewether had begun to wonder if he were not wasting time. Indeed, he had almost made up his mind last night to head back for Calcutta. Now, it appeared from the confident approach of those distant sails, his mission might be reaching a crucial phase after all. No use in sending the crew to quarters yet, he decided.

Merewether, staring at the horizon, suddenly wondered uncomfortably if he were a cad in his treatment of Miss Flora Dean. She clearly had understood almost from the beginning of their acquaintance that marriage was not in his plans, not to be considered in the uncertain state of his career in the Bombay Marine. He felt almost self-sacrificing for a moment, and virtuous in the thought that he had not tried to induce Flora or any other woman to share the hard bitter life of an officer in the Marine. Still, Flora had seemed to respond to him quite warmly, after that first kiss on the eve of his departure to meet Abercrombie. She had shown increasing ardor, even a hint of passion in their goodnight kiss. Merewether considered that he had probably taken advantage of her complaisant nature with no intention of doing more than amusing himself at her expense. God, that was the act of a cad!

He shifted his position uncomfortably, staring blindly out to sea, thinking of the evening before the report of the privateer. Flora's brother and his wife were away; only a servant lurked somewhere back in the house. He and Flora were in the dimly lighted parlor on the rattan settee, the breeze funneling in from the verandah. Conversation was desultory, aimless. Merewether on a sudden impulse reached for Flora and felt her melt against him, turning her lips to meet his. Passion awoke and gripped them both. Merewether had felt a reckless bravado. He pressed ahead regardless of consequences. He thought she would yield, only to feel her gently disengage and draw away, and place her hand over his lips, "No more, enough, Percival, stop!"

Merewether, thoroughly aroused by now, had been importunate, but Flora was entirely in control of herself. She lightly rebuffed his further advances and changed the subject. It was soon time to go. Merewether was convinced that had he told a facile lie, that he loved her, desired her, wanted to wed, the outcome would have been different. The temptation had come but he had resisted it—possibly, he thought cynically now, his only admirable act of the evening.

Merewether wondered if he had ever been really happy during the hard life he had led. He remembered the unhappiness of his first year at sea in an Indiaman, the secret tears shed on his pallet in a corner of the galley pantry in *Dunvegan Castle*. How bitterly he had resented his grandfather's callous rejection of his bastard grandson. Time, new sights, and the necessity to present an impassive face to a heartless world had hardened him. Ambition, stimulated by the learning imparted by Dawson in his classes, growth and maturity had all but obliterated those childish sorrows. But now he felt for the first time since his mother died that there was in the world a person who cared for him. He let his mind explore briefly a future with Flora Dean, a household with a wife, possibly children to cherish. Certainly, he was not unhappy now, in fact Flora had raised him out of his usually fatalistic mood. She fed his ego, made him feel desirable as a person and not merely a lofty and efficient captain in the arduous service of the Bombay Marine.

He shifted position on the scaffold. The schooner was hull up, now two points on the port quarter, maintaining the weather gauge and able to counter any maneuver *Rapid* might essay to escape. The French captain evidently knew his business. Merewether decided he would send the hands to quarters at eight bells, half an hour from now. He looked up to see if the red ensign was properly displayed. It should be visible in the Frenchman's glass by now. He fell again into reverie.

Merewether squirmed uncomfortably at the recollection of the balance of that last evening ashore. He had never been a lecher, had not set up one of the back-alley establishments in Bombay often maintained by unmarried officers, or even brought in the euphemistic Indian maid of all work to live in his quarters when ashore. Occasionally, simple biological necessity had sent him to seek transitory relief with one of the discreet women who plied their trade behind a facade of respectability, thereby supplementing the small pension from a dead husband in the Marine. But after he had left Flora that night, he had felt himself on fire, overwhelmed with lust, and had directed the coxswain to a landing near the center of Calcutta, sending the gig on back to the ship.

He had made his way through the dark streets, feeling the packed breathing humanity in the dwellings behind the woven screens, the buzz of voices, cries of children. He was thankful for his bright uniform and gold epaulets. It would be a brave or foolish thug or footpad who dared attack an officer of the Bombay Marine in Calcutta. He came out in a part of the city he knew, found his bearings, and proceeded to the place MacLellan had described to him months ago during long night watches in the South Atlantic. With lust coursing through his veins, he knocked at the heavy door.

Merewether heard the peephole pop open and stood impassively submitting to the unknown scrutiny. Then a chain clanked and the door swung silently open. He was admitted to a brightly lit vestibule. The door swung shut, and he saw an immense squat figure of a man, clad in a sort of green livery, a red tarboosh on his head. Merewether instantly recognized him for what he was, a eunuch, possibly Egyptian or Persian in origin, certainly not Indian. The eunuch examined him thoroughly, then said in heavily accented English, "Sah, you have business with Madame Salcedo?"

"Yes," responded Merewether, "I should like to speak to her." The eunuch had made a decision. Opening a door to the right, he gestured Merewether through into a large, dimly lit room. Blinking, Merewether finally made out a figure standing before him.

"I don't believe you have been here before, Captain," the figure said in a harsh throaty voice. "But you are Captain Percival Merewether."

"Yes," said the startled Merewether. His eyes became adjusted to the dim light, and he saw a woman standing rigidly before him. She wore a gown, black or green, he was uncertain in this light, without decoration, with high collar, long sleeves. Her face bore a pallor that contrasted with reddish-bronze curly hair and her eyes glittered in the lamplight.

"If you do not know my rules, Captain, five guineas gives you a choice of the house."

Merewether became conscious of other figures ranged about the room on chairs. His eyes flicked right. He saw two young Indian girls in saris, one shoulder and breast bare; a flaxen-haired girl, probably Dutch or German; a plump half-blood, two slender blond English women, a Malay, an Arabian houri. Part of MacLellan's tale popped into his mind. ". . . and then Wellesley, always fancied himself a lady killer, don't ye know, said 'I'll take Sallie here.' And Madame Salcedo fairly spit in his eye, says to him, 'You've not enough gold for that, Milord!' "

Merewether reached into his breast pocket. He extracted the

thin fold of pound notes he carried, counted off five, and laid them down on the table. Feeling Madame Salcedo's hard gaze still upon him, he counted off five shillings more to make the five guineas, and said to her, firmly, "You!"

Madame Salcedo instantly stepped forward, accepted his arm, guided him through a door at the left, as a sort of sigh breathed through the room from the other women present. She shut and barred the door as Merewether looked about the ornately furnished room, which was lit by a single lamp upon a pedestal near a huge circular bed.

"Here," she said, indicating a costumer. "Your clothing will take no harm here." She vanished into a room to the side. Merewether, still bold with desire, shortly had hung his uniform on the costumer and made his way toward the bed. He began, however, to be a little apprehensive that some game might be played upon him.

Madame Salcedo's reappearance coincided with the extinguishing of the lamp. Merewether had caught only a glimpse of ivory skin before the room was plunged into darkness and he had his arms full of a warm, scented female body. How long had it been? God, last New Year's Day with Beth!

Merewether had come awake at the first light, uncertain for a moment of his whereabouts. At last he oriented himself and arose. He dressed swiftly and quietly, picked up his hat, and started to unbar the door. Then he looked back at the figure on the huge round bed. For a moment Merewether hesitated, tempted to delay his departure. In the dim light, Madame Salcedo seemed a beautiful woman; in figure, a miniature Venus, only her high Slavic cheekbones betraying her origin somewhere in the Caucasus. But Merewether put temptation behind him. He tiptoed out through the large room, now deserted, to the vestibule, past the sleeping eunuch slumped in a chair, into the street. It was not difficult to get a boat to the ship from the dockyard. Flora was forgotten for a while.

CHAPTER 14

The first of eight bells sounding the end of the morning watch brought Merewether abruptly from his reverie. He saw the schooner two miles away, closing to port. He looked down and caught Larkin's eye. "Send the hands to quarters. Load the nine pounders with canister, the carronades with grape on top of round shot."

Merewether watched the hands man their battle stations, hidden behind the false bulwarks. Six months of drills and discipline had made this crew confident, efficient; they had met the enemy twice and had conquered each time. Now they had to meet a ship as well armed as *Rapid*, fully manned, no doubt ably commanded and as anxious to win. But Merewether had no doubts as to his officers and men. He and they were ready and would have the advantage of surprise.

"Signals," called MacRae. "Merchant convention, 'Heave to!' "

"Very well. Come right two points." The ship swung and squared off before the wind—the instinctive maneuver of a helpless country ship challenged by a stranger.

The Frenchman up to now had shown no colors. As soon as *Rapid* squared away before the wind, however, the schooner sent up a large tricolor, hauled the flag hoist to the dip, two-blocked it, and reiterated with emphasis the signal to heave to.

"Steady as you go," called Merewether, watching the schooner only half a mile to port now, and headreaching on *Rapid*. The two ships sailed along for possibly two minutes before the puff of smoke blossomed from the schooner's bow. A splash rose half a cable's length ahead. Merewether held on for a full minute more, then called to MacRae, "Heave to." *Rapid* came up into the wind, rolling in the swell.

Merewether watched the schooner go about and come running down with the wind, a bone in her teeth. She rounded to a little more than half a cable's length to starboard of *Rapid*. He looked forward. Larkin was poised at the break of the poop watching him, every gun captain in turn intent upon Larkin. The lines fastened to the canvas flaps concealing the gun ports were in eager hands; a pull and the ports would be exposed, guns ready to fire. Merewether swept the Frenchman with his glass. He noted her gun crews standing easy, the skylarking careless hands, exultant in this moment of triumph, savoring another prize.

Merewether turned and nodded to the quartermasters. One hauled down the red ensign, the other simultaneously ran up the striped red and white flag of the Bombay Marine. "You make take your aim. Fire when your guns bear, Mr. Larkin!"

Larkin raised his arm, and the canvas flaps were jerked up, exposing the gun ports. There was a moment of general adjustment, sighting, every gun captain making certain his gun was perfectly aimed. Now Larkin's arm dropped, and the broadside crashed out, the high-pitched reports of the nine pounders almost drowned out by the massive roars of the two twenty-four pounder carronades.

Merewether, high above the powder smoke, saw the execution on the deck of the schooner. Fully a third of her gun crews and deck force appeared to be down. Two guns were dismounted, the survivors in confusion. He heard the trucks rumble as his reloaded guns rolled back to battery. The second broadside blasted out, just as some desperate man on the Frenchman managed to fire a gun. The shot struck home in the waist, squarely on the false round-house, completely demolishing the wood and canvas structure. Well, thought Merewether, that saved having to use a working party to take it down. He heard the guns rumble up to battery again and looked at the schooner just in time to see the tricolor flutter down.

"Cease fire!" he shouted, as Larkin echoed and held both hands up in the symbol of "halt." He was too late to stop the fire of two guns. The Frenchman was now hoisting a white flag, double assurance that striking the tricolor was no accident.

"Hoist out the launch, Mr. MacRae. Jemadar Gunny, form your men up in the waist. Make sure your guns bear, Mr. Larkin!" Merewether had seen too many prizes lost through carelessness in the exultation of victory to take any chances now. The launch was hoisted out. Once the boarding party and the Sepoy Marines embarked, the boat crew pulled for the privateer, staying well clear of the line of fire. They boarded her on the side away from *Rapid*. The Marines shoved the French crew into groups on the forecastle and in the waist, routed out the men from below decks, and mounted guard. MacRae hoisted a signal on the Frenchman, "All secure. Need medical assistance."

Merewether found Dr. Buttram at his elbow. "Only one casualty, Captain," he reported.

"Casualty!" ejaculated Merewether. "How could that happen? Only one shot hit that canvas roundhouse, over the heads of everyone!"

"Mr. Burcham, sir." Oh, God! thought Merewether, only a lad, on his first cruise, and a casualty. "Flying splinter caught him on the cheek, slight laceration," continued Dr. Buttram. "Disinfected, treated, and bandaged; he's not disabled for duty, sir." He chuckled, "He wanted me to rub some salt and gunpowder in it, sir. Make a scar." Merewether felt Buttram's amused gaze, felt himself flush. The sincerest form of flattery, he thought, is imitation, remembering the apparent fascination with his scarred face that Burcham had shown upon their first encounter. Well, the boy had plenty of time to accumulate other honorable scars.

"Oh, Doctor, MacRae has signaled for medical aid. The Frenchman must be hard hit. Get your chest and assistants and I'll take you across in the gig."

Buttram hurried below, as the boatswain's mate called away the gig.

As the gig approached the privateer, Merewether made a careful inspection. Evidently no hull damage, the masts and spars were intact, some stays and halyards were cut, and the mainsail was shredded where canister and grape had gone through. He came on deck to find the side manned with four Sepoy Marines at attention, the boatswain's mate blowing his pipe. MacRae awaited him.

"They appear to have twelve dead, nearly fifty wounded, sir," MacRae reported. Merewether saw blood on deck, a row of silent forms ranged along the starboard bulwarks.

"Name of the ship is *Tigresse*, ex-*Claudia Peabody* of Salem. I have her captain and officers under guard in the wardroom, sir."

"See what aid you can give the wounded, Doctor," called Merewether. "Let's interview this captain," he continued to MacRae. They went below. At the wardroom door a Marine sentry presented arms. Inside, Merewether found Jemadar Gunny and two Marines on guard over four dejected men seated at a large table. They wore no uniforms other than the usual seafaring garb of merchant officers.

"Who is the captain?" inquired Merewether in English. The four men looked blank, uncomprehending. Merewether did not speak French. These men apparently spoke no English. An impasse.

Just then, Jemadar Gunny broke in, "Sah, with your permission, I shall serve as interpreter." He turned to the group, spoke briefly in French, and was answered. One of the men, short and stout with a luxuriant black moustache, stood up and bowed.

"Captain Boisdore of His Imperial Highness's privateer *Tigresse*," translated Gunny. "He says many of his men are wounded and he wishes medical aid."

"Tell him it is already aboard," instructed Merewether. "And ask him how many prizes he has taken and their disposition." Gunny jabbered, received a reply, jabbered again.

"Four, sir, the most recent two days ago off Madras, one of the Royal Navy's dispatch brigs. He manned them all with prize crews and sent them to Mauritius, sir." The French captain was saying something more. Gunny paused, listened, then continued, "He has twelve prisoners aboard, all officers of the prizes but one." Well, that was the usual precaution. Hold the officers who might foment and lead an attempt to retake the prizes, leave the seamen aboard leaderless, prisoners of the prize crew. "One prisoner, sah, he says, is an officer-courier of the Honourable Company's military forces, came off the dispatch brig." That was interesting, thought Merewether.

"I'll interview the prisoners at once. Where are they?"

"Locked in a storeroom below, sah. I did not wish to release them without orders."

Gunny led the way down a ladder to a door fastened with a large padlock. A Marine stood on guard before it. "Not against their escape, sah, but sometimes defeated men try to take revenge." The sentry unlocked the door and flung it open. He took the lantern off its hook and stepped inside.

In the dim light, Merewether saw the men seated on the deck about the room, backs against the bulkheads. In the group were two Royal Navy lieutenants, off the dispatch brig, no doubt, nine men in the nondescript dress of officers of country ships and one in the uniform of an ensign in one of the Honourable Company's European regiments. They looked up apathetically at the intrusion, then started up at the sight of the uniform of a captain of the Bombay Marine, their faces lighting up with hope.

"Well, I'm damned!" exclaimed one of the lieutenants. "The Bombay Buccaneers! Welcome aboard, sir!" Merewether grinned at the disrespectful greeting, the Royal Navy's nickname given the Marine in grudging admiration of its accomplishments, its willingness to fight against any foe and any odds at any time.

"We'll go on deck," said Merewether. "Easier to talk there. Any wounds?"

"No, sir." He led the way up the ladder, aft to what had been the French captain's cabin. It was not as large as the cabin in *Rapid* but was comfortably furnished with bed, desk and transom. Merewether sat behind the desk. He saw that pen, ink and paper were handy. "Your names, rank and ship," he said. He took down the list and said to the civilians, "You may go on deck, I'll leave you aboard this ship to assist my prize crew, if you don't mind." The nine civilians went out.

"And now," continued Merewether. "What ship are you gentlemen from?"

"HMS *Artemis*, dispatch brig, sir, four guns," replied one of the lieutenants. "I was her captain, Southfield, sir. And this is Mr. Monroe, my first lieutenant. We were the only two officers in her. The Frenchman took us in the early morning of July 11, just after we left Madras for Calcutta. Four six pounders and forty men, we had no chance, sir."

"Very well, Mr. Southfield," said Merewether. "And you?" he continued to the Company officer.

"Campbell, sir, ensign, Third European Regiment, assigned to the headquarters guard of the Governor of the Madras Presidency, sir, Lord William Bentinck. I was carrying the Governor's dispatches to Calcutta to the Governor-General, telling him about the mutiny."

"Mutiny!" exclaimed Merewether. "What mutiny?"

"Sepoy regiments at Vellore, sir; they rose against their officers and killed, I'm told, over two hundred of the British garrison. A hundred and seventy-odd escaped and reached Madras."

"When was this?" demanded Merewether.

"Three days ago, sir. That would be July 10. Of course, as soon as the news reached Madras, General Sir John Cradock sent all the troops he had to Vellore. But there's not enough to defeat the mutineers and they're holding the fort. Lord William sent me with dispatches to Sir George Barlow at Calcutta. Don't know what they say, but I guess he wants reinforcements."

"Where are your dispatches?" inquired Merewether.

"Don't know, sir. We were captured only ten hours out of Madras. French captain took them, I guess."

"Gunny," called Merewether. The door opened, and the erect square figure of the Jemadar appeared. "Ask that French captain where the dispatches are he took from *Artemis*. If he gives you any trouble, let me know."

In a few minutes the Jemadar was back with a bunch of keys tinkling in his hand. He handed them to Merewether. "Strongbox is under third cushion on transom, sah. Captain very unhappy. He has money there, too."

The third key tried turned the lock. Merewether lifted the lid, exposing a strongbox about two feet square. It was filled almost to the brim with gold and silver coins. On top were three canvas-wrapped packets of dispatches, their seals unbroken, each bearing a superscription addressed to the Governor-General.

"Are these your dispatches?" inquired Merewether. Campbell examined them.

"Yes, sir. Had three, two from the Governor and one from the General."

"Take possession of them," directed Merewether. "You will board my ship to complete your mission. Now, Gunny, get a chest, pack this money in it, and put it on the gangway under guard." Merewether considered that since he was responsible for this considerable sum, he would rest easier if it were in his own strong room. He went on deck to find MacRae.

"Signal *Rapid* to tell off and assemble the prize crew. Larkin is prize master, Dobbs his first lieutenant. The nine rescued officers will assist. I'll leave ten Marines and the Jemadar as a guard. Oh, and signal the Boatswain to send up the royal masts and yards. Tear off the false superstructure. Make all preparations for getting under way."

Merewether saw Buttram approaching, bathed in blood.

"She was badly hit, sir. Grape from the carronades was devastating. I've performed four amputations, three legs and an arm. French surgeon two more. It appears five are mortally wounded. I think the French surgeon and his assistants can take care of the rest now."

"Very well then, we'll go back to *Rapid*." The boatswain's mate signaled in the gig lying on its oars a hundred feet away. The chest of money was loaded. Buttram, Campbell, and Merewether embarked. They rowed for *Rapid*, arriving just as the launch pulled away with the prize crew. Larkin and Dobbs saluted as they passed. "Take her to Calcutta," Merewether called. "There's not too much damage to repair."

Rapid's royal masts were already up. Topmen were securing shrouds and stays and driving home wedges. The yards and sails were on deck ready to go aloft, seamen knocked down the false canvas poop and the wooden bow disguise, and removed the debris of the roundhouse in the waist.

Merewether saw MacRae and the Marine detachment, less ten, enter the launch and pull for *Rapid*. "All right, Mr. Burcham, you have the watch now. As soon as the launch is hoisted in, get under way for the Sandheads."

"Aye aye, sir," replied Burcham, scarcely able to disguise the tremor in his voice. Merewether noted the patch of plaster on his right cheek, his anxious look at the stolid quartermaster at the wheel and the boatswain's mate and messenger lounging at the lee rail. Shortly the launch pulled alongside and the Marines disembarked. Tackles were hooked on, lines taken to the windlass, the boat hoisted in and stowed in its cradle.

"All hands, make sail!" cried Burcham. The hands poured up to man the braces.

"Port, no starboard, yes, port your helm!" The impassive quartermaster spun the wheel. "Hands to the braces." Sails were trimmed. The ship paid off and spun around before the wind. She continued spinning about to starboard as the stolid quartermaster held the wheel hard over. Burcham, startled at the continuing swing, suddenly realized his omission; a quartermaster once given a direct rudder order held that rudder until another order to the helm was given. He shouted frantically, "Midships! Starboard helm! Meet her! Steady as you go!"

Rapid swung back and steadied on her course. Burcham consulted Mr. MacRae, who was standing silently by, a faint grin on his face. He self-consciously gave the helm the new east northeast course for the mouth of the Hooghly, thereby vesting discretion in steering to hold the course once again in the helmsman. He wiped his brow in relief; as MacRae prompted him he gave the orders to set studding and skysails, flying jib. The next cast of the log showed thirteen knots. Four hundred miles with a fair breeze: *Rapid* should be off the Sandheads tomorrow afternoon.

The masthead reported land just at the end of the afternoon watch next day. *Rapid* ran in and finally sighted the pilot lugger. She hoisted an urgent signal. Merewether, having twice traversed the Hooghly, felt he could take the ship up without assistance, but Company and Marine regulations were explicit: a pilot must be on board. After a maddening delay the lugger finally approached and the pilot climbed the ladder. He looked about the decks, as Merewether gave the command to get *Rapid* under way toward the channel. The pilot appeared startled.

"We best wait for morning, sahib," he approached Merewether. "River most difficult at night."

"Full moon by nine o'clock," Merewether told him. "It's most important I reach Calcutta." The pilot salaamed with resignation and took the ship into the channel to commence the ascent of the wild, treacherous Hooghly.

Merewether felt compelled to anchor at dusk and wait two hours for moonrise. He then continued with the tide making, conning the ship from his post at the foremast crosstrees. The Indian pilot on the quarterdeck relayed his commands to the wheel. Fortunately, the night was clear, the sky cloudless.

Rapid came to anchor off the dockyard two hours after midnight, the moonlight making the shore clearly visible. At the plunge of the anchor, Merewether saw lanterns appear at the dockyard landing and heard commands echo across the water. Some officer of the watch, alarmed at the appearance of a ship at this hour, must have suspected a raid and called out the military guard. Merewether called away his gig and sent for Ensign Campbell, who appeared still struggling with his jacket, cap awry, half asleep.

"You have your dispatches?" demanded Merewether. Campbell looked startled. He plunged back below, then reappeared clutching the bundle and entered the gig.

There was a brisk challenge at the landing from a squad of soliders in ranks up the bank. Merewether identified himself and vouched for Campbell. He requested a tonga and that Commodore Land be summoned. While messengers departed, Merewether and Campbell waited in the main gate guardhouse. A quarter hour later, a tonga trotted up, Commodore Land sitting rigidly in the back seat.

"What's up, Merewether?" he called. "Hell of an hour to rouse an old man out of bed."

"I must speak privately, sir." No hint of mutiny in King's or Company's forces must leak out among the troops here; it was often contagious, thought Merewether, remembering Spithead, and the Nore in '97. "I think, sir, we must call on the Acting Governor-General at once."

The Commodore whistled. "At this hour? Velloso's grog shop don't open till six o'clock." Merewether and Campbell entered the tonga. Merewether made a quick introduction and told Land briefly that Campbell bore dispatches of an urgent nature. They trotted off toward the Governor's Palace, as Merewether whispered what he knew to Land.

Outside the massive iron gates, a private soldier slouched along his post in the yellow light of two iron lamps suspended from brackets on the pillars on either side of the gates. Hearing the approach of the tonga, he stiffened to attention and presented arms as he caught the glitter of gold lace and epaulets.

"Call your officer," said the Commodore, dismounting. The private called, and a sleepy looking corporal poked his head through the door set in one of the large gates. When he saw gold lace, he disappeared; a moment later a sergeant emerged.

"Sir," he said. "The Palace is closed now. No admission until eight o'clock. Standing orders of the Governor-General, sir."

"Call the commanding officer of the guard," Land rapped. The sergeant goggled and hesitated a moment. Then he, too, disappeared.

A quarter of an hour later, a young man, coat half-buttoned, cap askew, came charging out of the gate. He wore the insignia of a captain, and plainly was in an unpleasant mood. "What the hell! . . ." he commenced. He subsided and stiffened to attention, saluting.

"Mister, I am Commodore Land, Senior Officer Present of the Bombay Marine, Master Attendant of Calcutta. I demand instant admission to the Governor-General!"

The young captain seemed to wilt. "Sir, it's worth my commission and career if I wake Sir George at this hour. He'll have me cashiered, probably shot before breakfast, sir." He looked pitifully at the unrelenting face of Commodore Land.

"Lead on, Captain. I'll take full responsibility."

The young man, in resignation, led the party through the gates, up the walkway to the Palace door. Here in a cubicle to one side they found an Indian watchman in the livery of the Governor-General's household, head down, fast asleep. The Captain shook him awake and told him to awaken Sir George. At this the dark-skinned Hindu actually blanched, spreading his hands in supplication. By an effort of supreme will, he opened the door and led the party into the ornate foyer, where taper in hand, he lighted two candles in a sconce on the wall. He disappeared through a door leading off to the right.

Some ten minutes passed, before he returned and opened the door. Now Locksley, the assistant secretary, yawning, hair tousled, belting home his robe, came through.

"Well, I'll be eternally damned!" roared the Commodore, his

face suffused with anger. "How many more flunkies before we see Sir George?"

At this, a door at the rear of the foyer crashed open. All eyes flashed toward it, and there, terrible as ever, stood Sir George in a crimson dressing gown, his bare feet thrust into slippers.

"This had better be good, Land," said Sir George. "Very, damn good, sir."

Commodore Land became instantly calm. "Your Excellency," he began, "we have news and dispatches of the utmost urgency. I judged they could not wait till morning. I take full responsibility for this intrusion. I must see Your Excellency privately." Sir George flicked his arctic gaze from Land to Merewether; then to Campbell, who stood frozen at attention, his bundle of dispatches in hand.

"Very well, this way." He marched back through the door and turned left into a paneled library with a large table in the center. Sir George seated himself and extended his hand for the dispatches. Campbell, frozen for a moment, was nudged by Merewether. He jumped and handed over the bundle.

Sir George turned the first packet over. He began by keenly examining the superscription, the seals. He next picked up a knife from the table and deftly slit the wrapping, extracting the dispatch. He now looked at both sides. "How did this courier come into your possession, Merewether?" he said, suddenly.

"Sir—Your Excellency," stammered Merewether, "he was a prisoner in *Tigresse*, had been captured in *Artemis*, dispatch brig."

"Oh, and you took the privateer?"

"Yes, Your Excellency."

"What was the butcher's bill?" inquired Sir George.

"Ah . . . ah, one midshipman slightly wounded, Your Excellency," Merewether admitted. This unthinking reply meant he would have to put young Burcham into his report and rewrite it, since he had made no reference to casualties.

Sir George pulled the candlestick closer and read the dispatch. His brows drew together in a frown. He reached for the second jacket, slit the wrapping, read it, his expression becoming blacker. He picked up the third dispatch, opened it, read it and threw it down. "I shall be eternally damned!" he shouted, his face for once betraying the fires within. "Those fools can't write a sensible connected sentence! Young man," he stabbed a finger at Campbell. "What happened at Madras or Vellore or wherever in hell it was?"

Campbell jumped. "Sir . . ."

"I am addressed as Your Excellency, young man, and don't you forget it!" Campbell's normally ruddy face turned pale. For a moment Merewether thought he might faint and braced himself to catch him.

Then Campbell spoke out, clearly and carefully, "Your Excellency, the Sepoy regiments at Vellore mutinied July 10, killing over two hundred of the British garrison. They hold the barracks, fort, all arms and supplies. I do not know the cause for the mutiny but the rumor at Madras was that it was because of religion, that British missionaries had influenced changes in the distinguishing marks of caste, dress, turbans and beards to convert them to Christianity. Sir John Cradock sent the Third Regiment to contain them, and I was ordered to deliver these dispatches to Your Excellency." Merewether breathed a sigh of relief. Young Campbell was not a man to become confused or inarticulate in a moment of crisis.

Sir George glared at Campbell for a moment, and resumed his impassive manner. "Thank you, young man," he said. "That was the first sensible news of the mutiny I've received." He flicked his gaze from Campbell to Merewether to Land. "All I make out from these dispatches is a bleat for help. That, of course, I'll send." He pulled a tasseled bell cord at his elbow. Locksley materialized as though by magic. "Send in that captain," barked Sir George. Locksley departed.

"How many men will your ship carry, Merewether?"

Merewether's memory went back to the interview with Sir William Foster six months ago in London. He remembered his estimate. "A half battalion, Your Excellency."

The door opened. The captain of the guard edged in, propelled by Locksley, mouth agape with apprehension. "Captain, you'll ride to Fort William at once. Take dictation, Locksley." The secretary produced a writing board to which was clipped a sheaf of paper, an inkwell in a socket on its corner, and a pen. "Command-ing Officer, Fort William," began Sir George as Locksley's pen raced across the sheet. In a moment the orders were dictated and written, handed to Sir George for signature, and another commenced. The first directed that upon receipt, a half battalion of His Majesty's 65th Foot would move for embarkation in *Rap-id*, equipped with full kits and gear for extended operations in the field. The balance of the regiment would march out for embarka-tion as soon as other vessels could be procured for transportation. The captain received the orders and departed.

"Land, you will commandeer any vessels suitable for this pur-pose. Move them to the port of embarkation not later than three P.M. day after tomorrow."

"Aye aye, Your Excellency."

"Merewether, the half battalion will be ready for embarkation by noon today or some heads will roll." Sir George briskly con-cluded the second set of orders to Merewether, signed them. Locksley now sanded the signature and handed them over, thrust-ing a receipt before Merewether for signature. He departed.

"Now, Merewether," continued Sir George, "are you acquaint-ed with the methods and theory of gathering and evaluating intelligence?"

Merewether goggled for a moment, uncertain what reply to make. He had often enough heard his seniors and even some junior officers speak glibly of gathering intelligence, evaluating it, and coming to a conclusion as to a given situation. He had on occasion taken a boat ashore by night, delivered a handful of rupees to a coast watcher, and received his report of ship move-ments. He had boarded many a country vessel to demand a report of sightings and conditions ashore. These routine matters had been dutifully reported to higher authority; possibly they had influenced the next operation, or order for the ship or squadron. But so far as consciously gathering intelligence, distilling it to a solution of a situation and acting upon it, Merewether had had no experience. He had heard of officers who, given the number of bullocks and bags of corn seized by foragers, could compute the force they would feed, but Merewether felt this was an accom-plishment far beyond his powers. Thankfully, there came a discreet knock on the door. In came a Hindu servant balancing a tray carrying a handsome silver coffee pot, sugar bowl and several delicate china cups.

Sir George pointed to the end of the table. The servant set down his tray, poured steaming black coffee into the cups and served them, setting spoons and napkins beside each.

"Well, gentlemen," said Sir George. "May as well be seated, have a cup of coffee. Should help us all at this hour."

Merewether, Land, and Campbell slid self-consciously into chairs along the big table. The servant served the sugar, a spoonful for Merewether. He had been reared from childhood on tea; had, in fact, only tasted coffee once before. Thus, he had no real idea of whether he liked it or not. He stirred the black brew, sipped cautiously. He decided that coffee was palatable, but that he still preferred tea.

"I haven't heard you reply to my question, Merewether," Sir George snapped from behind his cup.

"Your Excellency," said Merewether, "I have, of course, had experience in operational intelligence, but very little in evaluating it or deducing a solution." He felt deficient. Somewhere along the way he should have learned this art as he had that of taking a sun sight or computing a course.

"Any man who's a captain in the Marine should have had experience and be able to deal with such matters. Oh, well, you're not the only one lacking. Governor of Madras and Cradock have no conception of the situation, either, from their dispatches." Sir George paused as the Hindu refilled his cup.

"This mutiny," he continued, "is in my opinion merely a symptom of a much more serious malady. I have reliable reports that Bonaparte is about to make peace with Persia, has one of his pet generals with a party of engineers already there surveying a route through the country to attack India." Sir George sipped his coffee, patted his lips with the napkin. "Also, this fellow calls himself Tipu Sultan of Mysore is back in India from France."

At this Merewether started. He felt Land start, too. Sir George smiled thinly. "I know, Tipu Sultan was killed in '99 defending the breach at Seringapatum from Arthur Wellesley's troops; his family has been in exile, protective custody, at Vellore, ever since. This fellow is reputed to be a son of Tipu, grandson of Hyder Ali, and said to be braver and wiser than either and just as ruthless, though only twenty-two." Sir George sipped his coffee and signaled the servant to refill his cup.

"This boy was sent to France in '96. Twelve years old then, he was educated in the Academy in Rouen, then spent two years in public school in England during the peace. Tipu had a treaty with the French. They sent him a force of a hundred and fifty soldiers, arms, and supplies from Mauritius in '97. That caused his downfall. Wellesley attacked, destroyed him." Sir George stirred his coffee. "The son was picked up by Boney, given a staff commission in 1804, and disappeared last year. Our man in Teheran saw him at the Court of the Shah of Persia last fall. He was introduced to the Shah as Tipu Sultan of Mysore by the head of the French peace commission. I feel sure Bonaparte will make peace both with Persia and Russia before long; then he could move against India through Persia. Be that as it may, Tipu dropped out of sight until two months ago, when he was recognized in Mangalore. Reports two days ago say he made his way across Mysore, was received with joy by all the Muslims, and acclaimed as heir of his father and grandfather. Wellesley restored the old Hindu dynasty of Mysore in '99 in the person of a five-year-old boy ruling through a regent. You can topple that regime with a feather."

He paused, shook his head, pushed his cup away, and leaned back in this chair. "Merewether, you will accompany the troops ashore and proceed to Vellore. I want to know the whole situation. The causes of the mutiny, whether missionaries, French, Tipu Sultan, or the Devil himself. Report matters requiring urgent action to Bentinck, other matters by dispatch to me." Sir George stood up. Land, Merewether and Campbell pushed back their chairs and came to attention as he pulled the bell cord.

Locksley came through the door, writing board in hand. "Dictation," said Sir George. "Orders to Lord William Bentinck, Governor of Madras." He reeled off a dozen sentences that commanded the utmost assistance to Captain Percival Merewether of the Bombay Marine in the performance of a mission for the Acting Governor. He seized the order and dashed off his signature. Locks-

ley affixed the seal, wrapped it, handed it to Merewether, and
took his receipt.

"Now, Merewether," continued Sir George. "I can't anticipate
what conditions you may encounter. You'll have to use such sense
and judgment as you possess. You might even use that Hindu
pirate you rescued from the hangman to gather information."

Merewether jumped, "Sir! . . . Your Excellency . . ."

Sir George gave a mirthless laugh. "My knowledge of your
misprision of piracy, Merewether, is one example of my methods
of gathering intelligence which I expect you to employ. Your
steward is the only pirate in Abercrombie's crew subject to British
law. A Justice of the High Court of Judicature ruled last week the
Atjenese are protected by Bonaparte's letter of marque to Abercrombie since they're not residents of a British possession. The
decree took them away from Sheriff William Churchill and the
gallows, and delivered them to Fort William as prisoners of war."
He shook his head in disgust.

"Very well. Any questions? You are dismissed."

As they rattled back to the dockyard, Merewether took stock of
his situation. First, he must set in motion the preparations for
embarking the half battalion some eight hours from now. He
would have to refill the water casks emptied three weeks ago to
compensate for the carronades, regardless of any effect this might
have on *Rapid*'s sailing qualities. Facilities would have to be
improvised for the troops to prepare their food. Quarters must be
made available for the Major commanding and his officers. It
might take as much as a week to beat back to Madras against the
monsoon. He was brought back to the present by Commodore
Land as the tonga pulled up in front of headquarters.

"I'm sending lighters now to pick up the troops, Merewether.
Hope to be alongside before noon."

Merewether and Campbell went down to the landing and com-
mandeered a yard boat. They caught young Burcham by surprise,
the side not manned as they came to the gangway.

"Pass the word for all officers and warrant officers to report to
my cabin at once," he told the crestfallen Burcham.

The meeting was brief. The Purser and Cooper departed,

shouting for their mates. The Sailmaker remained a few minutes for explicit instructions as to three tents with canvas floors to keep out cobras and other ground vermin, vents protected by netting at the top to provide ventilation and keep out flying insects. The Boatswain and Carpenter left to rig landing nets, ladders and booms to embark the troops and their luggage. Merewether sat back at his desk, suddenly so weary that his head drooped onto his forearms on the desk. He almost slept, but was started full awake as Sangh came in, tray laden with tea, sliced oranges, toast and preserves. He was suddenly ravenous and quickly finished the breakfast.

The morning passed in turmoil, all hands hard at work preparing the ship. Just before noon, the messenger came below to report a lighter loaded with troops in sight upstream. The embarkation was orderly. The officers of the battalion seemed well in control of their troops. Water was aboard, the baggage being stowed, soldiers thronging the waist, curiously inspecting their new surroundings. Merewether had the word passed, "Make all preparations for getting under way." There was still over an hour before the ebb.

The messenger reappeared, "Sir, Mr. Burcham's compliments, and the French prize is in sight downstream." Merewether leaped to his feet and went on deck to call MacRae.

"Signal the dockyard to send a prize crew for the schooner and a guard to take off the prisoners. I want my crew and Marines back!"

Some of the lighters were still alongside unloading the last of the troops' luggage. MacRae called, "Dockyard acknowledges. I'll send these lighters ashore to pick up the crew and guards."

"Very well." An hour of frantic maneuvers ensued, at the end of which Larkin, Dobbs, Gunny, the prize crew, and Marines were alongside in the launch. He was no more than ten minutes later than he had planned for departure, and he had his full complement again.

Rapid cleared the Sandheads and dropped the pilot toward the end of the afternoon watch the next day. Merewether felt relief at having safely descended the Hooghly River once more. He decided it would be appropriate to invite the senior officers of the half battalion to dinner. He sent Sangh with a note to Major Lord George Cecil Laddington Montague, Baron Montague, commanding, and the two captains, and received their immediate acceptances. Apparently all were good sailors, though a number of their soldiers were already seasick as *Rapid* swooped quartering over the swell on the starboard tack. From his own officers, he invited Burcham and Buttram.

The group gathered, and were swiftly served by Sangh; gin for the Major and Merewether; Scots whisky for Captains Thomas and Carter; claret for Buttram and Burcham. Merewether found himself liking the young Major immediately. He did not stand upon his title, requested no formality. "Everyone calls me Lord Laddie," he explained, and soon had the party in high good humor with his store of droll stories and jokes. Merewether had heard of Lord Laddie before. He knew his reputation as a rake, and also as a competent soldier. The Major was dark, with close-cropped black hair, sparkling black eyes, a hawk nose, and a wryly humorous mouth. He bore two distinctions; he had become the seventh Baron Montague at the moment of his birth, his hard-riding, profligate father having been killed two months before when his horse broke a leg at a dead run; and he was reputed to be the most impecunious peer in England. He had not bought his commission, as it was customary for such sprigs of the nobility to do, but had entered the army as an ensign and been promoted on merit. However, since his mother had married a wealthy brewer, he was rumored to be in receipt of a handsome allowance.

Dinner was served. The merriment continued. It was the most entertaining dinner Merewether could recall. As the party broke up, Lord Laddie said, "Captain, I want to see you again when we get back to Fort William. My stepfather bought a villa for me out on Chitapur Creek. Have some high old times there with some of the other single officers."

"I should be delighted," said Merewether. He did not expect to hear of the matter again.

He came on deck, found rain beginning to fall, the sky clouded over, the night black as pitch. He looked at the compass, course southeast on a reach to a point where *Rapid* would have enough southing to beat back to Madras. Merewether gave Dobbs his night orders, and retired.

CHAPTER 15

At dawn the fifth day, the masthead reported a landfall. Merewether approached cautiously through a driving rainstorm and finally had the coast in sight from the deck. There had been no opportunity for evening or morning star sights. His dead reckoning from the noon observation yesterday put him south of Madras. He wore ship, headed almost due north. In an hour, the clouds lifted, the rain diminished, and he could see a range of hills inland. Ottivakam Hill, marked on the chart, was recognizable, bearing due west. He was only a few miles south of Madras.

The ship, before noon, had edged in as close as Merewether deemed prudent. She anchored in seven fathoms in Madras roadstead off Fort St. George. Merewether made *Rapid*'s number and signaled for shore boats to disembark the troops. The surf off Madras was nearly always heavy—most difficult for ships' boats to land in. His instructions through Major Lord Montague, commanding the half battalion, were to utilize the native boatmen with their double-hulled native craft for the landing. Merewether and Campbell were in the first boat ashore. Merewether interviewed the beachmaster, a taciturn boatswain of the Royal Navy. He demanded transportation to the Governor and was furnished a cart drawn by a bony mule driven by an Indian youth.

At Government House, Campbell was known. He gained quick admission for them. They waited in an anteroom to the Governor's chambers, while secretaries and aides came and went, and were finally approached by a very young and supercilious captain of His Majesty's Foot. "Captain Merewether, Lord William will see you now." The entire scene was much more relaxed than that around Sir George Barlow, Merewether considered, as he preceded Campbell through the door.

Lord William Bentinck was a young man scarcely older than

Merewether, and was already noted as a radical in England. He had a broad sloping brow, protruding china-blue eyes, and a bold aquiline nose above full lips. He stood behind a massive desk, inclining his head courteously as the aide made the introductions. He took the packet of dispatches from Campbell and handed them on to the aide. "Please be seated," he said, resuming his own chair.

"Your Excellency," Merewether began, a trifle nervously, "I have here a confidential order from Sir George Barlow." He handed the thin packet to Lord William, who read it swiftly.

"Very well, Captain. You shall have such facilities as I have available. You understand, we have the mutineers contained in the fort at Vellore and have moved up most of the forces from Arcot. With the addition of elements from the 65th Foot, the mutineers either will lay down their arms and march out, or we will overwhelm them." He looked at Merewether. "Transport is at a premium, of course. Only practical way to Vellore with all this rain is by cart, roads are almost impassable. Will you have much baggage? How many in your party?"

"My aide and servant" responded Merewether. "Baggage accordingly."

Lord William rang the bell and the young captain appeared. "Arrange for Captain Merewether to be furnished a high-wheeled cart, team of mules and driver at once."

The aide led the way out and, after calling one of the messengers squatting outside the anteroom, busied himself at his desk.

Merewether turned to Campbell. "I think this completes your duties with me," he said. "You brought your belongings from the ship? Well, you may report back to your command." Campbell saluted and departed.

Ten minutes later, the messenger reappeared with a pockmarked man of middle years wearing a southwester hat and crackling oilskins, dripping water on the handsome rug. "You wanted me?" asked the man truculently.

"Yes, Jolley," replied the aide. "The Governor requires a high-wheeled cart, driver, and team of mules at once. Best bring one with a cover. Deliver it to Captain Merewether here."

The pockmarked man looked at the young captain. Within

the confines of the anteroom he emitted a strong odor of horses mixed with rum.

"Gorblimey, sir, you must think I'm a bloody magician. Already scraped the country clean for horses, mules, anything with four legs. Have to move a half battalion's baggage, too, Major's raising hell to get started from the beach. And now this!" He rolled his eyes upward, then squinted at the aide to judge the effect of his protest.

The young captain looked up briefly and coldly from his desk, "Hop to it, Jolley. Twenty minutes, or you'll wish you'd never been born." The man rolled his eyes skyward again in resignation, turned and clumped out, Merewether at his heels.

At the beach, Merewether wished he had kept Campbell to stand guard over his cart. Sergeants and even a captain of the half battalion made successive essays to commandeer the cart. Finally, Merewether put his cocked hat, as a token of possession, on the seat beside the driver, loudly instructed him to wait under peril of instant decapitation and, bareheaded, was rowed out to *Rapid*.

Sangh had the baggage packed and waiting at the gangway, a tarpaulin protecting it. Merewether went below to take off the soggy full-dress uniform. This he handed to Sangh, before struggling into his oldest undress uniform. He pulled on the boots he had last worn two years ago when he led the landing force ashore at Bussorah, called Burcham, and departed for the beach.

Three and a half days of frustration, wet clothing, clinging mud, mosquito bites, and hard work at last accomplished the seventy-five miles to Vellore. The cart, with Merewether seated beside the driver and Sangh and Burcham curled on top the baggage, was challenged by a picket. Merewether gave the password and received directions to the headquarters of General Sir John Cradock, where he reported his presence upon special assignment. He was able to see the fort, a red flag flying over it, just as the mutineers at the Nore had flown one in '97. The encampment was along the bank of the Palar River. The breastworks and artillery emplacements had been hastily erected, and a battery of twelve field guns was positioned opposite the sally port. Evidently, Sir John considered his force not yet sufficient to move against the Sepoys.

Merewether took his cart on past the main encampment. He found a level spot just off the road and screened by a grove of palmyra trees, but still within the picket lines. Here he pitched camp. During the journey, Sangh seemed to have achieved some sort of ascendancy over the Tamil driver—probably some technicality of caste. Thus, with a minimum of physical effort on his part, but many shrill directions, he soon had the three tents erected, cots set up, a latrine dug, a stone hearth laid to support a charcoal brazier, and had commenced preparation of dinner. Merewether entered his tent, pleased to find a fresh, dry uniform laid out and a bucket of warm rainwater ready. He bathed for the first time in three days, pulled on the uniform, dug out the bottle of London gin, and took a medicinal dram before Sangh served dinner.

The dinner was truly remarkable. Somewhere along the road Sangh had acquired a fat hen. He had prepared it with rice, fresh vegetables, hot peppers. A delicious concoction! After ship's biscuit and salt beef for three days, Merewether found the gin had sharpened his appetite and soothed his sore muscles. The tasty dinner in turn imparted a feeling that all was well with the world. He had to haul himself back with an effort to the reality of the situation, to remember Sir George's explicit directions.

"Burcham," he commenced, lazily sipping a second cup of tea. "We must be out on our mission." Burcham assumed an expression of adolescent brightness and leaned forward to give attention. Merewether had not briefed him on the mission, had in fact brought him along as aide simply because he could best be spared from the ship. He looked up at the clearing sky. No rain had fallen since noon. The sun was setting in crimson splendor behind the hills to the west.

"Our mission," he continued, quoting Sir George, "is to discover the whole situation here, find out the true causes of the mutiny, whether missionaries, the French, Tipu Sultan, or the Devil himself, and inform the Governor-General. I think a stroll about Vellore before dark might be in order. Sangh!" he called. The little Hindu materialized inside the tent. "Can you speak enough of this dialect to be understood?"

"Yes, sahib."

"Then I want you to make discreet—I mean discreet—inquiry as to whether there are any European Christian missionaries in the area and their location. Find out, if you can, what the Hindus and Muslims think of them, whether they have made any converts, and what influence they have had. You understand?"

"Yes, sahib." The small man set out the newly oiled boots for Merewether, and went away. Soon Merewether could hear his shrill voice of command, catching enough of the sense of his orders to understand the driver was being directed to guard the premises with his life.

"Let us take our stroll," said Merewether to Burcham, clapping on his hat and slipping one of the handsome double-barreled pistols taken from Abercrombie in his belt under his undress jacket. He handed the other to Burcham. There were probably a hundred reasons for two officers of the Bombay Marine to be at Vellore at this juncture other than the real one.

CHAPTER 16

The town was much smaller than Calcutta or Bombay, but served as a trading center for a considerable area. Small boats could traverse the Palar River, now running banksfull, to bring in merchandise, fruits, timber, cloth, the myriad produce of the countryside. Merewether and Burcham shortly encountered a guard post and were passed in with warnings to be out by dark. They headed toward the river, where the current was running fully five knots. They found the main bazaar and noted guard posts at intervals, with soldiers of one of the Company's European regiments patrolling in pairs along the narrow streets, armed with muskets, bayonets fixed. Evidently Cradock was yet fearful of a general uprising of the populace, though this town was outside Mysore and appeared to have little reason to follow even a son of Tipu Sultan.

Merewether assumed the air of a sailor on shore leave. He looked about lackadaisically, bought a small brass elephant bell, a carved ivory figurine of a hideous god. Burcham, towering over him and the Indian passersby, was an object of awe to the smaller men, exciting jabbering comment as they passed. The sun was down. Dusk began to fall. Merewether bethought himself of the warning; no sense to run afoul of the Company's military forces. He turned to lead the way back to the camp.

The woman, obviously European, was marching with a stately stride down the center of the street. She caught Merewether's attention instantly, accustomed as he was to the omnipresent sari and headcloth. For her head was framed in a reddish-gold halo of braided hair that appeared at first glance to be a crown. She was clad in a shapeless black robe, with high neck, long sleeves, which billowed about her as she strode over the stone pavement. Around her neck was a thick white cord on which was suspended an ivory cross, dangling to her waist. In her left hand she clasped a Bible. It was her face that preempted attention, however, a face reddened and peeling from constant exposure to tropical sun, a skin so fair that it would never tan, piercing pale-blue eyes under heavy brows, long straight nose, and lips clenched in a rigid, almost colorless, horizontal line.

As Merewether and Burcham made their leisurely approach, the woman's eyes suddenly caught Merewether's. She raised her right hand, pointing her forefinger at his face, and continued her stately advance directly toward him.

"Stay, brother!" she said suddenly in a harsh high voice. Merewether halted, the finger six inches from his nose. Looking past it to the peeling face, into the hypnotic pale eyes, he became conscious that if he looked at the finger his eyes would appear ridiculously crossed. He was aware of Burcham's amused titter and felt a flash of irritation, both at Burcham and this apparition before him who was nearly as tall as he.

"Are you saved, brother?" continued the woman, fixing his gaze. This was a question Merewether had never consciously considered. At thirteen, he had learned his catechism under Dawson's tutelage and had been confirmed in a class of apprentices aboard *Dunvegan Castle* by a passenger Anglican bishop. Thereafter, he had dutifully attended church services aboard ship in the Company's service, and that of the Bombay Marine. He could not remember ever entering a church ashore, except St.

John's at Calcutta six weeks ago for Buttram's wedding. Since assuming command of *Rapid*, he had conducted simple services in accordance with regulations and officiated, he remembered, at two burial ceremonies at sea. As far as giving conscious consideration to whether his soul was in a state of grace, prepared for entry into a nebulous hereafter immediately following an enemy broadside, was a matter foreign to Merewether's naturally fatalistic nature. If a man did his duty to the best of his skill and ability and dealt honestly with his fellowman, there was little the church could add; or so Merewether had pronounced on the few occasions when some wardroom discussion raised the question of religion.

"Why—why, yes," he said. "Confirmed member of the Church of England."

The woman's compressed lips popped open. She almost spat, "Bah! You are naught but an idolator, a heathen, bowing down to ceremony and form, not the substance, not the true Jesus of Nazareth!"

Merewether heard Burcham snicker again. He felt irritation mount and started to push past the woman, then realized suddenly that here was, undoubtedly, a missionary, fortuitously delivered into his hands. He became aware that the woman had shifted her gaze from his eyes to his scarred and powder-burned cheek, saying almost as though to herself: "A man of war and violence. War is the affliction of mankind." Her voice rose again, "Oh, sir, you must be washed in the blood of the Lamb of God and be saved! Abandon this wicked life and follow our Savior!" Merewether heard Burcham titter once again.

"Sister, I would hear more from you, but I am under orders to depart for the time being. Where is your mission?"

The woman shifted her gaze back to his eyes. He met her stare unflinchingly and held it till her eyes dropped. "On the road to Bangalore, a mile beyond the town," she replied. "My father and I are there from dawn until midafternoon each day; then I pass through the lanes, gather up the sinners, and bring them to our evening services. I am Sister Jeanne, brother. Come and be saved!"

She stepped aside and resumed her stately progress through the darkening bazaar. Merewether watched her go, trying to evaluate the accent in her speech, it was an Irish brogue no doubt, but overlaid with a more exotic trace of some other culture. He and Burcham hurried back to the camp as darkness closed in.

Merewether entered his tent, where he found that the Tamil driver had lighted a battle lantern. Merewether pulled the netting back across the entrance and looked carefully around the interior, under the cot, behind his chest. The canvas floor of the tent should keep out ground vermin, but here in this far south province of India, cobras were a real menace. Often in the night, they sought warmth in a tent and could even surmount the foot high canvas threshold of the tent if large enough. He got out his leather writing and dispatch kit, which also contained his orders, sharpened a pen, and wrote his report to date. Then, blowing out the lamp, he slid out of his uniform and lay down on the cot. It was broad daylight when he awoke.

As Merewether was finishing his second cup of tea, Sangh quietly appeared before him and salaamed.

"Well?" he demanded.

"Sahib, the missionaries stay at a small bungalow a mile west of Vellore, on the road to Bangalore. They have been here four months, a man and woman. They already knew the language when they came. Last year there were others there, but two died of fever and one went back to Madras. They have made this time perhaps fifteen converts, most of them untouchables, but many more, mostly young Muslims, attend each night. The woman each afternoon walks through the streets, gathers in people to attend evening services. At first, there was only singing and preaching. Two weeks ago, a man, dressed as a Muslim, but European, began to come. He played a—" Sangh hesitated, searched for a word, then pantomimed the playing of a violin.

"Fiddle or violin," interposed Merewether.

"Yes, sahib. Then a second man, also dressed as a Muslim, but Indian, came a few times, played a flute for the singing." Sangh looked about him, then almost hissed, "It is said this second man is Tipu Sultan, come back to claim his throne!" The little Hindu evidently had little love for Muslim princes.

"Tipu has been dead these seven years," said Merewether. "He may very well be a kinsman, though. Do you know where these two live?"

"Yes, sahib. Across the road from the mission is a small estate, a villa owned by a Muslim merchant of Vellore. These two men and several others are staying there. This was all I could learn last night."

"Excellent, Sangh." The little Hindu's sad face actually creased in a brief smile at this praise. He salaamed and withdrew.

Merewether sat on his cot and tried to sort out the situation. The woman appeared to be a genuine fanatic. It would be hard to conceive otherwise of so consummate an actress. But then he had had no experience with these radical Protestant sects. He had heard of spurious priests, begging their way through the English countryside, obtaining a livelihood from the credulous, but accepting a post such as this in the hinterlands of a tropical Indian province was no safe or easy way to earn a living. Either these missionaries were genuine, or they were here on a much more important mission. He concluded that he must meet the man and try to ferret out the motives of the pair.

As to the visits of the European and Muslim musicians to the mission, this posed an even graver problem. Sangh's informants might be correct; this could, indeed, be the son of Tipu Sultan, waiting here outside of Mysore, for aid from Bonaparte. His relatives were sequestered in exile in the area and had been accused by Cradock of fomenting the mutiny. It could well be a calculated diversion, causing garrisons at Arcot, Bangalore, even Seringapatam, to march out to put down the rebellion and police the area afterward. But, Merewether thought, such a diversion would be wasted unless Tipu had a force in being, and was able to take advantage of it. This was the crucial point. He called Sangh.

"Have the team hitched to the cart," he directed. "Tell Mr. Burcham to come in at his convenience." In a moment Burcham pushed aside the netting, stumbled through the entrance, stooped over to accommodate his height in the tent. "Sit on the chest," directed Merewether. "I wish to go out to the mission this morning, to see if I can discover anything about those missionaries. I want you along, but out of sight. If my information is correct, some other people may be interested in my visit. You will remain in the cart, under the cover but so arranged that you can see out. It will be hot and uncomfortable but we will try to leave the cart in the shade. I am interested in the villa across the road, any movement or activity. You understand?" Merewether heard the creaking of the cart as it pulled up in front of the tent.

Outside, Burcham managed to haul his long body into the cart under the low cover. Merewether pulled the canvas flaps at either end together and secured them. Unless someone made a close inspection, Burcham was invisible, but could see out through the small gaps where the top was lashed to the bed. He mounted the seat beside the driver and the cart rattled off. The road was drying out under the sun. There had been no rain since noon yesterday; even the mules appeared to be in good spirits after a night's rest and ample fodder.

CHAPTER 17

It was no more than half an hour to the mission, which was instantly recognizable by a rude wooden cross set in the ground before a small, dilapidated bungalow, almost hidden behind an immense banyan tree. The cart pulled to a stop in the shade. Across the road from the bungalow was a pair of wooden gateposts, the remnants of gates propped against them. A thick hedge of thorny unpruned shrubs extended some distance on either side of the gate. The track leading in through the gates was well worn and showed evidence of the passage of many vehicles and horses. The villa itself was invisible from the road, but almost concealed behind one of the gateposts Merewether saw a man watching him. He wore an elaborate, large dagger in his belt and leaned on a substantial staff. Apparently the entrance was guarded.

Merewether swung down. He signaled the driver to wait and went slowly toward the bungalow. By its side, he now saw a space had been cleared and many benches had been set up, with an arbor of woven fiber erected to shield them from rain or sun. A rickety platform supported a rostrum on which there was mounted a small cross. As he circled the banyan tree, he caught a flicker of movement through the open door of the bungalow. A moment later, a slender man, nearly as tall as Burcham, emerged, blinking in the sunlight. His hair had been blond, but was almost white now. He came to the edge of the verandah, extending his hand, palm out.

"Welcome, brother," he intoned. "Welcome to the house of the Lord Jesus Christ who came into this world to save sinners. Except you be saved, there is no world to come."

"Good morning, sir," replied Merewether. "I am Captain Percival Merewether of the Honourable Company's Bombay Marine. Your daughter invited me yesterday to call here."

"Enter, Captain, and rest. We delight to spread the gospel among the military and naval forces. If we can bring enough of them to salvation, there will be no more war, only peace on earth."

Merewether pricked up his ears. Possibly there was some foundation for the rumor that the missionaries had either inspired or had taken advantage of the order changing the dress of the Sepoys. He followed the tall man across the verandah and entered the bungalow.

"I am John MacGuire, Captain," explained the missionary. "Born an Irishman and a Papist, but now a citizen of God. I was even a soldier for His Majesty once. I fought in the American War, before the Lord showed me his light and saved me from a life of sin and perdition." The man certainly had a gift of speech, Merewether thought: smooth, earnest, persuasive, overlaid with a soft Irish brogue.

The room, he saw as his eyes adjusted to the semidarkness, was simply furnished, a heavy table that served as a desk against the wall on which lay open a huge Bible, four simple wooden chairs, a low couch against another wall. Merewether caught a flicker of movement through the open door that led to the back of the house. He found himself staring at the tall woman as she came into the room, with her majestic stride.

"Welcome, brother! Welcome to this house of God. 'As God so loved the world, he gave his only begotten son to save sinners.' Come, walk in the paths of righteousness and sin no more!" In the half light, her eyes glittered under the bright crown of braided hair, her face appearing to float disembodied above the black robe. "I am Sister Jeanne."

"Well . . ." Merewether stammered, taken aback by the vehemence of her greeting and wondering what to say next. "I want to talk to you people first, to see if my soul is in any condition to be saved, to find out how you get this call." He looked questioningly at the man. "By the way, who is your sponsor in the Court of Directors or Proprietors of the Company?"

MacGuire laughed, "Not the Clapham Sect or the Evangelical Clergy and Laity, certainly. Our sponsor is The Society of Saint John the Baptist, which holds a letter of authorization from Charles Grant, who is, I believe, one of the Chairs. Does that answer your question, Captain?"

"Quite fully," said Merewether, noting with surprise the glib reply and the naming of the Deputy Chairman of the Company as a sponsor. Grant, he had heard, was an earnest churchman and might well have authorized this mission, radical though its present personnel appeared.

"We were about to have some tea before our converts begin to call, Captain. Will you partake? We generally see our people in the arbor," said MacGuire.

They went out around the bungalow, through the arbor to the rear where there was a rude table behind the platform with benches alongside. Sister Jeanne followed with three small native bowls nested in one hand, a pot of tea in the other. She set the bowls before MacGuire and Merewether. Was it Merewether's imagination that she had deliberately brushed against him and was now seeking to catch his eye?

"Ah," said Merewether appreciatively, raising the bowl to his lips with both hands. "I never get enough of this."

"Gluttony, Captain," she said in her harsh, high voice. "Gluttony. You should consume no more food or drink than your body requires." The tea was strong, unsweetened, almost corrosive in its taste. Merewether sipped again, gingerly, and set down the bowl.

"By the way," said Merewether. "You must have guessed why I'm in Vellore. I've brought reinforcements because of the mutiny. But is it true you or other missionaries caused the revolt, as they say in Madras?" Sometimes, he thought, an unexpected and direct question would elicit an unguarded answer.

Both MacGuire and Sister Jeanne looked at Merewether blankly, Sister Jeanne's clenched bloodless lips opened. "Ridiculous!" she said, her eyes flashing. "I've often enough seen the Sepoy soldiers in Vellore with their heathen beards and dress. One even seized me once on the road. He had been drinking in violation of his own religion—only good thing in it—but he was quite small. The good Lord saved me from him when I justly smote him!" Her lips resumed their bloodless line.

"Quite right, Captain," said MacGuire easily in his soft brogue. "Never had a Sepoy come here. We don't bother with the military, plenty of other souls to save. Rumors are completely false."

Merewether hesitated. This was a direct denial and certainly he had no evidence to the contrary. He changed the subject, finishing the bowl of tea with a suppressed shudder of distate. In time, he became aware of a small group of Indians standing humbly waiting before the rostrum. "You have visitors," he said. "I'll go, come again another day. Many thanks for the refreshment. You have given me food for thought." The woman stood and raised her hand in benediction.

"Go with God, brother. Seek out the light of salvation." MacGuire merely waved. Merewether walked through the arbor and emerged into the blinding sunlight beside the cart. The scene was unchanged. Even the guard at the villa gate still leaned against the post in the shade. Merewether mounted the seat, pointing back toward Vellore. The mules settled into a bouncing trot.

A quarter mile down the road, Merewether saw a level spot in the shade. The cart drew up and stopped. Merewether unfastened the flap, exposing the red-faced, sweating Burcham. He helped him out.

"Whew!" breathed Burcham, mopping his brow and stamping his feet to restore circulation. "Black Hole of Calcutta couldn't have been much worse!" Merewether smiled sympathetically.

"At least you didn't have to drink a bowl of acid and pretend you liked it," he responded. "See anything?"

"Yes, sir."

"Well, save it for the camp," Merewether told him, uncertain

of how much the Tamil driver might understand. They were back
in half an hour and found Sangh engaged in the preparation of
lunch. He somehow had come into possession of two canvas
chairs and had set them on a smooth bit of turf in the shade.
Merewether and Burcham sat down.

"Well?"

"Sir, a tonga, two men and a driver, came from the direction of
Bangalore about a quarter hour before you came back, turned in
at the gate to the villa. The guard bowed all the way to the ground
—prostrated himself as they say in the Bible—then spoke to them.
I couldn't understand but two words, 'Bombay Marine,' sir. He
pointed at the cart and the mission." Burcham leaned forward
toward Merewether, the faint red mark of the splinter scar visible
on his cheek. "Remarkable thing about it, I knew both men!" He
leaned back again.

"Well?" prompted Merewether.

"One's a Frenchman, M'sieur Lally. He was the French master
at Saint George's School back when I was in the third form."
Burcham hesitated. "Quite a scandal when he left. Headmaster
caught him kissing Henry Nelson in his room." He gave a short
laugh and actually blushed.

Merewether had encountered homosexuality before, both in
the Company's service and that of the Bombay Marine. Often, it
seemed to afflict men of virile appearance and considerable courage, as well as weaklings. It was no respector of person. He remembered as a boy in *Dunvegan Castle* overt advances being
made by a man or two, but even then the thought had been
abhorrent to him.

"Anyway, M'sieur Lally was sent packing, it must have been
1803. I know it was just before King George called the Navy back
to duty, because my eldest brother had been on half pay as a
lieutenant and he got an appointment to a frigate a week or so
later." He paused and thought a minute. "Yes, I'm sure, because
Hy Alley left school to go back to France on the same stage with
M'sieur. They both went down to Shearness to board a Dutch
ship before the blockade was declared.

"Hy Alley was the second man in the tonga today," he said
with a sort of wonder. "I almost didn't recognize him in that

turban affair, native dress, but that was Hy Alley sure as shooting!"

Merewether felt excitement well up. Hyder Ali was the father of Tipu Sultan, who was possibly the father, in turn, of the man reported to have come back to Mysore calling himself Tipu Sultan a few weeks ago. What would be more natural than for the boy, orphaned, but still well provided for in France, to adopt an Anglicized version of the name of his grandfather to escape notice when he went to study at an English school? It was entirely possible.

"This Hy Alley you mention, was he a student?"

"Yes, sir, at St. George's over a year. He entered the top form." Burcham's face took on a rapt expression of reminiscence. "Hy, even though an Indian, was the most popular boy in school. If he'd entered a little earlier, he would have been Senior Prefect. He spoke English perfectly. Jump and run, sir, you've never seen his like, and brave as a lion!"

He certainly had the heredity for courage, Merewether thought, remembering the legendary bravery of Hyder Ali and Tipu Sultan in the many wars of the Carnactic, with the Company and the British.

"Once we small boys—this was before I began to grow—went over to Gatling Green to a little shop that sold sweets. Some of the big village bumpkins began to knock us about and took our money. I had only two shillings left from my quarter's allowance. Hy saw our trouble, came bounding in and fair laid out four of them, all bigger and older than he. He made them give back the money, then faced down the town constable and took us back to the school."

Burcham fairly glowed at the recollection. Obviously the Indian prince remained a hero to this young man.

Merewether thought a moment. "Would Hy or Lally recognize you now?"

"I don't know, sir. I'm a foot and a half taller but my features haven't changed much in three years. I don't believe M'sieur would." Burcham laughed deprecatingly, "Never had a round enough bottom to attract his attention."

Merewether became aware that Sangh was standing by, a steaming tray of lunch balanced in each hand. He served them as they sat in the shade of the palmyra grove—fresh vegetables and salt beef somehow converted into a delicious substance topped with a spiced sauce, tea, ship's biscuit and jam.

As he slowly consumed the meal, Merewether considered the situation. There was no doubt in his mind after hearing Burcham's report that the son of the late Tipu Sultan was here, thus far unrecognized or ignored by the authorities at Vellore. He tied this information to that supplied by Sangh, that many young Muslims attended the nightly services. This was unusual enough; the average Muslim considered any Christian an infidel dog, lost to salvation. The circumstances suggested, however, that the mission might well be in fact a recruiting station for a revolutionary army aimed at Mysore and its thirteen-year-old Hindu ruler. The missionaries had been at Vellore now four months. Assuming only twenty recruits a night, this might well total twenty-five hundred men by now. If they had arms and supplies, such a force might overwhelm the weak Hindu dynasty of a child ruling through a regent and have the entire countryside rally behind a strong, intelligent son of Tipu Sultan, particularly with British and Company forces diverted by the necessity of containing the mutiny.

Merewether mechanically finished the meal, and sat almost in a trance as he sought a solution of the situation. Here, he was less than a hundred miles from Pondicherry, the old capital of French India. Pondicherry was now held by British forces, but still contained a number of French citizens possibly able to give assistance to a plot conceived by young Tipu Sultan to regain the throne of Mysore. It was mere conjecture, however, he told himself. He had no proof, no knowledge of how such a conspiracy might be carried out. Such an operation would require at least three thousand trained soldiers, as well as arms, ammunition and transport. For food, such a force could largely subsist upon the countryside, as did every British expeditionary force. Where such a force could be assembled without coming to the attention of some government authority was a mystery, as was the source of arms and equipment. Merewether squirmed uncomfortably in the canvas chair, becoming aware of the gaze of Burcham fixed upon him.

"Oh, Burcham, you may be excused, but don't get out of ear-shot."

The tall boy departed into the middle distance.

CHAPTER 18

Merewether turned the matter over in his mind again. Combining the information supplied by Sir George, Sangh and Burcham, he was in little doubt that the son of Tipu Sultan was present. Since his family was resident in exile nearby under surveillance of the authorities, it was possible young Tipu also was on the proscribed list and could be taken into custody. Merewether entered his tent and shifted into full-dress uniform with sword, feeling the sweat beginning to trickle down his body as he fastened his stock.

"Burcham," he called. The young man trotted up. "I shall call upon the Resident at Vellore. Wait here." The journey in was brief. After a single inquiry, he found the Resident's quarters.

A sullen half-caste Indian clerk intercepted Merewether to obtain his name and rank, though not the purpose of his visit. He disappeared down a corridor. Eventually he returned and informed Merewether in singsong English that he must wait. Fuming and still sweating, Merewether subsided upon a wooden bench; he watched the clerk count documents from one stack to another. These provincial Residents, Merewether thought savagely, were an arrogant lot, careless of another man's time. Finally a bell tinkled far down the corridor, at which the clerk beckoned and led him back.

In a large room, dimly lighted through shutters, a civilian sat behind a heavy table. He had removed his coat, rolled up his sleeves and was positioned beneath a large woven fan suspended from the ceiling. The fan, which swept back and forth, was propelled by cords leading outside and was undoubtedly powered by an Indian boy. The man was slender, gray-haired, with a bold aquiline nose and bright eyes.

"Yes, Captain?" he inquired. "I am Millard, Resident of this District."

"Sir, I am Captain Percival Merewether of the Bombay Marine, on an official mission for the Governor-General." He tendered the copy of the order given him by Sir George.

"Very well, quite in order."

"Sir, at present you have members of the family of the late Tipu Sultan of Mysore under restraint here." The Resident nodded. "I have reason to believe another member of his family is at large in the area and likely to create trouble. This man is reputed to be a son."

The Resident nodded again. "Yes, Captain," he said. "I have had such a rumor reported to me. I sent it on to Madras." He paused, tinkled the bell on his desk. The clerk appeared. "Get me the roster of the family of Tipu Sultan." He sat back, fingers pressed together in an arch. In a moment the clerk returned and handed the Resident a bound volume.

"Already made inquiries," he said. "This son was named at birth Haidar Ben Ali. He was in France in school, fifteen years old, at the time of the death of Tipu Sultan, and was overlooked by Wellesley in making this official list of proscribed members of the family to be exiled. We have no legal right to restrain him now, even if we could find him. If he's actually trying to foment a rebellion, the military should arrest him. Matter for it." The Resident yawned genteelly.

"Very well, sir," responded Merewether. "I had hoped there might be some way to restrain him. I think I have people who can identify him. Sorry to have troubled you." The Resident waved negligently as Merewether departed. He knew only too well the legalistic framework in which a Resident operated, the precise rules and formulas prescribed for each situation, with little room for the exercise of discretion. Outside he mounted the cart, directed the driver back toward the camp, then to the headquarters of the besieging forces.

Headquarters for the staff of Sir John Cradock, the Commander in Chief, had been established in a substantial house a mile north of the sally port of the fortress. A quarter mile away, a picket post commanded by a sergeant challenged him. He gave the password and was waved by. In sight of the house, identified by a large ensign flying from a pole in front, he was halted by another guard post. This time an ensign of His Majesty's Foot was in command.

"Sir," he wavered, looking at the gold epaulets on Merewether's uniform. "I must send an escort with you. Sniper almost hit the General last night with a shot, sir."

"Very well," replied Merewether. A lanky corporal climbed onto the cart, and they rattled on toward headquarters. Fifty yards from the door, a private challenged them again. The corporal replied, groaned, and climbed down.

"Must walk from here in, sir," he said in a broad Cockney accent. "Buggers really have the wind up, 'fraid of their bloody shadows." He led the way to the door where yet another sentry stood. The sentry hallooed over his shoulder while bringing his musket to present arms.

A sergeant major, splendid in scarlet coat, silver mounted cane in hand, strode majestically out. He saluted.

"I am Captain Merewether of the Bombay Marine. I have urgent business with Sir John Cradock, sergeant."

The sergeant examined Merewether up and down, almost as though he were on a parade inspection. Deciding the Captain was a senior officer of some foreign service, he replied, "Sir, General Cradock is away. His adjutant is in temporary command. I will inquire as to whether he will see you."

The sergeant about-faced. Two minutes later he returned.

"Colonel Thompson will see you, sir." He ushered Merewether in to a room lighted through slatted blinds. Four tables were set about the room, three covered with maps and piles of papers. The fourth bore a silver coffee pot, a tray, and dirty plates. Behind it sat a colonel of His Majesty's Foot, coat unbuttoned, sipping from a cup.

"Come in, Captain," he greeted, setting down the cup. "His Nibs is off on a scouting expedition." He looked penetratingly at Merewether. "Bombay Marine? Don't think I ever met one of you before. What brings you this far from the sea?"

"Colonel," said Merewether, extracting the order from Sir George again from his inside pocket and handing it to him. "I am here on a special mission for the Governor-General."

"Yes, Captain?"

Merewether plunged desperately into his story for the second time within the hour, ending with his recommendation that Tipu Sultan be seized and sequestered with the balance of his family. As he finished, Merewether realized he had wasted his time. The colonel's saturnine face had become expressionless, distant. He shook his head decisively. "No, Captain, direct orders from Sir John. Military is not to interfere with internal political affairs. If this Sultan commences a rebellion, we move. Otherwise, it's up to the civil authorities. Have you seen the Resident?"

"Yes," said Merewether. "He says it is a military matter."

The saturnine face suddenly creased in a roar of laughter, as Merewether felt a flush of anger and exasperation well up. "Looks like, Captain," Colonel Thompson cried, "as though it's up to the Bombay Marine!" He laughed again. "When I was a child, got into mischief or trouble, my nurse would always say, 'Call for the Bombay Marine!' It's supposed to be able to solve any problem." He sobered. "Captain, we have no jurisdiction in the matter. Mysore is under other authority, no provable overt act here, and our hands are full. We are only waiting for reinforcements from Calcutta to take these mutineers. With that," he pointed to Sir George's order still in Merewether's hand, "you have more authority than Sir John. What's to stop you from acting?"

"Lack of force," said Merewether automatically, but there was no use arguing with this colonel or giving away any more information. "Thank you, Colonel."

Merewether about-faced, strode out, picked up his corporal escort, and went back to the cart. He was in camp ten minutes later. He entered the stifling tent, unbuckled his sword, fought his way out of his coat, threw the cocked hat on the chest, ripped off the stock. Sangh would take care of them.

CHAPTER 19

Merewether came out, and went to his chair in the shade. Burcham wisely kept his distance, noting the black humor possessing Merewether. Almost immediately Sangh, tray in hand, was in attendance. "Lemonade, sahib," he explained.

Merewether thankfully seized the glass and gulped at the cool drink. Then he sipped more leisurely and tried to put his thoughts in order. He had reached no solution as to the maddening dilemma of two authorities, one civil, one military, each denying responsibility for action he was convinced must be taken to prevent another rebellion and the overthrow of the Mysore dynasty, when he found Sangh before him again.

"Sahib, the lady wishes to see you."

"Peace be with you, Captain." The tall, robed figure moved across the grass, pale eyes and reddish-gold hair glittering in the sunlight. Merewether came to his feet, conscious he was in his shirt, collar unbuttoned, to receive this unexpected female.

"Welcome, Sister Jeanne," he managed to say. "Be seated, pray. I am most honored." Sister Jeanne seated herself.

"Drinks, please, Sangh," said Merewether absently.

"I commence my evening crusade at the crossroad over there," Sister Jeanne explained. "I thought I'd stop, to see if you are ready to forsake war and evil for our Lord Jesus Christ." It was almost the same sort of thing she had said earlier, but somehow Merewether felt he detected a subtle difference in her speech. It was as though she spoke now from rote, rather than conviction; as though she had other matters on her mind and was only temporizing. Merewether decided that conversion and salvation of his soul was not as important to her as it had been even this morning. Sangh served Sister Jeanne lemonade with a napkin and poured Merewether another glass. Each sipped politely. Merewether noted that, relaxed, Sister Jeanne's lips were full and red.

"Were you born in Ireland, Sister?" he inquired to make conversation.

"No, Captain, in Paris." She looked at him unflinchingly. "My father came to France after the American War, and married my mother, a French woman. She died when I was three. We traveled with a missionary group, then came back to England, to the Gospel Haven in Sussex. It's hard, Captain, to spread the gospel. People don't believe. The priests and curates fight you most unfairly. Urchins throw rotten apples at you in Sussex." She bowed her head, paused, looked up almost beseechingly, "And the flesh is weak, Captain. I fell from grace in Sussex. I married a man, gloried in the pleasures of the flesh for half a year, till the press gang took my man away to drown at Spithead. The Lord gave me no child, a judgment on me; I came back to God and the church. I know the Lord will protect and save me, that salvation is worth all the ills and pains of the flesh, but sometimes I wish I were back in Sussex, settled in a cottage, my man and children to look after, instead of trying to bring these heathen idolators to Christ." The woman looked almost beautiful for a moment. The fair peeling skin, the long nose and pale eyes relieved by parted, trembling red lips under the crown of hair combined to produce a striking appearance.

Merewether felt distinctly uncomfortable. He would rather she were mouthing religious platitudes than talking this way. He felt a wave of compassion for this lonely, unhappy woman, but could conceive of no way to help her. And too, there was still the question of young Tipu Sultan and her connection with him. He felt sure that Sister Jeanne must have made this visit for a purpose, and suddenly realized she had wanted to see him again, that she was drawn to him.

Once more she looked at him with real concern. Good Lord, he thought, is she going to weep? She spoke again in a low tone of voice, "Your mission must be important to you, Captain, to come all this way from the sea. Believe me, we had no part in the mutiny, but there are others." She looked searchingly at him. "I know nothing—only suspect—this may be a very dangerous place. It is best, I think, you not come again to the mission." Merewether saw she was in dead earnest. He knew there was no trickery here.

"Thank you, Sister Jeanne. I shall bear your words in mind. More lemonade?"

"No, thank you."

He made a trite remark, but it served to change the subject. In a moment they were chatting about the Indian countryside, the heat, the flies, and a dozen other inconsequential matters. Merewether even essayed a small joke and evoked an appreciative laugh. Sister Jeanne looked at the sun sliding down in the west.

"I must go, brother," she intoned in her former manner, handing the glass and napkin to Sangh. "My people expect my evening crusade through the bazaar."

"You must return, Sister Jeanne," said Merewether. "It has

been a most delightful visit." He bowed, conscious again of his informal appearance. She swept across the grassy turf and went out of sight down the already dusty road.

Burcham ventured to come near. "Your soul well saved, Captain?"

Merewether was tempted to lash out at this impudent young popinjay and put him in his place. But realizing the boy's good intentions, he could not help but smile. "Salvation awaits me. Now, let us get our affairs in readiness for departure to Madras tomorrow. I think I must see the Governor."

Merewether at this point could see no other alternative. He had solicited the aid of the local authorities, both civil and military, without success. He was convinced that young Tipu Sultan, if left at large, could and would raise a force with the aid of the French to invade Mysore and recover his ancestral throne. Perhaps Lord William Bentinck would listen to his story, his deductions, and issue the order for the arrest of the prince upon the strength of the order from Sir George Barlow.

Still feeling a little resentful at the waggish remark as to the state of his soul, Merewether remembered the way the young aide to Lord William had dealt with the reluctant horseman in Madras. "Hop to it, Burcham," he said cheerfully and sat back to await dinner.

When he heard the whisper of Sangh's feet through the grass, Merewether expected a tray of the bountiful dinner that only Sangh could concoct. Instead, the little Hindu hissed, "Sahib, the man they say is the Muslim prince is approaching."

Merewether came out of his chair quickly, wishing he had the double-barreled pistol in his tent. This young man undoubtedly had spies in the civil government and probably the military, and was here to call him to account. He saw a figure in native dress fifty feet away, with the tall figure of Burcham bounding to meet him, to embrace him. "Hy Alley, you old rooster!"

"Billy Burcham, how have you grown so tall? Do you still like sweetmeats?" The pair came across the grass, Burcham beaming, arm about the shoulders of the other man.

"Captain," the capering Burcham shouted. "This is Hy Alley, my old schoolmate at St. George's, come back to India!"

"Delighted to meet you," Merewether said with the gravest

courtesy. "I gather you two are old friends." Burcham looked
surprised a moment. Then an expression of comprehension appeared on his face as he realized he was not supposed to know of
the presence of Hy Alley.

"Come, be seated," invited Merewether.

Alley was a man of almost the same height as Merewether,
smoothly muscled, clean-shaven except for a neatly trimmed
moustache in the French fashion. He had an olive complexion, a
straight, classical nose, but it was the eyes that were remarkable.
They appeared in this light to be an emerald green, piercing,
intense, yet somehow withdrawn and secretive. Tiny crow's-feet
already appeared at the corners, evidence that this man spent
much time in the sun.

"Sangh," said Merewether to the hovering little Hindu. "See
what refreshment Mr. Alley will have." He looked apologetically
at the visitor. "I usually when ashore have a bit of London
gin and lemon at this hour before dining, but I knew your
religion . . ."

"Perfectly all right, Captain," broke in Alley. "I am a devout
disciple of Mohammed, but I was educated in England and
France and learned to enjoy wines and spirits in moderation. I
will join you in a gin, if I may." Burcham merely nodded, eyes
glistening in admiration. Sangh left with a disapproving backward
glance.

Instantly, Burcham and Alley began to play the old games of
"Do you remember—?" and "What ever happened to—?" Names,
places, events flew back and forth as Merewether listened, interrupted only momentarily as Sangh served the drinks. It was an
excellent opportunity to size up this man who might very well
plunge the Carnactic into another upheaval, if Bonaparte followed through with the plans attributed to him.

Merewether recalled the stories he had heard of this man's
grandfather. Hyder Ali, as the British spelled it, had been a penni-
less mercenary soldier from somewhere out of the north of India,
perhaps even Persia. He had come south over sixty years ago, and
taken service in the army of Mysore. Rising rapidly through sheer
intelligence, ability, and courage, though he could neither read
nor write, he had soon become a general. Victorious in the field,
the adventurer turned upon the weak Hindu dynasty, pushing it

aside with the enthusiastic support of a majority of the people. Yet he had left it to his son Tipu to assume the title and the throne. It was said that he had boasted on occasion that he was descended from a Royal Duke of France, one of the crusaders of five hundred years ago. Looking at the young man, Merewether could well believe this legend.

Alley was perceptive. There came a momentary pause in the flow of reminiscence with Burcham, and he turned to Merewether. "You must forgive our enthusiasm, Captain. I have not seen an old schoolmate for more than three years. The war has made travel difficult. I only just arrived back here last month." He grinned ruefully, "I had to walk a good bit of the way because of your blockade." He sipped the gin.

"Royal Navy has been most efficient, I'm told," responded Merewether. The young man looked about. Sangh was squatted fifty feet away in the shade of Merewether's tent, within earshot for a summons, but too far away to overhear ordinary conversation.

"And now, Captain," said Alley in the same quiet conversational tone, "let us end the charades we are playing. You have learned or guessed, I'm not sure which, that I am Haidar Ben Ali, son of Tipu Sultan, whose name I have adopted." The green eyes fixed Merewether, burning into his with an intensity that was almost frightening. "My father died defending his capital against Arthur Wellesley seven years ago when I was a boy. I have returned from exile, even as did your Bolingbroke, the fourth Henry, to reclaim my own." His eyes bored into Merewether's. Merewether was the first to break the fixation, turning his attention to Burcham, sitting open-mouthed.

"I knew within moments of your attempts to have me imprisoned with my kinsmen," Alley resumed. "For your information, the civil and military forces will not act against me, and neither will the Governor of Madras." He sipped the gin and bit into the half lemon. "Barlow, that creature of Wellesley, acting Governor-General, would act, but he is too far away, and you, as his agent, have no force in this place." Now he looked penetratingly at Merewether. "Except that I am aware of the foolish scruples of officers of the Bombay Marine, I would offer you power and fortune, a future with me as Commander of the Naval Forces of all India, Admiral of the Fleet, if you chose that title, for I intended to reunite India under a single crown!"

Merewether looked at the strong face, the penetrating emerald gaze. He understood the power and intensity of the quiet voice, the pervading aura of intelligence and courage; the complete ruthlessness under the polite veneer. He realized that this young man meant exactly what he had said and quite evidently possessed the ability and force to carry into execution such a project. For a moment he felt that this was a man he might follow, a man who inspired loyalty and courage in his followers even unto death.

Then his eyes turned to Burcham again, still transfixed, under the spell of Tipu, and he realized this was ridiculous. Did he not have his sworn duty to do to King and Company and the Bombay Marine? He shifted his posture negligently in the canvas chair, tossed off the last of the gin, raised his hand in signal to Sangh, and the spell was broken.

Tipu politely refused more gin. He took courteous leave of Merewether and a curiously subdued Burcham and went out of sight behind the palmyra trees along the road.

Merewether sipped the second gin as he tried to determine his course of action. He thought the visit of Tipu had possibly two objectives: first to see, confront and evaluate the enemy in the person of Merewether; and, secondly, to deliver, in effect, a warning not to interfere. Merewether's requests for civil and military assistance today had been denied upon solid legalistic grounds, but Tipu had learned of the attempts almost at once. He therefore must possess at least a formidable intelligence organization in the area and might have much more than that.

Merewether wondered about the plans attributed to Bonaparte, the possible invasion from the north, the French elements still resident in Pondicherry, the long history of friendship with the French by Hyder Ali, Tipu Sultan, and now this young man. He came to a conclusion: however bold, able, and intelligent Tipu might be, he could strike no substantial blow without the materiel of war. He was sure these could not be obtained in this area by means other than outright capture. The recruiting of the Muslim army was useless without arms and equipment. There remained the French possessions to the south, their considerable sea power; with the British and Company naval forces spread across a four thousand mile front, it was impossible to anticipate or defend a landing. He sighed, finished the second gin, and decided he would carry out his original plan—to go back to Madras tomorrow, beard Governor Bentinck in his chambers, and insist upon imprisonment of young Tipu Sultan. Dinner was served.

CHAPTER 20

Merewether came awake in black darkness in cold terror, still hearing the scraping, slithering rustle of the cobra sliding on the canvas floor of the tent. He lay uncovered on the cot, conscious that the deadly snake could rear up high enough to strike over the edge—in his face perhaps—if he made the slightest movement or sound to attract it. He lay absolutely still, scarcely breathing, as the rustle approached the cot. Something brushed his cheek. He starred wildly, almost screamed in horror, only to hear the urgent whisper, "It is Sister Jeanne."

Merewether, convinced a moment ago that his life was in danger, was stunned beyond speech. He felt a hand brush his scarred cheek again and heard a muffled sob and felt warm breath upon his face. Suddenly, his lips were seized, he was kissed; his arms went automatically about the invisible shoulders, felt Jeanne's robe. As he responded he felt tears drop and run down his cheeks. "We have so little time, so little time! And I am wicked, sinful again. Oh Lord, the flesh is weak but it burns most devilishly! I am yet a woman and must quench the fire!"

She stood up suddenly. Merewether heard the rustle of cloth. Then she was back, in the cot, her lips seeking his, her splendid naked body pressed against him. Passion overwhelmed them.

It was much later when Merewether came back to his senses. Sister Jeanne still lay in his arms. She was whispering in his ear.

"What?" he whispered back.

"The arms for Tipu Sultan, they will be delivered by a frigate from Mauritius, within the next few days. That was what you wanted to know, wasn't it?"

"Where?"

"Somewhere near Pondicherry, I think. They do not trust a woman, but I overheard M'sieur Lally tell my father tonight that he must go meet the ship, not to send any more recruits for the time being, until they unload the arms." She grasped Merewether, kissed him, and rose. He heard the rustle of her garment in the darkness, a whisper, "Goodbye, Captain," the soft sound of the netting covering the door of the tent dropping back into place. The episode had been like a dream. Merewether, in the early light of dawn, was almost uncertain that it had occurred.

On an impulse, thinking of the sniper reported the night before, he dressed and picked up the double-barreled pistol on the chest. He had taken some three steps beyond the tent when the scream tore into the night from the direction of the road. Almost simultaneously there was a great orange flash from the trees fifty feet off, and the full-throated roar of a musket sounded as Merewether heard a charge of shot tear through the canvas just behind him.

Merewether ran toward the trees, cocked pistol in hand, expecting a second shot momentarily. He heard a short exclamation of surprise, a movement, and snapped a shot at it. There was a howl of pain. Something fell heavily. There was a thrashing of footsteps in the undergrowth. A voice cried, "I'm hit, don't shoot again!"

"Come out!" said Merewether, the second barrel of his pistol cocked. A shape came crawling towards him, one leg dragging, groaning. Merewether heard hoofbeats on the road, receding toward Vellore, then the sound of running feet behind him. "Hold on!" he shouted. "Don't shoot!" Burcham galloped up, and close behind him Sangh with a lantern.

"M'sieur Lally!" cried Burcham. "And he's wounded."

"Hold him here," said Merewether. "Give me the lantern, Sangh, and exchange pistols with me, Burcham." He set off toward the road.

Only a few feet from the road, he found Sister Jeanne. She was lying on her face in an attitude of repose, but the black robe was pierced and wet with blood that glistened in the lantern light. Merewether touched her and sought a pulse. He found none. She was dead, pierced from back to front by a long broad blade. He mentally commended her tortured soul to God.

"Wait here a moment, Sangh." He took the lantern and searched up and down the road, quickly finding where at least three horses had been tied. He decided the French master and two other men, one possibly Tipu Sultan, had been involved. He came back to Sangh. "Go into Vellore and inform the watch that the woman missionary has been murdered. Lead the authorities back here."

Merewether came back to where Burcham was standing guard over the Frenchman. In the lantern light he could see the pistol ball had struck him just below the right knee. With his clasp knife, he cut away the trouser leg and staunched the hemorrhage with his handkerchief. The leg appeared to be broken. The Indian teamster had now come up, shivering uncontrollably in the dawn chill. He sent the Indian and Burcham to bring a cot. They lifted Lally on it and carried him to Burcham's tent. Merewether handed his pistol to Burcham. "I'll dress and find a surgeon in the army camp," he said. "Guard this man with your life. No rescues!"

Merewether threw on his uniform and walked quickly the few hundred yards to the main encampment, to the headquarters of the battalion of Company troops posted on this flank.

The Captain Adjutant was awake and cooperative, once he had seen Sir George's order. He sent a corporal to wake the surgeon. As he waited, Merewether thought of the assassination attempt. His cot was riddled with a charge of shot, fired from a musket. He would surely have been killed if he had been in it. He had no doubts as to his enemy; the lines had been drawn with studied courtesy yesterday afternoon. Sister Jeanne had been summarily executed for her defection, though whether by Tipu or another, he could not say. With as ruthless and intelligent an enemy as Tipu, his life was in mortal danger in this place.

"Captain, I require for a few days a reliable sergeant with a squad of soldiers for a journey to Madras and a transport wagon for a wounded prisoner. Can you oblige me?"

The Adjutant hesitated. "I suppose I can, sir," he decided. "One squad more or less makes little enough difference." He shouted for an orderly.

"Full field equipment and rations for a week," continued Merewether. The orderly departed at a trot. A few moments later, a portly, red-faced man in the uniform of a surgeon came up, an Indian servant following with his medical chest balanced on his shoulder.

"Here is Dr. Allenby, Captain," said the Adjutant.

"Good morning, Doctor. Captain Merewether of the Bombay Marine. Come with me." They left, walking toward his camp, the servant following with the chest. "I have a prisoner I must take to Madras," continued Merewether. "Leg's broken, I believe."

At the tent, the surgeon squeezed in, the Indian carefully lowered the chest and opened it. Inside the tent the doctor gave off a powerful odor of stale rum. He fumbled for scissors, cut off the temporary bandage, looked at the wound. "Yes, sir, leg's broken," he agreed. "And the ball is inside. I must probe." He removed his instruments, and laid them out. Merewether noted his shaking hands, the sweat beading the florid face. It must have been a happy evening.

"Doctor, wait a moment." He slipped into his own tent for the bottle still half full of London gin. He poured a healthy measure into a cup and brought it to the surgeon.

"Gin, by God!" The surgeon downed the cup in three swallows and took a deep breath. "Now," he said. "I need some help to hold him down. I'm going to probe."

Merewether beckoned to Burcham, and together they grasped arms and shoulders while the Indian assistant held the legs. The probe slid into the flesh, as Lally heaved and groaned. A few turns, a gingerly withdrawal, and the surgeon held a flattened lead disc in his hand. "Ha!" he said, and laid it aside. The probe sank into the flesh again, and in a moment the doctor had withdrawn a bit of bloody cloth.

"I think that's all," he said cheerfully. "Bullet and a bit of his trousers. Fibia's shattered, tibia's only cracked. If no gangrene, I might even save the leg." He applied a noxious-looking concoction from a pot that smelled of pitch. Then a compress. Then a bandage. The Indian servant came back in with several narrow wooden boards. The surgeon fitted one on either side of the leg and secured them so as to hold it immobile, yet allow access to dress the wound.

"Now, sir," he said. "We can move him to the hospital on a litter. Give him a bit of laudanum first to make him drowsy."

"No," said Merewether. "No laudanum now. He goes to Madras. Put him in the wagon."

The surgeon's mouth gaped. "But, sir, with a leg in that condition, jolted in a wagon, he'll lose it sure."

"No help for it. Put him on a litter and lift him into the wagon." Outside, a sleepy-looking file of soldiers had drawn up with a heavyset, black-browed young sergeant at its head. A canvas-topped transport wagon drawn by four mules was behind the soldiers. That Adjutant was an efficient officer, Merewether decided, and deserved mention in his report, if he ever had time to write it.

"Wait here." He hurried off toward the road, a little surprised to find that it was now broad daylight. There he found a little group, including an Indian watchman with his truncheon and badge of office, Sangh, and another dignified Indian who appeared to be a submagistrate, gabbling back and forth over the body. Just then, Millard, the Resident, with his sullen half-caste clerk, came up.

"Bad business," he said. "She's dead, of course?"

"Yes," said Merewether. "Just as I found her."

"Bad business," said the Resident again. "You don't know who did it?"

"No, sir," said Merewether. "I only heard her scream."

"Those missionaries," complained the Resident, "go anywhere, any time, no way to protect them. Heard a drunken Sepoy attacked her a few weeks ago, but she beat him off." He sighed and turned to the submagistrate. "Get a cart. Take the body to the mission. I'll sign a certificate. You," he continued to the watchman, "make inquiries, see what you can find out."

"Yes, sahib."

"Sir," said Merewether. "I am packed to go back to Madras to consult the Governor. If you need me, communicate through him."

"Very well, Captain." The Resident washed his hands of the affair and went back to his carriage. Merewether looked again at the black-robed body, which seemed so much smaller in death than in life. Under his breath, he said, "May God have mercy on her soul." He returned to camp.

After breakfast, the tents came down like magic, as the Indian teamster, assisted by two Company privates, folded them under the shrill directions of Sangh and packed them with the baggage in the cart. The sun was barely visible above the trees to the east; it was not yet uncomfortably hot.

Merewether reluctantly concluded that his disagreeable task must be accomplished at once. He called the sergeant and gave explicit directions to station his squad as pickets around the campsite and to allow no one to pass. Entering the transport wagon, he now looked for the first time squarely at M'sieur Lally on his litter. A surprisingly small man, Lally was sharp-featured, with large brown eyes that opened widely at Merewether's approach. His forehead was beaded with sweat. Doubtless he was in shock and in considerable pain.

Merewether struck harshly. "When is the frigate due?"

A spasm of pain contorted Lally's face. He quavered a denial of any knowledge of a frigate.

Merewether's brow contracted in a scowl, his jaw clenched, and unconsciously he closed his right hand into a fist. "Tell me or I pull that leg right off you!" Merewether's left hand dropped to Lally's knee.

The Frenchman screamed, perhaps more in terror than in pain. He seemed about to faint. Merewether slapped his cheek, despising himself, but compelled to carry through the inquisition and elicit the vital information. "Speak!"

The Frenchman's eyes were filled with tears. He stammered, then managed to find his voice. "Three days from now, Thursday if she's on time."

"Where?" demanded Merewether, raising his hand.

"Off the mouth of the Palar River." The words came in a rush.

Merewether reconstructed in his mind the chart of the Coromandel Coast, visualizing the entrance to the river, the bar block-
ing passage to vessels of any draft. There were, however, five
fathoms only a mile offshore. It was almost exactly halfway between Madras and Pondicherry. There was an old French fort just
north, on the coast, now abandoned, and a village inland. It
dawned upon him that Tipu Sultan's army could easily be close
by that point, sparsely settled as it was, in formerly French
territory.

"What are the signals?" Merewether demanded.

Lally attempted momentary defiance, but subsided at the
perfectly diabolical expression that came over Merewether's
scarred face. "Two red rockets repeated three times from the
frigate, a yellow rocket from the fort followed by two red. The
lighters carry blue lights on their bows." A brief lapse, then, "A
light will be burned on the wall of the old fort from sunset on."

"And this is Friday night?"

"No, no, Thursday hight, between nine and midnight," the
Frenchman cried.

"Why did you come here tonight?"

Lally looked piteously up at him. "We found the woman was
missing and guessed she had come to warn you. She had overheard me talking to her father."

"Did you kill her?"

"No! No! And I did not fire at you!" cried Lally. Merewether
felt he was sincere. In any event the point was not important now.

"Very well," said Merewether. "Since you will be present, the
first thing I find false in your information, I pull that leg off!"

"It's the truth! The whole truth, everything I know! Saving, I
don't know how you'll escape Tipu's army! They're camped
outside the village and have a watch set at the fort. You'll never
get by them."

Merewether paused, dissembled. "Cross that bridge when I
reach it. Now, you'll stay with me. I'll feed you laudanum to ease
the pain. I'll turn you over to the best doctor in the Company's
service and save that leg if possible, but if anything you told me is
false, you'll walk on crutches the rest of your life, if you live at
all!" with that he left the quivering little man. He was not proud

of his actions but he hardened his heart with the recollection of Sister Jeanne's fate.

He called the sergeant over. The man appeared to be alert and intelligent, not one of "the scum of Europe" as the Member of Parliament had once termed the Company's military forces. "Sergeant, how long have you served in this area?"

The man thought a moment. "The better part of three years, sir."

"Do you speak the dialect?"

"Enough to get by, sir."

"Good. Can you hire me a boat and crew to go down the river and sail up to Madras from the mouth?"

The sergeant scratched his head. "River's in flood now, brim full, sir. You need a good-sized boat. I know a Hindu who has such a boat, took a party of us down fishing last spring."

"Find him. Make the best bargain you can, one half now, the other half at Madras." The sergeant departed, and Merewether moved over into the shade of the trees to wait.

CHAPTER 21

The Palar was not a large river normally, but with the recent rains it was running banks full and had flooded some of the lowlands. It had a considerable current, possibly as much as five knots. There had been no rain here for nearly thirty-six hours, but the rains must have continued in the western highlands where it had its source. If he could get a seaworthy boat, he could descend the seventy miles to the mouth in less than fifteen hours, sail thirty miles to Madras roadstead in another six hours and be back aboard *Rapid* by dawn tomorrow. It would take over three days by road with the distinct possibility of an attempt at the rescue of Lally by Tipu's men. It was nearly an hour before the sergeant returned.

"I found him, sir. No fishing in this high water. He'll go with his two sons," the sergeant reported. "Wants two hundred rupees."

"How large is the boat?"

"About eighteen feet, sir. I know the old man can handle it."

"All right," decided Merewether, handing a bag of silver rupees over. "Pay him one hundred rupees. Tell him to sail down the river five miles. There's a bend and a ferry landing I saw on the way here. Tie up on the north bank. The road passes only a few hundred feet from that point, and we will meet him there in not more than two hours."

Half an hour later the sergeant returned and assured him that the boat would move at once. Merewether called his party and mounted the seat of the cart beside the driver, while Burcham and Sangh disposed themselves in the back on the baggage. Two soldiers mounted mules; the sergeant and driver took the seat of the transport wagon; the others crowded in beside Lally or stood on the back step. They moved off briskly toward Vellore, crossed the river on a rickety ferry, and went down the road toward Madras.

Another hour and Merewether found the byway leading off to the ferry landing. The boat was tied up there: a native craft nearly twenty feet long, flat-bottomed, a matting shelter amidships, a stumpy mast forward and a lateen sail furled on its yard lying along the gunwales. A wizened old Hindu was in the stern; two younger men lounged on the bank. The old man greeted the sergeant.

"Here we are, Captain. This is Shaku and his sons. The sons speak a little English."

"Good," said Merewether. "Put Lally in the boat." Four soldiers quickly passed the litter down the bank and slid it out of sight beneath the shelter. Merewether's chest followed. "Now," he said, "Which of you is my size?" One of the privates appeared to be about the same height, though a little thinner. "All right, you take off your coat and cap. Put on these." He doffed his undress uniform jacket and took off his hat. The soldier slid into the jacket and perched the hat on his head. "You ride in my place on the cart."

"Yes, sir."

Merewether called Burcham and the sergeant aside. "You may expect to be followed and possibly attacked. I do not think it will be today. Too close to Vellore. But at dawn tomorrow or tomorrow night. Your friend Hy Alley is playing for very large stakes and wants Lally back. Defend yourselves. Give no hint of my whereabouts or that of Lally. Once at Madras dismiss the sergeant and his guard. I'll take Sangh with me."

Merewether and Sangh boarded the boat, as the two young men cast off. Once in the stream, the sail was set, and the southwest breeze moved them briskly down the stream with the current.

Merewether had time to look at the boat. Flat-bottomed, it was literally "sewed" together with coir, a fiber almost equal to hemp in strength. There was not a nail in it. It was amazing that it leaked so little, but he knew it must have a coating of galgal composed of resin and coconut oil on the bottom. Suspended over the leeward side was a leeboard to serve as a keel with the wind on the quarter. The contraption appeared strong and seaworthy. It might carry him to Madras.

Merewether crawled under the shelter, and administered a dose of laudanum to Lally, who shortly fell asleep. By sunset, pushed along by wind and current, they were almost at the mouth of the Palar.

"Bar is two miles ahead," said one of the younger Hindus. "Plenty of water over it now to cross."

Merewether just then in the dusk saw a primitive landing on the north bank. Moored alongside were two substantial lighters, both flat-bottomed and pierced for sweeps, each able to carry at a guess a burden of some fifteen tons. Up the bank was a wooden building. Merewether counted eight men in the clearing. Apparently they were cooking their evening meal on charcoal braziers. These must be the permanent crews of the lighters. They would have to add stevedores to handle cargo and man the sweeps.

The boat swept past with no more than a passing glance from the men. In a few minutes it was traversing the bar, which now lay submerged under the flood waters of the river. The old Hindu shouted. The two young men took in the sail and reset it on the port tack, then shifted the leeboard to the starboard side. In the open sea, the speed was greatly reduced, but the boat moved steadily northward toward Madras roadstead. Sangh produced tea brewed on a tiny brazier, ship's biscuit, a tasty morsel of roast salt beef, pomegranates for dessert. Lally was feverish and took only tea. Merewether administered another dose of laudanum. They sailed on through darkness.

CHAPTER 22

Merewether had been dozing when he heard a bell striking. He counted seven: near the end of the midwatch. He had sighted the riding lights of ships anchored in the roadstead an hour before. Now finally he could make out the light on Fort St. George and get his bearings. He directed Shaku toward *Rapid*'s anchorage. Soon the dim shape of the ship emerged a hundred yards ahead.

"*Rapid* ahoy!" he roared through cupped hands. "*Rapid* ahoy!" He waited for a response. Then coming down faintly against the wind he heard a challenge.

"What boat's that?" It must be Dobbs. He was sure MacRae or Larkin would have recognized his hail.

"*Rapid!*" he roared. As the two Hindus took in the sail, the old man used the last of the boat's way to lay alongside the starboard gangway. Jackson, boatswain's mate of the watch, took a line, and shouted for side boys. However, Merewether did not stand on ceremony. He was on deck before the side could be manned. Dobbs came bustling up with a lantern, his hat awry, carrotty hair sticking out, only a few minutes awake for the watch.

"Uh . . . welcome aboard, sir."

"Thank you. Please call Mr. MacRae, Mr. Larkin, Dr. Buttram and Gunny. I will be in my cabin." He went aft. Five minutes later, the officers, a little disheveled and confused, gathered in the cabin to meet a grimy, touseled, jacketless Merewether.

"Doctor, I've a wounded prisoner in the boat. Have Jackson rig a whip and hoist him on board. He has a leg broken by a gunshot wound, dressed by a Company surgeon in Vellore yesterday morning. I promised him you would try to save the leg if he cooperated." By now, the commotion had brought half the crew on deck. A buzz of conversation arose as the watch told the idlers and watch below that the captain had returned, bringing a wounded prisoner.

"Yesterday morning at Vellore!" marveled MacRae. "Three days at least to Madras. How did you come back so fast, Captain?"

Merewether chuckled. "Down the Palar River in that boat alongside. Beats a mule team any time." He turned again to the business of the moment, "Are there any Royal Navy ships present?"

"No, sir," replied MacRae. "Three Company transports brought in two battalions of troops yesterday from Calcutta. Pellew and the squadron are down near Ceylon, I'm told."

Merewether had hoped that some ships of force would be found here that could intercept the French frigate and sink or capture her offshore. *Rapid* certainly could not alone engage with any hope of success a thirty-six gun frigate.

"Too bad," he said. "Gunny, is your force at full strength?"

"Yes, sah." The erect military figure looked almost insulted at the question.

"Now, let me tell you gentlemen the situation." He was interrupted by a knock. "Come," he invited. Sangh entered. Merewether suspended the proceedings until all were served.

"Now," he resumed, and stated concisely the tactical and physical situation.

"Sir," said MacRae. "I've been in that fort. It's just outside a little village called Sadras. Hasn't had a garrison since the British took over Pondicherry. Serves no purpose at all to control river or sea. Three years ago there was only an old Indian caretaker, retired Sepoy petty officer, and his family living there. Tipu could take possession of it and no one discover it for months."

"Thank you," said Merewether. "I doubt he has any real force there, probably no more than a lookout party. His main body of troops would be inland, dispersed probably in the country around the village to avoid notice. The arms would have to be landed at the dock in the river."

Larkin spoke up, his keen blue eyes flashing under the long blond hair. "Sir, it's going to take at least forty men each to man the sweeps and move those lighters, and they must be Indians.

Two of these transports have lascar crews, and you're senior officer present."

Merewether absorbed this information almost with awe. Four Company vessels present and theoretically he could issue orders, move them as a squadron, even fly a broad command pendant. Those clumsy transports, armed with only six or eight guns each, would be worthless in a fight with a frigate, however. He sat, head bowed for a moment, while he collected his thoughts, fought off the fatigue that threatened to overwhelm him. He looked up to find all eyes fixed upon him. Larkin's keen mind had penetrated unerringly to the heart of the matter. The only alternative he had was to seize the lighters, hold off any interference from Tipu's army, some of whom must be armed, and try to obtain the arms from the frigate by fraud. The parts of the plan fell into place. He issued his orders methodically to the officers.

As the group went out the door, Sangh reappeared. "Sahib, the boatman is ready to leave." Merewether had forgotten him completely. From his chest he took the bag still containing one hundred silver rupees. Adding twenty-five more from his strongbox as a bonus, he handed the bag to the little Hindu.

"Convey my thanks. When you have time, I would like breakfast."

It was gray daylight through the ports, rain beginning to fall again. After breakfast, Merewether kicked off his shoes, stretched out on the bed, instantly was asleep. He came awake, hearing four bells strike, a deep sense of unease, foreboding suddenly possessing him. He had been asleep only a few minutes, but he was now fully awake, tense with anxiety, unable to relax. His mind turned over the situation and reached a sudden conclusion that his plans were faulty; he had underestimated Tipu. That energetic young man would never wait for dawn to attack and try to recover his French agent. He would surely have struck last night, perhaps even yesterday afternoon. When he found Merewether and the prisoner missing, he would certainly have guessed their mode of transportation, obtained a boat and descended the Palar to warn his men and take personal command of the operation. The only saving factor might be Tipu's necessity to return to Vellore to find a suitable boat. The road angled away from the river toward

Madras and he could not count upon a suitable small craft being found in the scattered settlements below the town. Possibly, he might just now be under way. It would be difficult even for Tipu to induce a riverman to brave the flood, the snags and floating logs, by night. Merewether leaped up, shouting for Sangh.

An hour later he had the launch under way south. The entire Sepoy Marine detachment had embarked with full landing-force equipment; lascars from HEICS *Leopard* were pulling easily at the oars. Against the monsoon, it would be a long, weary day, but he should be at the mouth of the Palar before dusk. The rain fell steadily, remorselessly, soaking the men and equipment. Merewether had removed his sword belt and the jacket with two pistols in the pockets. These he stowed in the locker under the stern seat, along with the tin box of pyrotechnics, tinder boxes, slow and quick match and spare keg of powder. He hoped they would remain dry. As for himself, he was soaked with the warm rain, but it was less uncomfortable than sweating under oilskins. He settled back and relaxed. Two Marines began to bail rainwater from the bilges.

By late afternoon, the rain had slacked off into a foggy drizzle with visibility so limited that Merewether directed the coxswain closer in to keep the shore in sight. The hills near Sadras were hidden, but he finally made out the fort. When he saw the breakers on the long submerged spit extending out to sea off the mouth of the Palar, he steered west to cross the bar. On the north bank of the mouth of the river was a lofty grove of coconut trees.

The launch grated on the bottom a hundred yards from the shore. Gunny and fifteen Marines went over the side, their muskets, with bayonets fixed, held overhead. "Remember, cold steel," Merewether called. They waded ashore and disappeared into the grove. The lightened launch backed off and rowed up the river holding close to the north bank. Merewether peered through the gathering dusk, saw the lighters moored against the dock. "Way enough," he called in a low tone. The launch ceased its progress, then began to drift back with the current. "Hold her," he directed. An oar on either side bit into the water and pulled to hold the boat steady in this nearly slack water by the bank.

It seemed an eternity—Merewether's watch was in his jacket

pocket in the locker for protection against the weather—but it probably was no more than a quarter hour when a figure appeared on the dock and waved a white rag tied to a bayonet. Gunny and his force had secured the dock and the lighter crews!

"Give way," said Merewether. The boat pulled up the river and hooked on to the dock. The painter was made fast by a Marine. Merewether opened the locker and considered donning the jacket. But he decided it was a useless encumbrance; the priming in the pistols would probably be wet and useless in this weather. He pulled out his sword, buckled on the belt and hauled himself up on the dock.

Gunny approached. "Sah, there were eight men here. No fight in them. We have them under guard in the warehouse. I have pickets posted up the path at the edge of the grove."

"Excellent," said Merewether. "We shall now take a party to the fort and make sure of it." Just then a low whistle came from the launch. Merewether saw the lascar coxswain point upstream.

"Boat coming down," he called.

Merewether looked upstream. It was getting dark, but the glow to the west outlined a boat, almost the mate of the one he had used yesterday, a quarter mile away, under sail and oars and heading for the dock. It was too late to try to conceal the launch; it must be visible against the dock. Even as he looked, the boat altered course and headed for the north bank.

"Quick, send a party to head them off," shouted Merewether. Gunny reacted instantly. Marines ran to intercept anyone who might land at the point two hundred yards upstream where the boat was now heading. Another party raced up the road leading from the dock to form a second line in case the boat's occupants penetrated the first. Merewether was suddenly certain Tipu must be in the boat. He ran up the bank as hard as he could, his left hand holding clear his sword in its scabbard so it would not trip him.

Merewether crashed through bushes and caromed off a tree, but finally reached a little clearing where it was light enough to see. He heard splashing sounds to his left, then voices, footsteps, the sound of someone pushing through underbrush. A figure emerged into the clearing. It hesitated, then plunged across. Stopped dead.

"Well, I'm damned!" a remembered, pleasant voice said in a conversational tone. "The Bombay Marine is already here!" In the half light Merewether could see the gleam of those green eyes set in that handsome face and hear the swish of the blade, as Tipu whipped a sword from its scabbard. He too believed in cold steel.

Merewether drew instantly, his left hand releasing the tongue of the sword belt. He dropped belt and scabbard so they would not interfere with his movements and possibly trip him. He remembered the Venetian fencing master in Bombay in '99, an old man, stranded far from home, who had established his little academy in an alley behind the graving dock and given lessons in swordsmanship to young officers of the Bombay Marine, the Company regiments, even an occasional Indian of noble birth. Two rupees was the fee for each for an hour of instruction, provided at least four officers took instruction at once. Merewether, conscious of his low birth, his rise from the lower deck, and lack of gentlemanly accomplishments, had been fascinated with the romance of swordplay; for six months while he waited for his ship to return and be refitted, he had managed to induce three other second lieutenants to go with him weekly for instruction. He had not fenced since, though he had swung and thrust a cutlass on a dozen occasions. He placed himself in the *en garde* stance.

Down on the bank he still heard movements, low voices. It appeared some equipment, possibly pyrotechnics for the signals, was being unloaded. He had no time to consider. Tipu was upon him with a slashing attack in the French fashion. Merewether parried, managing to escape the first flurry. He realized that Tipu was an excellent and practiced swordsman, superior in skill, and retreated to his right so as to put such light as remained in Tipu's face.

Tipu drove forward again. Merewether parried. He felt the blade slide down his, the sudden disengagement. By a partial parry, coupled with a sidewise leap, he escaped being spitted as Tipu lunged a second time. He remembered old Maestro Di Risio telling the class, "Swordplay is for gentlemen. It has the rules and customs of a thousand years of chivalry. If you merely want to kill, use a blunderbuss or axe. But," the old man had paused, "if you find yourself in a duel à *morte*, not an affair of honor, chivalry ceases and a sword becomes no more than an axe, a tool of execution. In such event, there are no rules, you may grasp your opponent's blade, trip him, use any stratagem to defend yourself."

Merewether found Tipu upon him again. He realized his parry was too high and too late and saw the blade lunge at his heart. Throwing up his left forearm, he felt the blade slice through it and grate between the bones. He twisted the arm to the left as the blade tore through his collar. Now he drove his own blade squarely through the center of Tipu's chest. His breath came cruelly. For a moment he blacked out.

A sound of running footsteps brought Merewether to his senses. Gunny and three Marines charged into the clearing. They slid to a stop as they saw Merewether swaying with a sword blade wedged through his forearm, bloody sword in hand, another man writhing on the ground. "The boat and crew are down there," Merewether managed to say.

The three Marines stumbled down the bank. There were sounds of a scuffle, sharp cries of pain, then silence. Merewether dropped his own sword. He thought to grasp the sword driven through his forearm. It was too much. He turned to Gunny. "Pull it out!" he demanded.

The Jemadar glanced at the man on the ground, Tipu had a bloody froth on his lips and was glaring with his green eyes at Merewether. "Damn the Bombay Marine!" The eyes glazed and the gasps choked off in a final hemorrhage.

Gunny seized the sword. Merewether set his teeth and held the forearm with his right hand. Gunny pulled. The blade remained fixed.

"Move your wrist, sah," directed Gunny. Merewether rotated the wrist and the blade slid out, followed by a considerable hemorrhage. He reached automatically for his handkerchief, but realized it was in his coat. Gunny pulled out a clean cloth, wrapped it about the arm, tied it. It was almost completely dark as Merewether heard the Marines come up the bank, herding three Indian boatmen along.

"Bring him along," said Merewether. "We must make sure of the fort." He walked lightheadedly back toward the dock, bumping into trees and bushes as before. In a few minutes, four lascars had brought the body of Tipu Sultan, or Hyder Ben Ali, or Hy Alley, back on an improvised litter and put it in a small room in the warehouse. Merewether wondered for a moment as to the whereabouts and welfare of young Burcham. He hoped he had survived a second meeting with his old school friend, Hy Alley.

Merewether sat gratefully on a bench and called Gunny. "Feed your men before we move," he said. The arm was on fire; the bandage was soaked with blood.

The Jemadar looked with concern at the bandage and called his surgeon's assistant. The two Marines dressed the wound again with a lint compress and bandages and rigged a sling to hold the forearm up. The bleeding lessened.

"Sah, you must eat," the Jemadar told him. The mess cooks had prepared field rations, and now Merewether drank a mug of scalding, highly sweetened tea laced with rum from some source of the Jemadar's own, and ate part of the bowl of peas along with a piece of ship's biscuit. Half an hour later, Merewether moved off with the main body of Marines, as Gunny ranged ahead with a patrol to scout the way to the fort.

The way was clear. A well-marked road served the dock and led to the fort and then to Sadras, three miles north of the river. An hour later they were close by the fort. MacRae had hastily briefed Merewether and Gunny on its physical situation, the main gate and sally port.

Gunny came back to organize his party for the assault. He left Merewether with six Marines as a reserve force. This was Marine's work, Merewether knew; there must be no interference with an officer so skilled as Gunny. Yet it seemed an interminable time, waiting in the wet mist; even the insects were subdued in this weather. Then a Marine came loping up to be challenged by the picket. "We hold the fort, sah!"

"Good!" Merewether and his party were led to the main gate and admitted by a sentry. Inside, he found Gunny in what must have been the orderly room of the old French garrison. Several lamps cast yellow light over a group of prisoners. There were an elderly man and woman, evidently the retired Sepoy petty officer and his wife, several ragged young men, and three Muslims who gave off an aura of rank and authority.

"These three," said Gunny, "are officers of Tipu's staff. They are here to make the signals." The three looked with bold, hate-filled eyes at Merewether. "They say," continued Gunny, "that Tipu will shortly arrive to destroy us."

"Very well. At the proper time, we shall deal with them. Secure them now. What have you found as to the signals?"

"Sah, there is a tub of tallow with a coir wick upon the seaward wall set in an angle. If lighted, it would be visible far to sea. We found no pyrotechnics here. Possibly the boxes in the boat contained them."

"Very probably," agreed Merewether. "In any event, I brought a sufficient quantity. Now, your pickets and guards are posted. There may be a party to relieve these men by morning. I suggest you let them enter the fort without interference before you seize them. Is there a place I might lie down?" Merewether felt suddenly giddy. The fresh bandage was becoming sodden.

Gunny led him out of the orderly room, around a corner to a room with a cot. Merewether thankfully kicked off his shoes and lay down. He was dimly conscious that Gunny and the surgeon's assistant were again dressing his arm. He subsided into sleep.

CHAPTER 23

When he awoke, Merewether felt weak, washed out. He looked at the bandaged arm supported on a pillow beside him. It was no longer bloody; perhaps the hemorrhage had ceased. He noted that the fingers still obeyed his command, but moving them caused pain. He lay back, relaxed a few minutes more, then felt the compelling necessity to be up, to make sure his force was ready for whatever might occur tonight.

Outside, still unsteady, he found himself at the edge of a weed-grown parade ground. The morning sky was reasonably clear with little promise of more rain. He found the Marine mess cook and obtained a bucket of water, and washed himself as best he could with one hand, feeling the bristles on his cheek. In his haste yesterday morning, he had brought no extra clothing or shaving kit, had even left his jacket back at the dock. He looked with distaste at the dried brown bloodstains on his shirt and trousers, but there was no help for it.

It was eight o'clock and a long day ahead. Merewether sat in the shade out of sight of the gate where a little band of ragged children was begging for food from the Marine sentry. There he drank the tea the mess cook had given him, and ate the biscuit. He felt immeasurably better. The shock of the wound had worn off. Whatever happened tonight, he doubted that anyone other than Tipu would now mount and lead a rebellion in Mysore.

Merewether felt a curious regret at having killed Tipu. He had, of course, had no choice and was extremely lucky to have survived the encounter. But the young man had had a magnetic charm, courage, intelligence and energy that merited a better fate than death in the dusk in a remote jungle clearing. His father had died gallantly defending the breach at Seringapatam; his grandfather, old Hyder Ali, was the ablest enemy the British had ever encountered in India, though he could neither read nor write. With that heredity and the excellent education received in France and England, young Tipu might well have achieved his ambition and driven the Company out, uniting India under a single crown of empire. He might have become a power for the world to reckon with.

Merewether came out of his thoughts to find Gunny before him. "Good morning, sah. How is the arm?"

"Fine," said Merewether, lifting it to demonstrate.

"Sah, I sent back to the boat during the night and brought up the pyrotechnics and supplies. The lascars are waiting at the dock under command of my guard. I think all is well for tonight, if the other crews arrive."

Merewether cursed himself, sitting here mooning over a dead rebel when he should have been looking after such essential matters. "Thank you, Gunny, I have been remiss. The balance of the crews for the lighters should arrive shortly before dark. You, of course, command the lighters. Once we make contact, have the signals answered, we can withdraw from the fort, bringing all our people to the dock. I have ordered *Rapid* to be off the river mouth by dawn."

The Jemadar looked at the arm again. "May I touch your brow, sah?" he said softly. Without waiting for an answer, he felt Merewether's forehead. "A little fever, sah, only natural with such a wound. I would stay quiet today, sah." He looked at the arm again with a curious concern, then marched away. Merewether decided to lie down on the cot again for a few minutes. When he awoke, it was almost dusk. The arm throbbed with pain, was badly swollen against the bandages.

The surgeon's assistant clucked. A small wound it was, but inflamed and angry, the arm swollen to the elbow. He applied unguents from a jar and bandaged with care. Here in the tropics, a scratch or mosquito bite could, by infection, kill a man in short order.

Another hour passed. Merewether followed Gunny up a stairway to the seaward wall of the fort. Fifty feet to the right they found two Marines with a tub apparently filled with tallow, a heavy cable of braided coir set in it, in an angle of the wall.

Merewether waited until black dark. There would be stars, but no moon until after midnight. "Light it," he told Gunny.

The party moved aside as the impregnated coir burned with a radiance that illuminated the whole area. Down around the angle in darkness they could see out to the east. Merewether made sure the rockets were set up in racks in the proper sequence and that a marine had a lighted length of slow match. He subsided against the wall, watching out to sea. Gunny departed for the dock.

Time passed. Constellations rotated. The huge flare lit the sky as Merewether kept a restless watch. He felt entirely alert, not in the least drowsy after a night and day of sleep. If his estimate of time was correct, it was nearing midnight and the frigate was late. He was not overly concerned. With navigation so chancy and the bad weather of the past few days, he was prepared to wait, if necessary, several days for the contact.

It came as a surprise when he heard the Marine call and saw for himself the two red pinpoints of light far offshore. Two more blossomed, then the final pair. The Marine was moving in the dark, blowing on the smoldering match. He applied the glowing tip to a fuze and stood back. The rocket ignited, soared upward, burst in a vivid shower of yellow sparks. Two more were ignited, rose, became red bursts. He repeated the signal. The reply had been made. Merewether knew that three miles to the south, Gunny must have seen the signals and would by now have the lighters moving out. He waited an interminable half hour, but saw no more signals. So with the Marines, he descended to the parade and crossed to the gate. There, Merewether paused. The four other Marines who had composed the skeleton guard in the fort joined them; they struck out briskly down the road to the dock. Merewether's arm hung heavily in its sling, full of sullen throbbing pain.

The lighters were gone from the dock, but *Rapid's* launch lay there, manned now with its own crew. Alongside were launches from *Leopard* and *Antelope*, which had brought the additional lascars down to the lighters, together with the men from *Rapid*. The prisoners were under guard by two Marines in the warehouse. Merewether called to Larkin and asked the time. It was nearly two o'clock. There was no way to know when the lighters might be loaded and the frigate under way again, except to wait for daylight. The lighters were under orders to steer north for Madras, once they were well clear of the frigate.

Finally it began to grow light in the east. Merewether decided to move out. He struggled up from the bench beside the warehouse and called Larkin. He saw the men awakened and pushed to their places at the oars. He mustered the Marines, sending one to recall the picket a quarter mile up the road.

"Bring out the prisoners," he told the guard. A dozen men were marched out. "You," he said to the three Muslim officers, "come with me." He led them to the small room where they had laid Tipu and pulled aside the tarpaulin. There, already a little bloated, lay the body of Tipu Sultan. "There lies your hope of empire," said Merewether. "I hope you will give his remains the honorable burial he deserves." One of the officers burst into tears; the other two remained impassive. "You are free," Merewether told them. He returned to the dock and descended to the launch.

By the time the three boats had cleared the bar, it was broad daylight. Just outside the five fathom line, Larkin called, "I see *Rapid!*" He pointed to the northeast.

Merewether could see nothing, but he was suddenly consumed

with anxiety to get back to his ship. "Launch rockets," he told Larkin. "Row, you men!" He shouted orders to the other two boats and told them to proceed to Madras.

Larkin, striking flint and steel, finally caught a spark in the tinder and blew it alight. He ignited the fuze; the rocket rose and burst—visible even against the rising sun. The launch was well past the five fathom line now, heading for the ship. Merewether could see her sails and see them alter shape, as she changed course and ran down toward them. In a matter of minutes, *Rapid* was hove to and the launch alongside.

Merewether managed to haul himself up the ladder with one arm. He was conscious of the appearance he must make to Mac-Rae, dirty, hatless, unshaven, his uniform stained with blood, arm in a sling. "Hoist in the launch," he told MacRae. "Then steer as near south as she'll lie."

The boat crew came over the side and the launch was hoisted in. *Rapid* paid off, heading almost south on the starboard tack.

"The French frigate has only a few hours start on us," Merewether told MacRae. "Perhaps we can find Pellew and intercept her."

"Yes, sir. Now, Captain, you need a little attention. I'll send Dr. Buttram to wait on you." Merewether did not protest. He went to his cabin, followed shortly by Sangh with tea—and by Dr. Buttram.

"Now, let's see that arm," Buttram began. "It looks like blood poisoning from here." He cut the dirty bandage off and looked at the small angry wound. "Yes. I'll have to open it up. A puncture like this is most susceptible to blood poisoning. It may hurt a bit." He extracted his probes and called over his shoulder. His two assistants sidled in, looking embarrassed at this intrusion. "Hold the arm flat," Buttram told them.

Merewether was not particularly sensitive to pain, but he groaned as the probe delved and was withdrawn. It was followed by a noxious reddish discharge. The arm was turned and the operation repeated. Buttram sponged the arm off with clear spirits and applied what appeared to be a poultice, then a bandage.

"I hope this draws the poison," he told Merewether. "Be well to repeat in two hours with a hot, wet dressing. Now, I prescribe two ounces of London gin and bed rest for the rest of the day." He grinned at Merewether, "And that's an official medical opinion, sir. Otherwise, I must certify you to be incapacitated for command."

Merewether was in no condition to argue; he would be useless on deck in any event. MacRae and Larkin could handle the ship in what might be a long, fruitless stern chase.

Several times during the day, Merewether was conscious that Buttram was again dressing the arm with something hot, heavy and wet, but he subsided into sleep each time. He struggled to consciousness late in the afternoon, he sun shining in his eyes through the starboard ports. The ship was lying well over on the starboard tack; the telltale compass showed a course almost due south. The arm had been dressed yet again, but now, apparently, only with wads of lint on either side strapped on by the bandage. The swelling had diminished, and the dull ache. He called for Sangh.

Shaved, bathed, in a fresh uniform, belly filled with dinner, Merewether came on deck at the end of the first dogwatch. Mister Dobbs had the watch and saluted, as Merewether looked at the compass, the log, the traverse board, and glanced aloft at the sails. *Rapid* was under all plain sail and flying jib. The last cast of the log indicated nine knots.

"Nothing sighted?" inquired Merewether.

"No, sir," replied Dobbs, as though he might be held accountable for this omission.

"Frigate probably is further east. She wants to stay clear of Ceylon and the Royal Navy squadron down there," said Merewether. He walked forward along the weather deck, as MacRae and Larkin came on deck.

"I didn't get a chance to tell you this morning," said MacRae, "but, First of the *Antelope* told me a semaphore message came in from Vellore last night. Mutiny is over, Sepoys will march out. One thousand lashes each for the ringleaders, sir."

"Sentence of death," said Merewether. "It would be kinder to hang or shoot them outright."

"Yes, sir. But you can't treat mutineers with kindness." Little MacRae was a stickler for discipline, and rightly so, Merewether told himself, but a thousand lashes was inhuman, monstrous.

Larkin smiled at him, "I think you're going to live, Captain. Could have made book against you this morning, just like on a pigeon race. Buttram must have worked a miracle."

Merewether lifted the bandaged arm. "I hope so. By the way, how is our prisoner with the broken leg?"

"Last I heard, comfortable," replied Larkin. "Here is the Doctor, he'll tell you." Buttram came aft from the direction of the sick bay. He looked keenly at Merewether, saw the normal color, the arm swinging at his side easily.

"I'll restore you to duty, sir," he said. "I was most concerned this morning."

"How is M'sieur Lally," Merewether demanded.

"Quite comfortable. I had to probe again. There was another bit of cloth still in the wound. With that out, he ought to heal, save the leg."

All the rest of the night, *Rapid* plunged southward. Merewether remained on deck until six bells of the first watch. When he reluctantly retired, he still felt washed out and helpless, but no longer fevered and morbid. He came back on deck just after dawn. There was still no sign of the frigate. He might have head-reached on her by sailing closer to the wind, which was highly desirable, provided he could find Pellew's force and ever contact the Frenchman again. He went down to breakfast with a real appetite.

By midafternoon, MacRae calculated they were almost due east of the shallow eastern entrance to the Gulf of Manar between Ceylon and India. It was in this area Merewether had hoped to find the eastward picket sloop or frigate of the Royal Navy Bengal squadron. Once alerted, the squadron could cut off escape to the southwest and Mauritius for the French frigate. As night fell, he directed Larkin to take in the flying jib and change course a point to the eastward.

Buttram came in to remove the dressings on his arm. It now appeared curiously shrunken; the wounds no longer swollen or bright and angry, but depressed, the edges grayish white in appearance. Buttram bent and sniffed on either side. "No more than a little laudable pus," he said. "Blood poisoning is gone, sir, it will heal now." Merewether felt disinterested, drained of all ambition for the time. After the arm was dressed, he dined and came on deck to sit in the canvas chair rigged on the weather side of the quarterdeck.

He thought of the mission Sir George had sent him on, the fact that he had not written his journal and reports since that first night in the camp at Vellore. He hoped he could remember the facts and give credit to that Company officer at Vellore for his assistance in making the escape down the river. He wondered for a moment where young Burcham was: dead in some thicket on the road to Madras or cooling his heels in makeshift quarters in Madras while he awaited the return of *Rapid?* He concluded he would bring matters up to date in the morning.

Off the starboard quarter, he saw flashes of lightning—an equatorial squall blotting out the stars. He decided the ship was beyond it and would not be struck, and settled into his chair more comfortably. He heard Dobbs admonish the helm on some minor error of steering. He thought of the woman, Sister Jeanne, deeply unhappy, hag-driven, seeking solace in religion, but unable to forget the pleasures of the flesh—now so suddenly and uselessly dead. He had felt a deep sympathy for her and might have felt more, given time. She had evidently been strongly attracted to him and he had only used her. He despised himself for a moment, then came back full circle to Flora Dean and despised himself even more for his treatment of her. He was a man, he decided bitterly, who could not deal with women of quality (a heritage of his low birth, perhaps), who might use and abuse women attracted to him, but could not deal honorably with them. Frustrated by one, he had sought a prostitute. Sought out by another for help desperately needed, he had taken advantage of her, gratified his desires, obtained the information he desired, callously let her go to her death in darkness. He squirmed in the chair and told himself it was not his fault. Yet he still felt the sense of guilt weigh him down.

He left the chair. Calling a good night to Dobbs, he went below. He sniffed the bandages on his arm and caught the faint odor of corruption; consoled himself that this must be the laudable pus. He poured and drank a glass of gin, no lemon, blew out the lamp, undressed and lay down. In spite of his burden of guilt, he was asleep in two minutes.

CHAPTER 24

Merewether heard two bells strike and opened his eyes to gray light through the skylight. Arising he deliberately made enough commotion putting his shoes on and slamming a locker door to alert Sangh. He was only buttoning his shirt when the little Hindu came in with the tray of tea and toasted biscuit, pot of preserves, and even a bit of butter, not yet rancid. He ate, marveling that he could use his left hand without pain, and went on deck. The bitter thoughts of the night before were gone.

MacRae, with the watch, had already plotted the ship's position. In the cubbyhole, Merewether looked at the chart. *Rapid* was well down the coast of Ceylon and would reach the point by noon at which a ship normally would take departure and begin the long wearisome beat southwest against the monsoon. Company ships, in their comfortable fashion, would wait for the northeast monsoon, but the Bombay Marine, French, and Royal Navy could not wait for favorable winds; they must make their way as best they could. He stood on the lee side of the quarter-deck, watching the huge red orb of the sun push up above the eastern horizon.

The hail from the masthead caught him by surprise. "Sail ho! Three points on starboard bow." He rushed to the starboard rail, but, of course, could see nothing in the haze to the westward. The lookout at the masthead could probably see the rising sun's reflection on the sails of the unknown ship to the southwest.

"What do you make out?" he roared.

"Looks like ship-rigged sloop or frigate, sir," came back the attenuated reply from aloft. If so, this probably was Pellew's outermost picket to the east. It would be under orders to stay within visual communication range of an inner picket, which, in turn, would be in communication with the squadron to the west and able to alert it to the passage of any vessel attempting to weather Ceylon.

Merewether caught fire and felt, for the first time since Tipu Sultan had driven that French sword through his arm, the thrill and desire for action. He made a decision.

"Lay the ship as close to southwest as she'll sail," he told Mac-Rae. "Make our number and signal 'Enemy to the east.'"

"Aye aye, sir." MacRae methodically changed course, trimmed sails, and put *Rapid* thrashing along on a course as close-hauled as she would lie. Only then did he send the signal quartermaster forward to the foremast halyards to hoist the signal.

Merewether had no hope of its being seen for a while. *Rapid* would be sighted against the sunrise, of course, but signals would be invisible against such a background until the sun rose clear of the horizon. He settled down for a wait. After a quarter hour, he could stand the suspense no longer.

"Any signals?" he hailed the masthead.

"No, sir." The picket's royals were now visible from the deck. Her lookouts should have seen by now the bright bunting on the signal halyards and reported it to the watch officer.

For the third time in the last three days, Merewether dipped into his precious pyrotechnics locker and ordered three rockets launched to attract attention. He might be making a fool of himself, but obviously the frigate had not passed within sight of the picket and was probably actually northeast of it, intending to give Ceylon a wide berth. If he could get the Royal Navy squadron to move eastward, he would feel free to try an interception and hope to drive the frigate into contact with the squadron.

Belatedly, the masthead shouted, "Signals!" MacRae went scrambling up the mizzen shrouds to the crosstrees and focused the glass.

"She's repeating, sir," he shouted down. "Must have another ship in sight to the west. Acknowledges our number and recognition signal."

Merewether turned to the quartermaster. "Signals: 'Am proceeding east,'" he told him. The rating pulled the bunting from the flag bag and hurried forward. In a moment, the new signal was two-blocked and acknowledged. MacRae came sliding down.

"Now, Mr. MacRae," said Merewether. "Can you put yourself in that French captain's shoes? Take your departure off the Palar for Mauritius, knowing there's a squadron probably waiting off the southeast point of Ceylon. What course would you set, and, assuming seven knots, where would you be now?" MacRae looked at him for a moment, then darted into the cubbyhole.

Five minutes later he emerged, a scrap of paper in hand. "Sir," he said, "my course in such a situation would be south, southeast. He should now be at five degrees thirty minutes north, eighty-two degrees twenty minutes east. Our course is east by southeast one half south to intercept," MacRae paused, one of his infrequent grins appearing. "This mythical ship."

Merewether smiled back at the saturnine little man. "Then set such a mythical course. We'll at least give Admiral Sir Edward Pellew a bit of exercise this morning."

Rapid wore round. With the wind on her starboard quarter, under all plain sail, she was logging ten knots and her motion was much easier.

"Send the hands to breakfast," called Merewether. There was just enough chance of action to justify disrupting the plan of the day by half an hour.

Rapid held the new course for two hours, the lookout reporting that the picket was still visible to the east and must be following. Evidently Sir Edward had reacted with his usual decision. A force would be in striking distance with the weather gauge if Merewether could make the interception and find the frigate. The hail from the masthead came as almost an anticlimax. "Sail ho! Broad on the port beam!"

Merewether turned to MacRae. "Ah ha! She should be dead ahead. There must be something awry with your computations."

MacRae looked indignant for a moment, then said, "She's not making seven knots either, sir."

"You're right. It was a magnificent calculation. We'll hold on east of her in case she tries to run with the wind. We'll try to force her into the squadron."

It was soon apparent that the frigate had sighted *Rapid* and also the picket sloop. Her silhouette changed shape as she wore around before the wind; studding sails, jibs were set and she headed east northeast. *Rapid* was on her starboard bow, head-reaching, steering to place herself ahead of the frigate in position to cut her off and give the squadron time to come up."

"Send the hands to quarters," Merewether told MacRae. The frigate was less than three miles distant, now on the port quarter. Merewether heard the gun captains and divisions reporting manned and ready as he saw the frigate alter course again and come south close-hauled.

"Hands to the braces!" roared Merewether. "Wear ship. Port your helm." The ship spun around, close-hauled, and plunged south, the frigate now on her starboard beam. *Rapid* no longer held the weather gauge. It had been an astute maneuver, Merewether realized. The French captain had made a feint to the east, then turned again to the south, confident he could at worst beat off two sloops and escape before any heavier vessels could come up. *Rapid* would have to beat westward, could not now intercept her. She had a clear run to the south between the Royal Navy sloop and *Rapid*.

Merewether cursed himself. He should have maintained the weather gauge and stayed behind her instead of confidently trying to cut her off; or else repeat his trick of placing himself ahead where his long nine pounders might shoot away a spar and bring her to bay. He now had a stern chase, the frigate to windward, the Royal Navy sloop already too far behind to catch up, and the balance of the squadron over the horizon, plowing ahead east with no chance of an interception.

He put the ship as close to the wind as she would lie, desperately clawing to windward, trying to get into position where he could take some action to force the frigate into the jaws of the squadron.

The masthead hailed, "Sloop's signaling." MacRae scrambled into the rigging again.

"Reporting new course of frigate, sir," he shouted down. Well, thought Merewether, that was a help. At least the squadron might turn south and not continue plunging blindly east seeking a fox that had doubled back.

The morning wore on. As the sun climbed, *Rapid* gradually closed to windward, but at the cost of dropping astern of the frigate. The masthead reported the sloop still in sight far to the west but losing ground. The men sought such shade as they could find behind bulwarks or guns. Finally, *Rapid* was two miles dead astern of the frigate, and could now counter any maneuver she might make. Merewether began to exercise every trick he knew to increase her speed, and close on the Frenchman. He sent men aloft with buckets of water to wet down the sails. He trimmed the braces to the last fraction of an inch.

Rapid crept up. A mile and a half. Closer. Then he saw the blossom of smoke and heard the flat delayed report; the frigate had fired a stern chaser gun. He could not see the fall of shot, but the French captain evidently thought he was close enough to justify warning him off.

"Mr. Larkin." The tall man unwound himself from his position of vantage ten feet up the weather mizzen shrouds. "You might, if you please, try a ranging shot with the forward pivot."

"Aye aye, sir." He dropped to the deck and hurried forward.

"I shall yaw to port," called Merewether. Close-hauled as the ship was, he might be taken aback otherwise. Larkin smiled over his shoulder and waved in understanding. The Frenchman fired again, the splash was far short.

The crew of the forward pivot gun swarmed about it. A cartridge came up, wads and shots were rammed home, the lock primed. Now Larkin's hand raised in signal of readiness as he crouched behind the sights. Merewether gave the command to the helm to ease a point to port. He saw the men rotating the pivot in obedience to Larkin's hand signals, the gleaming tang of the rear sight at maximum elevation, the pivot locked. Larkin stepped aside, negligently twitching the lanyard. The earsplitting, spiteful report of the long nine sounded. As the smoke blew to port, Merewether strained his eyes for the fall of shot. He wished his left arm was strong and steady enough to support a glass.

MacRae, from halfway up the mizzen shrouds, shouted down, "Just on the starboard beam!" Larkin waved in acknowledgment and twisted the deflection knob as the crew rammed home the shot. Merewether yawed again, watched Larkin take his aim and fire.

"Hit!" shouted MacRae. "Starboard quarter. I saw the splinters fly." It was a creditable enough feat of marksmanship, but not crippling; it would not bring the frigate to bay. The crew reloaded, as the frigate fired again. The shot fell a cable's length on the starboard bow, ricocheted and skipped three times from wave to wave down the starboard side, The slow rate of fire from the frigate indicated the stern chaser gun was unhandy—possibly mounted in close quarters and difficult to serve and load.

Larkin was ready again. Anticipating the yaw, he fired on the upward pitch of the bow almost before the pivot was locked. Quiet, undemonstrative little MacRae let out a whoop from his perch, "Hit!" The frigate's spanker gaff seemed to roll up on itself; the close-hauled sail disappeared, collapsed across the quarterdeck, quite evidently fouling the helm. The mizzen topsail and royal changed shape. Braces parted. Without a hand at the wheel, the frigate came up into the wind.

"Hands to the braces!" cried Merewether. He came left as a ragged broadside erupted from the starboard side of the frigate. All the shot fell well to starboard as Merewether headed to cross the frigate's stern. He could see the crew on the poop chopping away at the tangled mass of canvas, cordage and splintered spars, could guess at the party below decks rigging relieving tackles in the lazaret for emergency steering.

Larkin was ready again with the pivot trained out to starboard. He fired at relatively close range, striking the end of the mainyard. The ball continued through the fore-topsail, doing little damage.

"Stand by," called Merewether to Dobbs, in charge of the starboard battery. He heard the command echoed by the gun captains down the battery. The frigate fired again, her guns slewed around as far as they would train aft. One ball ricocheted and struck the starboard bow a shattering blow; several howled across the deck, cutting stays, holing sails. He was now out of their range, crossing the stern less than a cable's length away.

"Commence fire!" Dobb's echo of the command was lost as the six nine pounders, two twenty-four pounder carronades, blasted out in a sheet of flame. The smoke came back across the deck, as Merewether became dimly aware that the frigate's stern chaser had fired almost simultaneously, that its shot had ripped through the mizzen shrouds just below MacRae's perch. He caught a glimpse of MacRae's body soaring in a backward arc toward the water.

Merewether forgot his crippled arm and seized the life buoy hanging on the starboard bulwarks. He hurled it at the spot where the little man had disappeared. He looked at the Frenchman. The broadside had hit home; the stern lights were gaping holes, the mizzen-topsail yard shot in two, braces hanging loose, the working party on the stern vanished. She would not move from this spot without major repairs to her rigging. It was not his task to try to hammer her into surrender; having brought her to bay, he could await the Royal Navy. His only concern at the moment was MacRae.

"Hands to the braces! Stand by to go about!" The port gun crews leaped to attention, confident he was about to give them a chance at the frigate. "Port your helm!" *Rapid* spun about, came to the wind, and settled on the port tack, clawing back toward the bobbing white buoy. No more fire came from the stern chaser on the frigate, it must have been disabled by the broadside. It was almost an afterthought as he gave the anxious port battery crews the command to fire. The broadside struck home, but had little noticeable effect.

"Launch the gig," he told Dobbs. *Rapid* crept upwind as the hands hoisted out the gig and set out toward the bobbing buoy. Hove to, he was still out of the line of fire of the frigate's broadside. He took time to observe the progress of the Royal Navy picket sloop, which was now hull up with a bone in her teeth, signals flying, "Engage the enemy." He fancied he could see specks of white on the western horizon; possibly clouds, but perhaps Pellew's squadron.

Larkin was beside him, glass to eye. "Got him, by God!" he shouted. Merewether could see a commotion in the boat. Then oars began to move. The gig was pulling back.

Merewether beckoned the messenger. "My compliments to Dr. Buttram. Ask him to come on deck." The gig came alongside, a drenched MacRae sitting with an embarrassed smile beside the coxswain. He came over the side. There Buttram and his mates met him with a blanket and a cup of medicinal brandy. MacRae waved them away, however, denying any injury, and took his place as officer of the watch on the quarter deck. The puddle dripped from his clothes, soon dried on the steaming planks.

CHAPTER 25

Four hours passed. *Rapid* was making her way north, close-hauled on the port tack. The Frenchman had struck as soon as the squadron was hull up. Merewether had been summoned to the flagship and had made his verbal report to the sanguine, volatile Admiral Pellew, who congratulated him. A prize crew was in the frigate laboring to restore her rigging and get her into condition to sail to Columbo. Merewether told Sangh to prepare dinner for four guests; in weather as mild as this, the Boatswain could stand a dogwatch.

MacRae was still a trifle sheepish in his fresh clothing, as the party gathered. "A good thing I learned to dive for pearls," he said. "I thought I never would come up. When I did, the ship was already almost out of sight. Then I saw the buoy a hundred feet away. Just hung on till the gig came." He took brandy at Buttram's insistence. "No point to waste it," he admitted when Buttram told him he would not put it back in the flask.

To Merewether's embarrassment, he found Larkin most insistent, in his easy, engaging way, in wanting to hear an account of Merewether's shore adventure. Reluctantly at first, then as the second gin and lemon took effect, with some eloquence, he told his story, glossing over the part played by Sister Jeanne, minimizing the duel with Tipu, remembering to compliment Burcham, Sangh and Gunny—and wondering to himself what fate Burcham had met. In due course, Sangh announced dinner. Afterward, Merewether sat at his desk until the middle watch, bringing his journal up to date, with the report of his mission and today's action.

Two days later he anchored off Fort St. George in Madras Roads, made his number, and prepared to go ashore to report to the Governor. He hoped Gunny and the Marine detachment were ready for embarkation, that Burcham was waiting ashore. His signal for a shore boat was soon answered; two raced for the gangway. The mutiny was over and demand for boats had diminished; the three Company transports were only waiting to re-embark their troops to head back to Fort William.

The landing area, so crowded and confused the last time he had come here, was empty. No beachmaster. No transportation. In full dress, wearing a sword borrowed from MacRae, he walked sweating through the town to Government House and finally reached the young captain aide in the room outside the Governor's chambers. The captain recognized him and stood up respectfully. "Sir, the Governor is at Vellore winding up that business. Bad luck on your midshipman. I had the sergeant wait here to give you a direct report."

Merewether felt stunned, stupid. He had worried about young Burcham. This was confirmation of his worst fears.

"What happened?" he demanded.

"I don't know, sir. That's why I held the sergeant. Been a bit of a dustup here, you understand. Lots of confusion. You can leave your report with me, sir. I'll give you a receipt and see the Governor gets it." He rang a bell. A messenger popped in. "Bring that Company sergeant—Thompson, I think's his name—to the gate, to see the Captain here." The messenger departed. "Nothing more for you, Captain. Oh, yes, here's a copy of a receipt from the Provost Marshal for three thousand muskets, four field guns, ammunition, two lighters, turned over by your Marine commander. He and his detachment are at Fort St. George." The young man casually dismissed him.

Outside, Merewether waited at the gate for a quarter hour before he saw the heavyset, black-browed Company sergeant coming up. The man saluted, but looked nervous. "Speak up, tell me what happened," said Merewether brusquely.

"Well, sir, after you and the prisoner got in that boat we went on toward Madras. Got close to dark, we stopped, sir, started to feed and water the mules. Been driving hard, got a fire built. Happened so sudden, never had a chance, fifteen or twenty men jumped us. Then this good-looking young man wearing a sword came up, looked in the wagon, says, 'They're gone! Where did they go, Billy Burcham?' Mr. Burcham, all he says is, 'Hy, you'll never find them now.' Just as cool as ice. 'Too bad for you, Billy,' says the man and whips out this fancy sword, stabs it right through the boy, then weeps, real tears, says, 'What have I done?' Looks about, says, 'Down the river, of course, not too late yet,' and rides off. When I got to him, the boy was dead, sir." The sergeant looked even more upset. "Not a thing I could do, sir."

"Where is he?" demanded Merewether.

"Buried yesterday morning in St. George's Cemetery, sir. Chaplain, naval and marine guard and all, sir, full honors."

Merewether simply stared at the uncomfortable, sweating sergeant. He felt physically nauseated at the realization that the alert, intelligent young midshipman had been killed in cold blood while carrying out his orders. The boy had shown promise, courage, ability, energy, and would after a few years' experience have developed into an excellent officer. Yet he had been cut down needlessly, vindictively, just as had Sister Jeanne. He remembered with disbelief the regret he had felt the night he killed Tipu, felt instead a savage satisfaction that he had ended his career before it was well begun—one that might have become a monstrous thing. The courage, intelligence, and charm that had appeared on the surface was mere veneer to mask a spirit as ruthless and cruel as Attila the Hun.

Merewether returned to the present, to the anxious sergeant still standing stiffly before him. "Very well, sergeant. Most regrettable. Mr. Burcham gave promise of becoming an excellent officer. Give me your orders. I'll endorse them to proceed and join your unit immediately." The sergeant fumbled out a folded paper and handed it to Merewether. In the guardroom at the gate, he found the duty clerk, borrowed pen and ink, and wrote and signed the endorsement. The sergeant saluted with relief, took the orders, and fled. Merewether found a tonga, which he directed to Fort St. George. There he arranged for Gunny and the Marine detachment to be embarked. He returned to *Rapid* with them.

On board, he called all hands aft. "Mr. William Burcham," he began abruptly, "midshipman in this ship, was killed in line of duty four days ago ashore. I wish to offer a prayer for his soul." He could not help thinking, as he read from the Book of Common Prayer over the bowed heads of the crew, what effect this gesture might have had on Sister Jeanne. At the conclusion of the prayer, he announced, "I wish you all to drink in memory of a brave and able young officer. Mr. Davis, you have my permission to serve out a ration of rum to all hands." He called his officers together, and drank a solemn toast to young Burcham in the cabin, then told MacRae to make all preparations for getting under way.

Just before the end of the afternoon watch, Sangh appeared. "Sahib, Gunny wishes to see you."

Gunny saluted. In his left hand were two swords.

"Sah, I have here your sword and that of Tipu you left at the Palar." He laid them carefully side by side on the table, hilts toward Merewether. Merewether's sword had been bought from the widow of a Bombay Marine officer eight years ago and was plain and serviceable. Tipu's sword had a hilt of gold in the pattern of the French Army dress sword, and was set with rubies and pearls; in the pommel there was a ruby as large as a grape. The blade was sheathed in a regulation leather scabbard, but mounted with gold, again set with small rubies and pearls. A magnificent weapon fit for a prince of the Indies!

Curiously, Merewether withdrew the gleaming, double-edged blade, now wiped clean of the blood it had drawn. He saw the engraving etched into its surface, and twisting the blade in the light, saw the inscription was in French. Gunny translated: "It says 'To Tipu, Sultan of Mysore, Emperor of India, from his brother, Napoleon, Emperor of France, A.D. 1805.' "

"Remarkable!" said Merewether. The man had truly intended to become Emperor and reunite all India under a single crown, and he must have convinced Bonaparte he could do it. He felt the solid, balanced weight of the weapon; it was a magnificent and valuable trophy, with the gold, jewels and inscription, it might bring a thousand pounds from some wealthy collector. "Thank you, Gunny, I was most careless to leave them." The Jemadar saluted, about-faced, and went out.

Merewether sat looking at the sword. At the call for the first dogwatch, he came to a conclusion. "Sangh," he called. The little Hindu stood hands folded, awaiting his orders. "Send the Carpenter in," he told him. Five minutes later, he was telling the man, "I want this sword packed and boxed up for safe transport to England. Have it ready by the time we reach Calcutta."

The Carpenter took the sword with awe and withdrew.

"And guard it with your life," Merewether called after him. It would be worth paying the extra tariff to have it transported in the strong room of an Indiaman. He sat down at the desk, looked at the sheaf of reports completed through the action off Ceylon, wrote the brief addenda to the effect that Midshipman William Burcham had been killed near Vellore in line of duty.

He paused, laid out a fresh sheet, consulted the records in the strongbox, ascertained the names of Burcham's parents in Surrey, discovered with some surprise that his father was a baronet, and addressed himself to the unpleasant duty of informing them that their son was dead. He concluded, "Shortly afterward, Tipu Sultan was intercepted and killed by other elements of the Bombay Marine, I feel it only fitting that you should have Tipu's sword in recognition of your son's able service as an officer in the Marine. Respectfully, etc."

CHAPTER 26

At Calcutta, Merewether reported to Commodore Land; they went at once to Government House, waiting a bare half minute before Locksley came back beckoning. A red-faced Company dignitary came out the door, glaring at the two officers who had cut short his interview. Merewether followed Land in and marched to the spot before the table where he had first confronted the Governor-General—what, three months ago?—and been sent out full of anger and resentment with changed orders on an impossible mission.

"Good morning, Your Excellency," said Land. "Captain Merewether has returned from Vellore with his reports." Sir George's gaze moved coldly from Land to Merewether. His face was as hard, as obdurate as ever.

"Very well, Captain, you may give me a verbal summary of your reports." The blue eyes bored into Merewether's most disconcertingly.

Merewether commenced his account. He remembered to praise Burcham, Gunny, the Marine detachment, Larkin's marksmanship in the action of the frigate. He concluded with his belief that the missionaries had no direct connection with the mutiny, that it was largely due to Cradock's order, possibly partly fomented by Tipu and his relatives, but that the missionary MacGuire was a French agent.

"And you killed this Tipu in single combat," wondered Sir George. "God, what a glorious experience!" His impassive face for a moment assumed an expression composed of almost equal parts of admiration and envy. "Glorious," he repeated, then resumed his usual glacial calm. "Very well, Captain, leave your reports with Locksley. By the way, Lady Barlow and I are receiving tonight. I would be pleased for you and your officers to call."

"Thank you, Your Excellency," Merewether replied.

"Have we Your Excellency's permission to withdraw?" inquired Land carefully.

"Yes." They delivered the reports to the secretary, and went into the dazzling sunlight.

"Still need a gin at Velloso's," growled the Commodore. "When he's pleasant, it's often harder than when he isn't." They marched around the corner to the dim, cool public room. The old white-haired Portuguese served the London gin and lemons. Land raised his glass, "To Young Burcham," he said. "Liked the boy on first and only sight. Crying shame." They touched the glasses solemnly and drank. A single gin sufficed. They went back to the dockyard, Merewether on to the ship.

Merewether gave the names of his little party to the majordomo and heard them announced. He found Commodore Land close by and joined the procession to Sir George and Lady Barlow, who, flanked by other members of the Council of Calcutta, were receiving. They worked their way slowly forward, reached the official party, were introduced, bowed, finally reached Sir George, bowed again. To Merewether's surprise, Sir George grasped his hand and turned to Lady Barlow, the faded beauty with the bitter mouth. "My dear," he said, "this is Captain Merewether."

The woman looked at him with interest as Merewether made his bow. Suddenly, she blurted out, "You're the one that killed Tipu!"

Merewether was stricken. The others were looking at him. He felt color flood his face and could only murmur, "Yes, ma'am, afraid I did." He bowed again, escaped. He soon found himself at the punch bowl, thankful to have a cool drink in the company of his officers. He was still lurking in a corner when he saw a young ensign of His Majesty's Foot, splendid in scarlet coat and white breeches, come in. Hanging possessively on his arm was Miss Flora Dean, followed by Jason Dean and his wife.

For the first time in his life, Merewether felt jealousy take possession of him. Two minutes ago, he would have laughed at the suggestion that Miss Flora Dean meant anything to him, that anything she did was of concern to him. Yet, it suddenly became of the utmost importance to part her somehow from that popinjay ensign, with his curly blond hair, with his fair complexion not yet burned and marred by the Indian sun. He watched from his post of vantage as they proceeded by the members of the Council, Sir George and Lady Barlow, then came toward the punch bowl. The ensign was leaning over familiarly whispering some quip in Flora's ear, at which she laughed. Merewether stepped forward and made his most elaborate bow. "Miss Dean, delighted to see you again."

Flora was startled. Evidently the news of *Rapid*'s return this afternoon had not reached her. She actually stammered as she introduced Ensign John St. John. The two officers bowed, murmuring amenities. "When did you return, Captain?" she demanded.

"This afternoon, M'am. I had to report to the Governor-General. He asked me and my officers to this affair."

St. John broke in. "I expect you were down at Vellore. My battalion's still there. I was on leave when it went."

"Mutiny's over," said Merewether brusquely. "They'll be back soon." The man seemed decent enough. He must not be over twenty-one, a mere child, Merewether thought from the vantage of twenty-eight, sixteen years at sea. "May I bring you some punch?" he asked Flora.

He plunged into the crowd around the punch bowl and eventually emerged balancing three cups. He made his way back to where Flora and St. John had taken seats near the windows. He tried to make desultory conversation, to find out the trivial news of the past month, but soon gave up the effort. He reached for the empty cups. But St. John was ahead of him. Merewether let him take them back to the table.

"Can I see you tomorrow night?" Merewether demanded urgently.

"I'm sorry," replied Flora, looking at him coquettishly. "John and I are invited for whist."

"Then when?" said Merewether, seeing the scarlet coat approaching out of the corner of his eye.

"Friday is soonest," said Flora with a smug air of self-satisfaction that grated upon him.

"Very well," he conceded. He rose as St. John came up, then bowed and took his leave of the couple. He sought out Commodore Land and told him he was weary—yet weak from the wound and infection—and would prefer to return to the ship. Land promised to make his excuses to the Governor-General. Merewether went back to the ship and found Sangh ahead of him, lighting the cabin lamp as he entered. He said only one word, "Gin."

Over the half glass of gin, Merewether tried to analyze his feelings, to discover what possessed him, why he suddenly felt such hatred of an obviously nice and gentlemanly young officer, simply because he appeared to be attractive to a nice but not extraordinary young lady. His thoughts went back to the last time he had been with Flora. He had deliberately turned back, refrained from committing himself, had left her and sought out a prostitute. He was a fine figure to feel resentment because she, in turn, welcomed an honorable young man with conventional intentions. It was unreasoning, yet it was still torment. He could not rid himself of the jealousy or resolve his emotions in any logical way. A knock came on the door, upsetting his savage train of thought.

"Come," he called. The door opened and MacLellan entered, his big red face wreathed in smiles.

"Ah, Captain," he said. "Watch at the arsenal told me you had come back aboard. Been all day over at Fort William sitting on a board of survey on powder and pyrotechnics. Crying shame the way such things are spoiled with improper stowage. I thought I'd row out and say hello," he continued lamely, conscious suddenly that he had intruded upon a man with his mind on other things.

Merewether was genuinely fond of the big Scots officer. He forced the bitter thoughts out of his mind, rose and took MacLellan's hand. "I'm delighted you came," he told him. He saw Sangh at the door. "Scots whisky, Sangh. Now, Mac, tell me the news." Flora was forgotten for the time as MacLellan gently pumped out his story for the third time, clucked at the still bandaged arm, and related the newest scandal of the European community. He left just after midnight, as the other officers came on board from the reception. Merewether had no difficulty going to sleep.

Merewether found himself tongue-tied, unable to utter more than the most trivial of platitudes in reply to the bright conversation of Jason Dean, his witty wife, and Flora. Major Lord Laddie Montague and his half battalion of troops had arrived this afternoon in *Antelope*, Lord Laddie waving cordially from her quarterdeck as she passed *Rapid*. The news of the end of the mutiny was general now, the consensus of opinion reflected by Jason, that the French were behind it all in a sinister plot to conquer India from within. This was just near enough the truth to make Merewether even more uncomfortable in view of the injunctions placed upon him by Sir George and the Commodore not to discuss the matter. Otherwise, this would have been a pleasant little dinner party for the four of them. He found himself nervously drinking one more glass of port than his usual quota. Mrs. Dean arose to announce with an arch expression that she and Jason would visit the Willoughbeys, and made their withdrawal. Merewether looked for the first time that night squarely at Flora Dean.

There certainly had been enough to do the past three days to keep him from brooding. M'sieur Lally had to be moved to Fort William, a prisoner with an uncertain future. The Carpenter had made repairs to the bow, replacing the planks shattered by the ricocheting French shot; the Purser had a stack of requisitions and had drawn pay for the crew; new rigging replaced stays and braces damaged in the action; MacRae had become dissatisfied with the table of compass corrections and had the launch swing ship at slack tide. Yet this activity was insufficient to overcome the fires of jealousy burning in Merewether. No matter how he tried to rationalize and reason with himself, he found himself back in the same unreasoning, insane mood.

Merewether had tried to examine the matter dispassionately. He had known from the start that a girl like Flora was interested in marriage, and not to just anyone. She wanted someone she not only could love, but with prospects, a future. He had told himself cynically upon their first meeting that marriage was the major purpose of her visit to India, as it was of dozens of other young ladies in Calcutta, Bombay, Madras each year. He had felt, still felt, that he had no right to ask a woman to share the hard, bitter life of an officer of the Bombay Marine, the extended absences, the real day-by-day dangers of death or disabling mutilation, and of life in a country where every kind of fatal disease lurked, possibly even in the next mouthful of food. All these matters, Merewether pled in self-justification for his failure to declare his intentions. All, unquestionably, were valid reasons. Nevertheless he found himself actually considering making some sort of declaration that inevitably would lead to marriage. The whole process had been maddening. If he spoke, he was committed; if he did not, it was clear that Flora was lost.

Silence persisted for a moment after Mr. and Mrs. Dean departed. Flora and Merewether moved into the parlor as the servants cleared the table. The silence grew uncomfortable. He looked again directly at Flora. She was almost beautiful in this light. He saw the enhanced color, the bright brown eyes, a lower lip caught between white teeth. He realized that he need only speak and she was his. He failed miserably. He was unable to compel himself to utter the few simple words necessary. The moment was past, irretrievably lost, the spell broken, as a servant came in to inquire as to whether he would be needed further. In his cross-grained way, Merewether felt a sense of triumph; he had not permitted emotion to overwhelm sober judgment.

The evening passed in casual, stilted small talk, Flora appearing hurt and distant. He took his leave before Jason and his wife returned and made his way to the landing, embarking in the gig.

Halfway down to the ship, the sense of lost opportunity struck home; the jealousy flared up again. Now Flora became supremely desirable. He almost concluded to try to mend the affair and to order the gig to head back upstream. The thought of the effect such irresponsible conduct would have on the boat crew deterred him.

At the gangway, Larkin handed him a message. Merewether went aft. He threw off his hat, coat. He tore off the stock. He sat at his desk, slumped in the chair, despising his conduct, conscious that he had behaved irrationally tonight. Absently tearing open the note, he found it was an invitation from Major Lord Laddie Montague to attend an entertainment at his villa on Chitapur Creek tomorrow night. Merewether decided he would accept. To hell with Flora Dean, he thought savagely, as he wrote the brief note to Lord Laddie. Then he blew out the lamp, and fell into troubled sleep.

PART THREE

Grand Chop

CHAPTER 27

THE pounding on the door became intolerable. Merewether groaned, roused, pushed himself sidewise on the bed, and finally made his lips articulate, "Come!" Through blurred vision he saw a seaman messenger from the dockyard, hat off, escorted by Jackson, the boatswain's mate of the watch, holding out a document and a receipt. He seized the message, sought pen and ink on the desk, scribbled his signature on the receipt, and thankfully saw the pair about-face and go out, closing the door. He shuffled toward the bed, conscious only of his need for sleep, and found the sunlight in his eyes blinding him. The realization that the sun was high enough to be striking through the skylight finally awakened him.

His watch had run down and presently pointed to two o'clock. From the altitude of the sun, he realized that it must be well into the forenoon watch. He heard the bell strike three times and concluded he must have been back on board *Rapid* over three hours. He opened the message and tried to focus his eyes on it, then heard the door open and saw Sangh putting a tray of tea and toasted biscuit on the table. He staggered up, poured a cup, slopping the saucer half full, took an incautious gulp, and blew frantically, spraying out tea from his scalded mouth. The pain brought him to full consciousness, spluttering curses, feeling the throbbing ache extending from temple to temple around the back of his head. He felt blisters forming inside his lips, cursed again, drank cautiously, and looked at the message.

It was from Commodore Land. Report at once for an interview with the Acting Governor-General at a half after ten. Good God! Merewether ran his hand over the bristles on his chin and looked at the ruin of his clothing. He shouted for Sangh, then drank another cup of tea while he scraped the razor through blood-flecked lather. He fought his way into fresh clothing, and emerged on deck, sword belt looped over his arm, to descend to the waiting gig. By the time the boat touched the landing, he had made some adjustments, had the sword belted on, his hat on straight, and buttons in their proper holes.

Land was pacing outside his headquarters where a tonga was waiting. Brusquely he motioned Merewether in, not bothering to return the morning salute, and directed the driver off at a gallop toward Government House. Only after they were halfway there did he look at Merewether, sitting stiffly, holding on with both hands, eyes closed, fighting to overcome the nausea that threatened him.

"Good God, man!" exploded Land. "I've seen a man look more alive after being flogged through the fleet." He dug into his waist-coat pocket and extracted his watch. "A quarter hour yet. Go to Velloso's," he told the driver.

At the public house, he urged Merewether along and found the proprietor waiting, summoned by the jingle of the doorbell. "Two coffees," the Commodore told him. "One laced with brandy." The old white-haired Portuguese shuffled off and soon returned with two cups of steaming black coffee, one emitting a powerful aroma of Spanish brandy. "Drink it," directed Land.

Merewether put the cup to his blistered lips and felt the hot coffee and fiery brandy set them aflame again. He almost surrendered, and then drank down the aromatic brew with a shudder. For a moment, he thought it would come back up in spite of all he could do. Then he felt the draught take hold and expand through his body, carrying with it a sense of well-being. He felt almost human again.

It had been only two days since he had miserably failed to declare himself to Miss Flora Dean and had accepted Lord Laddie Montague's invitation to a social affair at his villa up on Chitapur Creek. Merewether had had no idea what to expect. He had thought vaguely of a sort of formal garden party with members of Calcutta society promenading about in a leisurely fashion, making polite conversation while sipping punch or tea with a group of musicians possibly playing in the background. This was the conception of an entertainment hosted by a member of the nobility which occurred to a backstairs child. He could not conceive of a blue-blooded baron conducting himself except with the utmost decorum.

The fact proved to be entirely different. Merewether had prevailed upon the Commodore to borrow the dockyard tonga, and arrived as invited in the late afternoon. The drive out the country road had been pleasant, a breeze was stirring. There was color in the small fields in late summer. They passed an occasional Indian farmer driving a bullock hitched to a cart full of produce for the Calcutta bazaar. The driver turned from the road down a lane through a grove of trees, and Merewether could hear voices in the distance, increasing in volume as the tonga rattled along. He had wondered absently what the laughter and shouting was about, what group would behave so boisterously near the villa of Lord Montague. The tonga emerged from the grove and pulled up in front of a long, low bungalow. The driver said, "Lord Montague's, sahib," and Merewether realized the sounds of merriment came from the bungalow itself.

He had been met at the door by a servant who took his hat, led him from the hallway into a large room nearly full of officers, mostly Army, a few Royal Navy, and Honourable Company gathered about gaming tables. Merewether's quick glance failed to reveal another officer of the Bombay Marine. He found his hand seized, look about and found Lord Laddie beside him, a smile wreathing his dark face.

"Welcome, Captain," he cried over the din that filled the room, "I am delighted you could come." He took Merewether's arm and propelled him into another room, less crowded, where he could talk in a normal tone. Here was a table with punch bowl, bottles, glasses, plates of cheese, meat, and fruits. It was presided over by a portly red-faced man wearing a white apron whom he recognized as one of the sergeants from Lord Laddie's battalion.

"It will be another four hours before dinner, Captain. Have a bit of refreshment and then you can join one of the games. There are tables of whist, vingt-et-un, hazard, and any number of dice games, take your choice." He clapped Merewether on the back, smiled, and dived out the door across the game room to greet a colonel of light cavalry just arriving.

By some freak of memory, Merewether was able to call the sergeant's name. "A gin and lemon please, Massey." The man beamed at the recognition, poured the glass, cut a lemon, and supplied a napkin.

"Here you are, Captain. Beats sailing up and down the bloody ocean, sir." His voice dropped. It became confidential, "His Lordship has a real surprise for you gennulmen tonight, wait and see!" He winked portentously as he turned to serve an impatient captain of the Royal Navy. Merewether drifted away, sipping the gin.

Merewether possessed no skill at cards or dice. Occasionally he had joined in simple games, won or lost small stakes, but he saw from the door that this was no gathering of small-stakes players. In one roaring vingt-et-un game close by the door, gold guineas as well as silver rupees were piled in front of the players and changed hands rapidly to cries of joy or despair. He immediately concluded that even though it was just past quarterday, his capital was insufficient for such a venture. He sidled about the edges of the room, watching first one game, then another. The whist players sat silent, no shouts from them, but the object of the game was a mystery to Merewether. He completed his circuit of the room, came back to the door to the adjoining room, and stood there as a succession of Hindu servants came and went, bearing refreshments to the players.

Sergeant Massey was jovial. Likely he had been sampling some of his wares. He provided a fresh glass of gin, lemon, and napkin. Merewether had found himself back at the table several times before darkness fell. Apparently dinner was delayed, he was feeling the effects of the gin when the butler appeared and made his announcement.

The dinner was served in a large dining room, bright with candlelight. It took all Lord Laddie's persuasive powers to get some of the guests away from the gaming tables. Merewether felt a little blurred. He ate mechanically. He drank the wine served with each course, as he listened to the buzz of conversation. He began to feel exhilarated and found himself loudly discussing an obscure point of horsemanship with a major of dragoons seated next to him. He subsided, conscious that he was drinking too much, and close to making a fool of himself.

After the dessert, Lord Laddie arose from his place at the head of the table and proposed a single toast to King George. Then he said, "We have a bit of entertainment before you gentlemen resume your games." He clapped his hands and through a door at the other end of the room came a servant carrying a pack of playing cards. "There are twenty-four of us here," said Lord Laddie. "Let each gentleman select a card." The servant proceeded around the table, cards fanned out, each officer drawing a card until all had drawn one. "Hold your cards, for they may be valuable later," he called, laughing. "We will play a game with a prize of consequence. And now, have on with jollity!"

From beyond the door there came a sudden tinkle of stringed instruments, the thud of a drum, clang of cymbals, and a squeal of flutes. Through the door a troupe of dancers came, swaying in rhythm with the music. Merewether had seen such performances a time or two before in Bombay. Such troupes traveled about India from the court of one native rajah or nizam to another, were sometimes employed for months to entertain the ruler, his family, and retainers. These dancers were Burmese, he guessed, beautiful, small, brown-skinned girls, bare above their girdles, only peacock feathers below, wearing bracelets about wrists and ankles that jangled with each movement of the dance. A sigh went through the assembly, but there was only one drunken whoop as the dancers went through their movements, keeping time to the music from beyond the door.

Merewether sat back, relaxed, and enjoyed the interlude, marking time with his foot. The small women went through their repertoire, their dark eyes, rimmed with kohl, flashing in the candlelight, the graceful bodies matching in time every nuance of the music. They slipped from one tempo into another and came at last to a flashing crescendo of movement and music, dominated by cymbals and drum; with a final thunderclap, they froze in statuesque attitudes.

Merewether clapped and shouted bravos with the rest as the

eight girls demurely genuflected, then resumed their poses. Lord
Laddie stood up, hands extended, seeking quiet, at last he said,
"And now, gentlemen, comes the crux of our game. We learn who
takes the stakes!"

The servant came forward again, cards fanned out in his hands.
He offered each girl in the troupe a choice, saw each of the eight
cards drawn. Merewether felt excitement mount as he picked up
the card he had so carelessly accepted an hour ago and looked at
it. The knave of hearts! It was certainly appropriate after his treatment of Flora Dean, and his unreasoning refusal to declare himself. He leaned forward tensely, awaiting the next move from
Lord Laddie.

"As you may have guessed, gentlemen," said Lord Laddie,
white teeth gleaming in his dark face, "the odds are three to one,
much better than Lord Derby usually enjoys at his race meetings.
Each girl becomes the property for this night of the officer who
holds her matching card. Thant here will call the winners." A
small Burmese man, evidently the manager of the troupe, materialized beside Lord Laddie, his wide grin displaying black, betel
nut discolored teeth.

The game suddenly became serious to Merewether, he found
himself straining forward to see and hear the results of the competition. He tried to tell himself that the whole affair was ridiculous,
a joke, something for Lord Laddie to laugh about in retelling in
later years. Still, the other officers present had become dead serious too, possibly because it was a competition and each wanted
to win the game. The small, almost naked women stood in their
file, dark eyes glancing about, giggling, as the Burmese called out
an incomprehensible gabble, apparently the name of one of the
dancers.

The leader of the troupe stepped forward and held out a card
for Lord Laddie to see. She was a beautifully proportioned little
woman with white teeth, not discolored by betel nut as some of
the others' were. "Knave of hearts!" cried Lord Laddie. "Step
forward, oh you lucky gentleman, and claim your prize!"

Merewether felt heat flood up and was conscious he was blush-
ing in embarrassment. A moment ago he had wanted desperately
to win one of the stakes. Now he was by no means so sure. Even

with the gin, the innumerable glasses of wine, the excitement of the dances, and the game, he felt reluctant. He was almost willing to hand the winning knave of hearts to one of the applauding officers. He managed a red-faced grin, conscious of his scarred face, crooked nose, stood up and held out his card. "I have it, sir," he croaked as applause deafened him.

"The Bombay Marine is first into action again!" sang out Lord Laddie. "Just hold your place until we complete the game, Captain." Merewether sat down, his face still red, as attention shifted again to the Burmese. He drained the glass of port before him and found it refilled almost instantly, as the next girl's card was matched by a major of light cavalry. So it continued until each of the eight girls had been claimed by an exultant or sheepish officer. Lord Laddie, still laughing, announced, "They belong to the winners until cockcrow tomorrow! And now, for the rest of us losers, back to the tables where all we may win is gold!"

Merewether found his hand seized in the general confusion of the end of the dinner. He looked down and saw the small brown woman smiling up at him. He had suffered himself to be led through a side door, across a bit of lawn, and into a small guest-house, one of several ranged about a garden. He had abandoned himself to enjoyment of the spoils of the game and came awake only after sunlight struck in the window. He left the little Burmese woman curled up, still asleep. Locating his tonga, he aroused the driver and made his way back to the dockyard.

Outside Velloso's, the Commodore and Merewether reentered the tonga, pulled around in front of Government House and entered the anteroom to the Governor-General's chambers. Locksley, at his desk arranging a pile of documents, rose and greeted them respectfully: "Sir Thomas Jeffrey has not yet arrived, sir. He should be here in a moment. Merewether sat down with relief, the residue of last night's wine and the brandied coffee had made him uncertain of his legs. He wondered briefly if he could stand at attention through an interview of any length before Sir George.

"God knows what's up now," growled Land, sotto voce. "This Sir Thomas is on the Council, and I can't guess what he would have to do with naval matters." Just then the door opened and a tall, elegantly turned-out man of some forty years came in. Locksley leaped to his feet, came forward, and greeted him with ceremony. He turned to the Commodore and Merewether: "Sir Thomas, may I present Captain Percival Merewether of the Bombay Marine? You are acquainted, of course, with Commodore Land." Sir Thomas acknowledged the presentation with a bow.

"You're the fellow," he said in a high nasal tone, "that killed that pirate Abercrombie. I just heard you killed Tipu Sultan, too. Damned good piece of work." Sir Thomas had thinning hair over a sloping brow, a large curved nose, full lips, and receding chin, but he gave an impression of resolution and force.

Just then, Locksley emerged from the Governor-General's chambers, bowed to Sir Thomas, greeted the Commodore and Merewether, and said, "Sir George will see you gentlemen now." He held open the door as Sir Thomas, the Commodore and Merewether marched in. It was a relief to Merewether to see the three chairs ranged before Sir George's table. Seated, he might survive this interview.

Sir George came from behind his table and took the hands of Sir Thomas, Commodore Land, and Merewether in turn. He indicated the chairs and resumed his place behind the table. "Gentlemen, I am delighted that you could come on so short a notice. I regret any inconvenience you have suffered, but I feel that events justify this hasty action." He sat back, his ice-blue gaze flicking from one to another. "You know, of course, I hold this post pro tempore, only until the Court and Government can agree on an appointment, perhaps Minto, Grenville, or myself. My sin is agreeing too wholeheartedly with Wellesley during his tenure."

"And quite rightly, George," said Sir Thomas. "He was the man who saw the chance to make an empire of India for the Company. Not quite a likeable man, but sound." He subsided into his chair as Merewether wondered at the easy ability to address the Governor-General by his Christian name. "Of course," he continued, "Wellesley is facing an inquiry into his governorship in the House now, can't be of much help."

"Water over the dam," said Sir George briskly. "He'll come clear because he was right, but meanwhile I have to govern India as best I can and try to make the Company profitable." He paused, picking up a paper from the table, as Merewether marveled at the phenomenon of a Sir George Barlow acting almost human, expressing the doubts of an ordinary man. "This dispatch came in this morning from the captain of *Surrey*, a new Indiaman."

Merewether pricked up his ears. The term was loosely used, it might mean a newly built ship on its maiden voyage, or it might mean one of the ships constructed after the defeat of the "Shipping Interest" in the Company a few years ago. The coffee and brandy had been effective; it had cleared his head enough that he could think again and recall what he had heard of that bitter struggle. The Shipping Interest was composed of those shareholders in the Company who owned the right to supply ships for the trade. This right was hereditary, passed from father to son, and constituted a most profitable monopoly until 1801, when outsiders were permitted to build and furnish vessels for the Company. Merewether himself had left *Dunvegan Castle* because of the lack of any future for him in the Company, but he owed his promotion to the enthusiastic recommendation of one of the leaders of the Shipping Interest, the owner of *Lord Exmouth*. He hoped he would not become involved in the dispute between the factions in the Court of Directors.

Sir George continued, "This report says *Surrey* and several other new Indiamen are held at Canton, cargo loaded, but are unable to obtain customs clearance—'Grand Chop' they call it— to sail. The official who issues it is the Hoppo, the head of the Chinese Customs Service. This fellow says none of the captains can see him, and the Select Committee says it cannot either." Sir George paused, tinkled the bell on the table. Locksley materialized through the door. "Coffee, please."

Merewether remembered Whampoa, the port for Canton, quite well, though it had been nearly ten years since he had been there. He had never been to Canton, not even ashore in the small allotment of the Company along the Pearl River. China was forbidden territory. The Select Committee, he had heard, was composed of old China hands, supercargoes who knew the language and customs. Its function was to serve as an agency between the Indiamen and the Hong merchants, arranging for a commission, the purchase and sale of goods and the payment of customs duties imposed by the Emperor. He could remember piping the side as a boatswain's mate in *Dunvegan Castle* when the Select Committee's chairman came aboard for dinner with the captain. If that powerful committee could not see the Hoppo, something certainly was amiss.

Sir George went on, "I suspect that the Shipping Interest has a hand in this. The last I heard, John Elphingham was chairman of the Select Committee at Canton, and his family owned the rights to two bottoms for the trade. It would be simple enough for a man in his position to use the Hong merchants to influence the Hoppo and prevent the issuance of Grand Chop."

"Quite possible, George," said Sir Thomas. "I am perfectly willing to go up there and see if I can get to the bottom of the affair. As you know, I have had a bit of experience in such matters."

"Precisely why I called upon you," agreed Sir George. "I knew of your diplomatic accomplishments in Portugal. I shall issue a commission to you as minister plenipotentiary in my behalf to deal with the Canton government. Merewether, I assume you can have your ship ready for sea in two days' time?"

"Yes, Your Excellency." Just then, the door was held open by Locksley and a servant brought in a tray containing a coffeepot and cups.

"Dictation, Locksley," growled Sir George over his cup. He dictated a commission to Sir Thomas, designating him as Envoy and Minister Plenipotentiary to the Government of Canton. "Have that engrossed on parchment, ready for my signature and seal," he told the secretary. "Now, orders to Captain Merewether." The Governor-General rattled off the stereotyped phrases as Locksley's pen raced across the paper. The order was sanded, signed, sealed, and delivered. Merewether signed the receipt, carefully folded the order, and placed it in his pocket. With the second cup of coffee, he was beginning to feel amost comfortable; the iron bands of pain around his head had relaxed into a mere nagging ache.

"By the bye, Merewether," said Sir Thomas, "I have a reception tonight for the Chief Minister of the Nizam of Hyderabad at my town house. I would be pleased if you and your officers could attend."

"Delighted, sir," murmured Merewether, unable to think of any excuses. This constant round of receptions and entertainments became abrasive after a while. The officers were under the necessity of having their full-dress uniforms sponged and pressed by a grasping cook's mate who expected his reward in rupees. "My officers will be performing duty in making the ship ready for sea, sir, but I shall attend."

Sir George looked at the small clock on the wall and stood up. Sir Thomas, the Commodore, and Merewether rose with him. "I shall see you gentlemen tonight," said Sir George in dismissal.

Back in *Rapid*, Merewether called his officers together and quickly acquainted them with the mission. He sent them out to obtain supplies, make preparations for the long voyage east, through the Straits, the crowded archipelagoes, to China. The word spread like wildfire through the ship; men who had carelessly diced away their pay an hour ago became tightfisted, debts were collected, and the liberty party sought goods thought to be in demand in China. These men were sophisticated; they had served as slavers in Africa, touched every port in the West Indies and Central America. But the magic word China was still one to conjure with, even as Cathay in the day of Marco Polo. Merewether took a light lunch, lay down and slept away the afternoon watch.

Feeling entirely recovered by the second dogwatch, Merewether bathed. He decided not to irritate the cheeks and chin lacerated by his hasty razor this morning, and dined in leisurely fashion. He sat under the vent enjoying the breeze diverted by the windsail on deck as his thoughts went back to Lord Laddie's party. God! What if the game the guests had played became known; some of the winners were married men, he was sure. The news might fly back to England, cause estrangements, possibly even bills of divorce. Still, he consoled himself, those officers would be discreet, even the losers would not spread the news, lest they be suspected as well. Uncomfortably, he realized that a story so scandalous as this would not be suppressed. Fortunately, he thought, he had no wife to account to.

Inevitably, the thought resurrected Flora Dean. He had put her out of his mind since three days ago and had concluded the affair was over. His miserable failure to declare himself was the end of what might have been a lifelong union. Yet he remembered her small straight nose, bright brown eyes, sweet clinging lips, and compact body. Most of all, he told himself, she had cared for a lonely bastard-born officer of the Bombay Marine. He shook off the thought. There was no use becoming maudlin; he had had his chance, and through some cross-grained impulse had rejected it. He rose, pulled on his uniform, and sent Sangh to have the boatswain's mate call away his gig.

Sir Thomas's house was blazing with light, carriages discharging their passengers at the door, servants in livery assisting them to alight. Merewether paused outside the light of the flambeaus and adjusted the hang of his sword and the angle of his cocked hat. He made sure all buttons were secure and started forward toward the door. He was checked by the sound of bugles and drew back as a squad of cavalry charged up the street, scattering the guests. Carriages and tongas pulled hastily out of the way. The horsemen were Indians decked out in green and gold frogged jackets. They wore white turbans, each displaying a jeweled device, and carried lances erect with ribbons flying. They reined to a halt before the door, wheeled at the salute, and a man of distinguished appearance rode up on a prancing gray charger, closely attended by two young officers wearing jeweled swords. Merewether realized he was witnessing the arrival of the guest of honor.

Sir Thomas, flanked by Sir George and all the members of the Council, was at the door. Merewether, hovering in the background with other curious guests, at last saw the Chief Minister and his bodyguards disappear inside. Circumspectly, he made his way in, escaped the majordomo, and found Commodore Land glumly lurking in a cloakroom.

"No spirits at this party, Merewether," he growled. "As if you needed any. The Minister is most devout, won't even enter where they are served."

Merewether grinned at the jibe. "I only want to report my presence to Sir Thomas and the Governor, sir. There's enough to do tomorrow without that." He peered out through the portieres at the entrance and watched the ceremonies continue for an interminable time. These influential Indian princes had to be treated with the utmost care lest they become offended at some unintentional slight and repay the insult with interest at some inconvenient juncture.

Finally, the affair tapered off, and Merewether saw Sir Thomas and Sir George make a withdrawal. He slid out the door, hurried to a point where he could make a casual interception, and bowed in greeting.

"Oh, hello, Merewether," said Sir Thomas. "Delighted you came. There's tea or coffee in the dining room." He moved briskly through a door to the left. Merewether turned to Sir George, and had opened his mouth to utter a respectful platitude when he was startled to hear this cold, hard man actually chortling with merriment.

Merewether had heard Sir George laugh dryly on at least two occasions, but chortling, almost doubled over with glee, was an aspect of the man he had never expected to witness. He stood there, mouth open, wondering if there might be a surgeon present who could treat or certify the Acting Governor-General, or at least get him out of sight, into privacy where he might be calmed.

The Governor-General straightened up, clapped Merewether on the back, and said in a low tone of voice, "You devil! Top winner at Lord Laddie's party and never a word! I was beginning to think you a bit of a prig, but still water runs deep!" He released his hand, clapped him again on the back, winked, chortled, and said, "Won with Lord Laddie's own cards, too." He turned abruptly and went through the door where Sir Thomas had disappeared.

Merewether felt like a fool. If Sir George had already heard the story, no doubt it was current throughout Calcutta. He fled back to the cloakroom and interviewed Commodore Land. "Certainly, I heard it at noon at the Officers' Club. The only thing unusual about it is that someone won first choice besides Lord Laddie." The tall man's black eyes sparkled. "I've been to three of his parties, and never held a winning card. Persians, Egyptians, or Malays, he always drew the prize. Something must have slipped."

Merewether stammered, "But the story—is it widely known?"

"Certainly, everyone knew what would happen. The only secret was the nationality of the girls and who won besides Lord Laddie. You're famous for a day, Merewether." The Commodore laughed at the red, embarrassed expression on Merewether's face. "Don't worry, there'll be a new scandal by tomorrow. By the time you're back from China, all will be forgotten. Now, I think I'll go on. I've a game of whist waiting." The Commodore put his hat under his arm and moved unobtrusively toward the door, skirting the group about the guest of honor.

Merewether hesitated only a minute. He had made his presence known to the host and Sir George, and felt no obligation to stay longer. He put his hat under his arm and, emulating the Commodore, flicked his glance at the glittering press paying homage to the guest. As he turned, he came face to face with Flora Dean on the arm of Ensign St. John.

Flustered, Merewether made a clumsy attempt to bow, and found himself cut dead by Flora. She threw her chin in the air, wheeled St. John hard left, and took departure toward the center of activity. He heard only a single word drift back over her rigid shoulders.

"Rake!"

CHAPTER 28

About the middle of the forenoon watch, Sangh came into the cabin, salaamed, and said, "Sahib, the servant and secretary to Sir Thomas Jeffrey are on board to make his quarters ready and stow his luggage." Good Lord, thought Merewether, a day ahead of time, and he had not given the matter a thought.

"Ask Mr. MacRae and Mr. Davis to come in."

When they arrived, he was blunt. "I am sorry to inconvenience you, MacRae, but I'll have to ask you to give up your room. Mr. Davis, see what quarters you can manage for the secretary and servant."

"Aye aye, sir," they responded, almost in unison. Merewether gloomily concluded he would have to provide mess facilities for Sir Thomas during the voyage in his own cabin. He was glad he had had the foresight to lay in a fresh supply of luxuries since his return from Vellore. The supercargo's cabin was certainly adequate even for a knight and member of the Council, but Merewether wondered if he possessed sufficient abilities as host for a distinguished diplomat and man of the world during a long, tedious voyage. He wished young Burcham with his education and fund of bright small talk had survived to share the responsibility of entertaining the envoy.

Sir Thomas came aboard at noon the next day, accompanied by his wife, a plump, cheerful woman, his daughter, a young lady of sixteen, several friends, Commodore Land, and Sir George Barlow. Seeing the approaching boatload of distinguished guests, Merewether shouted for Sangh and Davis and gave urgent directions for refreshments. He had Larkin man the side, and Gunny form up the Marines as an honor guard. Larkin swiftly rigged an armchair on a tackle and prepared to lift the ladies over the side in style. The signal quartermaster stood by with the Governor-General's flag to be broken at the main when Sir George reached the deck. Belting on his sword, Merewether hastened to the gangway and took his place.

Sir George nimbly climbed the ladder, the pipes squealed, side boys at salute, as the Marines presented arms. Sir Thomas and the Commodore followed, then the ladies, squeaking genteelly, were hoisted up in the chair and deposited on deck. Merewether escorted the group aft to his cabin, found the table decked with bottles, relishes, pickles, and fruit. Sangh was poised at its head in a white apron and fresh turban.

"Ha!" ejaculated Sir George, "Served by a pirate!" He laughed in his usual mirthless fashion, as Sangh salaamed, his sad little face impassive. The affair was brief and pleasant, a drink around; MacRae, Larkin, Dobbs, and Buttram presented to Sir Thomas and his family. It broke up with the echo of the Boatswain's hail.

"Make all preparations for getting under way."

The party reembarked, and the Governor-General's flag was hauled down as he swung into the boat. Larkin dismissed the honor guards and the boatswain's mate passed the word, "All hands, all hands, make sail!" The crew turned from ceremonials to hard work; the windlass clanked around, spanker and jib were hoisted, ready to be sheeted home.

MacRae shouted from the forecastle, "Anchor's breaking ground, anchor's aweigh!"

"Starboard helm," called Merewether. "Sheet home," he told the afterguard, echoed forward by MacRae. "Topsails, hands to the braces," *Rapid* caught the breeze and began to move on the starboard tack downstream. "Midships; meet her; steady as you go." He looked at the trim of the sails closely, then turned to Larkin and told him, "You have the watch, Mr. Larkin." The launch, fully manned, was towing alongside, ready to spring into action and tow the ship if necessary; as the ebb began to flow, *Rapid* moved swiftly downstream.

Merewether turned aside and found Sir Thomas standing quietly by, watching the scene. "Brings back old times, Captain," said Sir Thomas. "I was a midshipman, '82 and '83. When the French and American Wars ended, I resigned and went back to Oxford. I've often wished I'd followed a naval career. Might be an admiral by now." He smiled and moved out of the way as Larkin shouted orders preparatory to rounding the next point. Merewether felt a sudden warmth for this man; at least he had experience as an officer in the Navy and should not be unreasonable in his demands.

"Sir, I always remain on deck with the pilot while we are in the Hooghly, but you are welcome to use my cabin and have Sangh serve you lunch, anything you want. I usually have him bring a tray on deck."

"Quite all right, Captain, and I'll join you in a bit of lunch if you don't mind."

At the end of the dogwatch the next day, *Rapid* dropped the pilot off the Sandheads and took departure southeast for the Straits. MacRae came in to report the new course. "Wait a minute," he told him. He was now on detached foreign service, Merewether thought, and as captain he had the power to enlist, rate, or disrate any person in the crew, without reference to Bombay Castle, "Messenger, send in Sangh and Mr. Davis." In a moment, both entered. "Hold up your hand, Sangh," he told him. He administered the oath of allegiance. "Now, Mr. Davis, enter Sangh on your books as enlisted in the Bombay Marine." He turned to MacRae, "And enter in the log that Sangh has been rated Steward this date." He picked up a small bag of rupees from his desk and put it in Sangh's hands. "The King's shilling, so to speak, Sangh. I'm most grateful for your services." The little Hindu's sad face became even sadder, a tear rolled down his cheek.

"Thank you, sahib." He salaamed and made his withdrawal. *Rapid*, with the wind almost abeam, plunged over the swells of the Bay of Bengal toward the Straits of Malacca, as night fell.

They made their landfall on Sumatra, steered southeast through the Straits, then encountered a succession of storms, squalls, dead calms, and baffling winds. Merewether had hoped to sail northeastwardly through the South China Sea—taking the short course to Canton. He consulted with MacRae and Sir Thomas.

"Sir," he told him. "I think we must sail east, north of Java, and hope to make our way north through Makassar Strait. It's a longer way around, but with conditions so unsettled here, we may waste a month beating back and forth."

"Very well, Captain, I agree," said Sir Thomas, looking at the chart. Sir Thomas had been so far a most considerate guest, understanding and pleasant, full of droll stories and anecdotes to liven the meals he took in Merewether's cabin.

Rapid headed east, often in sight of the coast of Java, the light, variable airs making progress slow. Three days later, just after dawn, the masthead hailed.

"Sail ho! Two points on port bow."

Merewether hurried on deck, took a glass forward, and climbed to the foremast crosstrees. He steadied the glass, picked out the sail, and studied it. Here he might expect to sight Company, Royal Navy, and American ships, or, less likely, Dutch, French, or Spanish vessels. There were numerous smaller native craft about, but this sail belonged to none of them. He shouted down, altered course a point north, found the sail again in the glass and realized it was a Chinese junk of considerable size. On his new course, he should intercept it within the hour. He descended to the deck.

"Tell the cook to serve breakfast to the crew as soon as possible," he told Dobbs. MacRae was already on deck; with the bearing and apparent speed of the junk in hand, he offered a slight amendment to *Rapid*'s course for interception. Sir Thomas came up and joined the group.

"Sail ho!" came the hail again from the masthead. "Astern the first one on same course." This offered some interesting possibilities. These junks were a long way from China, but it was by no means unheard of for them to make such voyages. The Chinese had traded with the Dutch and Spanish in these islands for centuries, exchanging their wares for the produce of the islands. On their present course, the junks must be bound for Java, still under control of the Dutch. Whatever their nationality and cargo, they merited investigation, Merewether decided.

The mess cooks passed the word for breakfast. The sails were now visible to the naked eye from the deck. Half an hour later, Merewether told Dobbs, "Send the crew to quarters." He altered course a point north so as not to headreach.

"Hoist our colors," he told the Quartermaster. The red-and-white striped flag soared up, streamed out in the breeze. "Signals: Merchant convention, 'heave to.'" There was, of course, no assurance that the junks could read or understand the signals, but Merewether felt more comfortable in case of an inquiry with the signal duly recorded in the log.

The leading junk was now little more than a mile on the port bow, plowing sedately along, its two huge, many-sparred sails close-hauled. It made no sign of obedience to *Rapid*'s signal.

"Dip our colors and the flag hoist," called Merewether to the signal quartermaster. This sometimes added emphasis to a signal, but there was still no reaction. Through the glass, he could see a group on the poop of the junk close to her tiller, looking at *Rapid*. He could also see she carried at least four guns a side on deck, but they did not appear to be manned. The junk displayed no colors, not even a house flag. He came to a decision: the presence of such vessels in these waters under war conditions justified an investigation, even though they appeared to be Chinese. Quite likely, they carried contraband—supplies for the Dutch still in control of Java.

"Mr. Larkin, put a shot across her bow."

"Aye aye, sir." Larkin hurried forward, trained the pivot gun out to port, took his aim, locked, and fired. The splash arose two cable lengths ahead and caused an immediate flurry in the group on the junk's poop. A flag was hoisted, red and gold, with what appeared to be a dragon device emblazoned on it. These must be the colors of some local prince, Merewether decided, as he steered to close the junk.

"Another shot!" he called. "Close to her." The high-pitched, spiteful report of the long nine sounded again. The splash arose three hundred feet ahead of the junk, and she reluctantly rounded to, dropped the big clumsy sails, and lay wallowing in the trough of the sea. *Rapid* ran down, spun up into the wind, and hove to a cable's length to starboard. MacRae was already hoisting out the launch, and Gunny had his Marines formed up across the waist. Larkin had run out the starboard battery.

"I'll take the boarding party," decided Merewether. "You come too," he told Dobbs. "Would you care to accompany me, sir?" he asked Sir Thomas. "There might be a diplomatic matter here."

"Yes, I think I shall," responded Sir Thomas. The Marine detachment and boarding party were already in the launch as Merewether and Sir Thomas embarked.

The launch came alongside the junk and hooked on as a Chinese seaman reluctantly dropped a ladder. Alongside, Merewether could see that the junk was quite large; it must be three hundred tons burden at least. Gunny was up the side in a flash, followed by his men. By the time Merewether and Sir Thomas reached the deck, he had his Marines formed in two parties, commanding poop and forecastle.

A Chinese dressed in nondescript blue clothing met Merewether at the gangway. He spoke English in a sibilant accent, mutilating his consonants, "Sah, I am Ho Wong, supercargo of this ship, representing its owner, Lee Chin Chiang, the Mandarin of Canton. This is most unfriendly act. My master will be angry at the Company and its Marine." Merewether paused. It was a serious matter if this vessel was owned by a mandarin, particularly one at Canton, but that fact could not excuse the carrying of contraband to the enemy, and it was his duty to ascertain the junk's cargo.

"I regret any inconvenience," Merewether told Wong. "But I am Captain Percival Merewether of the Honourable Company's

Naval Service, the Bombay Marine. Why did you not heave to when I signaled?"

"I thought you had no right to stop me," replied the Chinese defiantly. "I still think you have no right."

"What is your cargo?" demanded Merewether, conscious of Sir Thomas at his elbow.

"General—mixed supplies, grain."

"May I see your manifest," persisted Merewether. If it was in Chinese, he would be no wiser, but since he guessed the cargo was intended for Java, it might well be in Dutch, and there was a Dutch sailmaker's mate in his crew. The Chinese still hesitated, finally walked off a dozen steps, then turned and came back.

"No use to try to hide it," he said. "We have among our cargo four tons of powder for the Governor of Java." He looked defiantly at them with his black eyes under the slanted lids. "We are at peace with the British and Dutch and you have no right to stop us."

Merewether glanced around at Sir Thomas, caught his eye, and walked forward, leaving the supercargo out of earshot. "Sir, he's partly right, but orders to the Royal Navy and Marine are explicit. 'Seize any ship carrying arms or contraband to the enemy, French or Dutch.' It's a matter for a prize court, but this mandarin, Lee Chin Chiang, at Canton, may be influential. If I take his junks as prizes, your mission might very well fail, sir."

"You are entirely within your rights, Captain, and fully covered by standing orders to take these prizes." Sir Thomas looked forward, Merewether following his gaze, and saw the second junk plowing placidly toward them, three miles away. "I shouldn't doubt from the size and cargo that you have a good many thousand pounds of prize money at stake. It's your decision, of course."

Merewether thought of the thousands of pounds, no other ship in sight . . . an opportunity to retire to a life of leisure, even go back to England . . . buy a manor and set himself up as a country gentleman. Or, he might form the partnership that MacLellan had mentioned months ago; with his experience and ability, he could manufacture arms of real quality in India and make a for-

tune supplying the Company, the friendly princes, even His
Majesty's forces. Flora Dean crossed his mind; she was bitterly
hurt by his conduct and his unintentional notoriety, but surely he
could convince her that he loved her, and would forsake such
ways, and had not intended the hurt to her. All he had to do was
issue a simple order, a single sentence would suffice, and he would
be rich, independent, a man of means. God! These decisions
came hard. He saw Sir Thomas looking at him impassively, with a
sort of concern in his gaze, almost as Gunny had looked at him in
the fort near Sadras as his wounded arm swelled with blood poisoning. He was in command, no one could make the decision for
him, but the loneliness in which his responsibilities placed him
was frightening.

"I shall release the junks," he found himself telling Sir Thomas. "Your mission to Canton is far more important to the Company and Sir George than prize money."

Once the decision was made, things went easier. The Chinese
supercargo signaled the other junk in after Merewether told him
briefly, "I shall let your vessels go, but you must jettison the
powder, and I want you and the supercargo of the other junk to
accompany me to Canton. I may need your evidence in this
matter."

Ho Wong folded his hands, bowed jerkily. "I shall be honored
to be your guest to Canton. May I give my orders to the master?"
After the powder was jettisoned, the launch picked up the supercargo from the second junk, reembarked the Marines from the
first, and carried Merewether and Sir Thomas back to *Rapid*.
"Make sail," Merewether told MacRae as he plunged below to his
cabin. He was writing his report when Sir Thomas rapped lightly
on the door and came in.

"Your decision was correct, Captain, and I shall say so in my
report. Hard lines to have to give up such prizes, though." He sat
in the armchair under the vent, waiting for Sangh to serve lunch
while Merewether finished his report and locked it away in the
strongbox.

"Can't be helped," said Merewether. "The Prize Court might
even decide the case against me if that mandarin complained to
the Company. All too often, it depends on who owns the ship
carrying the contraband." He was grateful for the courteous inter-

est of Sir Thomas and his willingness to let Merewether make the decision, though his own mission might be adversely affected. Sangh came in with his trays.

An hour later MacRae knocked and came in. "Sir, the barometer has dropped to twenty-nine twenty. Thunderheads are building up in the west, and the wind has pulled a little north of west. We're in for a blow, can't tell how bad."

"I'll come," said Merewether wearily. On deck, the sun was merely a bright spot in a leaden sky. The black thunderheads to the west towered into the sky, flashes of lightning passing through their folds. The wind was fluky, almost northwest, and the heat was stifling. Here in the shallow sea between Borneo and Java, a local storm could whip up waves of frightening proportions in short order. Merewether gauged the distance and intensity of the storm. "Reduce sail to jib, topsails and spanker with double reefs," he decided. There was no use being caught carrying too much sail in a squall that might last only five minutes, yet leave him dismasted. "Post double lookouts, this sea is dotted with islands."

"Aye aye, sir," said MacRae, turning to give the orders. Sails were clewed up and furled; when the howling squall struck a quarter hour later, *Rapid* staggered under the blow, but nothing carried away.

The unsettled weather persisted all night, with thunder and lightning, one squall after another out of the west, each sending the ship reeling eastward. Twice, the lookouts shouted frantic warnings as palm-topped islands loomed ahead in flashes of lightning and were avoided. During the midwatch as Merewether clung to the weather bulwark, a bolt of lightning struck the foremast, leaped down the lightning rod, and disappeared into the deck. The watch reported no injuries. By four bells of the forenoon watch, the squalls had disappeared eastward and a hazy sun had emerged. But the seas were still mountainous; *Rapid* groaned and creaked in every joint as she rolled and pitched, taking water over the bow. For the first time during his command, Merewether heard the pumps clanking continuously. This was no typhoon, merely a local series of squalls and storms, but in the crowded, shallow waters of the Java Sea it was not to be taken lightly.

At noon, MacRae was able to get a sight and compute the

latitude with some hope of accuracy. Longitude was a matter of guesswork after twenty-four hours of staggering blindly east.

"My reckoning puts us one hundred twenty-three degrees, twenty minutes east," he told Merewether anxiously. "I might be fifty miles off, at that. We are far past Makassar Strait and will have to go north through the Molucca and Celebes seas."

"Very well," Merewether told him. "Wait for star sights tonight, it will be soon enough to change course in the morning."

CHAPTER 29

Four days later, *Rapid* had Pulau Talisei, the northeast extremity of the Celebes, in sight on the port beam as she sailed from the Molucca Passage into the Celebes Sea, a brisk south wind giving her nine knots under all plain sail. The ship sailed now through sparkling seas, flying fish shoaling off in iridescent flights ahead, a giant ray, disturbed in his siesta on the surface off the starboard bow, making a thunderous report as he dived.

Just after dawn, Merewether came on deck. He looked through the glass briefly at Pulau Talisei, identified the bold cliff facing eastward out to sea, and joined MacRae in the cubbyhole. He watched him plot the ship's position, calculate the north northwest course that would take them to Basilan Strait into the Sulu Sea. There were no navigational hazards until they made a landfall on Basilan Island, a relief after the nightmare journey through the Java and Molucca seas.

He came out on deck just in time to hear the lookout report "Sail ho!" from the masthead.

"Where away?" cried Larkin.

"Broad on the port beam, right north of the island." There was a pause and then a shout, "She's firing rockets, sir!"

This brought Merewether up with a start. No one fired rockets without reason, distress, enemy in sight, or an urgent message.

"What's her course?"

"About east, sir. She looks like a snow."

Merewether was not concerned at this report. If she were a

snow, the odds were she was British. He knew of several such ships trading for the Company in these islands.

To Larkin, he said, "Come west and run down to her."

"Hands to the braces," shouted Larkin. "Wear ship." *Rapid* came smartly around, lay over on the port tack. "Set the flying jib." The snow was soon in sight from the deck.

"She's flying the red ensign, sir," reported Larkin.

"Signals," he called, glass to eye. " 'Require immediate assistance.' " Merewether picked up his glass, focused it, swept the horizon, and came back slowly. He could see nothing else in sight. The snow itself appeared to be in no distress, and seemed to be sailing toward *Rapid* in normal fashion.

"Good morning, Captain." Merewether turned and found Sir Thomas at his elbow.

"Good morning, sir. That fellow over there seems to be excited. He's been firing rockets; now he signals for immediate assistance. There's nothing in sight from here, no sign of fire, and she appears to be sailing normally. I regret the delay, sir, but I have to see what he wants."

"Quite right, Captain, I'm interested too."

The last cast of the log had shown eight knots. *Rapid* should be within hailing distance in less than an hour.

"Tell the cook to serve breakfast to the hands as soon as possible," Merewether told Larkin.

"Aye aye, sir," It was an age-old axiom of the sea that sailors fought or worked better on full stomachs.

By the time the crew was fed and Merewether and Sir Thomas had finished the trays brought up by Sangh, the snow was less than a mile distant. Now *Rapid* saw her heave to, hoist out a boat, and round to a cable's length away. The boat came dancing across the swells, pulled by four lascar seamen, the coxswain steering with an oar in the stern, beside him an enormously fat European. The boat pulled into the lee of *Rapid* and a hand caught the painter, as the oarsmen fended off. The fat man in the stern managed to reach the ladder and pull himself up to where hands could reach to help him over the side. Merewether met him at the gangway.

"Welcome aboard. I am Captain Merewether of the Bombay

Marine, commanding the Honourable Company's sloop *Rapid*. May I be of assistance?"

"Baynes, Captain, Resident at Amboyna. We have been attacked by pirates."

"Come to my cabin, Mr. Baynes. I would like Sir Thomas Jeffrey to hear your story as well." He led the man aft, caught Sir Thomas's eye, and made the presentation. They entered the cabin. "Be seated, gentlemen. Tea or coffee?"

"Tea, please, been so upset since last night, I did not have breakfast." The Resident looked a bit injured.

"Captain, we've had trouble out here for years with pirate raids, usually a quick landing, a few women abducted, storehouses robbed, perhaps a man or two killed, or a few houses burned. Never had more than two or three proas at a time, maybe as many as two hundred Magindanao pirates from the Philippines; the Company garrison would come out and drive them off. Three months ago a Bombay Marine cruiser caught three proas just after they raided Amoorang. Sank two of them, the third got away. It must have caused their chiefs to decide on revenge . . ."

The door opened and Sangh came in balancing his tray as *Rapid* rolled in the long swell. He swiftly served Mr. Baynes with toasted biscuit, jam, a cup of tea; tea for Sir Thomas and Merewether.

"Most appreciative, Captain," said Baynes, munching toasted biscuit. "Get upset when I forget to eat." Merewether and Sir Thomas waited courteously, sipped their tea, while Baynes finished. Baynes sat back, looking refreshed and happier.

"As I was saying, they must have decided on revenge. I was on an inspection tour. Usually travel in *Felicity* over there when she picks up cargo along the islands. We reached Amoorang late yesterday afternoon and found it overrun. Counted forty-one proas in the inner harbor and the town in flames. Must be two thousand pirates there. The Company compounds, fort, factory, and granaries seemed to be still in our hands, at least the flag was flying, but there are only two hundred Sepoys in the garrison, not much they can do." He paused, drank his second cup of tea, and declined more from the hovering Sangh. He continued, "Nothing we could do with two six pounders, so I headed out to try to find

Commodore John Hayes, he's supposed to have a squadron somewhere east of the Celebes, three ships. Lucky I found you so soon."

"I've not been in these waters before," said Merewether. "Tell me about these pirates, their ships and arms."

The Resident leaned his great bulk back and said, "They usually come from the north, Mindanao in the Philippines, I guess. The men are excellent fighters, usually armed with short swords, some muskets. The proas are over fifty feet long each, sails woven from fiber, able also to be rowed or paddled, and carry sixty to eighty men each. Most of them have a brass gun mounted in the bow, eight pounders, I'm told. Some also have small swivel guns, one pounders, along the sides, to fire small shot. Deadly at short range."

"And you counted forty of these vessels?" demanded Sir Thomas.

"No, sir. Forty-one," replied Baynes. "Most of them were pulled up on the beach, but at least ten were outside, fully manned, as a guard."

Merewether reached for the chart and located Amoorang less than sixty miles west southwest of *Rapid*'s present position. He pointed it out to Sir Thomas and said, "We can reach Amoorang by two bells in the afternoon watch. I should like your consent to turn aside from our mission." This was stating the matter politely. Merewether bore the full responsibility for the voyage and had the final word as to the employment of the ship; but since the ultimate mission was Sir Thomas's, it was proper to consult him.

"Go to it, Captain! I told you I was a frustrated admiral. I wouldn't miss it for a thousand guineas."

"Thank you, sir. Mr. Baynes, I suggest you remain aboard *Rapid* and send your ship on to try to find the squadron. We can at least interrupt the pirates." He pulled paper and pen from his desk, uncorked the bottle of ink, and continued, "You may write your orders and send them back with your coxswain."

"Quite, Captain." Baynes scribbled off a note. "I'll go to the gangway and give it to the coxswain." All three went out on deck. In five minutes, *Rapid* was again on the port tack heading west southwest, all sail set. The snow was out of sight in an hour.

Merewether had studied the chart and he and MacRae had cross-examined Baynes as to conditions, without much success. Baynes insisted he was no seaman and knew little of the naviga· tional hazards off the port.

"Mr. Dobbs," called Merewether. "I want boarding nets rigged. See that they are well secured, extend outward, and are loose enough to tangle a man. Harder to cut."

"Aye aye, sir." Dobbs hurried forward and soon had the hands stretching hammock nettings above the bulwarks, slanted outward on short spars.

"Don't mind how they look, leave them loose," directed Merewether. This was not for an inspection but to keep these Moro pirates from swarming on deck. He saw the Gunner and called him over. "You have an allowance of grenades?" he asked.

"Yes, sir, the cases have never been opened since we left Blackwall."

"Open them and test a few."

"Aye aye, sir." The Gunner hurried below to the magazine, soon emerging on deck with two of the oilskin-wrapped packages. He lit a length of slow match, came aft, and ripped the waterproof covering to expose the fuze. At the rail, he gingerly touched the glowing match to the fuze, watched it sputter, then eject a solid train of sparks, and threw the grenade high and far to leeward. Just as it appeared to touch the water, a white ball of smoke blossomed and the flat sound of the explosion came back across the water.

"Good," said Merewether. "No need to test another. Have a supply ready for the Marine detachment." The Gunner hurried forward as Merewether called Dobbs again. "Oh, Dobbs, make sure the windows and ports to the cabins are protected, too." With numerous small, handy proas, a boarding party might find its way in from below undetected.

"Aye aye, sir," said the harassed Dobbs, turning to shout another order.

Merewether took stock of the situation. His gun crews knew their business, and the Marines were superbly trained. They would man the tops and their deck stations under the command of Gunny and the two naiques with little supervision from him. He saw the gunner's mates laying out pistols on the hatch midships for loading and sending cutlasses to the racks at the base of each mast. Pikes were stacked along each battery, vicious weapons to reach out with and skewer a man trying to surmount the nettings. He felt *Rapid* and her crew would soon be ready, and went below.

In his cabin, he found Sir Thomas and Mr. Baynes chatting amiably, oblivious of the stir through the ship as she made ready for action against formidable odds. He called Sangh and requested an early lunch. His sword was laid out ready, and the two double-barreled pistols he had taken from Abercrombie and used at Vellore were on his desk, freshly loaded. He sat down and felt the tension and excitement mount in spite of himself. He decided a single gin and lemon would be medicinal and called Sangh again. Sir Thomas and Baynes joined him in a toast and sat down to a light meal.

Back on deck, Merewether watched the coast, saw the hills loom up in the background and feathery palms appear shimmering along the water's edge. There was a reef extending almost two miles offshore, apparent from the masthead by the discoloration of the water, then dropping off abruptly. A low, thickly wooded island came into view which appeared to be surrounded by reefs.

"The entrance is just beyond the island, Pulau Tetapaan, I think they call it," said Baynes. "A reef extends out from it a long ways, but the passage is west of it, I'm told." Merewether silently cursed: the resident possessed just enough local information to be confusing.

"Reduce sail, Mr. MacRae, topsails, jib, and spanker. Leadsmen in the chains." The ship's speed diminished; as he cleared the island, he could see the discoloration of the reef extending westward beyond it in the water. Merewether heard the leadsman report no bottom. He still could not make out the entrance to the bay, but he could now see a column of smoke inland that must mark the location of the village of Amoorang.

"Send the hands to quarters," he told MacRae. "Mr. Larkin, I am told these vessels are about fifty feet long, carry eight pounders in the bow and also small pivots. I suggest you use grape and cannister at close range, round shot when you think it advisable, but make every shot count. These proas carry sixty to eighty men each; if they ever get alongside and board, we are lost." He broke off, as he saw what appeared to be a break in the reef ahead with a prominent cape coming into view to the southwest. This must be Tandjung Mobonga marked on the sketchy chart as the landmark for the channel. He turned to MacRae again and said, "I am taking station at the foremast crosstrees and will have the conn from there. I want your two best quartermasters, one at the foremast and one aft to relay my orders to the helm."

"Aye aye, sir," said MacRae, watching the hands man their battle stations in a disciplined bustle. The jackets came off the guns and were stowed out of the way. Cartridges were brought up from the magazine, locks tested, a few flints replaced, and sand spread on deck to give purchase to the horny feet of the gun crews. Hands were swaying at the wash-deck pumps, filling an endless row of buckets with water, and a gunner's mate was passing down each battery lighting the lengths of slow match that would smolder in tubs ready for use if a lock failed to fire a gun.

As Merewether went forward, he passed Larkin, his pale blue eyes glittering, long blond hair flying in the breeze, pausing at every gun, emphasizing his instructions to the captains with fist driven into palm. Just abaft the mainmast, Merewether came face to face with Ho Wong and his counterpart from the second junk, Lee Fong. They had been aboard nearly two weeks, completely forgotten.

"You had best go below," Merewether told them. "We are going into action."

Ho Wong folded his hands, executed a jerky little bow, and said with his perpetual smile, "Sir, we wish to see how you fight."

Merewether laughed. "You are welcome to take your chances on deck," he said, "but stay out of the way!" He hurried on forward, and climbed to the crosstrees.

From this vantage point he could see the reef clearly, see where it broke off into deep water, which must be the channel. He shouted down his orders and heard them echoed aft by the quartermasters. The ship came to the wind, went about, and settled on the starboard tack with Tandjung Mobonga a point on the starboard bow. The channel appeared to be clear ahead leading toward the inner bay where the column of smoke arose.

Merewether put the glass to his eye and could now see a fort, compound, and other buildings beyond the village. Over the fort flew the British ensign, evidence that it had not fallen, though most of the village appeared to have been burned and was in ruins. He swept the glass forward, picked up a mass of vessels moored along the shore, and then saw the flotilla coming out of the inner bay, matting sails already hoisted. He tried to count and finally decided there were twenty-two proas under way moving toward him, possibly three miles distant.

He looked carefully about again. Once past the reef and into the bay, there appeared to be deep water ahead and to port. In the bay, with the cape and hills to the west and southwest, the breeze was variable, but it was now almost out of the west. It would be foolhardy to sail headlong into such a fleet, small as the individual units might be; only by utilizing *Rapid*'s sailing qualities to the utmost could he hope to stay clear of these massed warriors and destroy them. If one or more of them made contact with the ship, he could be overwhelmed. He made his decision.

"Hands to the braces!" he shouted down, heard the command relayed aft. "Come left two points, steer south southeast." He watched closely as the yards were braced around and the ship swung, then steadied on its new course. There appeared to be no coral heads or reefs ahead. It was comforting to hear the leadsman's cry of no bottom.

On the new course, settled on the starboard tack, Merewether put the glass to his eye again to observe the pirate flotilla. He saw it alter course to the east to meet him, dividing into two columns, one on either bow, hoping to make contact and give their wild fighting men a chance to get on *Rapid*'s deck. If he could lure them far enough to the eastward, to leeward, and leave himself enough sea room to the west, he might be able to deal with the fleet.

Just below him on the forecastle, Merewether saw the yellow flash of Larkin's hair at the forward pivot gun. He called down, "You may fire at will, Mr. Larkin." He was acknowledged with an upward glance and wave as Larkin called the crew to attention and trained the gun around to bear on the starboard column. He waited for what seemed an eternity as the proas and *Rapid* closed, then bent down, set the sight, took his aim and pulled the lanyard. The spiteful report blasted out. Merewether strained his eyes to observe the fall of shot, then saw the leading proa in the starboard column lose its masts, tip over sideways and lie swamped, a shattered wreck, men scrambling for refuge on floating timbers.

"Beautiful!" he shouted down to the gun crew as it sponged out and reloaded. It had been a remarkable hit at nearly three quarters of a mile, but it had no apparent effect on the other proas resolutely pressing on now, converging on either bow of the ship.

Merewether looked carefully to starboard and ahead. He could see no sign of reefs or coral heads, and the variable wind diverted by the cape and hills still appeared to be a little north of west. He heard the long nine fire again, could not see the fall of shot, and decided it was time to test his tactics.

"Hands to the braces!" he called down, hearing the command echoed aft by MacRae. He held on, watching the leading proa less than a quarter mile dead ahead, then saw smoke burst from her bow and heard the charge of musket balls and scrap tear through the rigging below him before he heard the flat report. The shot was echoed from the leading proa on the port bow; from further away, the charges fell short.

"Port your helm, steer south southwest!" *Rapid* swung to starboard, yards were braced up, sheets hauled in, and she clawed her way to windward. If the ship were taken aback now, her fate would be sealed. The inconstant breeze held for a moment, a moment more, and *Rapid* was to windward of both columns of pirates.

"Port battery stand by! Fire as your guns bear!" Merewether was conscious that several of the proas had fired, but straining his eyes for reefs and coral heads, watching the trembling luff of the close-hauled jib below him, he had no time to notice their effect. He heard Larkin's commands to the guns, heard the battery open up in single fire, the massive roars of the carronades punctuating the high-pitched reports of the nine pounders. Here, two hundred yards to windward of the pirate fleet, only one column could return his fire; the leeward column was blocked by the proas in its line of fire.

Rapid swept down the line as the proas turned into the wind, dead foul for them, pulling sweeps, paddles flashing, trying desperately to reach her. The nine pounders maintained almost continuous rolling gunfire at point-blank range, with Larkin moving forward and aft along the battery to point out the targets for the gun captains. A four-inch iron ball smashing from bow to stern through such a small vessel was usually sufficient to finish it; those that survived were raked with a charge of grape from a carronade. The pirates were courageous. They did not flinch as they saw *Rapid* bear down upon them. The brass guns in their bows were fired with defiance, charges of musket balls, and even round stones howled across the deck or thudded into the sides.

Rapid passed the last proa in the column which had now merged into one ragged line. It was high time to go about, Merewether decided, seeing another group of vessels under way from the beach ahead. The ruined village was now visible to the naked eye, nearly every house burned. He called down the command to wear ship, reverse course on the port tack, and try to destroy the survivors of his first passage. He took time to look about; nine of the proas were complete wrecks, smashed and sinking, drifting northeastwardly toward the reef. The others, under sail, sweeps and paddles, were still making every effort to close on *Rapid*.

Merewether laid a course almost due north, maintaining the weather gauge on the pirate fleet, but close enough to give the guns the opportunity to hit with every shot. He was walking a tightrope, between the wind and the enemy. If he miscalculated, were taken aback, lost a spar, he could be boarded by an irresistible horde of warriors and overwhelmed.

"Starboard battery, stand by," he called down. "Fire as your guns bear." The long nine pivots cracked out almost immediately, hit solidly. The broadside guns began to fire sporadically as gun captains found targets, now much wider spaced than on the first passage. Grape from the twenty-four pounder carronades tore two proas to bits. Merewether felt the battle was half won, and with deep water ahead, the reef still well to starboard, he was tempted to descend to the deck.

Where the proa came from, he never knew. It seemed to materialize dead ahead, with sweeps flashing, driving headlong into

Rapid's bow. Its brass gun belched fire and smoke, the charge tore through the forward bulwarks showering the crew of the pivot with splinters. There was no time to maneuver; collision was inevitable. Merewether clutched the shrouds, conscious of the lingering weakness of his left arm. He felt the shock and hoped desperately that *Rapid* would lose no spars.

The ship stopped dead in the water, every back stay strained to the breaking point, masts and rigging groaning. Men tumbled from their stations along the deck and the sails spilled their wind. Below him, he could see the proa, shattered but still afloat, against the starboard bow, men scrambling up lines they somehow had managed to attach to *Rapid*. They came pouring over the bulwarks in spite of the boarding nets, fanning out on the forecastle, heading aft, waving short, gleaming swords and screaming.

Somewhere below him, he heard the voice of Dobbs roar out, "Repel boarders!" and heard the command echoed all along the deck. The crew of the pivot gun was ringed around the mount, leveled pikes diverting the boarders as they raced toward the waist. Merewether heard the pop-pop-pop of pistols as he twisted about, seeking the back stay to slide down and join the fight.

The roar of the volley cut through the lesser tumult, swept the forecastle clear. A single Moro, left standing, made a desperate dive at Jemadar Gunny with his sword. He was spitted on a pike, and fell pouring blood across the deck. The file of Marines methodically poured in powder charges, spit balls into the muzzles of their muskets, rammed them home, primed the locks, and stood at the ready awaiting the next command.

Jackson, the boatswain's mate, was swinging an axe, chopping grappling irons loose from the bulwarks. As he struck the last time, the proa began to drift aft along the starboard side, a handful of shock-headed pirates still shouting defiance from its deck. Two Marines were tossing grenades to its deck. As Merewether reached the quarterdeck, he saw the immediate danger was over. MacRae had altered course to starboard and gotten way upon the ship again; she was now under control. Sir Thomas was leaning over the starboard side, firing one pistol after another at the few men remaining on the deck of the wrecked proa, his secretary standing behind him keeping the set of dueling pistols loaded for his use.

Merewether forced himself to observe the situation. He was much too close to the reefs to the northeast. The survivors of his second passage of the pirate fleet were a quarter mile astern by now, but the group of proas from the beach was rapidly approaching in a ragged formation to join forces with them and renew the fight. He must beat back against the wind to the westward, get the weather gauge again, and do his utmost to destroy the balance of the fleet. He saw the Carpenter knuckling his forelock, seeking his attention.

"We have two planks stove in below the waterline, right at the stem, sir. I've spiked timbers across, stuffed bedding in behind, but we're still taking water. The pumps should hold it, sir."

"Very well." The possibility that the ship might sink beneath him could wait. Merewether looked at the weather vane, then at the fleet massing again to the south. "Stand by to go about," he told MacRae. "Course as near southwest as she'll lie."

For a quarter hour, *Rapid* clawed her way southwestward against the wind as the proas slanted out to meet her from the south. The leadsman's chant of, "No bottom with this line," drifted back from the chains monotonously. The ship head reached on the proas until he decided he had enough westing, wore about and headed south again toward Amoorang. The pirate fleet was strung out now in groups and clusters, all still seeking to close on *Rapid*. He wore the ship about again to head northeast, altering course to run down upon clusters of the proas, yawing to give the broadside guns and carronades the maximum opportunity. The long nines conducted target practice; with his alterations of course, the carronades and broadside guns shattered proa after proa. Finally, as he drove down relentlessly, he saw the survivors square away before the wind in panic and head for the reefs and shallow water to the northeast. The sun was out of sight behind the cape to the west as the last shots were fired at long range at proas stranded on the reefs.

Off the village of Amoorang, the leadsman found bottom in forty fathoms, close ashore. Merewether dropped anchor, prudently carried out a stern anchor in the launch to the beach, and then set the boat to rowing guard against any attack from the surviving pirates. Within a few minutes, an outrigger canoe brought a lean, brown man in a dirty uniform to the ship.

Baynes introduced him. "Captain Merewether, this is Captain James Harris, Commandant of the garrison at Amoorang." Merewether bowed. The man's face was blackened with powder smoke, his eyes red.

"I'm most appreciative you came, Captain. We managed to beat off two attacks yesterday, and one this morning, but I don't believe we could have held out much longer."

Sir Thomas, still wearing a powder-grimed shirt, came in and was introduced. "You'll stay for dinner?" invited Merewether. "I must hear my reports and make an inspection." He went on deck to find MacRae.

"Sir, we have nine men wounded, one mortally, Buttram thinks. Two planks on the starboard bow are stove in. We're taking some water, but the punps are holding it. I'll go over the side in the morning and see if there is any other damage to the stem or bottom. The sides of the ship are pretty well peppered with musket balls and scrap, but there's no serious damage. We made some splices in the rigging, and with the strain from the collision, we'll have to take up on the deadeyes and drive home some wedges."

"Very well." The casualties of the action were less than he had feared. With luck, he might get under way late tomorrow afternoon. He saw the short, fat figure of Davis come into the yellow ring of light cast by the battle lantern. "You may serve out a ration of rum to all hands, Mr. Davis, including such of the wounded as the doctor may give consent to."

Merewether descended to the slave deck and found Buttram just washing up in a tub of seawater, his assistants mopping blood from the deck. Five cots were ranged forward with men on each. One man lay still, his head swathed in bandages, breathing stertorously. It was difficult to see the features beneath the bandages in the light of a battle lantern, then Merewether recognized Jackson, the boatswain's mate, who had fought beside him in his wild attack on Abercrombie. He last remembered seeing him chopping grapnels loose to free *Rapid* from the proa this afternoon.

Buttram came forward, drying his hands on a towel. "Too bad, Captain. He has a musket ball in the brain. He may live awhile, but will never regain consciousness."

Merewether felt regret. The man was a practiced seaman, energetic and courageous. He must be the seventh man to give his life for King and Company since *Rapid* sailed from London last January. Five of them he had known only casually as members of his crew. Burcham and Jackson had been much closer; both had served him well. The risk of death or injury was always present at sea, but it was still a shock when it struck.

"These other four all have leg wounds, Captain. There should be no amputations, barring gangrene. The other four wounded are ambulatory, but not fit for duty."

Merewether passed along the row of cots, speaking a cheerful word to each man, promising a ration of rum if the doctor would consent. He heard the pipe twitter on deck, joyous shouts as the word, "Up spirits!" was passed.

On deck again, he went aft, found Harris, Baynes, and Sir Thomas in the cabin. The round of toasts prefatory to dinner served to revive his spirits and send him to bed early.

CHAPTER 30

Shortly after daylight, MacRae stripped, lowered himself into the water from the launch, and lay back treading water as he took increasingly deep breaths. Suddenly he snorted and jackknifed over in a surface dive. Merewether could see his body flash through the rippled surface, then lost sight of him. He seemed to remain out of sight for minutes, then his shining black head broke the surface a dozen feet away with another snort. He lay back, treading water a moment while he filled his lungs with a half dozen breaths, upended and disappeared again. Upon resurfacing, he swam over to the boat and two seamen helped him over the side.

"The stem is notched, sir," he told Merewether. "There are some splinters that should be trimmed off and faired, but no major damage. Only two planks are shattered, but two sheets of copper have been pulled loose, and also need to be replaced."

Merewether looked at the situation. The smashed planks were no more than two feet below the waterline. The carpenter had reported the frames were sound. Possibly by shifting guns from the starboard side to port, he could heel *Rapid* over sufficiently to expose the damaged area. There was no suitable beach in sight upon which to careen and that would necessitate unloading the ship. He and MacRae came on board and called the Gunner, Carpenter, and Boatswain. In a few minutes, all hands were moving the guns cautiously across the deck with tackles and preventers attached lest a sudden roll free one of them.

It finally developed that some water casks had to be shifted as well, to expose fully the area to be recoppered. By four bells of the forenoon watch, the Carpenter and his mates had removed the damaged planks and were fitting new ones in their place. Planes, saws, drawknives, and chisels shaped the planks, augers made holes, and by six bells in the afternoon watch, the planking was replaced, caulked, and the copper sheets were nailed home. Guns and cargo were reshifted, Baynes and Harris took their leave to await arrival of the Resident's snow, and Merewether weighed anchor, heading north out of the bay.

As *Rapid* passed the wooded island and its reef at the entrance, several pirates could be seen along its shore. At least two proas had survived stranding and were pulled into shallow water to the east, far out of range. Possibly, they might reach home with news of the disaster. MacRae, turning the half-hour glass as was his duty, had reported the action lasted five hours, seven minutes. He had counted twenty-four proas sunk or smashed so badly as to be swamped; two had exploded and three had burned. Ten appeared to have wrecked on the reef or escaped, but the garrison should be able to deal with the survivors.

At the end of the first dogwatch, *Rapid* was twenty miles out to sea, with only a smudge on the horizon astern to mark the Celebes. Merewether told MacRae to heave to and call all hands. A melancholy procession came up from the sick bay, bringing the canvas-wrapped body of Jackson, the boatswain's mate, on deck. Buttram had reported his death at noon; Jackson had not regained consciousness. The bearers laid him on the plank, spread the ensign of the Bombay Marine over the body, and stood by as the crew assembled with none of the bustle or skylarking that marked other occasions.

Merewether stood quietly on the weather side of the quarterdeck as one of the purser's mates set up the little rostrum at the break of the poop from which he would read the Service for the Burial of the Dead at Sea. He held the Book of Common Prayer in his hand, finger marking the page, as the last stragglers from the holds joined the silent assembly. His thoughts went back to the two occasions off the Andaman Islands when he had read the service and his swollen nose had made his voice high and nasal. Burcham, at least, had had a proper clergyman to officiate, and now lay peacefully at rest at Madras, not in this lonely coral sea half a world from home.

MacRae saluted, "Sir," he said, "the crew is formed up for the burial services." Merewether straightened up and forced himself to march to the rostrum.

"Attention on deck. Off hats," commanded MacRae.

Merewether, himself hatless, hair flying and the pages of the prayer book ruffling in the breeze, plunged into the service, conscious of the beauty and sonorous rhythm of the Psalms he read. He reached the Sentence of Committal, concluding, "And the corruptible bodies of those who sleep in him shall be changed and made like unto his glorious body; according to the mighty working whereby he is able to subdue all things unto himself."

The plank tipped up, the shrouded body dropped into the sea with a sullen splash, and disappeared.

"Let us pray." Merewether led the crew through the Lord's Prayer and stepped back.

"On hats," commanded MacRae, looking at Merewether for the signal to dismiss.

Merewether was tempted for a moment to make some sort of maudlin speech about departed shipmates, then decided the truest appreciation of Jackson would be shown by an issue of rum.

"Mr. Davis, you may serve out a ration of spirits to all hands. Dismiss the crew, Mr. MacRae. Get the ship under way." He went below, followed by Sir Thomas. Sangh had gin and lemons on the table.

The passage of the Celebes Sea was easy. *Rapid* lost a day at

Basilian Strait due to squalls and contrary winds, but then emerged into the Sulu Sea and steered northwardly toward Mindoro and the South China Sea, keeping a sharp lookout for Spanish ships based in the Philippines. Two days later, she took departure off Cape Calavite northwestward for the mouth of the Pearl River estuary. Merewether was a little disappointed that he had sighted no Spanish ships so close to their Pacific capital. He had even let himself daydream a bit about a fortuitous encounter with the Manila Galleon, loaded to the deck beams with treasure.

With fair weather, a steady breeze out of the southwest, *Rapid* lay over on the port tack under all plain sail, making a steady eight knots across the South China Sea. Merewether came below for dinner and was informed by Sangh that Sir Thomas was indisposed and would not join him. He immediately went to the supercargo's cabin and found Sir Thomas lying in his bed, a bucket beside him. He evidently had been nauseated quite recently.

"What's the matter, sir?"

"Nothing but a bellyache," replied Sir Thomas. "If Sangh hadn't already proved himself a good cook, I'd think he had tried to poison me." The man's color was bad, a greenish pallor showing through his tan.

"I'll have Dr. Buttram wait on you," Merewether told him, and went on deck.

Buttram came below immediately, bringing his medical kit. "Let's see your tongue," he told Sir Thomas. "Where's the pain?"

"Just above the middle of my belly," said Sir Thomas. "Probably I only need a good purgative and I'll be all right in the morning."

"Pull up your shirt," Buttram told him. He placed his hand flat on the lower abdomen and gently pushed. Sir Thomas winced as the doctor palpitated the abdomen, working over to the right side. Here he stopped, Sir Thomas's brow was beaded with sweat.

He stood up, caught Merewether's eye, and told Sir Thomas, "No food or drink whatever. You may wash out your mouth with water, but do not swallow it. I'll be back shortly." He went out, and Merewether followed.

"Captain, he has a colic caused by inflammation and infection of the vermiform appendix, a bit of blind gut in the lower right quadrant of the belly. If I had ice, I might freeze out the infection, but all I can do now is put cold water compresses on, starve him, and allow him no liquids. Many cases heal themselves; in others there is a rupture and death follows from a general infection. In a few, a rupture will contain itself and form an abscess that I can deal with at a later date. I would like to borrow Sangh, if I may; with the secretary and servant, I want to keep cold compresses on around the clock."

"Certainly," said Merewether. "It is serious, then?"

"Can't really tell now. His right side is swollen rigid and the pain will soon localize there. I've dissected cadavers that died of a rupture and the infection spread throughout the abdomen. It would appear to be a simple matter to cut in and take the thing out, but in the few cases I've heard of, the infection caused death anyway."

Merewether sent Sangh to wait for instructions from Buttram and retired to his cabin. This could be a serious matter. He was less than two days out of Macao, and the diplomat he had brought all this distance was disabled, might even die. He opened the strongbox and reread his orders. They were quite simple, with no more than a passing mention of the mission and directions to give all assistance to Sir Thomas. He, of course, had been present during a brief discussion between Sir George and Sir Thomas, but they must have had other conferences and agreed on their course of action. He went on deck and watched an almost full moon rising on the starboard quarter as he gloomily pondered this dilemma.

The next morning, Sir Thomas was flushed and feverish, obviously in considerable pain. He managed to lie still as his attendants immersed towels in cold water, wrung them out, and laid them over his swollen belly in a steady succession.

Buttram came to Merewether's cabin just before eight bells of the morning watch. "Damn it, Captain, he's getting worse. I'm sure the thing will rupture in the next few hours. It would be such a simple thing to cut in and amputate that bit of gut. I've dissected enough cadavers, I know exactly where it lies. The infection should not be nearly so great as if it bursts. The only thing is, it's not like an amputation of a leg, you can't just strap him down, full of rum and laudanum, and cut away. The pain would make him move enough to make the knife uncertain, and I can't give him liquids at this point." He shook his head gloomily. "I hate to see the man die."

"Ask him if he will consent to the operation. If you have him strapped down and someone to hold him besides, couldn't you amputate the gut?"

"I'd probably break the thing myself, Captain. I don't believe you can strap or hold a man that tight and prevent all movement while you cut his belly open." Buttram shook his head again. "I'll talk to him." He went out as Merewether wondered what he might do if a surgeon plunged a knife into his belly.

Ten minutes later, Buttram was back. "He wants me to try it, Captain," he said, with wonder. "He says he can stand the pain and will take his chances on the infection."

"Are you absolutely sure it is necessary?"

"As sure as a surgeon can ever be, Captain. Of course, I can't guarantee a diagnosis or a cure. All I can do is use my best judgment and ability. I am convinced the gut will burst before noon. He may live several days afterward, but will almost surely die."

"Very well. If Sir Thomas has consented, you must make the effort," said Merewether. He was on an important mission, far from home, and the man charged with the mission so sick and disabled he could not carry it out. "Where will you operate, what do you need?"

Buttram looked out the stern lights, tested the movement of the ship. "I don't believe we need heave to, motion of the ship is easy now. I need shelter and good light, a table to strap him to, and room for my assistants to serve me and hold him. For that matter, Captain, this cabin with the skylight and your table would serve very well."

"All right," Merewether decided. "Make your preparations. I'll give you anything you need within my power." He went on deck and after a swift glance aloft and about the horizon stood staring blindly out to sea from the weather side of the quarterdeck. He was aware of some disturbance behind him, heard Dobbs's voice raised in irritation, and turned to see what the trouble was.

Ho Wong was at the break of the poop, evidently desirous of coming aft. Dobbs was intent on preventing him, technically a prisoner, from entering the sacred area of the quarterdeck. The Chinese had his hands spread and apparently was making a plea to the adamant Dobbs.

"What is it, Mr. Dobbs," called Merewether.

"Sir, this Chinee says, near as I can make out, he wants to see you. I'll send him packing, sir."

"Oh, let him pass, I'll see him," said Merewether testily. He waited as the Chinese came up, bowed, and looked at him with his half smile. "What can I do for you?"

"You allowed me to see you fight last week, sah. You fight very well, sah." He bowed again and Merewether fought off the ridiculous temptation to bow back like a marionette. "Your large man is sick, sah? Very sick?"

"Yes, Sir Thomas is indisposed," replied Merewether cautiously. He could not imagine what the Chinese was getting at. The word of Sir Thomas's illness certainly had spread through the ship, what with lights and the doctor and servants moving all night, changing the cold compresses.

"Sah, I hear your surgeon must cut upon him. Most painful, hard to keep him from moving, hurt himself." The Chinese bowed again. "Maybe I can help. I have opium."

Merewether thought a moment. Buttram had mentioned laudanum, a derivative of opium, and had said he could not administer it, or spirits, under the circumstances. "Thank you. We have opium, but the doctor says he cannot give the sick man anything to drink because of the nature of his illness."

The Chinese bowed again. "Not to drink, sah, smoke."

"What?" began Merewether. He had heard of opium smoking all his life. Opium was an important crop in Bengal for export to China, but he had never been in the trade and had no real conception of what it was used for, except that it was reputed to destroy a man physically and mentally in short order.

"A few puffs from the pipe, sah, and the large man will be asleep, feel no pain. I have such a pipe, do not use it, present to me."

"Wait here," said Merewether, suddenly comprehending what

the Chinese was trying to tell him in his sibilant English. He went below and found his cabin full of activity. His desk had been moved, the table placed under the skylight and covered with sheets. Broad canvas straps were being rigged by the sailmaker, evidently designed to hold Sir Thomas securely. Sangh was tending a charcoal brazier boiling a pot of water in which gleaming surgical instruments were immersed.

"Where's Buttram?" he demanded, then saw him come in the door, sleeves rolled high. "Come on deck, Doctor," he told him.

On deck, he called Ho Wong over, swiftly told Buttram what he had said, and demanded, "You have the opium, the pipe, and know how to smoke it?"

"Yes, sah. I do not use it, pipe is a gift, but I know how."

"Now, Buttram, assuming Ho Wong is telling the truth, if Sir Thomas takes a few puffs, he goes to sleep and becomes unconscious, would that help you?"

"Yes, Captain. I never once thought of the heathen custom." He paused, reflected a moment. "Won't hurt to try it. Bring it to the cabin." Ho Wong bowed again and went forward.

In a few minutes, six men moved Sir Thomas on a litter from his cabin to Merewether's and gingerly slid him onto the table. Sir Thomas, obviously in great pain, was nevertheless cheerful and joked with his attendants. In a few minutes Ho Wong came in carrying a small teakwood case inlaid with mother-of-pearl and with silver clasps to lock it. He opened it and exposed the long-stemmed pipe with its small bowl, a stylet, and a flat silver canister from which he twisted the lid to display a dark gumlike substance. Merewether thought it was for all the world like the cased set of dueling pistols that Sir Thomas had used against the Magindanao pirates.

Buttram took the canister, sniffed it, scraped off a sliver with is fingernail, and touched it to his tongue. "It's opium, right enough," he announced. "Now, Wong, prepare the pipe." He turned to Sir Thomas, lying, with his bright feverish eyes gleaming, on the table. "We're going to give you a treat, sir. I want you to tell me every dream you have, how many houris you chase and catch. You're going to smoke a pipe of opium!"

"Opium!" said Sir Thomas. "Well, I've heard of it all my life, but I never expected to smoke it. Is this medical advice, Doctor?"

"Yes, sir!" He turned to watch Ho Wong, cooking a pellet of opium on the stylet over the brazier. He saw him deposit the smoking, bubbling pellet in the tiny bowl, come over to the table, and offer the stem to Sir Thomas.

"Take long, slow puffs, sah. Inhale the smoke into your lungs."

Sir Thomas took the stem between his lips, sucked on it, almost choked, then drew slowly in and exhaled. A dozen puffs over the period of a minute sufficed, he dropped the pipe and became unconscious.

Merewether had seen blood spilled all his life, and it had never bothered him, whether his own or that of another. But the sight of a knife cutting into the rigid white belly of Sir Thomas was too much for him. He went on deck to pace forward and aft along the weather side of the quarterdeck, still hearing Buttram's commands to his assistants through the vents.

Half an hour later, Buttram came on deck, giving off a powerful odor of spirits. "I've amputated it, Captain," he reported. "Sewed up and bandaged him, well doused in clear spirits. The gut was almost black, full of pus and ready to burst. I think he has a chance now."

"Have you moved him?"

"Yes, sir, he's still asleep. I have his hands tied so he can't pick at the wound. They're cleaning up your cabin now. He lost a fair amount of blood."

Buttram paused and looked out to sea. "Old Dr. Pierce who taught me anatomy told the class that that bit of blind gut was to blame for most deaths blamed on flux or colic. He said several surgeons had opened the belly and removed it, but most of the patients died of the infection anyway. Of course, a naval surgeon counts any man with a wound into the body cavity as mortally wounded, but my instruments were clean and I have hopes he will survive." He shook his head, "The opium worked wonders, the man was entirely relaxed, no flinching, and I reached the gut with the first incision. All we can do now is wait and see." He went forward toward his sick bay where two seamen were still confined.

Merewether paced the quarterdeck for another two hours, turning the matter over and over in his mind, without reaching any solution. Perhaps Sir Thomas would survive long enough to brief him on a course of action, but *Rapid* should be at Macao by tomorrow night and some action must be taken shortly. Sangh appeared and informed him his cabin was clean again and lunch was ready.

CHAPTER 31

Rapid dropped anchor in five fathoms in the roadstead off Macao just before sunset the next day. Merewether had made his number, saluted the Portuguese fort, and had been acknowledged. There was another sloop of the Bombay Marine present, *Gazelle*, fourteen guns. The Chinese allowed no warships to go beyond Boca Tigre up the Pearl River estuary, and it was convenient to anchor here. He might need to see the British consul in any event. Sir Thomas had a high fever, his belly was swollen, and he drifted from consciousness into delirium and back again. Buttram appeared to be encouraged, however, and said the infection was far less than he had feared.

Merewether slept, conscious of the periodic passage of attendants outside his door, ministering to Sir Thomas. He awoke in daylight, the sun just coming up was visible through the stern windows. On deck, he encoutered a haggard Buttram heading for Sir Thomas's cabin.

"What is his condition?" Merewether demanded.

"Sir, I think he passed the crisis earlier this morning. Lucky he has a strong constitution. The infection was much milder than if the gut had burst, but it was still severe. He may live now."

"How long will it be before he can go ashore?"

Buttram hesitated, looked at the sky, and spread his hands. "A month, six weeks, if he's lucky. I don't know, Captain." He turned and plunged below, leaving Merewether filled with dismay.

At two bells in the forenoon watch, a launch came alongside, a second lieutenant of the Marine in the stern. Dobbs escorted him aft, knocked, and entered the cabin. "Merrill, sir. Third lieutenant of *Gazelle*," the officer told Merewether. "Captain MacLeod asked me to call unofficially and inquire as to who commands this ship and his date of rank. We have been out here over a year and *Rapid* is not on our list."

"Have a chair, Lieutenant," Merewether told him. MacLeod and he had been commissioned in the Marine the same day, at Bombay Castle in '98. "You may tell Norman that his old ship-mate, Percival Merewether, commands *Rapid*, date of rank as captain in the Marine, January first, 1806."

"Thank you, sir. Captain MacLeod ranks as first lieutenant from June thirtieth, 1804. He will be over to call within the hour." Merrill took his departure, leaving Merewether to wonder a moment at the subtleties of fate, that he should be a captain and Norman MacLeod, his old companion in arms, still a first lieutenant.

Half an hour later, Merewether received MacLeod at the gang-way with full honors. He had last seen him two years ago at Bombay, but the stocky MacLeod was little changed, hair as black and curly as ever, eyes bright. He was not one of the dour Scots, but lively, full of jokes and quips. He looked at Merewether's scarred face and cried, "Good lord, mon, ye need a barber with a steadier hand!"

Merewether laughed and led him to his cabin. Over tea they played the old games of do you remember? and whatever happened to? for an hour, then came to the present.

"I've been out here over a year," MacLeod told him. "We had two Indiamen attacked by Chinese pirates in big junks. They seem to have bases on small islands west of here, but I've not been able to locate them. I did catch two small junks, no doubt about them being pirates, but I couldn't prove it, and the Hoppo made me release them."

"The Hoppo!" said Merewether. "Do you know him?"

"Never saw him," replied MacLeod. "He simply sent word to Elphingham, chairman of the Select Committee, and orders came to me through the Company. Must have cost me a thousand pounds prize money." He shook his head in disgust.

"Have you heard of some ships being held at Whampoa because the Hoppo will not grant Grand Chop?"

"Yes, I've heard of it. One of the supercargoes came down and talked to me about it. I told him I had no power to do anything, it's entirely a matter for the Select Committee. Put a little money in the right hands, and I'm sure the problem can be solved," he continued cynically.

"Well," said Merewether. "It seems to be my problem now. My envoy is sick." He confided his mission to MacLeod. "What do you suggest I do? Sir Thomas will be disabled, the doctor says, for at least a month."

MacLeod laughed, "I'd sit here and wait for him to get well." He became confidential, said, "Surely you know what the game is? The ships that are tied up are new Indiamen, built on speculation with borrowed money. If they can be delayed a few weeks past the sailing date, the notes will fall due before they can return to England and deliver their cargoes. Some of Elphingham's family are connected with the creditor banks. They hope to pick up some valuable properties at a fraction of their value."

"How do you know this?" demanded Merewether.

MacLeod laughed. "I don't. It's only current gossip, but it's logical. The Hong merchants who went security for these ships are the smallest and weakest in the Co-hong. They have their silver for the cargo that's loaded, and no further interest in the ships, since they're sure they will never be back under the same ownership. Now listen here, Percival," he continued, "I've been out here long enough to learn something both about Canton and politics in the Company. You wait for your Sir Thomas to get well and carry out his mission. The Bombay Marine serves the Company and does not interfere with the politics inside it."

Merewether was silent a moment in thought, then said, "But this sounds more like common fraud, dishonesty, than politics."

"It may well be, but the Marine fights the outside enemies of the Company and does not take sides if there's an internal fight. If you want to keep your commission, my advice as an old friend is to wait and let your fancy dan envoy handle this!" Merewether could see that MacLeod was dead in earnest and concerned lest he become involved in a matter between two elements within the Company.

"I suppose I should go up to Canton and report my presence to the Company factory, at least," said Merewether slowly. "The

Chinese don't allow warships to anchor at Whampoa; what's the best way to get there?"

"I use a Chinese boatman with a lorcha, he knows the channels and is reasonable. I'll be glad to give him a hail. When do you want to go? It usually takes ten to twelve hours. Best leave in the late afternoon and get there next morning."

"I'll give you a signal."

MacLeod soon took his leave, and Merewether came back to his cabin.

MacLeod was probably right, he thought, this was not a matter for the Marine to interfere with. It was proper to carry an envoy on a mission, but if the rumors reported by MacLeod were true, this involved a scheme on the part of Company agents, possibly some of the members of the Select Committee, to ruin the owners of the ships. Merewether was sure this could not be accomplished without cooperation by the Hong merchants and the Hoppo. Of course, the Select Committee, with its broad powers to supervise the trade and its day-by-day contacts with the Co-hong would wield great influence and could accomplish this result. He decided he must try to discuss the matter with Sir Thomas, if his condition permitted.

On deck, he looked about the anchorage and at Macao over to the west. There were possibly a dozen ships anchored out here in the roadstead, Portuguese free traders mostly, probably smuggling opium. The Company had refused to enter the trade, though it appeared to be well on the way to becoming most lucrative. It was one commodity the foreigners had to sell for which the Chinese would pay in silver. He saw Buttram coming aft and called him over.

"How is Sir Thomas?"

"Mending, I think. The swelling has lessened in his belly and I've allowed him a little water. His fever is down and he's not been delirious since yesterday morning."

"Is he able to talk and discuss his mission with intelligence?"

"Sir, he's weak but his mind appears to be clear this morning. I don't want to tire or worry him. I'll go with you and see how he reacts."

Below, Merewether was shocked at the change brought about

in three days in Sir Thomas's appearance. From a vital man with a ruddy complexion, he had shrunk into gray-faced weakness. He must have lost nearly two stone in weight, burned off by fever and dehydration. His thin hands plucked listlessly at the sheet covering him, and he turned his head toward them with an apparent effort.

"Good morning, sir. How do you feel?"

"A bit better than I did, Captain," he replied in a thin, tired voice. "I hear we are at Macao, but I fear I will not be strong enough to carry out my mission for some time." He shifted his gaze to Buttram. "Could I have a drink of water, Doctor? I think I shall expire of thirst."

"Just a swallow, sir. There's still inflammation of the gut."

The servant brought a cup and gave Sir Thomas a swallow under the stern eye of the doctor.

Sir Thomas appeared to draw himself together. He spoke out a little stronger, "Merewether, I'm afraid I will not be strong enough to go ashore in time to solve this problem. These ships must move at the same time the others do or they will not be in England in time to deliver their cargoes, and meet the notes their owners have coming due." This was confirmation of the rumors related by MacLeod, Merewether thought, as Sir Thomas continued, "I had planned to see Elphingham in person and convince him that the scheme is not only fraudulent but most dangerous to the interests of the Company. If this succeeds, what's to prevent the Hoppo trying it again, any time he wants more squeeze? The ultimate result would be to raise the cost of doing business in Canton to the point where the Company would have to take severe measures, and it might even destroy a hundred years of trade customs here." Sir Thomas lay back, looking tired. Buttram caught Merewether's eye and signaled a withdrawal.

"No, just a moment," said Sir Thomas. "Merewether, I want you to go to Canton to call upon the Select Committee or its chairman, John Elphingham, and take a letter from me. Perhaps I can persuade him to come out here and discuss the matter."

"Certainly, sir. Shall I call your secretary?"

"No, not yet. I must rest awhile and compose my thoughts first.

I'll be ready in a few hours." Merewether and Buttram went out.

"He's quite weak, as you can see, sir. Wait a while yet," said Buttram, sotto voce. Merewether went to his cabin, dealt with some requisitions left by Davis, the certificate of health and request for pratique to the Portuguese Captain of the Port, and sat idly wondering whether Sir Thomas could indeed compose a convincing letter in his present condition.

At four bells of the afternoon watch, Sangh appeared. "Sah, Sir Thomas wishes to see you." Merewether went at once down the passage and entered Sir Thomas's cabin.

He found the envoy propped up with pillows, looking much stronger than he had this morning. His secretary sat by with a writing board across his knees. Buttram was lurking in the corner, evidencing concern for his patient, but reluctant to interfere. Sir Thomas spoke out, his voice stronger, "Read this, Merewether, and give me your criticism." The secretary handed over two sheets covered with clerkly handwriting. The letter, omitting formalities, was forthright and logical. It ended with an urgent request for a conference with Elphingham in person.

"Well put, sir," said Merewether. "I can think of nothing to add."

"I can," said Sir Thomas, taking back the sheets. He dictated a postscript and initialed it. It constituted Merewether the deputy to act for and in place of Sir Thomas.

"Sir," he began in protest. This was an honor and duty he did not desire.

"Captain, you're the only one I have to act for me. Chances are, you'll have nothing to decide. But if it's impracticable to consult me, you must have the power to make a decision. After all, Sir George says you're one of the few Bombay Marine officers he's known who'll assume full responsibility and make a logical decision." Merewether felt stunned for a moment. He had had no idea Sir George held so high an opinion of him, had indeed felt the Governor-General had little regard for an officer of his obscure background. He was still bemused and speechless as Sir Thomas delivered the sealed packet to him, together with the fair copies the secretary had made.

CHAPTER 32

The voyage to Canton by lorcha was an experience. Most of the journey was by night, through channels Merewether was sure he could never retrace. The Chinese captain and four men sailed the little vessel, or pulled sculls where necessary, propelling it through a constant flow of small boat traffic even in the early hours of the morning. Canton possessed a whole population that lived their entire lives on the water, often never setting foot onshore. Merewether had seen some of these river people before, years ago, but not so close at hand as from a small craft making its way among them. He slept fitfully in the smelly shelter, propped against the side, then came on deck at dawn. The vessel reached the landing opposite the Company's Hong with its impressive headquarters building well after daylight. Men were already moving about in the performance of their duties as Merewether disembarked and ordered the lorcha to wait for him.

Merewether's uniform carried him by the doorman with no challenge. Inside, he was directed to a clerk who stood at a tall desk within a railed enclosure making entries in a large book. The man answered his inquiry for John Elphingham with quiet courtesy.

"Sir, he comes in later. Have you breakfasted?"

"No," admitted Merewether.

"Then," said the clerk, coming out of his pen, "come in the dining room and have a bite, sir." He led him through a great formal dining room, hung with chandeliers, a life-size portrait of King George as a much younger man at one end, through another door to a smaller room furnished with several tables. A half-dozen men were seated at the tables eating.

"Anywhere, sir," said the clerk, and clapped his hands. A small Chinese servant came over immediately, pulled a chair out, and seated Merewether. Without a word he placed a cup and saucer and poured tea. In a few minutes he served fresh eggs, bacon, and soft rolls. After six weeks at sea, Merewether relaxed and enjoyed himself. These China hands lived well, he reflected, leaning back comfortably.

It was nearly two hours before the clerk appeared and beckoned. "Mr. Elphingham has come in, sir," he told him. "If you'll write your name on this paper, I'll send it in to him." Merewether carefully wrote his name and added, "Captain, the Hon. Company's Bombay Marine." It was another half hour before the messenger came seeking him.

Elphingham had a room in the corner of the second floor looking north toward the walls of Canton. Merewether's impression as he was ushered in was of color and opulence beyond his experience, bright silk curtains, a blue carpet on the floor, delicately colored pictures painted on silk stretched across the wall. A black lacquered desk, inlaid with mother-of-pearl and intricate designs traced in silver, was set diagonally across the corner of the room. Behind it sat a man of middle years, with a long nose, thin, tight lips, graying hair, and piercing black eyes.

"Good morning, Captain," he said, making no move to rise. "What brings the Bombay Marine to Canton? More pirates?"

"No, sir," said Merewether. "I have a letter for you from Sir Thomas Jeffrey." He handed over the packet and stepped back, conscious that for all the opulent furnishings of the room Elphingham occupied the only chair. He remained standing stiffly, staring out the window to Elphingham's left along the narrow international settlement to the city.

Elphingham read the two sheets swiftly, and looked up at Merewether without expression. "And just what does your Sir Thomas hope to accomplish by a discussion with me?"

"Sir," said Merewether a little anxiously. "I thought he had stated his purposes in the letter."

"The man must be a fool," said Elphingham dispassionately. "Certainly he and George Barlow should know that the Select Committee has no power over the Hoppo." He paused, darted a glance at Merewether, then leaned back, putting the tips of his fingers together below his chin, and looked over his head. "And Barlow should know he has no power outside India. What power he possesses there will be gone as well, as soon as Minto is confirmed!" He sniffed delicately and said, "Putting on airs like a viceroy, commissioning envoys and ministers plenipotentiary. I honestly never heard the like of it!"

Merewether had never before encountered a man quite like Elphingham. Even that Resident at Vellore, with his negligent manner and offhand dismissal of a threat to the British rule in India, had been warmer and more human. He remembered MacLeod's advice, do nothing but wait for Sir Thomas to recover. He wondered what the pleasant, outgoing Sir Thomas would have said to Elphingham, or, for that matter, whether Elphingham would have spoken in this tone to Sir Thomas. He could easily back away, play the innocent messenger that Elphingham seemed to consider him, and take a message or lack of message back to the ship.

Elphingham was speaking again. Merewether brought himself back and concentrated on what he was saying. "Sir Thomas, by postscript, seems to have appointed you his deputy to act for him," he said with a faint note of amusement in his voice. "Have you additional arguments to urge, Captain?"

Merewether felt himself fairly taken aback. He had not given the matter the slightest consideration, confident that a letter from a knight and commissioned minister plenipotentiary of the Acting Governor-General of India would overawe a simple supercargo—even though he might be chairman of the Select Committee at Canton. Ten years ago, the last time Merewether had been at Canton, he had been a boatswain's mate and had taken the captain of *Dunvegan Castle* in the gig to that same landing out there, but the Select Committee had been only a name to him. He had not realized the sophistication and immense independent power that these men possessed in this one port of China that was open to European trade.

He temporized, seeking time in which to arrange his thoughts. "Sir, can you read to me what is said in that postscript?"

Elphingham looked at him sharply, then picked up the letter, sniffed audibly, and read.

"Due to my inability to travel to Canton, in the event you find it impossible to visit me at Macao, I appoint Captain Percival

Merewether of the Honourable Company's Bombay Marine to act for me, and in my place and stead, and do hereby ratify and confirm all that he shall lawfully do as my deputy in the premises." Elphingham sniffed again. "It seems you possess the same powers Sir Thomas does, Captain," he said dryly. "Have you additional arguments to urge?"

Merewether stood quietly, trying to organize his thoughts. Read by Elphingham with his tone of amusement, the formal wording of the postscript sounded so stilted as to be ridiculous. Still this was a serious mission, and some thousands of pounds had been expended by the Company to make this voyage. Sir Thomas had confided a trust in him, and he could not meekly turn and walk away because a supercilious man made light of the trust.

He found himself speaking briskly. "Yes, Mr. Elphingham. I should like to be conducted to the Hoppo, together with the Hong merchants who are security for the ships which have not been granted Grand Chop."

Elphingham seemed to be stunned, astounded. His eyes opened wide and he stared at Merewether for a full minute before he said, "Well, I'm damned!" He continued to stare at Merewether, and then said, "Ignorance is bliss, fools rush in where angels fear to tread!" His face became quite red, his dispassionate tone of voice had vanished. He paused again, evidently to collect himself, made an effort, and spoke in his former tone, with a slight note of persuasion now. "Captain, you evidently do not know the customs here. The Hoppo is a Manchu, a kinsman of the Emperor of China. He does not grant audiences to barbarians. Even I," he expostulated, spreading his hands, "have never been in his presence. We deal only through the Co-hong."

Merewether felt that he had nothing more to lose and pressed forward.

"Then summon the Co-hong and let me present the case to it. Surely any grievances can be settled and the Hoppo then will issue Grand Chop."

Elphingham looked at Merewether incredulously. "You evidently have no conception of what you are asking. I've excused

you so far for your ignorance. Another word and I prefer charges
with the Superintendent of the Marine. I'll have you court-mar-
tialed and broken!"

Merewether thought of the long, hard fight to rise from bastardy,
ignorance, and the lower deck, to his present rank in the Marine, even thought fleetingly that if all went well, he might
make peace with Flora Dean and ask her to marry him. He was
conscious that his face had flushed and the scars must be a livid
white against the suffused cheek. His voice felt thick as he said
slowly and distinctly, "Put your refusal in writing, sir."

"I'll do nothing of the kind!" snapped Elphingham. "You may
inform your precious Sir Thomas that I shall not call upon him,
nor will I intervene with the Co-hong. As for the Hoppo, any
audience with him is unthinkable. The Select Committee acts only
between the ships trading into Canton for the Company and the
Hong merchants in contracting for merchandise. Payment of
customs is the duty of each Indiaman through its particular Hong
merchants to the Hoppo. He then grants Grand Chop, if he is so
advised, and all laws or customs have been complied with. If these
ships are in default, they must correct their deficiencies themselves." Elphingham paused and glared at Merewether. "Now,
Captain, I've been very patient with you and I have many other
pressing engagements. You may go."

Merewether found himself downstairs again. He had enough
presence of mind to thank the courteous clerk at the entrance and
went outside. He was still smarting from the cavalier treatment he
had received at the hands of Elphingham and his contemptuous
dismissal of Sir Thomas's request, without even the courtesy of a
note in reply. Yet, for the life of him, Merewether could think of
no course of action at the moment. The other Company functionaries here were concerned with bills of lading and exchange,
supplies, and making the ships ready to sail when the northeast
monsoon began to blow in the next week or so. They certainly
would not become involved with the powerful Select Committee
for the sake of a few new Indiamen, or for the Acting Governor of
India, for that matter. He saw no alternative but to go back to
Rapid and report his failure to Sir Thomas. He walked down to
the landing and reentered the lorcha.

CHAPTER 33

Merewether climbed wearily over the side a little after dawn the next morning. He went to his cabin, stripped off his wrinkled sweaty clothing, bathed and shaved. After breakfast he found Buttram, learned that Sir Thomas had continued to improve, and went in to make his report. He was brief, detailing without elaboration the interview, and Elphingham's refusal to take any action.

Sir Thomas was impassive. "I was afraid he might take such an attitude; there must be some truth in the report at Calcutta that his family hopes to profit by delaying these ships. I'm sure he would have turned me away as quickly as you, Captain."

"What would happen, sir, if the ships simply hauled up their anchors and left with the rest?"

Sir Thomas laughed. "In the first place, there probably are war junks anchored below Whampoa to prevent just this, and in the second place, the Company would never permit these ships to sail for it again. It has accepted very stringent conditions for the right to trade here." He paused and thought a moment. "I must give the matter more thought, though I confess I can offer no plan or suggestion at the moment."

Merewether went back to his cabin, called his officers to the cabin and directed that they have the ship in a state of readiness for departure upon short notice. He could see no solution for the problem and he doubted that Sir Thomas would be able to conceive one. The weariness of two sleepless nights in a small boat overwhelmed him. Kicking off his shoes, he lay down and did not awaken until five bells of the afternoon watch.

Merewether was awakened by the calling away of the launch to pick up the liberty party. MacRae had made inquiries and learned that liberty might be granted during daylight hours in Portuguese Macao, provided an officer of the ship went with them and reported to the Captain of the Port. Larkin had accompanied this party and he had little anxiety. The port was small, but it was on the Chinese mainland and already an incredible amount of oriental goods had found their way aboard.

He came on deck and idled forward examining standing rigging and spars, guns and brasswork for possible attention while *Rapid* lay here. On the forecastle, he came upon the two Chinese hostages, Ho Wong and Lee Fong, leaning on the bulwarks talking in Cantonese. Merewether felt a sense of guilt. He had been at anchor three days and had neglected to take any measures to land them. He should have made arrangements when he went to Canton to release them. He was greeted with quiet courtesy.

"Ah, Captain," said Wong with his little bow and half smile. "We are close to our home but remain on your ship."

"I am sorry," said Merewether. "I have been remiss. I shall make arrangements to send you to Canton, if that is your wish, in the morning." Both Chinese bowed. He continued, curiously, "Do either of you happen to know the Hoppo at Canton?" Little chance of that, if John Elphingham did not, he thought, even as he asked the question.

Wong replied, "I do not, sah, but my grandfather does."

"Your grandfather?" echoed Merewether.

"Yes, Captain. The Hoppo is a Manchu, kinsman of the Emperor, but my grandfather is Chinese, he ranks as a Mandarin of Canton."

Merewether was surprised: the little Chinese supercargo a grandson of a mandarin! He had heard vaguely that the Manchus had come out of the west a hundred and fifty years ago to conquer China with their barbaric horsemen and had established the dynasty that still ruled. He did not appreciate the distinction Wong had made when he said, "The Hoppo is a Manchu," while adding that his grandfather was Chinese. Still, the statement deserved some amplification.

"My cousin, Fong, is also grandson," continued Wong. "Our mothers were daughters of the mandarin, but he had no sons and loves us well."

"I understood that the Hoppo controlled the trade at Canton," said Merewether. "How does your grandfather rank with him?"

"Hoppo only collects customs, the Kuang Chou Fu, or as you would call him, governor of Canton, is Chinese and of higher rank, but he has not the power of the Manchu Hoppo. He only rules the Chinese people, and my grandfather is one of his counselors." It was confusing to Merewether; Elphingham, Sir Thomas, and even Sir George had appeared to consider the Hoppo the only significant official at Canton. This deserved further investigation. He invited the two young men to his cabin where Sangh served tea.

A half hour of questions and explanations made the matter somewhat clearer. The practical and grasping Manchu dynasty had placed its members in key positions where they could control the military, revenues, and trade, exerting power and influence out of proportion to their comparative rank with the older Chinese ruling class. It was content to leave many of these as governors and officials of the provinces, so long as Manchu kinsmen collected taxes for the Emperor.

"Now," said Merewether after this paradox became clear. "Could your grandfather see the Hoppo?"

Wong looked uncertain, glanced at Fong, thought a moment, and then said carefully, "He could if there were some important reason. Of course, this Hoppo is only a Manchu of low rank, much beneath my grandfather, who was educated as a scholar."

Such oriental distinctions were still confusing, but possibly no more unreasonable than the British system of nobility, ranging downward from the royal family to knights and landed gentry. Still, if there were some way to reach the Hoppo, even through another Chinese official, the possibility should be investigated. Merewether could see no danger in disclosing to Wong his mission to Canton. Elphingham and his committee were already fully aware of it.

He explained briefly to the two Chinese the situation, and found it understood immediately. These young men were intelligent and knowledgeable. They grasped at once the plot to delay the vessel's arrival beyond the due date of the notes; it was, Merewether suspected, one that would have appealed to them, similarly situated.

Wong stood up and bowed. "Sah, may my cousin and I have time to consider this matter?" Merewether rose and bowed as the Chinese took their leave. From being hostages, virtually prisoners

of war, they had assumed the status of honored guests. He looked
in on Sir Thomas, found him sleeping peacefully, came back and
had a gin and lemon before dinner. The liberty party came back
on board with a little loud talk and laughter, but Larkin made no
complaints.

Just after eight bells of the morning watch, Sangh announced
the Chinese. They came in bowing and smiling, and took their
seats. Merewether sat back behind his desk waiting to see what
these young men might have to say.

"Sah," Wong commenced. "My cousin and I have lost much
face by being captured and brought back to Canton in an English
ship of war." Oh, God! thought Merewether. Now their feelings
are hurt, no telling what they may want as squeeze to heal them.

The Chinese continued, "You fight very well, sah, and you have
been courteous to us in your fashion. My cousin and I have given
the matter much thought. We have no desire to interfere in a
quarrel between foreign devils." He paused, and Merewether
thought, the Chinese had no more of a solution than he or Sir
Thomas.

"What we desire, sah, is to be returned to the house of our
grandfather with honor and dignity, as befits the grandsons of a
mandarin. Thus we lose no face by being captured. If we go back
by lorcha, we are like stray dogs slinking home."

Well, thought Merewether, that request was not unreasonable,
but it brought him no closer to the answer to his problem. "Tell
me your desires, and I will see if I can accommodate you," he
said, wondering what impossible situation he might be getting
himself into.

"Sah, we wish to be taken to Canton by your largest boat;
launch? yes. Then we wish you and your Marine soldiers to march
with us to the house of our grandfather as honor guard. Yes, that is
it."

"What?" exploded Merewether. "You know that no foreigners
and certainly no military force may enter Canton!"

"Please," said Wong quietly. "I know this, do not worry. We
shall tell my grandfather the whole story, he will be pleased his
ships are safe, his grandsons home with honor, and perhaps he
will then tell the Hoppo the trick the Englishmen play upon
him."

The recollection of the supercilious Elphingham came back to Merewether; he could not guess that a Bombay captain might have entrée to a mandarin. The thing was dangerous, but he had lived his life in danger more acute than this, and the prospect of marching a detachment of Sepoy Marines through the forbidden streets of Canton was exhilarating.

"Wait," said Merewether rising. He went to Sir Thomas's cabin, and found him awake, spooning up the contents of a cup of barley gruel as his servant stood by. Evidently Buttram had broken the fast imposed upon the envoy. He looked much better, there was color in his face, and his movements were much surer.

"Sir," commenced Merewether, and detailed Wong's proposal. "I feel I should attempt it," he concluded.

Sir Thomas lay back, gruel forgotten for the moment, gave the matter thought, and then said, "I can't order you to break the laws of the Empire of China, nor can I condone it. If you do, it is a matter for you to decide and to accept any consequences." He pushed himself up in the bed against the pillows, and said, "I'd do it in a minute if I were able to get out of this bed!"

Merewether went back to his cabin, took his place behind the desk, looked out the stern windows, and then up through the skylight, endeavoring to give an impression of deep deliberation. He realized that the two Chinese had anticipated his answer.

"I'll do it," he told them flatly. "Twenty Marines and the Jemadar."

"And the trumpeter and drummer," added Wong.

Merewether laughed. The Chinese certainly intended the return to their grandfather's house to be with full ceremony. "Done!" he agreed.

He sent for MacRae, Larkin, Davis, and Gunny, quickly informed them of his plans, then directed that the masts be stepped in the launch, and that it be provisioned. MacRae was most reluctant.

"This is dangerous, Captain," he told him. "Landing an armed force in forbidden territory in China is a violation of Chinese law and Company treaties and regulations,"

"I am aware of that," said Merewether. MacRae sullenly subsided. "Gunny, your men have their drill sticks?"

"Yes, sah."

"I'll want them polished bright. No arms of any kind are to be carried. We will leave at the end of the first dogwatch. You will be in charge of the boat, Mr. Larkin." He dismissed the group and sat at the desk turning over in his mind the chance he was taking. He should have demanded that Sir Thomas give him written orders to carry out the mission; he might thereby shield himself behind them. Still, the ultimate responsibility for taking such a force ashore was his, and he felt compelled to make the attempt to carry it out.

CHAPTER 34

The launch pulled away promptly, rowing clear of the anchored vessels, then hoisting two lugsails, and making fair speed up the Pearl estuary with the wind on the port quarter. Wong evidently knew the area thoroughly; he directed the boat through a maze of passages, bypassing Whampoa, to emerge after daylight in the river off the international settlement. Here the breeze failed, and boat traffic was heavy. Merewether ordered the sails taken in, and set the hands to the oars. He stepped the staff bearing the flag of the Bombay Marine in the stern, and pulled up the river toward Canton.

As the launch came abreast of the Company landing, Merewether saw several men come out the door of its building. He focused his glass and recognized the tall figure of Elphingham with others he did not know, all staring out at him. The uniforms of the Sepoy Marines were certainly recognizable at this distance. He wondered what those gentlemen might be saying about him as the launch pulled upstream out of sight.

Wong directed the launch to a landing on the north side of the city. Wong and Fong disembarked, closely followed by Gunny. Wong handed a square brass coin to an urchin, and sent him off on some mission. In a few minutes, three sedan chairs borne by coolies came down the narrow street to the landing.

"Sah," said Wong. "You ride in the first, Fong and I behind.

The Jemadar leads, then the trumpeter and drummer, with the files of Marines on either side of the chairs."

"Very well." This young man had the affair planned exactly; Merewether gave orders to Larkin to wait in the boat anchored in the stream, permitting no one ashore. The Marines moved out and formed up along the landing. Their uniforms were spotless, brass buttons gleaming, in spite of twelve hours in the launch. Each Marine carried in place of his musket a rattan stick about a yard long, capped at either end with brass ferrules twinkling in the sunlight. They made an impressive spectacle, Merewether thought, noticing the crowd that had already gathered along the riverbank to see this unusual event.

Merewether entered the chair and the Marines filed up on either side, as Gunny, the trumpeter and drummer took their places at the head of the procession. Straight ahead, until the street ran into a gate, Wong had instructed Gunny. The Jemadar gave a command, and every stick flashed simultaneously as the Marines tossed them up to rest on their shoulders. The bugle sounded the advance, the drum began to roll in a slow beat, and the files marched off.

He estimated the party marched nearly a mile, through solid masses of Chinese in the narrow street, others jamming windows and balconies, attracted by the series of bugle calls and snatches of melody played by the trumpeter, and the steady roll of the drum in slow cadence. The crowd opened ahead of Gunny and closed behind the files almost as though the party was a ship cleaving through the sea. At intervals, Gunny barked a command, and the rattan sticks flashed in simultaneous transfer from right to left shoulder, and back again, or were carried upright, then horizontally for a time. Merewether wished he had a better view; the sight must be impressive.

The party crossed a small square containing what appeared to be a shrine. Bivouacked along one side was a squad of Manchu bannermen, soldiers of the Emperor, staring open-mouthed at the Sepoy Marines.

"Eyes right!" commanded Gunny, rendering a salute to the startled unit, then marching steadily on. Ahead, Merewether could see the street was blocked by a large gate.

Gunny brought the Marines to a halt before the gate, still marching in place to the cadence of the drumbeat. They performed a series of intricate maneuvers with their sticks, then as the gate swung open a crack, came to a halt, the drum falling silent. A Chinese appeared through the narrow opening and looked questioningly at the party.

Merewether heard Wong give a shrill command in Cantonese from behind him. The gateman bowed, stepped back opening the gate wide, and remained in his bow, hands clasped, as the drum sounded again. The Marines marched through the gate into a courtyard in front of a three-storied house. Wong called another command, the chairs stopped while the Marines marched on across the courtyard to the door. Here they halted, one file left-faced, the other right-faced, the sticks flashed up to the position of present arms, and the bugle sounded attention.

Wong and Fong emerged from their chairs and stood at the end of the two files of Marines. Merewether could now see that the door was open and a little party of men had appeared outside. One, he could see, was an old man wearing a long, straight robe, a flat cap on his head on which a large ruby sparkled. There were five others, two middle-aged and three quite young. He guessed that the old man was the grandfather, the two younger men the fathers of Wong and Fong, and the other three their brothers.

The drum rolled softly, Wong and Fong marched slowly down between the files of Marines for all the world as though they were side boys. Merewether followed at a discreet distance, saw them greeted with warmth by the group as they made obeisance to the old man, and be embraced by the others. He stood aside, waiting for the welcoming ceremonies to be over, and managed to whisper to Gunny, "Give an exhibition of drill and then pass in review."

Gunny gave a low command, one file about-faced, and the detachment marched across the court to the brisk rattle of the drum almost to the wall, executed a right flank, then a column right, another flank movement, and marched toward the party at the door. At the last possible moment, they whirled about in a to-the-rear evolution, and marched away across the court. Another right flank movement followed by a column right and flank movement brought the detachment passing the group.

"Eyes left!" shouted Gunny, saluting the group. "Front." They marched almost to the wall again, spun about and paused, the Marines marching in place to the cadence of the drum, then halted.

Merewether could see that Wong and Fong were pleased by the ceremony and their relatives appeared to be impressed. He hoped that enough face had been provided to encourage them to induce their grandfather to see the Hoppo.

He found himself being presented to the old man, and made his most elaborate bow, then bowed in turn to the others. His surmise had been correct: they were the fathers and brothers of Wong and Fong. Inside the house, he found himself in dim light, smelling an odor of incense. The big room was partitioned off by colorful folding screens, some of teak and silk painted with intricate designs, others of paper bearing pastoral scenes. He was led through an opening into a corner of the room where there was a black lacquered desk, richly decorated with inlays of mother-of-pearl sprinkled with gold dust, set under an octagonal window. Beside it was a handsome cabinet, doors open, filled with scrolls. He remembered that the old man was a scholar.

"My grandfather does not speak English," whispered Wong. "We first have tea, then I speak to him of your mission." Merewether took his seat on a small chair and waited. In a few minutes, a servant came in with tea and fragile cups, thin wafers sprinkled with sesame seeds, and sweetmeats. It was an almost adequate substitute for the breakfast he just now remembered he had missed.

When the servant had cleared the dishes, Wong stood up, bowed and addressed his grandfather sitting behind the desk. He spoke in Cantonese in a liquid roll of monosyllabic rhythm with scarcely a pause for breath. He was interrupted twice by the old man— apparently questions—and finally fell silent. The old man sat with head bowed, his eyes closed in contemplation. Merewether waited patiently for his decision, hoping that he had not jeopardized his whole career for a refusal now.

The old man raised his head and opened his eyes. He uttered a single sentence. Wong stood up, bowed, caught Merewether's eye and went out. Merewether bowed and followed him. Outside,

Wong led the way to another screened cubicle at the opposite side of the room and indicated a seat on a chest. "My grandfather will send a message to the Hoppo saying he will call upon him this afternoon." Merewether felt relief. At least his story would be brought to the attention of the proper authority. What might then be the result, he could not guess.

He bethought himself suddenly of Gunny and the Marines. "Shall I send the Marines back to wait in the boat?" he inquired.

"No, sah. I have given instructions to the cooks to feed them and put up awnings to shelter them from the sun." This young man apparently thought of everything.

A sudden outlandish thought crossed Merewether's mind. Without pausing to examine it, he said to Wong, "Is there any way that I could see the Hoppo when your grandfather calls upon him?"

Even the inscrutable Wong showed surprise at the question, then laughed, "If you could become Chinese, sah, you might serve as one of my grandfather's retinue accompanying him to the audience." He laughed again, then said, "Wait." In a few minutes, he was back accompanied by Fong and a blue-clad servant. Fong seemed to find the proposition hilarious and for a moment Merewether considered withdrawing it. Before he could speak, the servant had put his fingers under his chin and gently raised his head, pushing his chin from one side to the other. He spoke to Wong in Cantonese, was answered, and went out.

The metamorphosis was astounding. A black wig with a formal cap set upon it; cheeks and hands, even the scar, stained to a yellowish hue; eyebrows blackened with ink and cunning lines drawn at the corners of his eyes to give the impression of a fold, made him unrecognizable. He must only remember to keep his eyes narrowed to slits. There were no blue-eyed Chinese, but even a Chinese might have suffered facial wounds. He slid into the sandals and adjusted the formal robe constituting the livery of a retainer in the house of the Mandarin.

Wong explained to him, "We enter with my grandfather and escort him to the chamber for the audience. Then we stand behind a screen beside the door while he talks to the Hoppo. When my grandfather leaves, we bow to the Hoppo and then follow him out. My grandfather thinks it will be great joke upon the haughty Manchu to have a foreign devil present at the interview!" Merewether thought so too, though he was beginning to have some misgivings.

Outside in the courtyard, they found a sedan chair drawn up at the door. Merewether looked to see how the Marines were faring and found them taking their ease at one end of the yard under woven fiber awnings, pots and bowls on low tables giving evidence that they had dined. He went over toward Gunny, the robe whispering along the ground as he walked, and saw him start up.

"Make sure you keep these men out of mischief, Gunny," he said in his normal tone of voice and saw the impassive Gunny for once lose his composure, show complete surprise, mouth open, eyes wide, stuttering as he managed finally an "Aye aye, sir."

The old man emerged and took his place in the chair. The procession went out the gate down the narrow street, a servant with a banner bearing a device in gold preceding the chair, another servant on either side of it, with Wong and Merewether following behind. People stood courteously aside as the old man passed during a journey of perhaps a quarter of a mile.

They stopped before a gate in a wall surrounding a three-storied house, quite similar to the one they had just left. The gate bore a dragon seal of the Empire and several ideographs. The group was instantly admitted to the courtyard, the chair set before the door, and the Mandarin emerged. He was greeted with great ceremony by a Chinese in an opulent robe who appeared to be a major functionary. He preceded the Mandarin in, struck a gong, and made an announcement.

The old man went through an elaborately decorated passage formed by screens, some of silk, others of paper, decorated with jade, mother-of-pearl and gold dust, Wong and Merewether following two steps behind. The passage turned to the right with an opening to the left. The functionary went through, followed by the Mandarin. Merewether felt Wong stop in the entrance. He halted, as the old man made a ceremonial bow and greeted the Hoppo.

The Hoppo sat in a gilded chair before a lacquered desk even more elaborately decorated than the one Merewether had seen this morning. He was a moderately obese man in a rich robe, wearing a gold chain about his neck upon which was suspended a glittering jade seal. His features appeared to be coarser and harder than those of the Mandarin, evidence of his Manchu blood, but his manner was one of courtesy.

Merewether felt movement beside him, and saw that Wong had slid to the right behind the screen. He followed suit, position-ing himself so that he might see the room through the joint in the screen. Apparently there were some formalities to go through before the actual business commenced, a tiny cup of tea, a wafer, short speeches in liquid monosyllables. Finally the preliminaries were over and the Mandarin launched into his report. He was interrupted once by what appeared to be a question and shortly concluded his statement. The Hoppo sat quietly for a moment, then rang a gong. The functionary came in from the other side, received instructions from the Hoppo and disappeared.

"He has sent for the Co-hong," whispered Wong. "He told my grandfather that the customs duty has not been paid by the mer-chants, and that is why he has not issued Grand Chop to these ships."

Merewether stood behind the screen for what seemed to be an eternity while the Hoppo and the Mandarin made what appeared to be polite conversation in Cantonese. Just when he felt that he could not stand it a moment longer, he heard the gong sound at the front of the house, and the functionary came in leading five dignified men in robes down the passage. Merewether remembered to close his eyes to mere slits, but they passed into the room without a glance at the two retainers behind the screen.

The Hoppo's manner changed abruptly. In stern tones, he ad-dressed the five merchants. They stood in an attitude of deepest respect, then one who appeared to be the spokesman for the group made a brief statement. The Hoppo replied brusquely and the spokesman made a longer statement, glancing sidewise at the old Mandarin with the ruby glittering in the center of his hat. The Hoppo again replied, impatiently, it seemed, then sat straight and delivered what appeared to be a judgment. The five merchants bowed almost in unison and went out passing close beside Mere-wether.

Wong whispered to him, "Be ready." The Mandarin was standing, bowing, apparently making a speech of farewell and thanks. He came out and Merewether followed him alongside Wong to the door and outside where the old man entered his chair and the party retraced their steps to his house.

Once inside, Wong told him, "The merchants said that the Indiamen had paid them the amount of customs duty, but the chief man of the foreign devils' committee had ordered them not to pay the Hoppo until after the other ships had left. The Hoppo has fined them double the amount of customs as a penalty for listening to him. Grand Chop will issue as soon as the duty and fines are paid tomorrow."

"Thank you, Wong," said Merewether. "Thank you!" The mission had been accomplished; now he had only to wait for the retribution he was sure Elphingham would try to visit on him. "May I express my thanks to your grandfather before I go back to the ship?"

Wong looked at him for a moment. "Please do not be in a hurry, Captain. Fong's father and mine have planned a banquet for us to celebrate our safe return tonight. Our grandfather will be there and you may make your speech then."

"What about my Marines and the crew of the boat?" protested Merewether. It certainly would be a hardship on Larkin and the crew of the launch, moored out in the stream. The Marines seemed to be perfectly comfortable in their impromptu bivouac in the court.

"We have planned to feed them and will take food to men in boat," said Wong. Merewether surrendered, but salved his conscience by sending Gunny with a message to Larkin explaining the delay.

"I will call the servant, I get you out of that robe and wig," continued Wong. "Best, I think, you wear uniform to the banquet. Our guests are the students of English and be most interested in how another Englishman talks."

"Another Englishman?" inquired Merewether. He had heard of no Englishmen in Canton other than those in the international settlement.

"We have foreign devils here many years who teach those of us who trade beyond the empire English, Spanish, Dutch, French, some Portuguese. The Emperor not favor this, but he not forbid it also. A few of us can speak English are valuable."

Merewether persisted. "But what about your laws, the treaties with the Company?"

"Oh," said Wong negligently. "We give them a paper, what we call a 'Freedom of the City,' issued by Mandarin of the ruby class. Can live in Canton, but not to travel outside."

Merewether found that while he had been dressed in the robe, someone had sponged and pressed the wrinkles out of his uniform. He washed the stain off his face and hands, but found that the black ink in his eyebrows was there to stay. Dressed, he waited in his cubicle for Wong to come for him. It had become dark outside and he hoped Larkin and the hands in the launch had dined well. Gunny had reported them to be in satisfactory condition, though anxious to be under way.

Finally, Wong came for him. He was now dressed in a magnificent robe, a gold chain about his neck holding a jade seal. He led Merewether through a maze of passages formed by screens to a large room, apparently at the rear of the house. Here he found the two fathers of Wong and Fong and three younger brothers, he was not sure of which, Wong or Fong, all equally dressed in splendor. Soon a steady procession of guests began to arrive. He found himself introduced to one after another, who spoke English in varying degrees. He had a cup of wine pressed into his hand, drank sparingly, remembering the fool he had made of himself with wine at Lord Laddie's party. He wondered when the dinner would commence. With only a bit of tea and some wafers today, he would be ready at any time.

Another robed figure was introduced to him. He started to bow, when the figure said in almost the words of Abercrombie, "Well, I'm damned! If it isn't little Percy Merewether, and a captain now!"

Merewether looked again. The figure had thickened with middle age, but the eyes were still nearsighted and kindly. Though it had been nearly ten years, Merewether realized that this was Dawson, the mentor of his youth, assistant purser in old *Dunvegan Castle*.

"But how . . ." he began, wondering if he were dreaming the whole affair, if he were really in Canton and this was Dawson.

The man laughed. "Yes, it really is old Dawson. I left *Dunvegan Castle* the same voyage you did, but after she reached China. I took a position ashore with the Company, six months at Canton and then six months at Macao. And after a year or so, I became acquainted with some of the Chinese who desired to learn a little more than pidgin English. They arranged for me get a certificate to live in Canton. I teach them English and navigation, such other arts as I know and they desire." He looked a little diffident, but proud, and continued, "I have a wife and three children now, live in a handsome house with servants. Entirely different from what it was at sea."

Merewether would have liked to talk at length. He owed more to this man than to any other man on earth, but the Mandarin came in, the banquet commenced, and he had all that he could do to give proper attention to Wong, Fong, their fathers, brothers, and the old Mandarin. At the proper point, he rose and made a speech of thanks to the old man, Wong translating simultaneously. Other speeches were made, poetry recited, even some cacophonous songs sung. As the affair broke up, he thought to find Dawson again and discovered that he had gone. The little man seemed happy enough, back in his profession of teaching, the sea forgotten. Merewether wondered briefly if he too might abandon the sea and settle into some snug billet ashore.

Wong led him to a cubicle on the second floor. Merewether had had just enough to drink to feel carefree and to forget that he had broken the laws of the Emperor and the Company today, and might be brought to account. The young Chinese said quietly outside what appeared to be a real door and not a screen, "I have taken the liberty to provide you with company, Captain." He smiled, bowed, and disappeared down the passage.

A little bemused and confused by the cryptic remark, Merewether entered the room. A wick burned dimly in a pottery lamp on the floor, giving just enough light for him to see the black hair above bright eyes peering at him from the pallet over the edge of the sheet. He found her both accommodating and accomplished.

When Merewether awoke, it was daylight, the sun already

shining through a window. The woman was gone, but a jar of water was outside the door, still hot. He scrubbed face and hands, conscious of the bristles on his chin, put on his clothing and went out. Downstairs, he soon encountered one of the younger brothers who spoke a little halting English, and told him that he must go. Wong, Fong, their fathers, the other brothers, and finally the old Mandarin gathered at the door to see him go. Gunny already had the Marines formed up, more pots and dishes indicating that they had been fed breakfast.

Merewether caught Gunny's eye. In a moment, the Marines were marching and countermarching through the courtyard, the drum beating, the bugle sounding, the Marines shifting their glittering drill sticks from shoulder to shoulder, as the servants crept out from the house and women looked out from upper windows at the sight.

The old man, with a bow, handed Merewether a scroll. His seal in red was stamped at the bottom. Merewether took the paper, bowed, and took his leave. He signaled the Marines to pass again in review, saluted the party, and marched off at the head of the column. A quarter hour later they were at the waterfront, hailing in the launch, with a thousand people lining the bank to see them go

They came back alongside *Rapid* just as the second dogwatch ended. MacRae met Merewether at the gangway, quite evidently relieved to have him back aboard. He handed him two messages, one from the British consul at Macao who had called in his absence, the other from MacLeod in *Gazelle*. The note from the consul was formal: he regretted missing Merewether; the message from MacLeod invited him to dine tomorrow night. He scribbled an acceptance and gave it to the watch with instructions to deliver it in the morning. A day in an open boat after a night of festivities sent him to bed.

The next morning he waited upon Sir Thomas and found him sitting in a chair, apparently well on the way to complete recovery. Merewether made a detailed oral report of the mission, including the fact that he had accompanied the Mandarin to his audience before the Hoppo in the guise of a retainer, but omitting mention of the ultimate hospitality afforded him by Wong.

Sir Thomas was a little anxious. "I hope I have not encouraged you into doing something that will damage you, Merewether. You have solved the problem, but certainly not by orthodox means. I shall do all that I can in my report to Sir George to make it plain that I concurred with you, and the defense offered by the Co-hong as to their motivation makes it plain that Elphingham should be relieved of his post. Still, we have a violation of laws and treaties." He shook his head in doubt.

"You could still give me written orders directing me to take the action I did," suggested Merewether hopefully.

"No, of course not," said Sir Thomas. "Even if I did direct you to disobey the law, it would be your duty to refuse to do so, and I am sure that a court of inquiry would so hold. It would not constitute a defense. Oh, well, it's a long way from Canton to Bombay, and Elphingham may be content to let sleeping dogs lie in the hope that his own criminal conduct will not be examined too closely."

Back in his cabin, Merewether was for the first time worried about the affair. Sir Thomas's view of it had dashed cold water on the high exhilaration he had carried away from its successful conclusion. Morbid imagination pictured him before a stern tribunal at Bombay, his conviction and sentence of dismissal from the Marine, his loss of any chance at happiness with Flora Dean, even a pitiful picture of him begging his way through the streets of London in a snowstorm. This last imaginative vignette was enough to arouse his sense of the ridiculous, and he was able to cast off his doubts for the time being. He shouted for Sangh and sent him to summon the officers to his cabin for a conference. He hoped to be under way for Calcutta within two days.

CHAPTER 35

The dinner with MacLeod in *Gazelle* was pleasant. He had told him of his exploit before the other two officers MacLeod had invited came in. The Scots officer was most complimentary of the manner in which he had solved the problem. "Man, I'd never have thought of going to see the Hoppo dressed as a Chinee!" he said admiringly over a glass of Scots whisky.

"Well," said Merewether feeling a little pride in himself, "I thought that if I had gone to all that trouble to get the message to the Hoppo, I damn well wanted to see it delivered." He realized that he was talking too much, almost boasting, and compelled himself to change the subject. In a few moments, the first and third lieutenants came in and the dinner was served.

Just as the affair was breaking up, the third lieutenant had already gone on deck to call his gig alongside, Merewether heard the first lieutenant say to MacLeod, "By the way, Captain, Abbott took passage in an American schooner for Bombay this afternoon."

This simple statement meant nothing to Merewether, but it obviously did to MacLeod. "Good God, Merewether, Abbott's the secretary of the Select Committee. Elphingham must be sending a report to Bombay Castle!" He shook his head gloomily, and continued, "Damn it, I told you to sit and wait for the fancy dan to get well and carry out his mission, but you had to go ahead. I do hope it doesn't mean trouble." The doubts and worries of the morning came back tenfold. Merewether dissembled, took a hearty leave of his old friend, and rowed back to *Rapid*. As he came on deck, he became conscious of a change, the breeze was light and variable, a hint of moisture in the air. He looked aloft; broken clouds were scudding across the stars heading southwest. He realized that the northeast monsoon had commenced.

He found Dobbs and MacRae on the quarterdeck, sniffing the breeze and looking at the sky. The roadstead off Macao offered no shelter from the northeast winds. MacRae came forward. "I'd like to carry out the bower anchor, sir. This bottom is none too good and we may have a squall or two before morning."

"Very well. I think we might make all preparations for getting under way tomorrow." There was nothing to hold him here any longer, and he had a seaman's dislike of being on a lee shore.

There was a minor squall just before daybreak, wind and rain, that brought Merewether on deck. Larkin had a bearing on the light displayed on the tower of the fort and reported that the anchors were holding. He could see signs of activity on other ships in the roadstead, lights bobbing about decks as boats were lowered and anchors carried out. He was glad he did not have to turn up all hands now for such an evolution in darkness and a choppy sea. Day broke with the sky completely overcast, a light but steady rain falling, and the wind now definitely out of the northeast. He could anticipate unsettled weather, perhaps even a typhoon, for an indefinite period to come. His tentative intention of the night before crystallized. He sent the launch ashore to notify the consul of his departure and to pick up mail and dispatches for Calcutta.

By noon, all departments had reported ready for getting under way. MacRae supervised getting in the bower anchor and then the stream anchor was brought to short stay. Once under way, he had enough sea room to clear Ilha de Coloane and its surrounding mud flats and islets. Close-hauled on the port tack, he clawed out into the great Pearl estuary to the eastward until he could set a course south into the open sea. By nightfall, he was clear of the scattered islands in the approaches and altered course a half point to the west of south. Almost before the wind, he had a two-day run to the point where he would alter course to south southwest for the thousand-mile voyage to the eastern approaches to Malacca Strait.

By dawn, the second day, the weather had moderated, the rain had ceased and the sun rose hazily in a brassy sky. The sea was choppy and the breeze, at first light and variable, soon hauled around toward the north. To the northeast, clouds were building up, and as the day wore on, the sea unaccountably rolled upon itsself, becoming a crosshatch of competing rollers, breaking in foam and flying spray. The barometer had dropped to 29.15 inches when MacRae approached him on the weather side of the quarterdeck.

"Sir, I recommend we reduce sail to storm jib and trysails. I think we are in the path of a typhoon." He looked again to the northeast at the ominous bank of clouds. Far up at their peak, fragments appeared to break off and be swept away to nothingness. The wind here was yet moderate, but in the confused sea, the ship was rolling and pitching, rigging groaning as stays alternately tightened and slacked off.

"Quite right," Merewether told him. "And have all loose gear secured and blocks placed under the trucks of the guns. Double up on the hold-downs on the boat cradles and spare spars. Have the Cooper make certain the water casks are secure." These were elemental precautions, taken whenever a blow of consequence threatened.

"Aye aye, sir." MacRae turned to go forward. Merewether looked again at the towering clouds to the northeast, they were more threatening than any he had ever seen, though he had been through a typhoon not far from here in '95 in old *Dunvegan Castle*.

"MacRae," he called. "Have the boatswain rouse out that sea anchor and bend the anchor cable to it. Be sure it is sheltered from the wind."

This was an all-hands evolution. The sails were brailed up, then furled with doubled gaskets. The Sailmaker and Boatswain hauled the sea anchor, not used since the journey to the Andaman Islands, on deck, bent on the anchor cable and then lashed it to the bulwarks on the starboard bow where it could be cut loose in a moment. Davis, the Purser, was seeing that the boats had water and provisions in them, though that was slight comfort if this were a real typhoon. Merewether considered that he had done all that he could to prepare *Rapid* for the storm. He went below, looked again at the barometer, saw it was now 29.10 inches and went to the supercargo's cabin to see how Sir Thomas was faring.

The diplomat was obviously not happy. The swelling of his belly had subsided, and he was able to move about and sit in his chair, but the motion of the ship would have troubled a sound man. Merewether called an encouraging word in the door as he saw Buttram and his servant easing the pale Sir Thomas into his bed, a bucket prudently set close by. He proceeded to his own cabin and found that Sangh had secured all the movables, and fastened down the ports, windows, and wind vents. To his surprise, it was almost noon, and he ate the light lunch that Sangh set out before he went back on deck.

As he came out of the companionway on deck, the wind whisked his hat off and sailed it up the deck over the starboard bulwarks into the sea. *Rapid*, still on the port tack under reefed storm jib and trysails, was plunging southward at close to ten knots. The wind must be at gale force, almost out of the north-east. To the east, the cloud bank was solid, looking like rugged cliffs against the horizon, tendrils breaking off from its top to whirl into nothingness.

MacRae came up and shouted over the howl of the wind, "It's hauling to the east, sir, and the barometer is still falling, 28.90 now. I recommend we wear about on the starboard tack and heave to. I think we are in the path of the storm and we cannot outrun it!" Merewether looked at the compass, saw that the wind was shifting to the east, and agreed. He had enough sea room to the westward, but there was the Dangerous Ground beginning a little over a hundred miles southeast, a vast area of reefs and islets, uninhabited and unexplored.

Hove to, the ship rode easily at first, taking a little water over the bow from time to time. Then the wind began to shift to the north again, increasing in force. Visibility in the early afternoon diminished. A fine rain, mixed with spume, blew horizontally, so hard that it stung the flesh as it struck. The clouds were no longer on the horizon, but now seemed to be all about the ship as she staggered under the force of the wind, driven now almost south-eastward.

MacRae fought his way from the cubbyhole to where Merewether clung to the shrouds. "I think we are on the left semicircle of the storm and being driven southeastward toward the Dangerous Ground. I recommend we launch the sea anchor!" Masts and rigging provided enough sail area to move the ship at a smart rate, though hove to. A few hours of this and the ship might strike an uncharted reef or island unless her drift could be minimized.

"Very well." MacRae fought his way forward against the howling gale and roused out the watch sheltering under the break of the forecastle. They managed after a quarter hour struggle to get the ungainly mass of canvas over the side and into the water out of the clutches of the wind. A hundred fathoms were veered out before the cable was secured and the ship rode to the anchor. It was impossible to be sure with nothing to measure against, but Merewether felt that the drift to leeward was greatly lessened.

Lifelines had been fastened across the deck. The two quarter-masters at the wheel had taken turns of line about their waists and

secured the ends to ringbolts in the deck. Their task of keeping
the bow into the seas had been eased by the sea anchor, but they
must still be alert for every plunging movement of the ship.
Merewether took a turn of line about himself and fastened it to
the weather shrouds. He was soaked, but the wind was not cold,
and he remained alert for any emergency.

Late in the afternoon, the wind seemed to build up to a crescendo. He could see the masts actually bend, every stay rigid as
an iron bar. MacRae was in the cubbyhole again, making calculations based on dead reckoning to approximate the ship's position. Dobbs and the Boatswain were forward keeping vigilant eyes
on the anchor cable that made a straight line ahead until it disappeared into the foaming sea.

Merewether was looking directly up at the mizzen-royal mast
when it happened. Perhaps a gasket was carelessly tied or rotten,
or simply could not stand the strain any longer. In any event, the
outboard gasket securing the mizzen-royal sail parted, the wind
forced its way between layers of canvas, snapping the remaining
gaskets like twine. The royal sail suddenly expanded, ballooned
out with the wind with a crack like thunder, and was driven back
against the mast and yard, filled with all the force of the typhoon.
The royal mast may have been strained or cracked from the
collision with the proa at Amoorang. It broke off just above the
top mast, bent over backward, the sail still filled with wind, tore
loose its stays and shrouds and disappeared aft like an arrow shot
from a bow.

Rapid was jerked violently backward when the sail filled, then
released when the mast and sail parted company with the ship.
There was another shock, and the ship staggered, her head fell off,
she almost broached as the helmsmen fought the wheel and
finally managed to hold her on the starboard tack.

A melancholy hail drifted aft over the howl of the wind. "Cable's parted, sir." Merewether could see confusion forward, evidently the end of the rigid cable had recoiled and struck down a
man. He could see the crumpled form lying on the deck, spray
driving into him, in danger of being washed over the side.

Merewether tried to loosen the line that secured him to the
shrouds and make his way forward to give assistance. Then he saw

the thickset Dobbs crawling forward against the wind and sea, reach the man and drag him slowly aft to where the others could lower him gently to the shelter beneath the break of the forecastle. He managed to make his way to the companionway, slide back the hatch, and shout down for Buttram to go forward.

The ship by now was going downwind at a great rate. Fortunately, the storm sails had not carried away, and she was still hove to on the starboard tack. Merewether made his way forward by inches, from handhold to handhold, to the forecastle. The Boatswain reported that he had already notified the Sailmaker to commence making a new sea anchor, but it would be a matter of hours at best before it could be ready, and they might be ashore by then.

Merewether looked about the deck for some object that might serve the purpose. His eye lit on the rack in which the spare studding-sail yards were stored. They might just be strong enough. In the howling wind, they lashed four of them together, wrapped the framework with a bolt of new canvas and attached a bridle to it like a kite. A ten-fathom length of chain gave the contraption weight enough to sink. They bent it on to the spare cable and managed to cast it over the side. The cable became taut and *Rapid* rode to the makeshift sea anchor, her drift checked.

Merewether made his way aft, found MacRae with his gloomy report that *Rapid* was much too close to the Dangerous Ground for comfort and resumed his post at the weather shrouds. It was dark by now, the wind shrieking through the rigging, the ship rolling, pitching, and twisting in the confused sea. The cooks had managed to get food, cold salt beef, biscuit, and cold beans, to the hands.

The sea anchor held all during the night as the wind drew westward, so that by dawn it was almost due west. Merewether fought his way down to the cubbyhole and joined MacRae to examine the chart. Even in this shelter it was necessary to shout to be heard over the howl of the wind.

"My best guess puts us about 12 degrees, 10 minutes north, 113 degrees, 30 minutes east, sir," shouted MacRae. "Might be two hundred miles off in any direction, but we may be close to Danger Island here on the chart."

"I don't know anything we can do," Merewether shouted back. "Looks like we are on the lefthand semicircle of the typhoon. If wind would moderate, I'd try to run for it to the south." He ducked into his cabin, drank a cup of cold tea and devoured a biscuit before he went back on deck.

It was now daylight, but visibility was extremely limited by the flying spray and the fact that *Rapid* spent a great deal of time in the trough of the seas which seemed to loom over her as high as the mainyard. He saw Eldridge, maintopman in the watch, sheltering beneath the break of the poop. He had had in mind rating him boatswain's mate since the death of Jackson at Amoorang, but had not found the time.

"You," he called. The man came toward him, pulling hand over hand on the lifeline rigged along the deck. "Can you get aloft in the mizzen and see if you can see anything?" Without hesitation, the man leaped to the shrouds, and made his way up. The mizzen without its royal mast was a stumpy thing, but high enough to get above most of the flying spume. He clung to the shrouds, clothes plastered to his body by the wind, and looked about the horizon, then pointed astern and shouted something that the wind carried away. Merewether signaled him down.

On deck, he shouted, "I can see what looks like breakers right astern of us!"

Merewether did not hesitate, he climbed up the shrouds, thankful that he had been a topman himself in his time. Before he reached the topmast, he could see the breakers no more than three miles astern, flung fifty feet in the air as they swept over what appeared to be a low island. He would be on it in another quarter of an hour at the present rate of drift unless he could somehow alter course.

Back on deck, he called MacRae, urgently told him to get in the sea anchor and to call all hands to make sail. MacRae looked at him as though he had lost his mind, then turned and fought his way forward on the pitching deck. The windlass began to clank around, the men slipping and straining to get in the cumbersome sea anchor. Merewether called Larkin and Dobbs. "I'm going to set enough sail to move us south on the starboard tack," he told them. "I want you to tend the sheets on the jib and trysails, and I'm going to set a staysail aft!"

This was easier said than done. The sail threatened to blow right away in spite of all the afterguard could do. It was finally bent on, and the hands stood ready at the sheets. Merewether tried to look aft where he had seen the breakers, could not see for the spray, and held himself tense, expecting any moment to feel the horrendous shock of the ship striking rock. The windlass clanked on interminably, taking in a hundred fathoms of cable against the strain of the sea anchor.

Merewether had almost decided to cut the cable, when MacRae signaled that the anchor was in sight. He sent a hand forward with directions to cut the remaining cable. He saw Larkin and Dobbs at the trysail sheets, MacRae at the jib, standing tense and ready. With stern way on the ship, it would be tricky to get her head about to the south without broaching. The axe flashed up and down twice and the cable parted.

"Port helm!" he roared. The ship, still with stern way on, staggered, rolled so far to port he thought she might go on over, then steadied as the bow began to swing to the left. He might very well continue the swing, be caught broadside to the wind and capsize. Watching with agonized intensity as the swing went through four points, Merewether shouted, "Midships! Meet her! Sheet home!"

He knew that MacRae, Larkin and Dobbs were out of earshot, but they had their eyes glued upon him and the party tending the after staysail. They acted instantly. The sails filled with thunderous reports, but did not fly to shreds as he had feared. The stern way was checked.

"Starboard helm! Midships. Steady as you go. Your course is south." With four ridiculous scraps of sail showing, *Rapid* staggered off to the south, clawing away from the breakers that all hands could now see on the port beam less than a mile away. The hands stood by the sheets all the rest of the day, tending them as though their lives depended upon it, which, Merewether considered, was the absolute truth. They lost each of the tiny sails at least once, shredded into tatters in an instant by a fluke or gust, but never all at once.

By the beginning of the midwatch, it was apparent that the wind was lessening, though the sea was still making up. MacRae was confident that they were making their way out of the path of the storm, which he now estimated was traveling northwestward. At dawn, there was a clear patch in the sky and enough of a horizon for him to observe the altitude of three stars and obtain a rough fix. *Rapid* was clear of the Dangerous Ground.

The ship changed course to southwest before noon as the wind backed around again to the northeast. This was the normal monsoon, and enough to convince Merewether and MacRae that they were well out of the track of the typhoon. The third day the sea had moderated to the point that they decided they could replace the mizzen-royal mast and rigging. Fortunately, among the spare spars was one that with some fitting would serve. They hove to for a day and a night while they made the repairs.

CHAPTER 36

Sir Thomas came on deck for the first time in nearly a month as the Boatswain was supervising the final tightening of the braces and deadeyes during the forenoon watch. He was able to walk now without assistance. The Purser set up a canvas chair along the weather rail for him to give him the benefit of some sun after his long confinement.

Merewether was in his cabin overhauling his journal, bringing matters up to date, when he noticed that it was Sunday. It had been so long since he had observed a Sunday that with the successful completion of the repairs to the ship, he felt suddenly that he should call the crew together and give solemn thanks for their survival of the typhoon. His mind went back to Vellore and to Sister Jeanne. His conscience still throbbed at the thought of her useless death, and he thought fuzzily that a service of thanksgiving might be a token of honor to her. In any event, he called Sangh, had MacRae summoned and directed him to call all hands for worship.

The service was brief. Merewether made a short statement of the trial the ship had just been through, expressed his thanks to the hands for their performance of duty, read the Twenty-Third

Psalm from the Book of Common Prayer, then the Thanksgiving for a Safe Return from a Journey, and concluded with the Lord's Prayer. The crew shuffled their feet and cleared their throats in anticipation of dismissal.

"Eldridge, step forward," said Merewether. The topman came toward the rostrum, knuckling his forelock. "By virtue of the Articles for the Government of the Bombay Marine and the powers vested in me as the commanding officer of this vessel, I hereby rate Eldridge, boatswain's mate. Enter this in the log, Mr. Mac-Rae, and change your pay records accordingly, Mr. Davis. And in view of the many braces that have been replaced these last two days, I think an issue of spirits is in order. You may dismiss the crew, Mr. MacRae." The crew gave him three cheers as he ducked below.

Rapid raised Bintan at the approaches to the Strait of Malacca just before dusk four days later. As a matter of prudence, Merewether lay to during the night intending to enter these narrow waters by daylight. The weather was fine, no hint of the typhoon of a week ago a thousand miles to the north that had almost overwhelmed the ship. The crew appeared to be in excellent spirits. There was a great deal of trading going on with the items they had managed to acquire at Macao, the produce of China. Porcelain, swatches of silk cloth, ivory carvings and delicate fans, articles of brass, and even some of silver and jade, were displayed by some of the hands, while others had only the memory of rum and brandy drunk or the present affliction of painful disease to remind them of the hard-earned pay they had squandered there.

Merewether remained awhile on deck in the group around Sir Thomas in his canvas chair, listening to his tales of service in Portugal as a diplomat, the glittering balls which he had attended in Lisbon before coming out to India. The man was entertaining; he had the gift of telling a story vividly, keeping his own part in the background. The mention of the social affairs reminded Merewether of the ones he had attended in Calcutta and inevitably brought to mind Flora Dean and the effect his last party had had on her. He tried to put the matter out of his mind. He had hurt her enough by his failure to declare himself. To become

the scandal of Calcutta by his performance at the party hosted by
Lord Laddie was inexcusable. He drew away from the chattering
group of officers and went below.

Here just above the equator, the interior of the ship became
unbearable with heat during the day, but the northeast monsoon
diverted into the cabin by the windsails through the vents made it
comfortable after sunset. He opened the strongbox and took out
his journal and the reports of his mission completed to date.
Having let them grow quite cold since he had written them, he
read them through critically, searching for mistakes or for a better
way of expressing himself. After all, he might very well be tried
upon the information contained in these documents once they
were submitted to Sir George and the Marine. Half a dozen
times, he reached for the pen, tempted to make an interlineation
or change a word, then decided he had used the correct expression
in the first place. He replaced the reports in the strongbox and sat
under the vent, drinking in the breeze, collar open, sleeves rolled
up. Sangh placed a glass of gin and a lemon before him without
his consciously noticing the act.

Merewether's mind was black on Flora Dean again. He tried for
the hundredth time to analyze his feelings and motives toward
her. Granted, she was a nice, reasonably attractive young woman,
with good intelligence. Yet he had met a dozen like her in the past
eight years since, as a commissioned officer in the Marine, he began to attend social functions. Possibly, it was the fact that she
seemed to be drawn to him that had made him reciprocate. His
self-justification for drawing back from the prospect of marriage—
that it was not fair to a woman to be married to an officer of the
Marine—was disproved by the scores of officers who were married
and whose wives seemed to thrive. That, he concluded, had no
real validity as an excuse. He must look deeper within himself for
his inability to take a step that meant marriage to as vital a young
lady as Flora. He sighed, found the glass empty and Sangh standing by with the bottle. He took a second glass.

Possibly, it was the fact that he had no family, that inevitably
in a marriage, the fact would become known, at least to the wife,
that he was fatherless, a bastard, with no respectable heritage to
pass on to his children. He tried to examine the fact dispassion-

ately, to say that it did not matter where a man came from, that it was his own deeds and way of life that counted. He could give lip service to this proposition, but he did not believe it himself. Reared as a backstairs child in a house of wealth and family, the necessity of an impeccable ancestry had been ingrained upon him by the time his mother had died. It had not been weakened by the callous action of his grandfather, no more than a groom himself, in making immediate disposition of this embarrassing descendant of his. The years in an Indiaman, with its hierarchy of wealth and family, had served to impress the matter still further upon him. His thoughts went to the new republic, the United States, and its lack of hereditary nobility, but even its first President, Washington, came from a noble family in England through a succession of younger sons. Merewether came to a reluctant conclusion; he knew his abilities as an officer, but he had no faith in himself as a person. It was silly, but the fact remained, he had withdrawn, failed to declare himself for the simple reason that he feared the inevitable discovery of his origin and the effect it would have upon a woman as proper and conscious of such matters as Flora Dean.

The second glass was empty. He waved Sangh away and went on deck just as the midwatch was called. Dobbs was already on the quarterdeck receiving the situation from Larkin. The moon was up, the horizon clear except for the loom of Bintan far to the southwest. The motion of the ship was easy and he went to his bed feeling a little as though he had taken a cathartic. For the first time in his life, he had faced up to himself, and admitted to a fear that he had tried for sixteen years to bury out of sight.

CHAPTER 37

The journey through the straits and northwestwardly across the Bay of Bengal was uneventful. *Rapid* picked up the pilot off the Sandheads and two days later came to anchor off the dockyard. Buttram refused to allow Sir Thomas to climb down the ladder to the gig, and to his disgust, he was lowered into the boat in a chair.

By the time the gig reached the landing, Sir Thomas's wife and daughter were present, as was Sir George Barlow. The ship evidently had been reported from far downstream.

Sir George was solicitous, though his face fell, when he learned that his envoy had fallen almost mortally ill before he arrived at Canton. He evidently was prepared for disappointment. Davis came up to the headquarters from the launch with his working party bringing the mail and dispatches from Macao, Canton and *Gazelle*. Merewether had his own reports wrapped in a canvas packet which he handed to Commodore Land while the reunion was taking place. He and Land waited courteously to one side until Sir George called them over.

"I've prevailed upon Sir Thomas and his wife to dine with Lady Barlow and me tonight to give an informal report of the mission. I'd be appreciative if you two would come as well and bring your reports."

"Aye aye, sir," both officers responded in unison. Sir Thomas, his wife, and his baggage soon departed in a carriage supplied by the Acting Governor-General. Land and Merewether separated the reports and dispatches due Sir George from those for forwarding to Bombay Castle, and Land put the copies for Sir George in his pocket. Merewether returned to the ship, changed quickly into full dress, and came back to the dockyard. It was almost dark as they drew up at the great gate outside the Governor's Residence.

Sir George, at home among friends, displayed little of the coldness that was his official manner. "I've some dry sack here I'd like your opinion of, gentlemen," he said. "Just came in. The vintner says it is not contraband, but was laid down during the peace." Merewether decided that contraband or not, it was an excellent wine. They shortly went in to dinner in the great dining room.

After dinner, the gentlemen gathered in the library where he had delivered the courier with the news from Vellore. Sir George, Sir Thomas, and Commodore Land lighted up aromatic cigars as a servant served coffee and Spanish brandy.

"Now, Thomas," Sir George commenced, puffing out an immense cloud of blue smoke. "Tell the story of the voyage, leaving out nothing. I've learned that Merewether here is a little too fac-

tual to be a good minstrel, and I can read his report tomorrow."
The group laughed, and Merewether found his cheeks a little hot,
though the remark was meant as praise.

Sir Thomas did make an interesting account of it, from the
unsettled weather east of the Strait of Malacca through the encounter with the Chinese junks off Java, and the engagement with
the Magindinao pirates at Amoorang. He made this battle sound
in the telling as though it were another Trafalgar or St. Vincent,
stressing the ship handling that maintained *Rapid* on the weather
gauge and prevented the pirate proas from approaching close
enough to board. Merewether was embarrassed at the praise and
completely unprepared when Sir Thomas paused.

"Several days before we reached China, I became disabled with
a colic and had to have my belly cut open. I have no very clear
recollection as to events until Captain Merewether returned
aboard some days later and reported that the mission had been
accomplished. I shall have to call upon him to complete the
account."

Sir George, Sir Thomas, and the Commodore all looked at him
expectantly. He pulled together his thoughts and launched into
his report, trying to remember the terms in which he had written
his account now reposing in the Commodore's pocket. He was
factual in telling of the interview with John Elphingham, the
proposition made by the two Chinese hostages for their delivery
home with honor, the *quid pro quo* he had proposed, and had
seen carried out. He made no mention of encountering an old
friend, now a teacher in Canton, or the entertainment that night.
He had verified the next afternoon that Grand Chop had been
granted the Indiamen. He mentioned the typhoon only in passing
to account for the delay in his return. As he fell silent, he found
the three of them gazing raptly at him.

Sir George was the first to speak. "Excellent!" he said. "You
broke the laws of China, but you were not apprehended, and you
accomplished the mission." He paused a moment, then continued, "This John Elphingham has powerful friends in the Company, but so do I. Your report shall go the Committee of Secrecy in
London by the next ship and I doubt that he will hold his post
this time next year."

"Just one thing," said Merewether anxiously. "I am told that Abbott, the Secretary of the Select Committee, took ship before *Rapid* left, bound for Bombay. I expect that he will make a report to the Superintendent of the Marine."

"May do it," said Sir George carelessly. "I can't see Campbell paying much attention to it though."

The talk changed to other matters, and in a few minutes they rejoined the ladies briefly before Land and Merewether took their departure.

Another period of the doldrums descended upon *Rapid* for the next week. In two days' time, she was revictualed, watered, the marks of battle and typhoon erased with new rigging, putty and paint. The prudent hands had disposed of their Chinese merchandise in the bazaars for silver rupees, and the others had a quarter's pay to squander in the back alleys of Calcutta. Merewether pumped MacLellan for news of events while he was gone. No one had seen or heard of Flora Dean, it seemed. There were no social events to which the officers of the ship were invited. Merewether found himself wishing that something would happen, even a reception, to break the monotony.

Zebra, a twelve-gun brig, came to anchor in the Hooghly one lazy afternoon. She had dipped her flag to *Rapid* as she passed, so Woodruff, a year junior to Merewether as a first lieutenant, must still be in command. He idled on the quarterdeck, watching her lower her gig and then her launch. The gig pulled away for the dockyard, followed by the launch with bags of mail piled midships. He had gone below, kicked off his shoes, and started to lie down for a nap when the messenger came.

"Dockyard's signaling, sir. 'Request Captain come ashore.' "

"Signal affirmative," Merewether told the messenger, putting his shoes back on and sliding into the coat Sangh held for him. He had a sense of foreboding; such messages heretofore had resulted in an immediate interview with Sir George and sent him out on impossible missions. He heard the gig called away and went on deck.

Commodore Land was brisk. "*Zebra* brought a whole set of dispatches from Bombay Castle I haven't bothered with, but here's one addressed to you personally, marked Private-Official."

He looked at Merewether with a sort of concern. Reprimands and letters of admonition to an officer were always delivered in this manner. For that matter, specifications of charges and orders to appear before a Court of Inquiry when an officer was not already under arrest were so delivered.

Merewether felt a chill of fear flash through him, then strove to appear impassive. He borrowed Land's penknife to slit the stitches in the oilskin covering to expose the envelope and examined the seal. "Sir James himself," he said lightly and broke open the covering.

The covering orders were brief. "You will depart Calcutta, or such other place as these orders may find you, immediately and proceed to Bombay Castle, there to present yourself before a Court of Inquiry for trial in accordance with the specifications of charges against you herewith enclosed." It was signed by Sir James Campbell, Superintendent of the Bombay Marine.

Merewether unfolded the other sheets. His eyes leaped immediately to the second paragraph. "First: That the said Percival Merewether, being then and there a Captain, commissioned in the Naval Service of the Honourable East India Company, and serving as commandant of one of the ships of its service, did willfully and unlawfully on the 29th day of September, 1806, and thereafter, enter the city of Canton, of the Empire of China, in violation of the laws of the said Empire of China, and of the Treaties and Regulations of the Honourable East India Company and its Naval Service, to the prejudice of good order and discipline in said Service." The second specification followed almost word for word, except that it added that he had unlawfully taken under his command an armed detachment of the First Marine Battalion into Canton.

Merewether laughed bitterly. "It appears that Abbott reached Bombay and Sir James did pay attention to him!" he told Land, handing him the specifications of charges. The Commodore read them slowly, then looked at Merewether.

"Sir James is a civilian and a bit of a fool," he said dispassionately. "The Court of Inquiry will, of course, be composed of officers of the Marine of the rank of captain or above. I feel sure the Court will understand the matter once Sir George's orders are brought to its attention. Be a sorry affair when an officer is punished for carrying out a lawful order of a superior."

Merewether hesitated, then said carefully, "Sir, my orders were only to transport Sir Thomas to Canton and assist him. Carrying out his mission may be within the spirit of the orders, but they do not spell it out, and I'm sure Elphingham knows this. I did what I thought had to be done, but not under orders."

"Well, I'm damned!" exploded Commodore Land. "A sea lawyer splitting hairs, and against his own interest at that!"

"I am only stating the facts that I am sure the court would bring out, sir," Merewether said gloomily. "I asked Sir Thomas for orders, and he declined to issue them, but said he would do what I proposed to do in a minute. I shall have to take the full official responsibility."

Land continued to look at him for a full minute, his mouth a little open and an expression on his face that Merewether had never seen before. Then he snapped his mouth shut with an audible click, and said, "You require legal counsel to consult with you, render an opinion, and represent you in the trial."

"Perhaps so," said Merewether. "But I do not know any lawyers, though I am sure there are some in Bombay."

"Bombay!" cried the Commodore. "Bombay, when the finest advocate in the Marine is within a stone's throw of us now!"

"You, sir?" ventured Merewether, confused by the heat and apparent agitation of Land's manner. He was still a little stunned by the reality of the fact that he had been charged with an offense that upon conviction would effectively end his career in the Marine. It had been one thing to worry about the possibility at Macao and quite another to face the fact.

"Not me, you ninny! As your commanding officer for the time, I am disqualified. I share, at least by association, your guilt. MacLellan has represented officers at six Courts of Inquiry and the worst his man has gotten is a verbal reprimand!"

"MacLellan," murmured Merewether, with wonder. He had known the big Scots officer now for ten months, counted him possibly his closest friend, but no hint of this ability had reached him. Granted, the subject had never come up, not even on the long night watches in the South Atlantic and Indian Ocean, when MacLellan had rambled on through the politics and gossip of the

Company and the Marine, the Wellesley clique in the Council, and the foibles of Calcutta society. "I never heard that. Do you think he would consent to serve as my 'friend,' sir?"

"In a minute," said Land firmly. "He thinks you hung the moon, and I shall see that he is given orders to Bombay Castle for this duty." He looked down at the specifications again. "I wish to consult with Sir George before I actually issue any orders. His deposition should carry some weight in the affair, as should that of Sir Thomas. I suggest that you take these specifications over to the arsenal, and acquaint MacLellan with the facts."

Merewether walked reluctantly over to the arsenal. He found MacLellan in a rare moment of relaxation watching a party brushing thick black paint on a row of gun carriages. He forced himself to greet him in his usual manner, make small talk, listen briefly to the trials and tribulations of an ordnance officer plagued with workmen whose hands were all thumbs. He could not bring himself to broach the subject here, finally invited MacLellan to dinner, and waited for him to wash up and shift into a fresh uniform before they rowed back to the ship.

In the cabin, Sangh brought gin and Scots whisky. Over the second gin, Merewether finally began his story and brought out the packet of charges. MacLellan's manner changed instantly. He pursed his lips, narrowed his eyes, and read the specifications with care, his lips moving as he scanned the lines.

"Now, Captain," he said in the burr that he assumed in moments of stress, sitting back in his chair and putting his fingertips together below his chin. "Tell me exactly what happened and what you did at Canton."

Merewether felt for a moment like a truant schoolboy summoned before the master, though this officer had served as his first lieutenant for six months and had been his close friend and confidant. He sat back, gathered himself, and told the story baldly, trying to give every fact without elaboration or omission. When he finished, he looked at MacLellan. The big red face had assumed the rapt, distant expression that indicated his technical abilities had been challenged.

MacLellan sat quietly for perhaps two minutes, eyes almost closed. Then he asked in a quiet voice, "And these Chinese you had on board asked you to take them to their home in Canton?"

"Yes," said Merewether. "After the contraband powder was jettisoned from the junks, I thought I should have hostages in case some complaint was made, and I brought them to Macao, intending to have them make a statement to the consul. I never got around to it, though, what with Sir Thomas being disabled. It was a matter of face for them to return home with honor, rather than as whipped dogs, as I recall Wong said." He paused, thought a moment, and continued, "Of course, in exchange for this, I asked that they induce their grandfather to intervene with the Hoppo, which he did, successfully."

"Of course," said MacLellan reprovingly, "these witnesses are some three thousand miles away and not available to testify before the court." He sat back again, eyes closed, then leaned forward. "Do you have anything in writing, other than your bare orders, as evidence that might be introduced in your favor?"

Merewether was conscious that Sangh had been hovering inside the door for the past quarter hour, ready to set dinner on the table. "I don't think so, but let me think. Shall we dine?"

By mutual consent, they both steered the conversation into other directions during the meal, but as soon as the table was cleared, MacLellan came back to the subject.

"Best let me read the copies of your reports and journal, Captain. So far, you have convicted yourself of both specifications by your own story." Merewether felt his spirits sink again, went to the strongbox, and removed the copies of his orders and reports. Jammed in the corner, half crumpled, was the scroll the old Mandarin had handed him as he departed from Canton. He laid the stack of papers on the table under the lamp.

MacLellan read rapidly through the orders and then the reports, laying them back neatly in the proper order. He picked up the scroll, smoothed and unrolled it. Merewether had only examined it briefly on the way back to the boat from the Mandarin's house. He vaguely remembered that it contained a drawing of a figure, a number of Chinese ideographs, and a red seal stamped at the bottom.

MacLellan snorted. "Where did you get this, Captain?"

"Why, the Mandarin gave it to me as I left his house," Merewether replied, puzzled.

"Do you recognize yourself?" demanded MacLellan, thrusting the scroll across the table to him.

Merewether looked at the scroll. At the top was a drawing of an officer in the uniform of the Bombay Marine. Though less than two inches high, the detail was exquisite, from the buttons on the coat, the crooked nose, to the scar along the right cheek and the missing earlobe. It was a beautifully rendered miniature of himself.

"Well, I'm damned!"

"Of course, you don't know what it says?"

"No. Oh, Wong said something about giving me the freedom of the city. Perhaps that is what it says."

"Perhaps!" exploded MacLellan. "This appears to be a most important piece of evidence in the affair, and you don't know what it says." He shook his head. "I don't know what it says either, but I intend to find out if I can find a Chinese scholar in Calcutta. I have three Chinee artisans, but they're not scholars. Perhaps they know one who can read it. If you don't mind, I'll take this with me for the night."

"Certainly," said Merewether. Suddenly he felt bone weary, unable to endure a moment more of this even from MacLellan. He was relieved when MacLellan announced that he would go ashore. He went to sleep immediately, to awaken at the call for the midwatch, and toss feverishly until daylight.

CHAPTER 38

The dockyard signaled for him at two bells in the forenoon watch. In the headquarters, he found Commodore Land and MacLellan waiting for him. "Conference with Sir George," explained Land briefly, as they entered the tonga.

"Well, Merewether, I was wrong," said Sir George briskly. "I shall do all that I can to see that a man carrying out orders I've given does not suffer for it. I have already dictated a deposition in the strongest possible terms, and Sir Thomas is prepared, if Buttram will permit, to go with you to Bombay as a witness."

"Thank you, Your Excellency," murmured Merewether.

"Now," continued Sir George. "I am informed that Lieutenant MacLellan will be your 'friend' at the court of inquiry. I have ordered my staff to give him every assistance in preparing the defense. Only thing we cannot find in Calcutta is a Chinese scholar, but MacLellan says there is one at Madras, and I've issued orders to Bentinck to make him available to you, if his services appear to be necessary."

As they rattled back to the dockyard, MacLellan explained. "My best Chinee artisan had a cousin, a scholar, who lives at Madras. He thinks he is still alive, though he would be quite old by now. If we can't find him, he has another cousin at Goa and even one at Bombay, though he doubts the scholarship of the Bombay one. My man can read just a little, but he thinks this paper you have is what they call a 'freedom of the city,' given to important visitors. If he's right, we'll diddle them yet."

"You must be under way day after tomorrow," said Land. "Three days they usually allow. Although the orders did not say so, I'm sending you in *Rapid*. There's precedent for it in the Royal Navy. Nelson sent Calder back last year to England for trial in his own ship."

"Thank you, sir." Merewether felt a sense of warmth at these people, from Sir George down, rallying to his defense.

Two days later *Rapid* weighed anchor and made her way down the Hooghly. MacLellan, Sir Thomas, and the Chinese artisan from the dockyard were on board. They reached Madras and anchored off Fort St. George. MacLellan, Merewether, and the Chinese went ashore where Merewether reported to Governor William Bentinck with the orders from Sir George. The same brash young captain was in the outer office, rising respectfully as he recognized Merewether.

"Sir, no need to bother His Lordship, I'll take care of this." Bells tinkled and people appeared, MacLellan and his Chinese artisan disappeared under the escort of a sergeant major. They were back within an hour, looking downcast.

"Sir, Lee's cousin died six months ago. No other Chinese scholars in the city. We'll have to stop at Goa."

Merewether felt that fate must be conniving at his ruin. He had no real faith in this defense that MacLellan set such store by, but deferred to his superior judgment. One thing struck him. He must not depart from Madras without paying tribute to young Burcham, cut off in the flower of his youth, and buried over there in St. George's Cemetery. He requested a carriage, bought a handsome display of blossoms, and laid them on the grave with a silent prayer as MacLellan and the Chinese stood by with bowed heads.

Merewether realized almost as soon as they left the burial grounds that his visit had been a mistake. It had served to revive memories of events better forgotten. He came back on board *Rapid* and gave MacRae terse orders to get under way south again. He remained on deck until the course was set, then went below. Sitting at his desk, depression overwhelmed him as never before.

He had deliberately sent young Burcham to his death as a decoy to draw Tipu away from him while he made his escape down the river. Looking back, he felt he should have taken Burcham with him and left the Company detachment to go on to Madras alone. He tried to reason with himself, for it had appeared essential at the time that the party traveling by land closely resemble the party as it departed from Vellore. Now, he was convinced otherwise.

The gloomy thoughts of his guilt in the death of Burcham inevitably revived the recollection of the useless death of Sister Jeanne. Here again, he felt guilt weighing him down. The woman had come to him with vital information, and he had taken advantage of her infatuation. He thought now, the least he could have done was escort her back to the mission. He tried to tell himself that even that gesture would not have shielded her from Tipu's vengeance, but a blow in the dark in the heat of anger at a betrayal was quite different from carrying out a deliberate execution.

His present difficulties were a judgment on him, Merewether concluded. He remembered in disbelief the exhilaration he had felt at Canton, with his Marines marching ahead of him through the crowds to the sound of trumpet and drum, the journey in disguise to the audience with the Hoppo, and the lighthearted entertainment afterward. He wished desperately that he had taken the sound advice offered by MacLeod and had waited for Sir Thomas to recover to carry out his mission, even though it might have fatally delayed departure of the Indiamen.

He thought again of the specifications of charges against him to be heard by the Court of Inquiry. As MacLellan had pointed out, his own reports convicted him, with one immaterial exception; the Marines had not been armed. MacLellan appeared to set great value on the scroll from the old Mandarin, and spoke glibly of offering to the court something known in law as a "plea of confession and avoidance." So far, Merewether thought bitterly, they had been unsuccessful in finding a Chinese scholar to translate the scroll, and his confession might well stand alone at Bombay Castle without the semblance of an avoidance. Few Chinese were to be found in India, and fewer still had the education to decipher the black brush marks beneath the miniature portrait. He broke his usual custom of abstinence at sea, drank four gins, and slept the afternoon away.

Two days later, *Rapid* was challenged by the picket sloop of the Royal Navy squadron off Ceylon. MacRae hoisted the recognition signal and her number as the ship plunged on southwardly, then west to weather Ceylon, and north northwest up the coast of India in the Arabian Sea. The swiftness of the journey appalled Merewether. By this time next week, he might be under sentence of dismissal from the Marine, he realized. He found it difficult to converse with Sir Thomas, or even MacLellan, both of whom dined with him in the cabin. The bitter self-reproaches after the Madras visit had subsided into a sullen conviction that his career was ended in spite of the cheerful optimism of Sir Thomas and MacLellan.

The ship approached Goa in a driving rainstorm near dusk. Merewether decided to lie to, well offshore, until daylight before trying to anchor. Sir Thomas had agreed to accompany MacLellan and his artisan ashore to serve as an interpreter with the Portuguese authorities, but daylight found *Rapid* blown further offshore, with the necessity of working laboriously back almost in the eye of the wind to an anchorage. The weather continued bad, with MacRae concluding that a heavy storm was raging to the north. It was noon before the launch departed for the shore.

The afternoon wore on as Merewether fidgeted in his cabin. The sea was making up, and the force of the wind increasing. MacRae requested permission to veer out more cable. It was almost dark when the launch came pulling through the crosshatched seas. As soon as the boat was hoisted in, Merewether had the hands at the windlass, and then stood out to the northwest. He had noted subconsciously that there was an added man, making a party of four that came back aboard. He remained on deck until the ship was well offshore.

When Merewether finally left the deck to Larkin and went below, he found MacLellan, Sir Thomas, and the Chinese artisan in his cabin, grouped about an incredibly ancient Chinese seated in the chair behind his desk. The Mandarin's scroll was laid out on the desk, its corners held down by spoons. A reading glass and MacLellan's fine magnifying lens lay beside it. There was an air of complete despair about the group.

MacLellan turned as Merewether came in. His burr pervaded his announcement. "We found the scholar, Captain, but he's too blind to read!"

Merewether felt no reaction. He had lost all hope a week ago when he left Madras. It was a judgment on him, but he would not let these men see it. He looked at the lamp swaying with the movement of the ship, already smoke-stained and grimy, and told them, "Wait for daylight, give him a night's rest. With this blow, we'll be delayed in reaching Bombay."

Four days later, *Rapid* came to anchor in the broad harbor off Bombay Castle. Within half an hour, a string of flags went up. " 'Captain, report ashore,' " interpreted MacRae.

"Acknowledge and affirmative," Merewether told him, and went below to find MacLellan and Sir Thomas in his cabin. "I am ordered ashore," he told them. "I shall probably be placed under arrest and restrained there until the trial. I should be most appreciative, Mr. MacLellan, if you would accompany me to the Castle and ascertain the details of the trial." He called Sangh, had his chest packed, shifted into full dress with sword, and went on deck.

At the dock, he found Evan Tollett, promoted captain exactly a year before his own promotion, there to greet him. Tollett was ten years older than he, already a little thick about the middle, but noted in the service as sure to achieve the rank of commodore at an early age.

"Ah, Merewether, I regret that we meet again under these circumstances. I'll not take your sword," he said quickly, seeing Merewether's gesture to surrender it. "Time enough for that. It's not as though it was a hanging offense. I must place you under restraint, however, in Bombay Castle. All the members of the Court are present. They expected you would arrive a week ago."

"We had quite a blow coming north," Merewether explained cheerfully. "You know Lieutenant MacLellan? He will serve as my 'friend' before the Court."

Tollett had a seaman with a handbarrow waiting. The chest was loaded on it, and the party proceeded to the gloomy pile of Bombay Castle. There were formalities; Merewether found himself before a young second lieutenant who read the specifications to him in a high strained voice and required him to affirm that he had returned for trial upon them. Eventually, he was delivered to a small, severe room, looking out to the north, and informed in writing that the trial would commence at noon tomorrow. Somewhere along the line, he had lost MacLellan, but he knew the big Scots officer was about his duties and would appear.

It was two hours before he knocked and entered. "I ran into some old friends, Captain. Had to stop and chat a bit." He gave off an aroma of Scots whisky and was in high good humor. "My friends say Abbott, Secretary of the Select Committee, has been here a month, wining and dining everyone who would accept his invitations, and boasting of your ruin. He's told his story a dozen times, and I'm sure the members of the Court have heard every detail. Elphingham sent him in a lorcha to follow your boat and make sure you landed in Canton, but he does not know where you went or what you did after that." He chuckled, then became serious. "No need for me to stay here. I'll go back to the ship and have our witnesses ready for the trial tomorrow."

After MacLellan left, Merewether tried to relax. While he technically was under arrest, he had the freedom of the Castle and could visit other officers in their quarters, or dine at their invitation in their mess. Yet he had no desire to renew old acquaintances. He felt the stigma of being ordered before a Court of Inquiry for trial, and feared the well-meaning sympathy that might be expressed. Whatever the outcome, to a certain element in the Marine, the mere fact that charges had been made was proof of guilt. He began to pace across the narrow room to the window and back. It was a relief when the Indian servant came to invite him to dinner at Captain Tollett's table.

Tollett was pleasant, and took a glass of gin with Merewether before dining. He mentioned in passing that he now had a son twelve years old and a daughter ten over in Bombay. Merewether realized that this officer had deprived himself of a night at home to be with him on this eve of his trial. He tried to be lighthearted, steer the conversation away from his ordeal, but after a bit, found Tollett returning to the subject.

"You know who's on the Court, don't you?"

"No, I left that to MacLellan. If there's any prejudice, he'll deal with it."

"Commodore Morris presides, he's first-rate. Then Captain Glenn, a stickler for regulations; Captain Johnston, fair but easily persuaded; Captain Gregory, don't know much about him; Captain Jarvis, hard but fair, he came up from the lower deck as you did; Captain Kersey, old man now, but still alert; and Captain MacAllester, he's a bear if there ever was one."

Merewether had met all of them at one time or another, and had served two years as a second lieutenant under Kersey. Running over the seven names in his mind, he concluded that it would be a fair Court of Inquiry.

"Who is the Recorder?" he asked. The Recorder was the officer charged with the prosecution.

"Dan James," replied Tollett. "This was a matter of luck. You might have waited two years and never found this many captains at Bombay at one time." Merewether thought bitterly that events had conspired to bring him to trial at the earliest possible moment. In two years, the facts might have been forgotten, Abbott back in Canton, Elphingham relieved and sent back to England.

As they finished their dinner, a group of half a dozen first and second lieutenants came over from a table across the room. Some of them Merewether knew, the others were introduced. One, a pockmarked, weatherbeaten first lieutenant, had had just enough to drink to lose all inhibitions. He clapped Merewether on the back and cried, "No need to worry a minute, Captain! You have

Iron Mac to defend you. Six times, he's come to Bombay Castle, and six times he's cleared his man!"

Merewether laughed. "I hope there's no charm to the seventh! I'm appreciative of your confidence." Soon after, he pled weariness and escaped to his room, expecting to pass a sleepless night. He awoke in broad daylight.

CHAPTER 39

The seven members of the Court were ranged behind a long table set at the end of the room so as to put the backs of the members to the narrow windows opening to the west. Merewether marched in behind Tollett and the master-at-arms immediately after the sullen report of the gun signaling the convening of the Court had sounded. They halted at a point five feet before the table, saluted, and Tollett announced, "Captain Percival Merewether present, sirs." Merewether saw his sword on the table before Commodore Morris, the hilt to his left. If he were found guilty, it would be turned with the blade pointing toward him.

MacLellan and Captain Dan James, the Recorder, followed with the chief clerk to the Superintendent of the Marine. They took seats behind a smaller table to the right of the Court, while MacLellan carried a portfolio to a table set to the left, leaving Merewether standing alone before the Court.

Commodore William Morris looked left, then right, cleared his throat, and announced: "This Court of Inquiry will come to order. I have orders here from Sir James Campbell, Superintendent of the Bombay Marine, transmitted through Commodore Sir John Waldron, Commandant of the Marine, to Commodore William Morris to convene a Court of Inquiry at Bombay Castle to try Captain Percival Merewether of the Marine upon certain specifications of charges thereto attached. I read the orders." He proceeded to do so, then inquired, "Is there any objection or challenge of the convening authority or of any member of this Court?"

"No, sir," said James.

"No, sir," echoed MacLellan.

"I now read the specifications of charges." The Commodore did so, then looked up at Merewether. "And how do you plead to these charges, Captain Percival Merewether?"

"Not guilty to each specification, sirs," said Merewether firmly.

"Captain James, you will record the plea of the defendant."

"It is so recorded, not guilty, sirs."

"You may proceed with the case, Captain James."

James rose, cleared his throat, and said to the court, "Sirs, in view of the nature of the charges involving a violation of the laws of the Empire of China relating to entry of foreigners upon her territory, I ask the Court to acknowledge the existence and validity of such laws. Otherwise, I shall proceed to prove them by the introduction of treaties entered into between the Company and the Empire."

MacLellan rose ponderously. "No objection, may it please the Court."

James continued, "I shall then proceed to read a report written and signed by the defendant, Captain Percival Merewether, October 3, 1806, addressed to the Commandant of the Marine, by way of the Acting Governor-General of India, and by him endorsed and forwarded."

"Objection, sirs," said MacLellan quietly. "If the Recorder intends to read the defendant's reports, he must first lay a foundation for them by reading the original orders given the defendant and all other reports of action taken thereunder up to the date of this report. Standing alone, it is meaningless."

The Commodore looked left, then right. "Clear the Court," he told the master-at-arms. Merewether and the others filed out. James was a little red in the face and spluttering in the ear of the chief clerk.

Five minutes later, the master-at-arms appeared in the doorway and the group filed back in. The Commodore said. "The Court is reconvened. We are of the opinion that the defendant's objection must be sustained. If the prosecution intends to rely upon a report, a proper foundation must be laid."

"Very well, sirs," said James. He whispered to the chief clerk, who gathered a stack of documents, stood up and adjusted a pair of steel-rimmed spectacles on his nose. "May it please the Court, I shall have Mr. Smith read into evidence the orders and reports of the voyage of Captain Merewether to China."

The clerk commenced to read the orders issued at Calcutta by Sir George Barlow and continued through the series of reports of the events of the voyage. The man had a felicitous tone of voice and manner of reading, he waxed almost lyrical as he read the factual account of the capture of the junks and detention of the two supercargoes, the engagement with the pirates at Amoorang, the illness of Sir Thomas, and the interview with Elphingham at Canton. Merewether could see that the members of the Court were following the reports with close attention. Then came the report of the landing at Canton, "At the invitation of Wong and Fong, citizens of that city," Merewether heard the clerk read. He had inserted the phrase at a time when he attributed no great importance to the matter. The clerk concluded and sat down.

James stood up. "Sirs, I submit that the first specification is proved by the report of the defendant himself, and the second specification proved, except for the matter of 'arms' carried by the Marine force. I call Mr. St. Clair Abbott as a witness." The master-at-arms went to the door and shortly returned with the witness.

Merewether had never seen Abbott before. He proved to be a man of forceful appearance, in his early thirties, with penetrating gray eyes and a bold nose. He bowed to the Court, and stood erect.

"Please state your name and the position you hold with the Honourable Company," said James.

"I am St. Clair Abbott, Secretary of the Select Committee at Canton, sirs."

"For the record, state the nature and function of the Select Committee."

"It is a committee composed of experienced supercargoes of the Company Service which acts as intermediary between ships trading to Canton and the Co-hong merchants to arrange for cargoes and payment of customs duty to the Empire of China."

"Were you so acting on September twenty-ninth of this year?"
"Yes."

"Have you ever seen or met the defendant, Captain Percival Merewether?"

Abbott turned and looked deliberately at Merewether. "I have seen Captain Merewether, but I have never spoken to him."

"Please state the circumstances under which you saw the defendant."

"Early on the morning of last September twenty-ninth, I was called to the door of the Company factory in the International Settlement at Canton by John Elphingham, our chairman. The Captain was pointed out to me in a launch being rowed up the river toward the city of Canton. In the boat with him were more than a score of Marines of the Company's service, in uniform and bearing arms. I was directed by Mr. Elphingham to follow the launch and ascertain its destination. I did so in a lorcha. I saw the launch land near the center of Canton where the Captain and the Marines disembarked. The Captain and two men who appeared to be Chinese entered sedan chairs and departed up the street led by the Marine detachment."

"Were the Marines armed?" demanded James.

"They appeared to be; they shouldered what appeared to be muskets as they marched off. I could see brass flash in the sunlight."

"And where was this point at which the defendant and the Marine force landed?"

"In the old city of Canton, Empire of China, the morning of September 29, 1806."

"Thank you, sir." James turned and bowed to the Court. "Are there any quesions the Court may wish to put to the witness?" There evidently were none. James bowed formally toward MacLellan. "Your witness."

MacLellan rose slowly, bowed to the Court and to James, and said deliberately, "No questions, may it please the Court."

Merewether felt a little anxious. Surely MacLellan could make Abbott admit that he had not been close enough to identify the drill sticks as muskets. Then he relaxed; he had Gunny to prove the fact.

"The prosecution rests, may it please the Court. I submit that the specifications are proved in full," said James.

Commodore Morris looked left and right at his three colleagues on either side. "Clear the Court. We recess for a quarter hour before proceeding with the defense."

Outside, Merewether looked at his watch. Only a little after one; at this rate, he might be under sentence of dismissal within the hour. MacLellan drew him aside. "Under the rules, you must testify first, Captain. Speak out, stick to the facts, and answer any questions fairly. At least Abbot didn't try to embroider the facts."

The master-at-arms appeared, and the Court reconvened. Merewether found himself bowing to the Court, and at MacLellan's urging, telling again the story of the voyage. His voice appeared to be steady, but a little higher than normal, and he was conscious of dropping an *h* along the way, proof that he was under stress. He concluded, "I landed in Canton in obedience to the letter and spirit of my orders given by Sir George Barlow, Acting Governor-General of India, to give all assistance to his envoy, Sir Thomas Jeffrey, who was then physically disabled and prevented from carrying out his mission. In addition to acting upon the direction in my orders, I was invited ashore with my Marine detachment by Wong and Fong, citizens of the Empire of China. I offer, in proof of this, a document giving me the Freedom of the City of Canton, issued by the Mandarin of Canton." He laid the scroll on the table before the Court.

The balance of his testimony he had learned by rote from MacLellan. "I therefore do freely confess that I entered the environs of the City of Canton, Empire of China, on September 29, 1806, but I avoid any imputation of wrongdoing by reason of my orders, the emergency arising whereby Sir Thomas Jeffrey was prevented from carrying out his mission, and the invitation of citizens of that Empire, evidenced by this document which grants me the freedom of Canton."

There was dead silence in the room for a moment. Commodore Morris gingerly picked up the scroll and unrolled it. He looked carefully at it as though he was reading it, then up at Merewether. "This picture shows no sword. Did you wear one?"

"No, sir." The Commodore handed the scroll to the officer on his right, and it passed from hand to hand between the members of the Court.

Captain Jarvis finally tossed the scroll to the center of the table, where it lay across Merewether's sword. "This may all be quite true, Merewether," he said. "But what does it say?"

"I am not a Chinese scholar, sir," replied Merewether, anxiously. "I know only what I am told of its contents."

Captain MacAllester leaned forward and barked, "Surely you have a translation?"

MacLellan stood up. "All in good time, sirs. Does the Recorder desire to ask Captain Merewether any further questions?"

"No, may it please the Court." Merewether stood aside, thankful that the ordeal was over.

"Call Jemadar Gunny," MacLellan told the master-at-arms.

The Jemadar came in, erect and spotless, every button gleaming. Merewether could see the critical appraisal of the Court, how every eye caught the gold medal for valor hung on the Marine's chest. He was quickly identified and proceeded to testify.

"Was your force armed upon this landing in Canton?" asked MacLellan.

"No, sah. We carried a drum, a trumpet, and twenty drill sticks, sah."

"What is a drill stick?" asked MacLellan.

"No need for that, Lieutenant," broke in Commodore Morris. "This Court knows what they are, and the Jemadar's statement is sufficient. That portion of the second specification is now held, 'not proved.' Thank you Gunny." The Marine saluted, about-faced, and marched out.

"Call Sir Thomas Jeffrey," MacLellan told the master-at-arms.

Sir Thomas was fully recovered now, step firm and color good. He was respectfully greeted by the Commodore, who called for a chair. Sir Thomas declined graciously, saying, "I'll testify standing like everyone else, gentlemen."

MacLellan led him through the events of the voyage, his illness and disability, then asked the direct question. "Sir, did you direct Captain Merewether to go to Canton and try to carry out your mission?"

"No, sir. I had no authority to do so." He paused as the Court leaned forward to hear him. "When Captain Merewether told me of the invitation by our Chinese hostages, I told him I'd do it in a minute!"

The Court leaned back, old Captain Kersey whispered in the ear of Captain Jarvis, who then whispered to Captain Gregory. Captain James, the Recorder, rose slowly.

"As a diplomat, I assume you do not know much of naval matters, Sir Thomas?"

"Quite the contrary, sir," replied Sir Thomas briskly. "I had the honor to serve as a midshipman under Admiral Lord Howe some years ago in the Royal Navy. I have kept abreast of such matters since. I think a man who carries out the spirit of his orders in time of emergency is to be commended!"

James bowed to Sir Thomas and the Court. "No further questions, sirs."

Merewether watched Sir Thomas bow to the Court and withdraw. He had done all he could for him, he thought, but he had admitted that he gave no orders, only encouraged him to break the laws of China. Still, the Court seemed impressed. He heard the next witness called, a Chinese name.

The ancient wisp of a Chinese found at Goa entered the room on the arm of the master-at-arms. This time, Commodore Morris's request for a chair was followed, and the old man was seated. MacLellan rose, spoke clearly and loudly with no trace of his Scottish accent.

"Please tell the Court your name, age, and citizenship."

The old man looked blindly toward him. "Huasin Lin. In years, seventy. I am a native of Pekin."

"Are you a scholar, can you read and write the language of the mandarins?"

"I can if I can see it. I am almost blind."

MacLellan came forward and picked up the scroll from the table, handed it to the old man, and said, "Can you see and read this?"

With the light in his face from the windows, the old man held up the scroll. "No, sir."

"Turn about, take it to the window, use the magnifying glass if you wish." The old man staggered to his feet, turned to place the light to his back, held the lens before his eye, and said, "Yes, I can read it!"

"Tell the Court what it says," MacLellan told him.

"First is a picture of a man, I think it is this man here," said the Chinese, stabbing a finger at Merewether. "Then it says, 'Foreign devil Captain of the sea is given freedom of the City of Canton.' This is the seal of Lee Chin Chiang, the Mandarin of Canton."

"All right," persisted MacLellan, "does it show a date?"

"Yes. In your time, the twenty-ninth day of September, 1806."

"You may examine him," said MacLellan, turning away.

The reading of the deposition of Sir George Barlow was an anticlimax. MacLellan announced that he rested the defense. The court was cleared, and Merewether found himself outside. Inwardly, he was trembling with anxiety. He had no idea of how his case had sounded to a Court composed of officers who had no reason to favor him, or Sir George Barlow, and possibly many reasons to side with the Select Committee of the Company.

Merewether stood to one side in the corridor. Abbott and several local Company functionaries gathered in a little group beside the door. Sir Thomas and MacLellan whispered to one another a few feet away. Events assumed a dreamlike quality to Merewether as he forced himself to stand quietly and await the verdict.

The opening door caught him by surprise. He had to hurry to enter in his proper place beside MacLellan, just behind Captain James and the chief clerk. He was halfway across the room before he remembered to look at the table for his sword. The hilt was toward him!

"The Court is reconvened." said Commodore Morris. "The defendant will step forward." Merewether did so.

"It is the unanimous verdict of this Court of Inquiry that Captain Percival Merewether of the Honourable Company's Naval Service is not guilty of either of the specifications of charges preferred against him. We therefore most honorably acquit him and order that he be restored to duty." The Commodore paused and looked about the quiet room. "I might say that the Court reached this conclusion without reference to the writing exhibited by the defendant, which purports to give him the 'Freedom of Canton.' We do not disallow the validity of that writing, but we prefer to base our verdict upon the ground that Captain Merewether carried out his orders in time of emergency to accomplish the mission assigned him. The carrying out of a lawful order of a superior under difficulties is in accordance with the highest traditions of the Bombay Marine. This Court of Inquiry stands adjourned without day."

Several members of the Court, led by Commodore Morris, came around the table to shake his hand, as did Captain James. MacLellan handed him his sword, and then turned to face a swarm of admirers congratulating him upon his seventh victory before a Court of Inquiry at Bombay Castle. All Merewether desired now was to get back aboard *Rapid* and try to forget this ordeal. He was moving blindly toward the door when Tollett intercepted him.

"Merewether! I've planned a small dinner tonight before the Superintendent's Ball. You'll be my guest?"

Merewether hesitated only a moment. As much as he desired to be alone for a while, this officer had been most courteous to him.

"I would be delighted, sir."

He found MacLellan at the head of the stairs and went down through the gate to the dockside. He had no premonition until the bugle blew attention and the drums began to roll. He found himself passing through the files of the Marine detachment, their drill sticks rigidly at the present. Face red, he marched down to the boat landing as the Marines followed, drums rolling, the bugles playing snatches of melody, to the delight of a hundred idlers, while the drill sticks performed flashing evolutions in the sun. He came alongside *Rapid* to find the hands manning the rails, even a few along the starboard yardarms, cheering him. He shook hands self-consciously with MacRae, Larkin, Dobbs, and Davis, as the pipes squealed.

"You have permission to serve out a ration of spirits," he managed to tell Davis and went below. Sangh had both hot tea and the bottle of gin set out on the table. He took neither.

CHAPTER 40

The Superintendent's Ball was a glittering affair, the massed candles making the room uncomfortably warm for Merewether after treading four successive movements of the dance with Mrs. Tollett, Mrs. Morris, Mrs. James, and stout, vivacious Lady Waldron, wife of the Commandant of the Marine. He finally escaped to the cloakroom he had marked as the lair of MacLellan and MacRae. Dobbs and Larkin were already in the midst of the next set, partnered with two agile young ladies, twin daughters of the Comptroller of the Company at Bombay.

"Ye require asylum, Captain?" demanded MacLellan as Merewether entered. He and MacRae were seated against a window, a bottle of Scots whisky and two glasses set before them.

Merewether mopped his brow, unbuttoned his coat and held it wide against the night breeze through the window. The dinner had been cordial. Commodore Sir John Waldron and Commodore Morris had joined them for a glass of wine and dessert after leaving the state dinner given by the Superintendent for the Company officials.

"A wee nip, Captain," urged MacLellan.

"No, thank you, Mac. I've certainly had enough to drink already." After the acquittal, he would not have it said that he drank too much tonight. Feeling refreshed, he went back to join his party.

He found Commodore Sir John Waldron alone in the cluster of chairs. The others seemed to have joined the dance or withdrawn for the time. Merewether had scarcely spoken two words to the Commandant before tonight; he had been only a name signed to orders and addressed in reports. In person, he was a short, broad-shouldered man of fifty, with a bald spot gleaming at the back of his head. He had commenced service as a midshipman in the Royal Navy, transferred to the Army just in time for the surrender at Yorktown in the American war, then accepted a commission in the Bombay Marine. Merewether knew he was well connected in the Company, and feared he might have resented the action of the Court this afternoon.

"Ah, Merewether, we seem to hold the castle alone; all else have fled."

"Yes, sir. Deserted myself for a moment."

"Before I forget, HMS *Scorpion* arrived this afternoon from the Red Sea. It brought dispatches delivered overland from the Mediterranean. There are several private-official dispatches for you from the Court of Directors and the Committee of Secrecy. You weren't in trouble with them before you left London?"

Merewether was startled. The only private-official communication he had ever received during his service in the Marine had been the orders and specifications of charges last month, on which he had been tried today.

"No, sir. Not that I know of," he replied carefully.

"Come by my office in the morning and sign receipts for them. Now, let me say, Merewether, I was delighted with the verdict of the Court, and particularly the fact it saw fit to base its decision on your carrying out your orders, not the Freedom of the City you produced. In this service, we must have officers who will act upon their own judgment to accomplish their mission in time of emergency. If you had waited for that envoy to recover, the mission would have failed."

Merewether managed to stammer out his thanks as he saw Sir John rise and turned to greet Lady Waldron and the others. It was a long evening.

Merewether was waiting outside the Commandant's quarters when a yawning clerk arrived at seven o'clock. He had slept well, he reminded himself, the night before his trial, but the trial was a known peril to which he had steeled himself. The contents of these sinister "private-official" dispatches held the terror of the unknown. The clerk turned and languidly rummaged through a stack of mail.

"Not here," he announced in triumph. "Must be locked in the strong room. Private-official you said? Can't get in until Smith comes with the key."

Merewether sat on the hard bench in the anteroom for an hour before the chief clerk arrived. He looked narrowly at Merewether as he repeated his request for the dispatches, then went into the other room. There was the metallic sound of a lock and squeak of hinges.

"Here you are, Captain," said the chief clerk. "Now, if you'll just sign these receipts, I'll lend you a penknife, and you may use my office over there to read them." He paused, and in a confidential tone, continued, "I was most pleased with the verdict of the Court, Captain."

"Thank you," said Merewether absently, accepting the dispatches and the knife.

He went into the small office and shut the door. It was furnished with only a desk and a chair. He laid the oilskin-wrapped packets in a row. By the superscriptions, two were from the Committee of Secrecy, and one from the Secretary to the Court of Directors.

"Senior command first," he told himself, and slit the wrapping.

There were two sheets and a bill of exchange drawn upon the treasury of the Company at Calcutta. He read the first sheet with amazement:

Percival Merewether, Master and Commandant, The Honourable Company's Ship, Rapid

Sir:
I have the honour to enclose herewith a bill of exchange drawn upon the treasury of the Company at Calcutta in the amount of 15,000 pounds, payable jointly to you and the Commodore, Commandant of the Marine, to be distributed as prize money to said Commandant and the officers and persons thereto entitled while serving in the Company's ship Rapid, *February 12, 1806, during an engagement with the French ship of the line,* Canonnière, *in accordance with the Regulations for the Government of the Honourable Company's Naval Service.*

Matthews, Gen'l Secty

"Well, I'm damned!" said Merewether. He picked up the second sheet, a fair copy, addressed to the Court of Directors.

The High Court of Admiralty adjudged the late French ship of the line, Canonnière, *a prize of war, May 1, 1806, and ordered her sold as such. His Majesty, through his Commissioners for executing the Office of Lord High Admiral of England, purchased her into His Majesty's service for the sum of 60,000 pounds nett. It appearing from the undisputed evidence that His Majesty's ships* Growler, Defiance, *and* Buxton, *and HEICS* Rapid *participated in the taking of said ship, and that the capture was east of Cape Aghulas in the Indian Ocean, the usual area of operations for said* Rapid, *the Court ordered the proceeds of said sale to be equally divided among said ships.*

> *Stovall, Proctor in Admiralty*

"Well, I'm damned!" said Merewether again. He remembered his bitter resentment as he left the three seventy-fours boarding their prize after MacLellan had crippled her with his marksmanship. In eight years as a commissioned officer of the Marine, he had never drawn a shilling of prize money. Now, for the first time in his life he possessed funds in excess of the slender packet of pound notes, the small bag of gold guineas stored in the strongbox, and the three hundred hard-earned pounds on deposit with the Company.

He weighed the other two packets, one in either hand, tossed the right one on the table, and ripped open the covering of the other. It was a single closely written sheet he recognized as a fair copy addressed to Sir William Foster, Secretary of the Committee of Secrecy.

I have carefully examined the reports concerning the recovery of 23,000 pounds alleged to be the spoils accumulated by the pirate, Abercrombie, and recovered by one Percival Merewether of the Honourable Company's Naval Service. This occurred on an island, a part of Sumatra. As you well know,

His Majesty, George III, has many claims to Sumatra, and is only temporarily balked of occupying it as is his right. The man, Abercrombie, was, without dispute, a British citizen, and was in possession of Pulo Rondo as such. The specie was found concealed below ground. Under all the precedents, particularly Rex v. Harlow, House of Lords (1742), I am constrained to rule that this sum constitutes treasure trove, and is the exclusive property of the Crown. I might remark, it is customary in such cases for the finder to present a proper petition for compensation, which His Majesty may consider.

Buckminster, Attorney General

There was a brief endorsement by Foster, "Such a petition has been submitted by the Company's solicitors."

Merewether sat back looking at the opinion of the Attorney General. It had never crossed his mind that the hoard might constitute treasure trove, and he had made no claim to the proceeds of Abercrombie's piracies. He tossed the letter aside, and picked up the third packet. There was a brief covering letter from Sir William Foster addressed to him.

My Dear Captain Merewether: I forward herewith certain enclosures furnished me by the Honourable Cecil Lynde in appreciation of your services and that of your officers and men to them. Commodore Welchance joins me in congratulating you upon the success of your mission.

Your ob't servant, etc.

Merewether turned the page to a second letter addressed to him. It was signed by Cecil and Lady Catherine Lynde and was couched in extravagant terms. It concluded, "Our families, being sensible of your valor in rescuing us, desire to reward you and your crew, and request that the sum represented by the enclosed bill of exchange drawn upon Barclay's Bank be distributed as prize money in accordance with your regulations." The bill was drawn in the amount of 10,000 pounds.

Merewether was too stunned to repeat the expletive. Twenty-five thousand pounds in prize money meant that he had what amounted to a small fortune coming to him as his share. Properly invested, he might live out his life upon the income, even support a wife and family!

Flora Dean, absent from his thoughts the past month, popped into his mind. He could visualize the bright eyes, smooth skin, sweet lips, firm body. He had hurt her terribly by his illogical failure to declare himself. He had compounded the injury by his unintentional notoriety gained at Lord Laddie's entertainment. Now, there was no impediment; he had enough resources to support a wife and family. He gathered together the letters, folded them into a single packet, and made for the door. He must see the Commodore, make arrangements for the negotiation of the bills of exchange, and somehow persuade him to order *Rapid* back to Calcutta. If he left now, he could be there by Christmas. He would make amends to Flora, declare himself, be her slave, somehow defeat Ensign St. John, and make her his own in lawful matrimony. He might be, he thought hotly, a wedded man by New Year's Day!

The chief clerk was coming toward the door as he emerged. "Commodore wants to see you, Captain."

Merewether felt as though he were treading on air. He was ushered into the severe chambers of the Commandant of the Bombay Marine, past the marine sentry standing at the door, and came to attention five feet before the table.

Commodore Sir John Waldron sat behind the big table with Commodore Morris and Captain Tollett in chairs to his right. "Good morning, Merewether, we seem all to have survived the festive occasion. Be seated, please."

Merewether took the indicated chair to his left, facing the other officers. He restrained himself with difficulty from blurting out the news in the dispatches and demanding orders on the spot back to Calcutta.

"Now, Merewether, we've had a bit of a council of war. Since you're restored to duty, we must decide where to employ you." Good Lord, thought Merewether, probably duty in the Arabian

Sea against the Joasmi pirates. He might never see Flora again! He opened his mouth to protest, and thought better of it.

"During the last four months, eleven prizes have been taken in the Bay of Bengal by French privateers. Pellew says he has insufficient force to deal with them and can only post pickets off Ceylon, the approaches to Madras and the Hooghly. I have an earnest representation from Sir George to provide a force for the protection of shipping off Bengal." He paused and looked over Merewether's head for a moment.

"The real solution, of course," he continued, "is to take Mauritius and deny them a base, but neither the Royal Navy nor the Company has sufficient force at the present time to mount such an operation. I have assurances from London that possibly next year the force may be forthcoming. Meanwhile, I think we can spare more ships for Bengal." He looked at Captain Tollett. "Tell Merewether the plan you recommended to me."

"Yes, Commodore. This French privateer *Tigresse* you took last summer was condemned as a prize by the High Court at Calcutta in October. We have just received authority to purchase her into the Marine. We have a crew, survivors of *Hasting*, wrecked two months ago. We propose to send the crew in *Rapid* to Calcutta to man the prize, her Marine name will be *Comet*. Three officers survived from *Hasting*, but we feel none has sufficient experience to command her in this operation. The Commodore offered her command informally to MacLellan last night, but he prefers to remain at the arsenal." Tollett paused and glanced at Waldron. "I was tempted to take her myself, but Commodore says no."

The Commodore shook his head, and smiled. "Still no."

"We have in mind appointing your first lieutenant MacRae to her as commander, providing you consent."

"Certainly, he is entirely qualified for the command, sir."

"If you concur, we will issue an acting appointment as first lieutenant to your American officer, Larkin, I believe his name is."

"Larkin is entirely deserving of promotion, sir."

"We can also give you a second lieutenant, Charles MacCamy, and possibly a midshipman."

The Commodore broke in. "I have in mind a young man,

seventeen, but with six months' experience at sea, Roy Hamlyn, son of one of my oldest friends."

Merewether was suspicious. Transfer of a midshipman after only six months at sea was unusual, but he certainly would not quibble if the Commodore desired the appointment. He decided to test the matter.

"I shall be delighted to have both officers, sir, but I might point out that Mr. Dobbs is ranked as a passed midshipman and acting second lieutenant. I feel he is entitled to the permanent rank, having satisfactorily performed all the duties of the third lieutenant for the past six months."

Tollett looked at the Commodore. "Quite right," he said. "The boy is on the list, and I shall see that the commission issues before you leave." Merewether thought quietly that he had advanced the promotion for Dobbs by some months."

"Now," said Tollett, "*Rapid* and *Comet* are provided for. We propose to order *Tiger*, brig, ten guns, to your squadron."

Merewether jumped. His squadron!

The Commodore looked searchingly at Merewether. "I have in mind ordering you as commander of the Bengal Squadron, haven't had one over there since Welchance left. It will be additional duty, but it will entitle you to fly a broad command pendant, and to use the courtesy title of Commodore. Do you accept?"

Merewether took a deep breath. Yesterday he had been under threat of dismissal from the Service, or some lesser punishment that would have merely wrecked his career. He thought of dazzling Flora Dean with the title Commodore, even of the proclaiming of the banns at St. John's Church, "Commodore Percival Merewether and . . ."

"I accept, sir."

"Very well. Your orders will be forthcoming, and you may sail as soon as your passengers return from leave next Monday."

Commodore Morris and Tollett stood up, as did Merewether. He had almost forgotten his private-official dispatches.

"Sir," he said to the Commodore. "I have another matter to bring to your attention."

"You gentlemen may be excused," the Commodore told Morris and Tollett.

Merewether quickly informed Sir John of the contents of the dispatches and delivered the bill of exchange drawn on the Company treasury to him. The Commodore whistled. "First prize money we've gotten away from the Royal Navy in years. Someone must have blundered. I'll put it through for collection in the official mail to Calcutta with directions to pay over *Rapid*'s share there."

"Thank you, sir. I have another bill in the form of a reward from Lynde's family to be shared as prize money as well."

"Well, I'm damned! I'll send it through, too. Quite a day for the Bombay Marine!"

CHAPTER 41

The journey to Calcutta was slow against the northeast monsoon. Merewether made a long reach southeast of Ceylon to a point where he was able to set a course for the Sandheads.

MacRae had accepted his appointment as Commander of *Comet* with his usual impassive expression. He called his officers together, worked out a watch, quarter and station bill, and had his crew engaged in general drills as *Rapid*'s hands stood by grinning to see them sweat. He told Merewether he intended to commission *Comet* without a moment's delay.

The voyage was slow enough to infuriate Merewether. He boiled with impatience and was short with his officers. The new second lieutenant MacCamy appeared to be competent, but he accompanied his watch with a continuous tuneless whistling he apparently could not control that set Merewether's teeth on edge. The midshipman Hamlyn was a young man of fair complexion with brown hair he wore longer than was fashionable in this climate, and a thin moustache that was his pride. He appeared a little slow and sulky at first, but after a private interview with Larkin, began to improve.

The long night watches in fair weather found Merewether on deck into the midwatch night after night. MacLellan and Sir Thomas found him uncommunicative and soon drew away. He turned over in his mind tactics and strategy, how he might approach Flora most winningly and convince her of his love and desire to wed. His mind drifted into fantasies in which she stood in bridal white beside him at the altar in St. John's Church, or met him at the gate to a flower-bedecked bungalow with a kiss. He tortured himself with thoughts of Ensign St. John playing the cavalier with her, being admitted to the intimacies that Merewether had enjoyed last summer. The voyage became interminable. He was on fire with impatience to reach Calcutta and claim Flora Dean as his own.

Rapid came to anchor off the dockyard before noon on Christmas Eve. Merewether had the dispatch pouches out of the strong room and loaded in the gig before it was hoisted out. He fumed as he waited for the baggage of Sir Thomas and MacLellan to be loaded and then for them to take leave of the other officers. Finally, he reached the headquarters and found Commodore Land waiting beside a carriage occupied by Lady Jeffrey. The formalities seemed interminable, receipts for the pouches to be written, a cordial farewell with thanks to Sir Thomas for his evidence at Bombay, even a drunken, overleave seaman reeling into the party to be handed over to the master-at-arms.

Finally, Land said, "Time for lunch. You'll be my guest at the Club, of course?" Merewether hesitated, then resigned himself. In any event, he should not go charging out to the Dean residence at this hour without notice. Possibly he should send a polite note requesting permission to call first. The practicalities of the matter and employment of the proper niceties of etiquette gave him pause. Perhaps at lunch, he could get a bit of discreet advice from the Commodore on the subject.

"Delighted, sir."

The Club was well attended; evidently Fort William had declared the holiday. There was a short wait before the majordomo led them to a table by the window. Off to one side was a long table at which several of the senior officers of His Majesty's Sixty-fifth Foot sat sedately.

Commodore Land ordered two gins, then indicated the table with an almost imperceptible gesture and said, "A month ago, you couldn't have heard yourself think with all the laughter from

that table. Lord Laddie would have been presiding at the head
and keeping the rest in stitches, but no more."

"Why, what happened to Lord Laddie?" asked Merewether, a
little startled.

"He dines with Lady Montague now, no more wild parties for
him."

"Lady Montague? He's married? I'd never have dreamed it!"

Commodore Land chuckled. "No more the rest of Calcutta. It
all started with the Sixty-fifth's regimental ball, oh, a day or so
after you left for Bombay. Some junior officer, they say he was a
bit serious about her, brought a young lady to the affair and introduced her to Lord Laddie during the evening. Fair swept him off
his feet, she did, had him begging to see her again, dancing attendance on her at every affair that came along. In a week he'd
proposed and been accepted; in two weeks, they were married.
Even obtained a special dispensation from the Bishop waiving the
second and third publication of the banns. Oh, quite a romantic
affair! They tell me she leads him about by the nose, and he
glories in it."

"Well, I'm damned! Never expected Lord Laddie to be smitten
so hard," said Merewether smugly, conscious that he had lost his
own heart and expected to take similar action at the earliest
possible moment. "Who was she?"

"A young lady out from London; I believe you'd met her some
time back. She was Miss Flora Dean before her marriage."

The pain had subsided into a mere aching void as Merewether
led his little party of officers into the Governor-General's Christmas Ball. The effect of the bombshell delivered innocently
enough thirty-four hours ago by Commodore Land was wearing
off. Merewether even forgot it for a few minutes as he made sure
MacCamy and Hamlyn were delivered into the proper hands for
introduction into their contemporary circles. There was no receiving line at this affair, but he saw Sir George and Lady Barlow
holding informal court across the room and felt obligated to greet
them.

He went over slowly and stood by as others drifted away. An
opening developed, and he stepped forward to bow to Sir George.

"Ah, Captain, or I might more correctly say, Commodore. I am delighted to have you back, most honorably acquitted."

Merewether was conscious that Lady Barlow was facing away from them, intent upon a conversation with a plump dowager. Beside her was a taller figure whose reddish-gold hair blazed like a crown in the candlelight. It was uncanny; from the back she was Sister Jeanne, dressed in emerald instead of shapeless black.

Sir George was growling on, ". . . been insisting to Waldron ever since Wellesley resigned, the Bengal Squadron must be reestablished. Now it's done, and under competent and resolute command."

Lady Barlow turned as the dowager departed and Merewether bowed to her.

"Good evening, Captain, but it's Commodore now, isn't it?" She touched the elbow of the tall figure beside her, "Caroline." The young woman turned, and Lady Barlow continued, "May I present Commodore Percival Merewether, my niece, Lady Caroline Austen."

Merewether bowed. As he straightened up, he found himself looking into a pair of violet eyes under the crown of red-gold hair. Sir George was saying, "I hope you'll find it convenient to join our little party for supper, Commodore."

"I shall be delighted, Your Excellency," Merewether replied with complete sincerity.

Bibliography

THE Bombay Marine carried on its operations for the Honourable East India Company from 1613 to 1830 when it became the Indian Navy. It has been almost forgotten, since all its records at Bombay Castle were destroyed in 1860, and it has been over ninety years since a history of the service was published by private subscription. Among the many authorities consulted, I found the following works most useful in providing the historical situation and background for this novel, and extend my thanks to their authors:

Cambridge History of England

Cambridge History of India

Evan Cotton, *East Indiamen*, Batchworth, 1949

Ainslee Embree, *Charles Grant and British Rule in India*, Columbia University Press, 1962

William Foster, *East India House*, London, 1924

William Foster, *John Company*, London, 1926

Holden Furber, *John Company at Work*, Harvard University Press, 1948

C. R. Low, *History of the Indian Navy*, London, 1877

B. B. Misra, *The Central Administration of the East India Company, 1773–1834*, Manchester University Press, 1959

C. H. Phillips, *The East India Company, 1784–1834*, Manchester University Press, 1961

C. Lestock Reid, *Commerce and Conquest; the Story of the Honourable East India Company*, C. & J. Temple, 1947

United States Oceanographic Office, Publication H. O. 64, *Sailing Directions for the Bay of Bengal*, 1966

Bernard H. M. Vlekke, *Nusantara, a History of the East Indian Archipelago*, Harvard University Press, 1944

Phillip Woodruff, *The Founders of Modern India*, St. Martin's Press, 1954